JANICE PRESTON

Unexpected Inheritance

Quills

Two classic historical stories

CONTENTS

THE EARL WITH THE SECRET PAST

Janice Preston grew up in Wembley, North London, with a love of reading, writing stories and animals. In the past she has worked as a farmer, a police call handler and a university administrator. She now lives in the West Midlands with her husband and two cats and has a part-time job as a weight-management counselor—vainly trying to control her own weight despite her love of chocolate!

Author Note

It's hard to say goodbye, and last year I bade farewell to my series centered around the Beauchamp family. Regular readers will know I enjoy writing stories set in the same Regency world, where familiar faces pop up in a supporting role, and so when I was thinking about what to write after finishing Alex's story (*Christmas with His Wallflower Wife*), I decided to write a complete standalone.

I didn't anticipate how hard that would be.

I've been immersed in the Beauchamps' world for several years, and as I wrote one, the next would be percolating inside my brain and each book started off on familiar ground. This was different and I felt like a fish out of water at first—much as my hero, Adam, does when he discovers his first thirty-six years have been a lie and he enters the alien world of the *haut ton* as an earl.

In the end, I couldn't resist including two tenuous links to "my" Regency world in *The Earl with the Secret Past*: one name and one (very) secondary character. I wonder if anyone will spot them.

This is a second-chance-at-love story, where Adam meets up again with widow Kitty, the seventeen-year-old he fell in love with fifteen years ago. I adored both Adam and Kitty, whose confidence has been eroded by her past although she is very good at hiding those insecurities. I hope you enjoy it.

To Kim Deabill and Irina Wolpers, and all the other followers of my Facebook author page who rose to the challenge of naming two of the characters in heroine Kitty's novel.

The names I picked were Kim's suggestion of Sidney, for the villainous uncle, and Irina's suggestion of Minerva, for Sidney's flighty and mercenary betrothed!

Prologue

Hertfordshire

'You *said* you loved me!'

Adam Monroe gazed into huge grey eyes drowning in tears. His throat thickened as he thrust his emotions down.

'I do, Kitty. I… I care for you. Very much. But it's impossible…ye must see it.'

She clutched his hands, her nails digging urgently into his skin. He wrenched his gaze from hers and concentrated on her hands: the slender fingers, the soft white skin, the neatly shaped nails.

It's impossible! She doesna understand the world as I do.

'Kitty… I canna… I can *never* give ye the kind of life ye're accustomed to.'

Too late to regret his weakness in succumbing to that instant attraction that had flared between them the very first time they met. Too late to realise the risk he had run in their clandestine meetings. Those meetings…they had been innocent: walking hand in hand in the woods where they would not be seen, talking and laughing, a few shared kisses, murmured endearments. He'd been naive, not deliberately cruel. He hadn't understood how the heart could so quickly become engaged, how a lonely girl like Kitty might read more into their meetings than he ever intended. Not that he wouldn't elope with her given half a chance. But he had not one tenth of a chance! Not one hundredth! He, an architect's apprentice, she, an earl's daughter.

'Your father…never would he consent to such a lowly match for his daughter and ye know it.'

Adam had never even set eyes on the man, who was away from home, in London, leaving his only daughter alone with just the servants and an elderly great-aunt for company. It was no life for a young lady who craved excitement and company in her life.

'We could run away. We could elope. In Scotland, there is a place…'

Adam laid his fingers against Kitty's lips.

'We canna. Ye would not do that to your father.'

Her head jerked back, away from his touch. 'I would!' Her eyes burned into his. 'I *must* get away before he comes back. You don't understand. *Please*, Adam. Take me with you.'

'Ye would come to resent me. I'm still apprenticed tae Sir Angus for another year, so I canna marry even if I wanted to. I've no income until I build my reputation as an architect. And that could take years.'

And before he could begin to establish his own name as an architect, Sir Angus McAvoy had promised to fund a trip for him to Italy, to study the architecture in Florence and Rome and Sienna. If he searched deep in his heart, he knew he couldn't pass up on such an opportunity; it could be the making of him and of his career. Neither would he betray Sir Angus McAvoy's trust in him, not after the man had been such a good employer and friend to Adam's widowed mother, who had worked as Sir Angus's housekeeper since the death of Adam's soldier father when Adam was barely out of leading strings.

'I would not mind, Adam. I…we could live as man and wife until you finish your apprenticeship. And I can be thrifty. I know I can.'

Adam's heart clenched at the sound of her voice, small and defeated; at the sight of hope dying in her eyes. He closed his own eyes and summoned his strength. Would that he'd had the foresight to avoid this—he should never have indulged himself in meeting with her, but that realisation came too late. He loved her and the thought of never seeing her again tore him apart. But she was only seventeen. Four years younger than he. And it was up to him to be the man. To be strong.

Better she hate him and believe him a scoundrel than she grieve over what might have been.

'Marriage is no part of my plans; not for many years. I'm fond of ye, Kitty, but this was never more than a pleasant way to pass the time when I had an hour to spare. I thought ye understood that.'

She swallowed, her long, slim throat moving. Adam clenched his hands into fists to stop himself reaching for her, comforting her…

'You do not know what I must endure at my father's hands.'

He frowned. Was this some kind of ruse to persuade him to change his mind? She had never before hinted at trouble at home. Loneliness, yes…how could she not be lonely at times, with just herself, her father and her father's aunt rattling around in that huge house? He understood the loneliness of an only child with just one parent. And the natural wariness of a daughter under the control of a strict father.

'Tell me.'

The words left his mouth even as he realised that, whatever her reasons, they could change nothing. He and Kitty still came from, and lived in, two separate worlds and, all at once, he was afraid of what she might reveal—afraid that what he learned might render it impossible for him to leave her. Afraid…selfishly…that, if he felt compelled to act, both of their lives would eventually spiral down into regret, blame and destitution.

He raised his hand, palm facing her, silencing her reply. 'No. On second thoughts, say nothing. It can make no difference. I will still be an architect's apprentice and ye will still be an earl's daughter.'

She was clean, well dressed, well fed. She showed no signs of neglect and he had never seen a bruise marring her white skin. She spoke of endurance…but he had seen the state of the people who lived crammed into the tenements in Edinburgh's old town. There could be no comparison.

He hardened his heart again, knowing he must break hers.

'Return to your father's house and, in time, ye'll see I was right. What ye feel for me isna love. It's infatuation. And, even were we equals, I am but one-and-twenty and in no mind to marry for a verra long time.'

He succumbed to the urge to touch her once again. He cupped her face and looked deep into those tragic grey eyes, the eyelashes spiky from her tears. 'When you meet the man who will be your husband—a man who is your equal in society—ye will look back and ye will see I was right, and ye will be grateful to me.' His hands dropped to rest briefly on her shoulders before sliding down to clasp her upper arms. He squeezed gently before releasing her and then stepping away. 'I have to go. We leave at first light. God bless ye, Kitty.'

He spun on his heel before she could reply; before her pleas could wring a promise from him that he could not honour. A clean break. It was for the best…he must do the right thing for Kitty even though it tore his heart into shreds.

He strode off through the woods, the fallen leaves crunching beneath his boots, his throat aching as he tried, unsuccessfully, to hold back his tears.

He did not look back.

Chapter One

Edinburgh—fifteen years later

'I lied to you. I've been lying to you for a long time.'

Adam Monroe's mother stood gazing out of the window of the Edinburgh town house where she had lived and worked for as long as he could remember—the home in which he'd grown up. Ma's back and shoulders were rigid, but Adam didn't miss the tremble of her hand as she tucked a straying lock of hair away under her cap.

'So you *are* ill?'

Adam's gut churned…he couldn't bear to lose Ma. It had always been just the two of them. Well, them and Sir Angus McAvoy, who employed Ma as his housekeeper and had long stood as Adam's benefactor.

Adam crossed the room in two strides, gently took hold of her shoulders and turned her to face him.

'Tell me.' His voice rasped. 'Anything is better than leaving the worst to my imagination. What is wrong with ye? We can fight it together.'

She jerked away from him. 'I'm not ill!'

Adam studied her face: her pallor; the quiver of her mouth; the tear-washed eyes. She *looked* sick, to his inexpert eyes. 'What have ye lied about? What happened while I was away?'

He'd been to Lincolnshire, to oversee the completion of his first-ever commission south of the border. He'd travelled home, excited and full of pride at the success of the new stables and carriage house he had designed for a William and Mary country mansion, and with the praise and the grateful thanks of the owner—a Member of Parliament—ringing in his ears. This could be the breakthrough he'd been working for. The chance to attract a better—that was, wealthier—clientele. The chance to get his name known among men of influence. He'd arrived home to find his mother, pale and frail, her eyes haunted, her hands wringing at waist level.

Now, she sucked in a breath and straightened her back, her chin up.

'Sit down, Adam. I have something to tell you.'

He obeyed, sitting at the small circular table in the housekeeper's room, and Ma perched on the edge of the opposite chair. There were only two chairs...there had only ever been two chairs...there had never been any visitors. Ma had always kept herself to herself, even after Sir Angus took Adam on as his apprentice and they were away on jobs for weeks and months at a time.

He waited.

'Your father... I've been lying to you all along. He didn't die. I left him. Ran away and took you with me.'

The air left his lungs in a rush, leaving him to struggle

to draw another breath. Ma stayed silent, her expression a mask. No shame. No remorse. No apology.

He ignored the flare of anger that fired his gut. His quickness to anger was now ingrained in him, fuelled by his bitterness at a society that—despite his honesty and his hard-working ethic—deemed him unworthy of an earl's daughter and had cost him his first love, Kitty.

First love? Only love, for he'd never forgotten her and he still had regrets.

He'd learned to control his anger over the years; learned that it was more productive to allow his emotions to subside and his head to clear rather than to launch angry tirades in which words spoken could not be unspoken, even if subsequently regretted.

'He's alive?'

His soldier father...a rifleman...decorated for his bravery. A true hero. Alive?

Adam shoved back his chair and surged to his feet. 'I want to meet him.'

All his life he had regretted never having the chance to know his father...the heroic soldier. And now...and now...

'You cannot. He died six months ago. I'm only telling you now because they're searching for you. Again. But this time...' Ma slumped, her shoulders drooping, her shaking hands lifting to cover her face. 'You deserve to know the truth. He was never a soldier. He was never the man...the father... I told you about. I made it all up.'

Adam frowned, scrambling to make sense of her words. His father was not...? 'Then who was he?'

'An earl.' She looked up at him, her face drawn. 'And you were his only son. I have written to the trustees of his estate and one of them is coming here to meet you and to confirm your identity before escorting you to London to register you as his successor.

'Congratulations, Son.' Her upper lip curled, as though she tasted something nasty. 'You are now the Earl of Kelridge.'

How can I ever forgive her?

His mother had sobbed bitterly after her confession, saying only that she had done it for Adam's own good. But he had only been two years of age when she'd spirited him away from his Hertfordshire home and his father. How could that possibly have been for his own good? And although he could understand why she had not told him the truth as a child, he was now six-and-thirty. There could be no excuse: her silence over all those years had robbed Adam of any chance of ever knowing his father.

Now his imagination was bursting with all kinds of lurid speculation about the father he had never met as Ma stubbornly refused to answer any of his questions about the man, or about why she had snatched Adam away.

'It is only right ye should learn for yourself what sort of a man your father was,' she eventually said, when Adam tried yet again to wring an answer from her.

His temper—sorely tried and brimming close to the surface—erupted. 'And so might I have done had ye told me about him *before* he died!'

He wrestled his anger back under control. Ma buried her head in her hands yet again.

'I did what I thought best at the time, Son. Now, though, I am thinking maybe it *was* a mistake to keep this all a secret and I will not now compound my error by painting his character for ye using the palette of *my* distant memories and experience. You will find out more about him from those who knew him better than I. It's been thirty-four years, and he might have changed since I last set eyes on him. I cannae know the truth of that.'

She lifted her head then, to pierce him with the same blue eyes he saw every time he looked in the mirror. He caught a glimpse of her usual steely determination emerging from the depths of her distress and guessed he was unlikely to get any more from her.

'I willna whine and make excuses for what I did,' she said. 'I acted as I thought best and we were happier without him.'

She might have been happier. But what about him?

More bitter resentment, aggravated by a deep sense of betrayal, settled in Adam's gut over the following few days as he awaited the arrival of his father's trustee. His rage and hurt stopped him from any further attempt to coax the truth from Ma, for to do that he must soothe her, cajole her and tell her he understood.

But he didn't damn well understand.

As the initial shock of the news about his father—and the huge change in his own circumstances—subsided, Adam's thoughts returned often to the past. To Hertfordshire. Remembering the time he had spent there fifteen years before.

Remembering Kitty.

His gut churned with angry regrets, made infinitely worse by the slowly emerging realisation of what might have been.

He and Sir Angus had spent several weeks at Fenton Hall, overseeing the restoration of a wing destroyed in a fire that had also stolen the life of Lady Fenton, the mother of four young children. It had been a tragic story…and when he was not working Adam had taken himself away from the grief as much as possible by going for long walks in the grounds and surrounding woodland, straying beyond the Fenton boundary on to the neighbouring estate, Whitlock Manor. And that was where he'd met Kitty, only daughter of Lord Whitlock.

And Adam had lost his heart to a girl who was so far beyond his reach she might as well have been an angel descended from the heavens.

But now…the truth was that he and Kitty *should* have grown up as equals and as neighbours. He'd consulted a map and Whitlock Manor was less than seven miles as the crow flies from Adam's new home, Kelridge Place.

What might have been possible, had he occupied his rightful place in this world? He'd broken Kitty's heart and guilt had plagued him ever since, even though he'd done it to protect her. Had his mother not snatched him from his father, he and Kitty could have met on equal terms. Their love could have blossomed, instead of withering under the blast of practicality and principle.

If I had known…if only I had known.

And, at first, he'd wished Sir Angus was home, for Adam longed to be able to talk this through with his mentor. But he was working on a project far to the north and wasn't expected home for weeks. Then the second blow fell, when Adam happened to mention Sir Angus to his mother one day.

'I need to tell ye the truth about Angus, too.'

'What truth?'

'He is my cousin, on my mother's side. We were always close as children and, when I came here to build a new life for you and me, he took us in.' She then felled him with another blow. 'Did ye never wonder why a man would take on a woman with a young child as housekeeper? Or make that young child his apprentice?'

He had believed Sir Angus had seen Adam's talent and recognised his hard work and found him worthy of taking on as his apprentice. Adam had been proud of those achievements which, it now seemed, owed nothing to Adam's abilities. It had been sheer nepotism. His sense of betrayal was complete. Sir Angus—his father figure and, as Adam had grown up, his friend—had been complicit in her lies all this time.

How could he ever forgive either of them?

If only I had known the truth.

Where was Kitty now? Would they meet? Would he recognise her? Would she remember him? She'd been seventeen then and fifteen years had passed. They would both have changed and she was bound to be married by now, but he couldn't curb his joy at the thought of seeing her again, even though any meeting would be bittersweet with the knowledge of what might have been.

He couldn't help but wonder how long she had mourned their impossible love—the Earl's daughter and the architect's apprentice.

Two weeks later

'We're here, my lord.'

Adam jolted awake. The carriage had indeed drawn to a halt and he gazed out at the Mayfair town house, with its five steps leading up to the front door and its stucco finish. He craned his neck to fully view it—four storeys, plus a half-basement—taking in the twelve-paned sash windows and the classical stone-pedimented surround to the black-painted front door, which was topped by a batwing-patterned fanlight.

He twisted on the bench seat to view his travelling companion—a compact, humourless solicitor by the name of Dursley, from the firm of Dibcock and Dursley. Once Ma had provided him with the evidence that she was indeed the missing Countess of Kelridge and that Adam was the rightful heir, Dursley had been briskly efficient in apprising Adam of the full extent of his change in circumstances, following which he had maintained a meticulously professional courtesy towards Adam throughout the journey from Edinburgh. There had been no relaxation of his formal manner: no hint of warmth, no friendliness, no reassurance.

'I shall collect you at eleven o'clock tomorrow morning and take you to petition the Attorney General, Sir Robert Gifford. As long as he is satisfied with the validity of your claim to the title of the Earl of Kelridge—and I am confident the documentary evidence your mother provided will prove sufficient—he will recommend the exercise of the royal discretion without reference to the House of Lords or the Committee for Privileges. The Clerk of the Parliaments will then record your name in the Register of Lords Spiritual and Temporal, following which you will receive a summons to take your seat in the House of Lords.

'In the meantime, your butler—Green—will acquaint you with your new household. I instructed the servants to come to London in order to prepare your town house for your occupation.' Dursley inclined his head. 'Good day, my lord.'

Adam blanked his expression, keeping his scowl from his face. Dursley owed him nothing, other than the legal service he was paid to provide but, surely, common decency dictated he should at least escort his client into the house and introduce this Green fellow? But he swallowed back his angry reaction to the solicitor's treatment, suspecting he would need all the goodwill he could get in this alien world. It would not do to make an enemy of his solicitor.

'And good day to you, too, Mr Dursley. Thank you for providing the transport to London.'

Dursley allowed himself a wintry smile. 'Oh, the cost will be reimbursed from His late Lordship's estate, my lord. You owe me no gratitude.'

Adam contented himself with gritting his teeth and a silent vow to appoint a new firm of solicitors as soon as possible. One nugget of information that Dursley had let slip during the journey was that Adam's heir—his uncle, Grenville Trewin, who would, in time, have inherited the earldom had Adam not been found—was also a client of Dursley's firm and he was clearly a firm favourite with Dursley himself. Unlike, it would seem, Adam's late father, upon whom the solicitor resolutely refused to be drawn. No wonder the fellow looked as though he was sucking a lemon most of the time. He would clearly be happier had Adam *not* been found.

Still, Adam was here in London now and it would be a relief to be released from the confines of the carriage and Dursley's not-so-scintillating company. The man had even flatly refused to stop at Kelridge Place on the way south, deeming time to be of the essence in establishing Adam in his new rank and status.

The sound of the carriage door opening grabbed Adam's attention. A footman in dark green livery stood to attention, his gaze fixed straight ahead. Adam stifled a sigh.

He'd visited, and even stayed in, a few aristocratic house-holds for his work and he really did not care for the rigid structure, the divide between the family and the servants who cared for them. Nor, if he was honest, had he much cared for the arrogance of many of those same aristocrats—the way they simply accepted subservience from others, including Adam, as their due. He supposed that, with Ma being a housekeeper—and he still could not quite believe that, all this time, she had been a countess—he instinctively identified with the servants rather than their masters.

A glance at the front door revealed a man dressed in black tailcoat and grey trousers waiting on the threshold, hands clasped behind his back, and further figures lined up along the hallway. Adam hauled in a deep breath before descending the carriage steps to the pavement. His new life awaited, with not one familiar thing about it to help him come to terms with all this change. Even his name was not his own, he had discovered. He was no longer Adam Monroe, Scottish architect, but Ambrose Adam Trewin, the English Earl of Kelridge. And he not only had an Uncle Grenville about whom he knew nothing, but he also had a cousin—Grenville's son, Bartholomew, who was thirty years of age.

The weighty dread that had settled in the pit of his stomach over the past two weeks now seemed destined to remain lodged there because, as far as he could see, he had little to look forward to. The only people he knew in this world were those who had hired him as an architect and he was not yet well enough established in his profession to help bridge the gap between him and the rest of the aristocratic world. Neither could he believe those same clients would be overjoyed to find him joining their ranks. He had attended a small boys' preparatory school in Edinburgh, with the sons of bankers, lawyers and business owners, and had not attended university, so he had never mixed with these people, but he must now make his home in this city of strangers and at his new country estate, Kelridge Place, in Hertfordshire.

Adam did not even have the comfort of his mother. Their relationship had remained strained until he left and although, at the last minute, he had invited her to accompany him, she had refused.

'I am content here, Adam. It's been my home for many years and I have no wish to face the censure of those who remember me from before. You will have a hard enough time gaining acceptance without me reviving that old scandal. You are better off without me.'

'What about *your* family, Ma?'

'There is no one, other than Angus.'

The only truths she'd told him of her own past was that she had been born in Scotland, she was an only child and her parents were dead. He had not known that her father— his grandfather—had been a wealthy banker or that she had gone to London for a Season, chaperoned by her mother and a hired companion. It had been there that an heiress, without male protectors, had proved all too easy prey for the impoverished Lord Kelridge.

'Have you no old friends?'

Her lips had pressed together at that and she would be drawn no more upon the subject. And he—God help him— had not argued, resentment at her betrayal still smouldering deep within him. Now, though, he found that the further he got from Edinburgh and the more distance he put between himself and his mother, the more that resentment gave way to hurt.

Hurt that she had never trusted him enough to tell him

the truth. Through his boyhood they'd always been so close. He'd always felt as though they'd shared everything, but now it felt as though his whole life had been a lie.

Now, as he trod towards the front door of his new home, Adam wished he had been more forgiving. Maybe then she would have relented and come with him.

'Welcome to your home, Lord Kelridge. I am Green. Your butler.' Green bowed, stiff and correct, then held out his hand for Adam's hat. 'Please allow me to introduce your staff.'

'Thank you.'

Adam scanned the entrance hall. It was dark and cheerless, papered in dark green stripes above the dado, but the cornices were crisply moulded and showed promise. Dursley had said his fortune was large…he would arrange for the house to be redecorated. Maybe then it would feel more like home?

Give yourself time. Don't rush into hasty decisions.

It was true. He'd only just stepped inside the front door. He would wait. He would see what this new life might offer before he changed anything, including his staff, not one of whom met his gaze or smiled during the introductions. He looked back along the line. They resembled soldiers on parade, standing rigidly, eyes forward. He sighed. It was not their fault. They would behave as his father had expected them to behave.

But…he was not his father and he did not have to continue any of his traditions if he chose not to. And he did choose not to. He was the Earl. *He* could dictate the mood of the house. The only other example he had was the happy household in which he had grown up, that of Sir Angus, who had always treated Ma more like a friend than an employee. *That* was the example he preferred.

Except, a sly inner voice reminded him, *do not forget they were family. Not employer and servant, after all. So how would* you *know what is correct and what is not?*

Even more confused, he vowed again to take his time.

'Aye. Well!' Adam clapped his hands together and then rubbed them briskly. He saw the momentary shock upon Green's face when he heard the Scottish accent and the devil inside him prompted him to exaggerate it. 'I hae been travellin' a week or more and I'm fair grubby and weary. Mrs... Ford, is it, aye?'

The housekeeper dipped a little curtsy. 'It is, my lord.'

'I should like to bathe, if ye'll arrange for water to be heated, please. And...' his roaming gaze paused on the chef 'Monsieur Delon, I should very much like a cup of tea while the bath is being prepared. Green... I will inspect the rest of the house, from basement to attics, after I have bathed.'

Green's lips compressed. 'The late Lord Kelridge relayed *all* domestic instructions through myself, my lord. And Monsieur does not make tea. Aggie...' he crooked a finger at a kitchen maid '...will see to that.'

'I see.' Adam scratched his ear. 'But, ye ken, I am *not* your late master. And if I wish tae communicate my needs directly tae the person most able tae satisfy them, then I shall do just that.' He smiled at the butler. 'I do hope we'll no' fall oot over this—or any other—wee detail, Green.'

The butler stood to rigid attention. 'No, my lord.'

'Verra good,' Adam murmured. 'Now, will ye show me the ground floor while Aggie fetches me that cup of tea?'

Chapter Two

'Stepmama? Are you in here?'

Kitty, Lady Fenton, laid aside her quill pen with a quiet sigh. 'I am.'

This was the problem with trying to write here in London—at least at home at Fenton Hall she had her own parlour where she could remain undisturbed, whereas she could hardly bar members of her family from entering the salon of their town house. Kitty twisted in her chair to find her seventeen-year-old stepdaughter, Charis, regarding her with a smile and a teasing light in her eyes.

'I am sorry to interrupt you, but I have such exciting news I cannot wait to share it with *someone* and Robert has gone out. *Again.*'

Kitty suspected that Robert—Charis's older brother, and thus Kitty's stepson—had not gone out, but had yet to return home from last night. A not uncommon occurrence. At twenty-six, however, that was his affair—he was his own man and Kitty had neither the inclination nor the right to interfere in his life. Fortunately, her relationship with all four of her stepchildren was an affectionate one and she trusted Robert—Viscount Fenton since the death of his father five years before—not to succumb to the wilder excesses of some of his peers.

It was a relief Charis was far too innocent to realise the half of what her brother—and most young men in the *ton*— got up to.

And long may she hold on to that innocence.

Love for her stepdaughter filled Kitty's heart as she rose to her feet, then linked her arm through Charis's and gently urged her towards the sofa.

'Then you shall share it with me, love. I dare say it is time I took a break from writing…the words prove somewhat reluctant this morning and I fear my prose is somewhat stilted.'

She bit back a smile at the disgust in her own voice. When would she accept that it would never be an easy matter to transfer the images in her head into interesting, or even compelling, phrases and sentences on paper? The late Miss Jane Austen had made the entire process seem so much easier than it proved. Kitty's attempts to follow in her footsteps had resulted in the publication of one novel—albeit anonymously—but it was proving even more daunting to write a second and, try as she might, it seemed impossible to confine her story to family and community as Miss Austen had done with such sly, observant wit. No. Kitty's characters inevitably seemed to stumble into thrilling dramas and her own prose veered towards exaggeration no matter how hard she tried to rein it in.

'You may tell me about it later,' said Charis, who delighted in Kitty's covert double life as a novelist and often

helped her to work through any sticky patches that arose
in the plots of her romantic adventures. 'But, first... I received this from Annabel.' Miss Annabel Blanchard and
Charis had been firm friends from their first meeting at
the start of this Season, when they had both made their debuts. Now, Charis thrust a note covered in painstakingly
neat writing—presumably Annabel's—under Kitty's nose.
'Talaton has spoken at last!'

'At last?' Kitty laughed. 'You young girls are always in
such haste! To my certain knowledge, Annabel only met
Lord Talaton for the first time this Season. So that is...now,
let me see...' She tapped her chin, puckering her brow and
raising her eyes to the ceiling as she pondered.

'You are teasing me, Stepmama.' Charis pouted, then
nudged her shoulder into Kitty, who dropped her pose and
laughed again.

'Well, how could I resist? Your delight in such exaggeration makes you a most satisfying target for my poor attempts
at wit. But it is true, nevertheless. Annabel and Talaton only
met two months ago and that is a very short time in which
to form a lasting attachment.'

Kitty clamped down on her mind's attempt to drag those
old memories from the depths where they had lain safely
buried for fifteen years. She had long made it a personal
rule not to look back. Not to tolerate regrets of any sort. She
lived in the present and she looked forward to the future.
It was enough. But she did not forget that hard-learned lesson in how easily the heart could be fooled into thinking
itself in love.

'Well, *Annabel* was certain of her feelings from the first
moment they met and now her father has given his consent, and it is *all arranged*. I cannot wait to hear all about

his proposal.' Charis clasped her hands together in front of her chest, her hazel eyes shining. 'It is *so* romantic. I wonder when it will be my turn.'

Kitty fought the compulsion to warn Charis to be careful, loath to quash her natural enthusiasm. She could not help but worry for her stepdaughter, lest she lose her heart to the wrong man—Kitty's own painful experience had left her determined to guard her own heart well, but she tried not to allow her fears to curb her stepdaughter's youthful dreams.

She contented herself with saying, 'Do not be in too much hurry, Charis. This is only your debut Season and you are still very young to be thinking of marriage.'

Charis pouted. 'Annabel is not the first of my friends to be betrothed.'

'Have you a particular young man in mind?'

'No. No one.'

Kitty almost laughed, Charis sounded so despondent, but she managed to swallow her laugh and, instead, she hugged her stepdaughter and dropped a kiss on her fair head.

'Don't despair, sweeting. The right young man will appear to sweep you off your feet one day. In the meantime, shall we call upon Annabel and her mother later and share their excitement?'

Charis threw her arms around Kitty and hugged her. 'Thank you, for I know you do not much care for Mrs Blanchard. You are the *best* stepmother anyone could ever wish for.'

'I am in wholehearted agreement, Charis,' drawled a voice from the doorway, 'but is this excess of enthusiasm due to anything in particular, or is it merely a general statement?'

Kitty looked up, laughing, at her stepson—tall and broad

with his father's golden-brown hair and dark brown eyes—
who filled the doorway. He was clean-shaven and dressed
in his riding clothes and looked nothing like a man who had
spent the night carousing, so she had clearly done him a dis-
service in suspecting he had not returned home last night.

Not for the first time, she counted her blessings. Edgar,
her late husband, had been over twenty years Kitty's senior,
but their marriage had been quietly content despite Edgar's
tendency to treat her as a surrogate daughter in need of instruction. His motives, she knew, had been good and he
was a kindly spouse, but his gentle comparisons between
Kitty and Veronica, his first wife—in which Kitty inevitably came off worst—had left her with the feeling of never
being quite good enough.

Ironically, being a mother—or, strictly, a stepmother, as
she had never been blessed with a child of her own—had
been the one role at which she had surpassed Veronica, who
had not been the maternal type. And even there, Edgar had
not failed to puncture Kitty's self-esteem with his monthly
'joke' that it was fortunate he had already produced his heir
and spare when Kitty, yet again, proved not to be with child.
Kitty had found that joke unfunny to begin with but, as the
years passed, it became increasingly hurtful, especially as
she became aware that her barrenness, in Edgar's eyes,
was all about him. He never once seemed to consider that
Kitty might be upset by her failure to become a mother in
her own right—and she had hidden her distress from him,
and from the children, for she could not love any of Edgar's
four children more had they been of her body.

Robert was the eldest, followed by Edward, currently
serving in the army, and Jennifer, who had been married for
two years now. Charis was the youngest and Kitty deeply

regretted Edgar had not lived to see her grow into such a fine young woman. Since Edgar's death, Robert had become more like a brother to Kitty than a stepson—a steadfast support and ally. She was happy and secure, both in her stepfamily and in her place in society. She had her marriage portion and the Dower House if she chose to live there, but, for the time being, she still happily remained at the family home, Fenton Hall, running it on Robert's behalf until he was ready to settle down.

'Good morning, Robert,' she now said. 'Your sister's enthusiasm is her customary over-exaggeration at my offer to visit Miss Blanchard to share in her celebration. But I must allow Charis to tell you the details, as it is her news to tell, not mine.'

'Where were you, Rob? I looked for you first because I was bursting to tell—'

'*Bursting?* That is hardly a ladylike expression, Charis.'

Charis pouted as Robert continued, 'And I was not here because I went out to pay a visit to an old…acquaintance, I guess would be the correct description. But tell me your news first, Charis, and then I shall tell you mine. Although I doubt it will mean much to either of you, as you never knew the gentleman in question.'

Charis quickly relayed her news to Robert, who—to the disappointment of his sister—failed to match her excitement.

'I dare say they will suit well enough,' he said dismissively, 'but you need not envy your friend, Charis, for Talaton is an awful windbag. You should hear him prosing on in the Lords. But, never mind that…now for my news. You will both be thrilled… I know how hostesses vie with one another to be the first to present a prestigious newcomer to their guests. There is nothing quite like stealing a march on one's rivals, is there? Well. Be prepared to crow over the rest of 'em, for *we* are to be the first to welcome the new Earl of Kelridge to our dining table. Tonight! I've listed a few names we might include on the guest list.'

He reached into his pocket and thrust a sheet of paper covered in his heavy black script at Kitty. She glanced down at the list of ten names—three couples plus a few unattached ladies and gentlemen, all Hertfordshire residents. She frowned up at Robert.

'They finally located Kelridge's heir, did they? They believe this one to be genuine?'

Over the past few years, as the late Lord Kelridge's health failed, the search for his missing wife and son had intensified, but to no avail. Several charlatans, however, had tried their luck, claiming to be the missing Ambrose Trewin. Their claims had been easy to disprove, but of Lady Kelridge and her son there had been no trace.

'There is no doubt. Lady Kelridge wrote to the executors of Kelridge's estate herself…she is still alive and living in Scotland. I'd have paid good money to see Grenville Trewin's face when he found out—I'll wager he was spitting feathers! To get so close to the prize, only to have it snatched away again…one could almost feel sorry for him, although it would have been at least seven years before the Committee for Privileges would even consider declaring Kelridge's son and heir dead.'

'*I* cannot help but sympathise with Mr Trewin's son,' said Kitty. 'It would have meant a very different life indeed for Bartholomew Trewin, who has always struck me as a pleasant gentleman.'

Robert smiled. 'He *is* a good man and a good friend. Let

us hope the new Lord Kelridge will have a temperament more like that of his cousin than his late father.'

'Indeed.' Kitty had heard tales of the late Lord Kelridge's violent temper. 'Well, I admit it will be quite the coup to be the first to entertain Lord Kelridge, although—'

'Although you do not consider yourself in competition with the rest of the hostesses?' Robert grinned. 'I know you always protest against any hint of competitiveness, but can you not admit you will enjoy a certain smug satisfaction at being first in this instance?'

Kitty laughed. 'Well, just between us, I *shall* admit to it, if only because I shall not then have to listen to the other ladies boasting of their success. But, how did it come about? Why is Lord Kelridge to dine with us? Did you meet him last night?'

'No, but I met up with Tolly—that is, Bartholomew Trewin—and *he* told me his cousin had trained as an architect and you will never guess! He might be a stranger to most of the *ton*, but not to me. He actually *stayed* at Fenton Hall.'

An architect? Unease stirred, deep inside Kitty.

'Ooh! Then do I know him, too?' Charis's face lit up.

'Not you, Sis. You were too little. And it was before Father married Stepmama, so I doubt they would have met.' Robert's brown gaze settled on Kitty's face. 'Do you recall when the library wing was rebuilt after the fire?'

Those stirrings lurched into boiling, roiling agitation. She nodded, her mouth dry, those locked-away memories clamouring to be set free.

'Well, the new Lord Kelridge—it turns out he was the architect's apprentice. They stayed at the Hall during the final stages of the restoration and although Adam, as he was then called, was much older than me—I was eleven at the time—he was always patient and made time for me, although I am sure he must have cursed my impudence at times, following him around like a lost puppy as I did.'

A vivid memory struck Kitty, stealing her breath—Adam Monroe, tall and dark, laughing as he described giving young Robert the slip in order to meet up with Kitty. But there had been no malice in his laughter and he'd also spent some of his free time fishing with Robert, knowing the lad was grieving the loss of his mother. She'd thought him a good man. She'd fallen in love with him, wholeheartedly believing that he loved her in return. But he had let her down, with his lies, and she had grieved for his loss— her foolish, tender heart in pieces—when he'd left. She'd dreamt about him at night and fantasised about him during the long, lonely days while she waited for her father's return. *Dreaded* her father's return.

Her father...the one man who should have had her safety and happiness at heart, but another man who had let her down.

Her throat thickened.

'I presume your path never crossed with his, Stepmama,' Robert continued, 'even though we were neighbours.'

Kitty's heart thudded in her chest as though it would beat its way free and disgust at her naivety scoured her stomach. Adam had made so much of the fact they were unequal in status and yet the entire time he had been the son of an earl.

'We were never introduced,' she said. And that was no lie. 'And...this Adam...did he never tell you the truth of who he was?'

'No. And that is the strange thing...it appears that *he* did not know his true identity. He knew nothing about Kelridge until a few weeks ago.'

Kitty felt marginally better. But only marginally. Was that true? He had lied before, about loving her. He might easily be lying again.

'And Lord Kelridge is to dine with us tonight, you say?'

'Yes. I hope you have no objection? I was aware you had no plans to dine out tonight and, as I said, it is the perfect opportunity to steal a march on the other hostesses.' Robert slung his arm around Kitty's shoulders to give her a quick hug. 'Not that you care for such petty rivalries, of course. But many of the others *do* care...a very great deal.'

He winked, and Kitty couldn't help but smile at the wicked twinkle in his eyes even though her insides were in turmoil. She scrabbled for an excuse. Any excuse.

But—if this is the truth, and not some dreadful night-mare—I shall have to meet him some time. He will be our neighbour in Hertfordshire. I cannot avoid him for ever. And would it not be better to meet for the first time when I am prepared for it? Adam. Oh, dear God. Adam.

She swallowed down the swell of emotion. Ignored the heat that washed beneath her skin. Pressed a hand to her belly to help quell her agitation as the memories she'd held at bay for so long shot to the surface, one after the other.

The taste of his lips.

His scent.

The feeling of rightness, of safety and security in the haven of his arms. The feeling that was a lie.

Kitty... Kitty...what are you doing to me?

Those words that were lies.

Kitty quelled a shudder, quashing those memories, forcing her attention back to the matter under discussion.

'Have you spoken to Lord Kelridge? Has he accepted your invitation?'

'That,' said Robert, 'is where I have been this morning. To call upon His Lordship and remind him of our connection. He was happy to accept.'

'And is there a Lady Kelridge?' Her breath stilled in her lungs as she awaited Robert's reply.

'No. He is a single gentleman. And, now I think about it...' Robert tweaked the list from Kitty's slack grip and scanned the names, '...this may be a touch overwhelming for him—all these strangers. Should we restrict the guest list to a chosen few? Two or three couples, perhaps?'

A shudder ran through Kitty at the thought of being so exposed. Better by far to be one of many rather than risk bringing his attention to her too often.

Will he remember me? Will he even recognise me?

She would be introduced as Lady Fenton. Their...*friendship*...had taken place over a matter of weeks, fifteen years ago. Why should he remember her? She shouldn't flatter herself it had meant as much to him as it had to her. He'd made it quite clear—*brutally* clear—that he'd merely been dallying with her affections. Oh, and how easy she had made it for him...so desperate to escape her father and his plans for her that she had practically begged Adam to wed her. She had even, God help her, lowered herself enough to offer to live with him unwed. It was a miracle she had retained her innocence for, looking back, she had been so besotted she had little doubt she would have succumbed to any attempt at seduction. Willingly.

Another wave of heat—this time the burn of shame—swept over her skin, resulting in another shudder.

'Stepmama?' Charis frowned as she eyed Kitty. 'Are you quite well?'

Again, Kitty tore her thoughts out of the past, the years of controlling her emotions—hiding them from both her father and from Edgar—coming to her rescue. She gathered her customary poise and stretched her lips in a smile.

'I am quite well, my love. No need for concern. I was simply pondering the issue of the guest list. Robert... I think we should invite as many as we can sit. With us three, and Lord Kelridge, that makes ten other couples—twenty-four in total. Charis, you may assist me in compiling the guest list and writing the invitations and, Robert...will you ask Vincent to request Mrs Ainsley to attend me at her earliest convenience to discuss the menu?'

'Will we still have time to call upon Annabel?'

Charis's hesitance suggested she knew the answer, but Kitty refused to put Adam before her beloved stepdaughter. 'Yes, my love. We will *make* time.'

Her nerves continued in turmoil as the rest of the day unfolded, but she did as she always did—rose above her personal concerns and concentrated on the practicalities of what lay before her. Life with her father had instilled in her the belief that, for a female in their world, duty outweighed all other considerations.

The passage of time, however, had never been less predictable: on the one hand, it dawdled past with the speed of a snail and yet, in complete contradiction, the dinner hour swept towards her with the speed of a runaway horse. She approved the menus Mrs Ainsley presented to her; she arranged flowers; she and Charis called upon Mrs Blanchard, staying for no longer than the usual thirty minutes; and, between all that, Kitty visited her bedchamber on at least three different occasions to examine her gowns, each time making her choice, only to return later, having changed her mind.

She prayed Adam, or Kelridge, as she must now think of him, wouldn't recognise her. Yet, as soon as that prayer formed in her head, she realised she couldn't bear it if he had forgotten her—her heart would rip to shreds if he had no memory of those romantic trysts that had meant the world to her. And while she was woman enough to hope he would still find her attractive, she determined to treat him as no more than an ordinary guest, with the reserve and courtesy expected of any society hostess.

And as the clock ticked by, so her thoughts and her insides jumbled and tumbled.

'Which gown do you wish to wear tonight, milady? I shall need to press it for you.' Effie, her maid, looked at her enquiringly when Kitty wandered, yet again, into her bedchamber.

'Oh. I...' She could not continue to prevaricate, but... which gown should she select? She thrust away her disgust at her fickleness. It should not matter what she wore or what she looked like. But it did. 'Why do *you* not choose, Effie?' Kitty smiled winningly. 'I want to look my best— something simple and elegant without frills or fuss. Which gown do you suggest?'

A delighted smile lit the maid's face. 'Ooh, milady. I've always loved this one, but you so rarely wear it.' She reached into the press and withdrew a gown of butter-yellow silk, simply adorned with a few silk rosebuds and with a trim of blonde lace at the neck and the hem. 'It shows off your hair something lovely, it does.'

It was a gown Kitty had not even considered. And yet...

yes. It was perfect. It skimmed over her slender figure, the skirt falling in graceful folds that swayed as she moved. The scooped neckline was low enough to be flattering, but not brazenly so.

'Thank you. Yes, I shall wear the yellow silk. With my wedding pearls, I think.'

There, Mr Adam Monroe—or Lord Kelridge, or whatever your name might now be. You might not have wanted me, but someone did.

Edgar's gift for his young bride had been an exquisite pearl necklace, matching drop earrings and a pair of pearl bracelets.

Thank goodness for Edgar. Without him...

Once again, she dragged her thoughts out of the past. Edgar might have been insensitive at times, but he was at least gentle, clean and respectable and they had each rescued the other and fulfilled a need. His, for a mother for his young children and a life companion for himself. Hers, to escape her debt-ridden drunk of a father and his petrifying plan to clear his gambling debts by selling his young daughter's hand in marriage to Algernon White, the lecherous owner of several gaming clubs. White, her father had informed her, had ambitions to expand his business empire and was therefore eager to gain respectability through marriage into the aristocracy. And, as for her—well, what use was a daughter unless to make an advantageous marriage? Her father had never forgiven her for being born a girl and she had never forgiven him his cruel plan.

Thank goodness for Edgar indeed. Kitty had been grateful for his solution to her dilemma and she had tried to be a good wife to him, even though she was sadly aware that she had never quite measured up to the perfection of Veronica.

Chapter Three

Two days after his arrival in London and Adam's feet had barely touched the ground.

So much to take in about this new life…none of which he had asked for or, if he was honest, much wanted. He'd spent much of his time with his solicitors, all of whom, so it appeared to Adam, subscribed to Dursley's opinion that the earldom and the Kelridge estates would be far better off with Adam's uncle, Grenville Trewin, at the helm. Not that they said it outright, of course. It was the subtext of what they said, under the guise of educating Adam about his new responsibilities…the sly insinuation that the estate was bound to deteriorate under new stewardship. More than ever he was determined to appoint new solicitors as soon as all the legalities around his return had been completed.

He'd received his summons from the House of Lords and had taken his seat yesterday, his skin prickling with the weight of so many stares even though, according to one speaker, attendance in the chamber was surprisingly thin.

Adam sat there, watching and listening, feeling nothing like a lord. He did not belong in this world of the aristocracy where, although everyone was curious about him—where he had been, where his mother was, why he had not come forward until now—still he could sense the reserve of the people he met. He had always prided himself on getting along with any man, no matter his birth but…this was different. It was no longer simply a matter of polite interaction with these people. Now, he must, somehow, fit into this world. *Their* world.

He'd enjoyed the debate, in which he had not taken part as he knew next to nothing about the application of duties to imported timber. When he'd returned home, however, the thought had come into his head that he perfectly embodied that old saying, a fish out of water. His servants had resisted all his efforts to create a less formal relationship with them. It seemed they had their own peculiar pride and had no wish to serve a master who, in their opinion, crossed the line between upstairs and downstairs. They wanted a master they could take pride in serving…not one who tried to blur the boundaries between his world and theirs.

Adam belonged neither with the aristocracy nor with the servants and, during the night, he had decided to cut his losses with London and its strict hierarchy, and travel to Kelridge Place that morning.

Until Robert knocked on his door.

Robert, Earl of Fenton. How strange…unsettling, even… to realise the scruffy, grieving eleven-year-old lad who had dogged Adam's footsteps during his stay at Fenton Hall was now a man. And another lord. How many were there in London? It seemed every person he met had some kind of a title within their family. And the remainder of the population seemed to exist simply to make the lives of this privileged elite easier. He'd known, of course, it was the case and that it was the way of the world, but never before had it been thrust in his face in quite such a blatant manner.

So now, Adam had an invitation to dine with Robert and his family that evening which meant he must delay his departure for his Hertfordshire estate. And this afternoon, rather than venture forth to sample the delights of the promenade hour in Hyde Park, where he would be subjected to even more stares and speculation, he opted to stay at home with a bottle of claret and…brood, Ma would call it. He huffed a laugh. She'd be right, too. He *was* brooding…all these changes—so many in so short a space of time—dominating his thoughts until he had little space left to think about anything else.

He jerked to attention as the door opened and Green entered the room to present him with a card.

'Mr Bartholomew Trewin has called, my lord. Are you at home?'

Adam frowned at yet another example of the stiff formality he so disliked.

What if I was to say, no, I'm not at home? This house is not so vast that my cousin could fail to hear Green speak to me.

But he was curious to meet his cousin, and so he said, 'Yes. I will see him, and please bring another glass and a fresh decanter, Green.'

His cousin had evidently been the one to inform Robert that the new Earl of Kelridge was the same person as Sir Angus McAvoy's apprentice, who had stayed and worked at Fenton Hall fifteen years ago. As ever, the thought of that time sparked memories of Kitty. He'd discreetly enquired about her father, only to discover he'd died and the title and estate had been inherited by a distant cousin. Adam had been reluctant to include Kitty in his enquiry because they'd never officially met.

He stood up as a gentleman walked in through the door. Green glided across the room and set a fresh decanter and a second glass on the table next to Adam's chair before silently leaving and closing the door behind him.

'Mr Trewin?' Adam bowed. 'I am Adam, your cousin. Please, take a seat.'

His cousin bowed, then strolled across the room to take a chair near Adam, giving Adam the opportunity to study him. Thirty years of age, according to Robert, Bartholomew had until recently been a captain in the cavalry and was a veteran of the war against Napoleon and of Waterloo, that epic battle where the tyrant was vanquished at long last. He had a handsome, boyish cast to his face, if one ignored the livid scar that slashed diagonally from forehead to left cheekbone. His missing left eye was covered with a brown-leather patch and his light brown hair was carefully styled to conceal the upper part of the scar, but did nothing to hide the scar that puckered his cheek.

'I'm pleased to meet you, Coz,' Bartholomew said, his tone—as with so many in this world, Adam had discovered—a light, amused drawl. 'Do call me Tolly. All my friends do. That is, if you care to be friends... Rob tells me you seem a decent sort and I trust his ability to read a man's character.'

'Tolly it is, then.'

Adam didn't know Robert the man well enough yet to know if his judgement was truly sound, but he'd told Adam that Tolly was a good man and Adam was willing to believe it until proved otherwise.

'Claret?'

'Thought you'd never ask.'

Adam grinned and poured another glass of the rich red wine, handing it to his cousin.

'Robert tells me ye served in the cavalry.'

Tolly grimaced, lifting his hand to his eyepatch. 'I did. I got this at Waterloo. Best to get that out of the way from the start, otherwise it becomes the one thing nobody dares to mention and that's enough to stifle many conversations.'

'It must have been painful.'

Tolly shrugged. 'It has its compensations. The ladies seem to love the piratical look…happy to soothe a fellow's pain. They're not called the caring sex for nothing, y'know.'

He raised his glass as though in a toast, then swigged the wine. Adam puzzled over that hint of sarcasm…almost as though Tolly were mocking himself. Then he caught up with his cousin's purpose.

'And in the spirit of getting awkward subjects out into the open…' Adam favoured the straight approach, too '…how do ye feel about my reappearance after all this time? It would be natural if ye bore some resentment towards me.'

Tolly put his glass down and leant back in his chair. 'I knew I'd like you. Rob said you were direct. And to answer your question, I am pleased you have returned. My old man—your Uncle Grenville—would die rather than admit it, but the burden of responsibility is beginning to weigh on him.'

'He's been running the estates since my father fell ill, so I understand.'

'And before that! He resigned from the cavalry thirteen

years ago, went home to Kelridge and took over. Your father, my Uncle Gerald, was never interested in the estate, or in dealing with business matters, and was happy to leave it all to my father.'

'Why?'

At Tolly's questioning look, Adam elaborated. 'I mean, why was my father not interested in the estate? And why would *your* father be content to give up his independence and take on such responsibility?'

'Near as I can fathom it, my uncle was too busy living the high life after your mother left and cared not if the estate went to rack and ruin as long as the rents came in and funded his pleasures. My father, on the other hand, adores Kelridge Place.' Tolly shrugged. 'It's his family home… taking over meant he could live there after he left the cavalry and that he could run it in the way he saw fit. It suited them both.'

'So…' Adam frowned, thinking. 'Your father…he is unlikely to welcome my return?'

Tolly's eye narrowed. 'It *could* prove a little awkward after all these years of him being in charge. He is a mite set in his ways and you may need to tread warily at first, until he gets used to you. But *I* still think your return is a blessing in disguise for him.'

'Thank ye for the warning. What about…does your mother also live there?'

'No. She died when I was seventeen. It's just Father and me now.'

Tolly left soon afterwards, leaving Adam with plenty to think about until it was time to change for his dinner engagement at Robert's house.

* * *

Some time later, Adam trod up the steps to the elegant town house belonging to Robert, Lord Fenton. The door swung open before he reached the top.

'Lord Kelridge.' And still he felt like an imposter saying that name.

The butler bowed. 'Good evening, my lord.' He clapped his hands and a maidservant hurried forward. 'Allow me to take your hat and then please follow me.'

As the butler handed the hat to the maid, Adam took in the surroundings—the graceful open-string staircase, with its triple barley-twist balusters topped by a polished dark wood handrail that finished in an elegant spiral at the foot of the stairs. He then followed the butler upstairs to a pair of double doors, which he flung open.

Adam stepped past him and over the threshold into a spacious salon papered above the dado rail in a fashionable grey-green floral design wallpaper and crammed, it seemed, with people. He halted, striving to keep his expression blank. Robert had assured him that they would dine *en famille*, with one or two additional guests. This…*this*… was too much. Every muscle in his body tensed as a hush descended upon the room. Without exception, every single person was staring at him. Appraising him. *Judging* him. His mouth dried and his breathing quickened, causing his pulse to pound as he stared back at the pale, featureless mass of faces. Then a movement broke the moment and Robert emerged from within that mass, striding towards him with a smile on his face, allowing Adam the time to recover his composure, determined to conceal how uncomfortable he felt in his new situation.

'Kelridge! Welcome, my friend. Come…' Robert ushered Adam further into the room '…allow me first to introduce you to my stepmother, Lady Fenton, and my sister, Miss Charis Mayfield.'

Adam's mouth stretched into a polite smile as his gaze skimmed over the two ladies. He bowed. 'Delighted to make your acquaintance, ladies.'

Is that correct? Should I have said Lady Fenton and Miss Mayfield?

Neither lady appeared scornful or, worse, laughed at him, so he hoped he had not committed a faux pas in front of all these strangers. He breathed easier as the two ladies bobbed curtsies, Miss Mayfield—a pretty girl with greenish-hazel eyes and fair hair—eyeing him with unabashed interest while Lady Fenton lowered her eyelids and had yet to look directly at him. As she rose from her curtsy, however, the crescent of her thick, dark lashes lifted to reveal a pair of clear grey eyes and, as their gazes collided, recognition hit Adam with the force of a lightning bolt.

Kitty!

He had hoped they might meet, but he'd not expected it so soon. He'd even wondered if she might prove difficult to find without revealing their previous acquaintance. Deep inside him, a bud of pleasure unfurled, radiating happy contentment. But even as his lips began to curve in a smile, so he recognised the signs that Kitty did not share his joy at meeting again. There was the frosty directness of her stare. The tight line of her lips. The fine groove etched between her eyebrows—a groove that deepened by the second. The stubborn tilt of her chin—a familiar habit from fifteen years before.

Adam blanked his expression yet again, recalling the

bad terms on which they had parted, realising that while *he* knew he had denied his love for her in order to protect her from a naive mistake, Kitty had not been privy to his reasoning. There was no chance for explanation, however. Not yet.

'Welcome to our home, Lord Kelridge. I am pleased to meet you.'

Not by a flicker did Kitty reveal they were already very well acquainted and the spread of joy that had already stuttered to a halt now shrivelled and died.

Adam studied his hostess. Robert's stepmother...but *Robert* was Lord Fenton, which made Kitty a widow.

No. Not *a* widow. *The* widow...of the Lord Fenton who had appointed Sir Angus to design and oversee the restoration of his fire-damaged house; the Lord Fenton who had lost his wife, the mother of his children, in that same fire. Robert's father who—so Robert had informed Adam that very morning—had married unexpectedly within two weeks of Adam leaving Fenton Hall.

Two weeks! She swore undying love and claimed her heart was breaking, yet, within days, she accepted another man's hand?

Adam's head spun. Had she lied? She *must* have lied! If she'd truly loved him as she'd claimed, she could never have given herself to another man so soon. He had never quite recovered from his youthful love for Kitty—no other woman he had met had come anywhere close to banishing his memories of her—and yet she had forgotten all about him within two short weeks and married another man. And not just any other man, but Lord Fenton.

God, I'm such a fool! A stupid, blind, trusting fool!

Fenton must have been...what? At least forty years old

at the time Adam had known him. Forty years to Kitty's seventeen? Adam's gut clenched. What the devil had possessed her to throw herself away on a man so much older than her, a man with four children already, to boot? No wonder she did not look happy to meet him again. He was no doubt an unwelcome reminder of her youthful infatuation and would be mortified should her stepchildren discover the truth of her behaviour.

Adam struggled to rise above his pain, vowing never to let her know for how long he had ached for her after his return to Edinburgh...not when she had moved on to another man without a second thought.

Lies! They all lied to me—Ma. Sir Angus. And now Kitty.

He reined in his anger and struggled to contain his sense of betrayal as he continued to study her.

She was still relatively young—only thirty-two—and she had matured into a fine woman indeed. Her pale yellow gown draped enticingly over a slender but lush figure—curvier and more womanly than he remembered. Unsurprising in view of her youth when they had last met. He wrenched his attention from her body to her face—the same face that had haunted his dreams for many months after his return to Edinburgh. It was older, but no less appealing: the plump smoothness of a young girl's cheeks had given way to high, sculptured cheekbones; the rosy robustness to a more subtle creamy glow; the brief smile she afforded him was measured rather than eager to please—no sign now of the dimples he had adored—and the eyes that had been a window to her every thought and feeling were now guarded. The full pink lips were the same, as was the glossy mahogany-brown hair, but they were physical features—they did not reflect the person...the character...

She was a stranger now, that was the truth.

Who knows what has happened to her in the past fifteen years, or what sort of a woman she is now? And this... He cast a glance around the salon and its occupants. *This is a new world to me...the* haut ton...*the aristocracy... Mother warned me how disapproving this world can be.*

He would be wise to move through society with a cautious tread until he could better understand it and, if Kitty chose not to reveal their past acquaintance, then he would respect that wish.

'I am honoured by your invitation, my lady.'

Another smile flickered over her lips and was gone. 'Robert will introduce you to our other guests, sir', and she turned away to greet the arrival of yet more guests.

Robert guided Adam towards the nearest of his fellow diners and the following half an hour became a jumble of names and a blur of faces, although he found his gaze drawn frequently to Kitty despite his best efforts to ignore her.

Robert assured Adam there were no more than four-and-twenty diners—all of them, evidently, Hertfordshire residents and, therefore, neighbours of Adam's seat, Kelridge Place—but it seemed like twice that number. Some of the guests were cautiously friendly. Others appeared more suspicious. But every one of them was curious and they vied with one another to slip intrusive questions about Adam's past into the conversation, as though trying to catch him out.

Just as he began to despair of ever reaching the end of the introductions, Robert gripped his elbow to turn him, whispering into his ear, 'This is the last of them, I promise. I should warn you, though...she is the highest-ranking lady in our area of Hertfordshire and she expects to be treated according to her consequence. But she's not a bad old trout.' He raised his voice. 'And this is the Marchioness of Datchworth. My lady...please allow me to present the Earl of Kelridge.'

The Marchioness had swept into the salon only moments before and Adam bowed for what felt like the hundredth time. The lady in question was around sixty years of age, with an upright posture and a sprightly, energetic step that surely rendered the slender cane she carried in her right hand superfluous. She was dressed in a peacock-blue gown and sported a turban of the same hue, trimmed with a fluttering white feather. In her left hand she held a white lace fan.

'I knew your mother.' The Marchioness pinned him with a piercing look from her sharp blue eyes. 'Has she ever mentioned me? Araminta Todmorden? That was my maiden name.'

'I'm afraid not.'

'You are very Scottish-sounding.' She continued to eye him suspiciously.

'Aye. That is because I *am* Scottish.'

'Do not be ridiculous! You are as English as I. You were born in Hertfordshire. I remember it very well.'

'Aye...well...' What the devil did the woman want him to say? 'I—'

'Lady Datchworth...'

A floral scent with a hint of citrus wreathed through Adam's senses. He half-turned and there was Kitty at his elbow. The scent was unfamiliar...it did not conjure up the girl of his past. He must get used to it. *That* Kitty was gone...vanished into the mists of the past...and this lady, this stranger, occupied her space in the world. But he couldn't deny she had matured into a very attractive woman—one who stirred his blood as effortlessly as the younger Kitty, despite the pain caused by that revelation of her speedy marriage to Fenton.

'It is time to eat,' Kitty said. 'Will you take Fenton's arm to lead the way to the dining room, ma'am?'

'Not on this occasion.' The Marchioness, although shorter than Kitty by a good three inches, still managed to look down her nose at her. 'Kelridge will escort me. I expect him to be seated next to me. I have *questions*.'

Far from looking put out by Lady Datchworth's edicts, Kitty bit back a smile as her eyes danced with amusement.

'Of course, ma'am.'

The Marchioness snapped her fan closed and tapped Kitty upon the arm. 'Do not imagine me blind to your insolence, young lady. You always were too opinionated for your own good. Young gels these days…full of new-fangled notions and opinions. It wasn't the same in *my* day. Come, Kelridge. Let us proceed. I know my way, even if you do not.'

Adam slid a sideways look at Kitty, intercepting her glance at him. Her expression was as blank as he strived to make his own, leaving him at a loss as to how to she truly felt about them meeting again and about his change of circumstances.

He vowed to speak to her privately before the evening was out.

Chapter Four

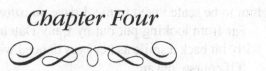

Trust Lady Datchworth to tread her own path, Kitty thought. Had anyone else suggested that Lord Kelridge give her his arm, she would have speedily pulled rank for, as the lady of highest precedence, she would expect to be escorted by—and seated next to—Robert, her host. Kelridge and the Marchioness strolled from the salon and Lord Radwell, as the highest-ranking gentleman, proffered his arm to Kitty, who accepted with a gracious smile. The remaining diners would, she knew, follow in no specific order, unlike at a formal dinner where they would enter, and be seated, strictly according to order of precedence.

For the first time she wondered how Adam would adjust to the unwritten rules and etiquette of this world so alien to him. Nothing would come naturally to him.

Her eyes sought him, taking in his height and the breadth of his shoulders. He was so much larger than she remembered—his sheer size as intimidating as his direct blue stare—but he was just as handsome. She guessed he was not a man to be thwarted as she watched him lean over to listen to what Lady Datchworth was saying, nor one to be easily controlled…and Lady Datchworth was a woman who thrived on manipulating others into doing her bidding. But Her Ladyship's acerbic tongue concealed a kind heart for anyone in trouble and Kitty hoped Adam would be patient with her when she annoyed him, as she surely would.

Kitty cast her mind back to the young man she had known. Had he been patient? Impatient? She was hard put to recall.

He had lied to her. *That* she remembered. He had broken her heart.

The manner of their parting overshadowed all that had gone before and all that had raised her young hopes. His fine words had proved false. Words with no meaning or substance or truth in them. Words to cajole and persuade a young starry-eyed girl to relinquish her heart…and thank goodness it had not been her body, too. She did owe him thanks for that, for he had never even attempted to go further than a few kisses and caresses—although she doubted the man he had become would be so hesitant.

She had not missed the admiration in his blue eyes when they first came face to face, or his subtle scan of her person, and she was conscious of the number of times he had sought her out with his gaze in the interlude before dinner was served. Her fear he would not remember her had proved groundless. He remembered her all right and he clearly still found her attractive. But she would not allow herself to be flattered into lowering her guard against him. Never again. So many men could not be trusted…she had learned that hard lesson early, from both her father and from Adam.

'Lady Fenton?'

She turned to Lord Radwell, seeing the kindly concern in his eyes.

'You tutted.' A smile creased his face. 'Is there aught amiss?'

She smiled back. 'No, indeed, sir.'

He quirked a brow. 'I am pleased to hear it.'

She need not elaborate and he would pry no further, of course. He was a gentleman. He had been a close friend of Edgar's and he and his wife had proved a great support to the family when Edgar died.

Radwell helped seat Kitty at the table and sat by her side. Adam was at the far end, between Robert and Lady Datchworth and, throughout the meal, Kitty responded by rote to her neighbours' conversation, drawing on her years of practice as a hostess. She even initiated a change of topic by referring to the forthcoming coronation of George IV in July but, the entire time, her attention returned again and again to Adam.

But that did not mean her interest was in any way personal. It was natural curiosity. It was understandable.

Everyone here is curious about this newcomer...why should I be exempt?

His hair was still dark as night and he still wore it a touch on the long side. Was it still as soft? His face...it was the same, but older, of course. And, perhaps, harsher—no longer the open, sunny smiles of his youth but all hard planes and chiselled, brooding looks, with dark brows drawn low over those percipient blue eyes. And his mouth...his lips...

The memory of his kiss shivered through her and she shook it off, only to find Lord Radwell watching her with a slight frown. She smiled at him.

'Tell me, my lord…how fares your mother these days? It is several years since I have seen her in town, I believe?'

'She grows frail,' he said. 'But that is only to be expected for a lady almost eighty. She is not strong enough to travel and so must remain at the Manor and hope for the occasional visit by friends and neighbours.'

Oh, dear. And now I am obligated…

'I am sorry to hear that. When we return to Fenton, I shall make sure to call upon her.' Radwell Manor was less than ten miles from Fenton Hall. Many of their guests, deliberately, had been drawn from their local society in Hertfordshire, for the same families were also neighbours of Kelridge Place. 'And how are the rest of the family?'

While the Earl told her about his adult children and their families, Kitty's thoughts returned to Adam.

Should I try to talk to him? In private?

But she shied away from the idea. What was there to say? Nothing she hadn't said to him at the time and nothing that could possibly alter the fact that he had walked away from her, having lied.

I must be grateful for Lady Datchworth's interest…she will no doubt keep him occupied for the rest of the evening.

But Kitty had not reckoned on Lady Datchworth developing the headache and leaving before the gentlemen finished their port.

'I am so sorry you are unwell,' Kitty said, as she escorted her from the salon, having already instructed Vincent, their butler, to order Her Ladyship's carriage to be brought to the door.

'As am I, for I had hopes of finding out more about the newcomer in our midst. He plays his cards close to his chest, does that one—bluntly refused me his mother's direction, would you believe, even though I demanded it outright! I am persuaded she would not object, for we were friends in our younger days, you know, and I wish to write to her, but he simply would not budge.'

Kitty smiled at Lady Datchworth's outrage—being thwarted was a novel experience for her—as they made slow progress down the stairs.

'Mayhap his mother does not wish to revisit her past?'

'Stuff and nonsense!'

Male voices reached them from the landing above as the gentlemen began to leave the dining room. Lady Datchworth halted.

'I shall pay my respects to my host, my dear, if you would be good enough to summon him?'

'Of course.'

A hand stayed Kitty as she turned to climb the stairs again. 'And, while you are there, you may tell Lord Kelridge that I wish to speak to him before I leave. He is an interesting man and he would, I believe, be a splendid match for that stepdaughter of yours. Do you not agree?'

'*Charis?* No, I do not. He is far too old for her.'

'Poppycock, my dear. Look at how content you were with Fenton…there were more years between the pair of you than there are between Kelridge and Charis. And think of the advantage in having her settled so near to Fenton. Not like poor Jennifer, so far away in Yorkshire. I am convinced you will be happy to have Charis so near.'

With no idea what to say without revealing her prior acquaintance with Adam, Kitty merely nodded and continued up to the landing. She passed Lady Datchworth's command on to Robert, who grinned good-naturedly and headed for the stairs. Kitty scanned the other male guests as they quit the dining room. Adam was the last to emerge and his gaze immediately settled on Kitty, capturing hers. She swallowed past the sudden constriction of her throat.

'Lady Datchworth is indisposed and is about to leave. She expressed a wish to speak with you before she goes.'

A sardonic smile stretched his lips but failed to reach his eyes. 'A wish, you say? I should rather believe it a command. I suppose there is no getting out of it? An excuse ye might pass on to Her Ladyship on my behalf?'

'You suppose correctly, sir.'

'Sir? There was a time ye called me Adam without hesitation, Kitty.'

Anger flashed through her, shocking her with its intensity. Hearing her name on his lips…as though he believed he had the right—No! He forewent any such right the day he walked away from her and left her to the mercy of her father and his greedy, heartless scheme.

'It is Catherine, Lord Kelridge.' She kept her tone measured. Not for the world would she reveal how rattled she was by his reappearance in her life. 'And that was in another lifetime. Time has moved on and I with it.'

How many years had it been since anyone had called her Kitty? Edgar had always preferred Catherine, deeming Kitty childish, and she had raised no objection because the name brought back too many painful memories of Adam. She drew in a breath and straightened her shoulders, raising her chin.

'I should deem it a favour if you forget we ever met.'

His expression gave nothing away, the planes of his face hard and still, his eyes shadowed by the fall of hair over his forehead.

'As ye wish.'

He spun on his heel and headed for the stairs. Kitty followed, her heart thumping erratically, her mouth dry.

They descended to the hallway where a maid was helping Lady Datchworth to don her tippet ready for the journey while Robert waited patiently by the open front door. Her Ladyship waved her hand at Robert in regal dismissal as Kitty reached the ground floor.

'I have already thanked you for your invitation, Fenton, so you may go now. Catherine will see me out. You must attend to your guests.'

Robert flicked a sideways glance at Kitty, and his lips quirked. He bowed to Lady Datchworth. 'Goodnight, my lady.'

Adam also bowed. 'I'll bid ye goodnight as well, my lady.'

'You may hand me into my carriage, Kelridge.' Her Ladyship's gaze shifted to Kitty, then back to Adam again. 'And do not imagine I have forgiven your stubborn refusal to give me your mother's address, for I have not.'

'It seems I am doomed to disappoint the ladies this night.' Kitty steeled herself not to react to his jibe. 'Yet I have offered to forward your letter to my mother—whether she then chooses to share her whereabouts with you is, I would suggest, her prerogative. My lady.'

Lady Datchworth peered down her nose at him, but then she caught Kitty's eye to reveal a twinkle in her own blue orbs. 'This one,' she said, 'will need watching, Lady Fenton. He is a rogue.'

With that, she marched out into the street, ignoring the groom standing ready to assist her into the carriage, and waited for Adam to hand her in. It was only when she was

settled on to the seat that she deigned to say goodnight to
Kitty, who was therefore obliged to stand outside as well.
She shivered as the carriage pulled away and turned for the
warmth of the house.

'It is chilly for the time of year,' she remarked as they
went indoors.

'Not in my experience.' Adam stood aside to allow Kitty
to precede him. 'You southerners are no' hardened to a cold
climate.'

Vincent closed the door behind them and then trod se-
dately towards the back of the house as Kitty began to
ascend the stairs, back straight, chin high, incredibly conscious of Adam following behind her. At the top, he grasped
her arm. His touch on her bare skin set her nerves tingling,
and her breath caught in her throat.

'Kitty. Give me a minute. I have something I need tae
say to you.'

He stood close to her, his sheer size almost intimidating, but there was no fear in her heart. Rather, his touch
and his nearness resurrected memories. Memories that, in
their turn, dragged long-suppressed feelings to the surface
and stirred forgotten yearnings that Kitty could not bear.
She could not allow him to sweet talk her into…into…into
anything. She snatched her arm from his grip and drew her
shoulders back.

'Unhand me, sir! You will bring scandal to me and to my
family and I will not allow it.'

He took her hand this time and no amount of tugging
could break his hold as he stared down at her.

'There is no one tae see us and we will hear should anyone approach.'

She stilled, loath to give him the satisfaction of struggling against him, but if he imagined she would fall for his false charm again he was sorely mistaken. 'Say what you must and then allow me to return to my guests.'

'I…'

His chest rose as he heaved in a breath and his thick brows drew tight into a frown. She averted her gaze, feeling her nostrils flare with anger. How dare he come here, to her home, and put her in this odious position?

'Say what you have to say.' She aimed her words at his chest, determined not to be put at a disadvantage by looking up at him.

'I know ye're angry with me, Kitty. But *I* behaved as I did for the best. I explained it tae you that day and—even were ye then too young and innocent of the ways of the world tae fully understand—ye *must* look back now and know I was right. But *you*…' He paused.

They were so close she could smell his cologne…musky and spicy…and feel the heat radiating from his body and the warmth of his breath as it stirred her hair. Slowly, his words penetrated the fury that clouded her brain. Even though she longed to throw his words back at him, she could not deny he had been right about the impracticality of what she had asked of him fifteen years ago. What she had *begged* of him.

But it does not change the fact that he lied to me. Over and over.

She reassembled her righteous anger and glared up at him.

'But I?' she prompted.

'Ye wed just *two weeks* after I left!'

'I—' Her eyes narrowed. 'How do you know that?'

'Rob told me. Ye lied tae me…ye swore ye loved me, but ye didna!' As his anger strengthened so, too, did his accent, bringing the young man she had known even more force-fully to mind. 'It wasna *me* ye wanted—ye'd take *any* man tae be your husband, ye were that eager to snare some poor soul...sae desperate ye'd even take a man auld enough to be your own da.'

Only as those accusations tore from his mouth, as though ripped out of him, did Kitty understand that his desire to speak to her without being overheard had nothing to do with currying favour, or with trying to cajole her...to re-kindle their love, or passion, or friendship, or whatever it had been...but everything to do with venting *his* anger. And that realisation revived, in all its heart-wrenching agony, the pain he had caused her.

She was the injured party here. It was she who had suf-fered...what right did he have to be angry?

'And I bless the day I married Edgar.' She snatched her hand away again, this time freeing it. She clutched the hand-rail on the balustrade to help steady her trembling frame, for she was shaking with fury at the injustice of him blaming her when it was he who had led her on, raising her hopes with his false declarations of love. She dragged her gaze up and down him, allowing her scorn full rein. 'You were *nothing*! He, at least, was a real man. And I still mourn the day of his death.'

She fled along the landing, heading for the safety of the salon and other people. Once inside, she crossed the room to sit with Lady Radwell and Lady Charnwood to join in their conversation about the last few weeks of the Season, including Lady Charnwood's ball the following night. Once again Kitty conversed by rote, at least half of her thoughts occupied with a silent diatribe against that despicable rogue, Kelridge. How dare he twist everything, insulting her and accusing *her* of inconstancy? Although, in all fairness, he *was* right that a match between the two of them would have been a disaster, given their unequal places in society. If, of course, he hadn't known all along that he was the son of an earl. How was she supposed to know the truth when he had lied before?

She fixed her gaze on her two companions and resolutely refrained from looking to see if he had followed her into the room.

She did not care.

She would not care if she never saw him, or spoke to him, ever again. And she didn't even want to *think* about him. She hoped he would soon tire of his new life and return to Scotland and leave his estates in the hands of his uncle and his steward, who—it was said—had run the place during much of the late Lord Kelridge's time. Eventually, however, a shadow fell across their trio and, when her companions fell silent, Kitty had no choice but to acknowledge Adam's brooding presence.

His bright blue eyes bore into Kitty. 'I must bid you goodnight, Lady Fenton. My thanks for your hospitality.'

'You are most welcome, Lord Kelridge. I trust meeting so many new faces has not proved too onerous?'

'Not at all.'

'Lord Kelridge,' Lady Charnwood addressed Adam. 'If you are free tomorrow evening, might you honour me with your attendance at my ball?'

Kitty stiffened in dismay. How had she not foreseen that he was likely to be invited to the same entertainments as her family? She needed time, and space, to think about his return without being thrust headlong into his company. It would be nigh on impossible to avoid him for the remaining weeks of the Season. Her nerves skittered as her stomach turned over.

Adam bowed to Lady Charnwood. 'It would be my pleasure, ma'am.'

'Splendid. I shall send the invitation in the morning...no need for a formal reply.'

Adam smiled at her before returning his gaze to Kitty. 'I wonder if I might beg the indulgence of a private word, Lady Fenton?'

Kitty kept any sign of emotion from her expression. If only she could refuse without giving rise to speculation and rumours she would do so, but the wretch knew very well good manners would force her to agree. She rose unhurriedly to her feet, smoothing down her skirts with hands that trembled with that suppressed fury.

'Pray excuse me, ladies,' she said and trod steadily and deliberately over to the nearby window.

'What more can you possibly have to say to me? Have we both not said enough?'

'I regret my outburst and I apologise. Blame my upbringing if you will.'

His wry tone indicated that he knew all too well the rumours flying around the *ton* about his life as a boy and a youth. Few facts were known about those years and the man himself was less than forthcoming, so speculation filled the void. All that was known of him were his professional qualifications and glowing testimonials for his work as an architect from a handful of well-connected clients, but they revealed nothing about the character of the man.

Kitty forced herself to face him, fixing her gaze on his mouth...a mistake, as it happened, because her treacherous mind insisted on conjuring up the slide of his lips over hers…the stroke of his tongue…and her heart, annoyingly, fluttered in her chest. She did not want these memories, or the feelings they aroused, but…*oh*, those kisses! She stifled her sigh. Edgar had never kissed her in such a manner. She did not even know if it was natural, for she had never kissed a man other than those two. She dragged her gaze from his mouth to his eyes.

'I will,' she said. At the lift of his brows she elaborated. 'I shall blame your upbringing. A true gentleman would never say such things to a lady.'

'Ah. No. Of course he would not.'

'Have you quite finished? I must return to my guests.' She started to step past him.

'One more thing.'

Kitty paused. 'I am listening.'

'When we meet, might we agree to do so with at least the appearance of civility?'

Civility! Who would have thought all that youthful passion could be distilled down into mere politeness? Kitty buried her hurt, telling herself it was a false emotion, borne out of memories and broken dreams, and it had no place in the present.

'I pride myself on my civility, sir, no matter the circumstances, and you have my word that I shall treat you no differently to any other gentleman of my acquaintance when our paths cross during what is left of the Season. Now, it has been interesting to renew our acquaintance, but I see our guests are beginning to depart and I must say goodbye.'

She inclined her head and moved past him to join Robert as he bade farewell to the Radwells. There was a flurry of departures and, when Kitty had the time to notice, Adam had gone.

Chapter Five

The following evening—quite late, as it was already dusk—Adam presented himself at the Charnwoods' house for Lady Charnwood's ball, his mind full of Kitty, as it had been all day, even after he'd lain awake half the night, going over every single word, every single look they had exchanged the night before. He told himself it meant nothing. There was nothing left between them...certainly no tender emotions. Only hurt and rejection and deceit. But despite that, and despite his hurt at the speed and the ease with which she had recovered from their ill-fated romance, he had looked forward all day to seeing her again, knowing she would, without doubt, be here tonight.

He entered the ballroom and stopped short. If the Fenton dinner had been intimidating, *this* was utterly overwhelming. So many people. So much chatter and laughter. The ballroom soared two storeys with three massive chandeliers suspended from its high ceiling, and wall sconces all around were lit. The effect was magical as jewels glittered, reflecting the candlelight, and gowns in a myriad of hues swished and swirled around the dance floor. The dancing had already begun, accompanied by a quartet of musicians sitting on a raised dais at one end of the room, and the combined heat from bodies and from candles was already tangible despite the row of French windows along the wall opposite having already been flung wide.

Adam tamped down his unease as he searched the crowd for his hostess and finally spied her standing with Tolly and another lady. His anxiety subsided. At least he had two acquaintances in this heaving mass. He threaded his way through the guests and bowed to the group.

'Good evening, my lady. Tolly.'

'Oh, you have come. I *am* pleased.' Lady Charnwood turned to the other lady in their group—a stunningly beautiful female of around twenty, he guessed, with hair of a deep golden colour and eyes the exact same hue. If ever a woman could be described as the epitome of femininity, it was surely this one. 'Lady Phoebe Crawshaw, allow me to introduce Lord Kelridge.'

Adam bowed as Lady Phoebe curtsied. Her unusual eyes examined him with a frankness he found refreshing. 'I am pleased to make your acquaintance, my lord.' Her voice was deep and somewhat husky. 'I have been wondering when we would meet.'

'How so, my lady?'

She shrugged gracefully. 'You must know you are much discussed and speculated upon in these circles. And I...' she slanted a look through her lashes at Tolly '...am of a naturally curious disposition.'

Tolly sucked in one cheek and his eye narrowed. Tonight...presumably in honour of the occasion...he had swapped his leather eyepatch to one made of silk. 'You will not persuade me, my lady, so you may as well save your breath.'

Lady Phoebe pouted. 'Then there is no point in conversing with you further, Mr Trewin. Lord Kelridge...a waltz is about to begin and I am in sore need of a partner. Would you care to ask me to dance?'

Adam bowed. 'It will be my pleasure, my lady.'

He held out his hand. Lady Phoebe laid her gloved hand in his, but then hesitated.

'I presume you do know how to waltz?'

Adam laughed. 'Scotland is quite enlightened, my lady. Aye, we know the waltz.'

He led her on to the floor and found a space, conscious of the many looks in their direction, not all of them benign.

Adam placed his hand on Lady Phoebe's waist and took her right hand in his left.

'Why do I get the feeling there is something here I dinna understand?' he asked. 'We appear to be the centre of attention.'

She shrugged and smiled up at him prettily. 'The men are envious of you and I imagine the ladies are envious of me.'

She was no shy miss with her opinions, that was for sure. 'And what is it that Mr Trewin will not be persuaded of by you?'

She laughed, revealing small and even white teeth. 'I *knew* you and I would get along. I do like a man who gets straight to the point. I requested to see Mr Trewin's scars and he is being most disobliging in that respect. That is all.'

Adam laughed and, as he did so, he glanced across the room, his gaze clashing with Kitty's as she stood in another man's embrace awaiting the opening bars of the music. The suddenness of it took his breath away and his heart lurched in his chest. He tore his eyes from hers, cursing inwardly, telling himself again that it meant nothing.

He forced himself to concentrate on dancing because—for all his brave declaration about the waltz—in truth he was not at all well practised in the steps. Time and again, though, he found his attention on Kitty as she glided gracefully around the floor in her partner's arms, her pale blue gown floating around her ankles.

'Are you acquainted with Lady Fenton, or is it Lord Silverdale commanding your interest, sir?'

His partner's slightly mocking question jerked Adam's attention back to her.

'I dined with the Fentons last evening,' he said, 'and I was wondering where I had seen Her Ladyship's partner before. Now you have said his name, I do recall it was in the House of Lords the other day.'

He forced himself to concentrate on Lady Phoebe until the end of their dance, when he led her from the floor, back to where Tolly stood with Robert, Lady Charnwood having moved on. The other men immediately vied with one another to pay Lady Phoebe the most extravagant compliments and Adam took advantage of their preoccupation to take his leave of them. He then patrolled the perimeter of the ballroom, scanning the guests. It wasn't long before he spotted Kitty at the very moment she slipped out through one of the French windows. Adam headed for the open window nearest to him and paused.

He welcomed the cool of the night air after the heat of the ballroom and breathed deeply as he took stock of the narrow, stone-flagged terrace outside. Lamps were set at intervals along the house wall, throwing alternating areas

of light and shade across the paving. There were a handful of others on the terrace but, of Kitty, there was no sign.
A growl of disapproval rumbled in Adam's chest and he
stepped out on to the flagstones even as his common sense
roared at him not to be a fool, that to follow her outside
would be to suggest an interest in her that even he was not
certain existed. A wise man would bide his time and sort
out his own inner turmoil first.

He ignored his own advice.

He would just make sure she was safe. He strode to the
balustrade that edged the terrace and slowly rotated. Finally,
he spied her, standing at the far end of the flagged area, in a
patch of shadow, her back to him and her head tipped back
as she gazed up at the night sky. The new moon was a mere
crescent suspended above the neighbouring rooftops while
innumerable stars spangled the vast darkness overhead.

'Ye shouldna be oot here alone.'

He spoke softly, but she started none the less and spun
to face him. He could not read her expression here in the
shadows, but he *could* recognise the tension in her body.

'Why ever not?'

'Someone might take advantage of ye.'

She laughed, folding her arms. 'Nonsense. I know all
the guests here tonight and this garden is entirely enclosed.
You may leave me, safe in the knowledge I shall come to
no harm.'

Adam stepped closer. She stepped back. He halted, his
hands itching to stroke the bare skin of her arm above her
glove, and he closed his fingers into his palms, clenching
his hands to keep them from straying. How could she have
this effect on him? How could he yearn to touch her and
yet, at the same time, long to fling her perfidy in her face

again? *Her* heartbreak had lasted a mere two weeks, and the urge to retaliate…to hurt her in return…beat deep inside him. But…alongside that urge was the desire to simply talk to her. Connect with her. *Understand* her. And he retained enough awareness to know that would not happen if they argued every time they met. He swallowed down that myriad of confusing emotions.

'I saw you dancing,' said Kitty. 'What did you make of The Incomparable?'

It soothed his wounded pride a little to learn that she had noticed him.

'What is The Incomparable?'

'Not what. Who. Lady Phoebe Crawshaw. That is what she is called by the gentlemen—it is the fashion to be in love with her, you know.'

Adam's eyes had adjusted to the dim light on the terrace and he searched Kitty's expression for a sign…*any* sign… that she experienced anything like the tumult of emotions that churned within him, but her expression was serene. His gaze lowered to her décolletage. Did her bosom rise and fall more rapidly than it should? Or was that mere wishful thinking?

'Is it indeed?' he said.

'It is. So I hope you will prostrate yourself at her feet at some point before the end of the Season, or you will be declared a very poor sort of a fellow.'

Her tone lightly mocked. Surely she could not speak of such matters so casually if she still felt anything for him? Not that he *wanted* her to feel anything for him…other than as a sop to his pride. He forced a laugh.

'I concede the lady is beautiful, but I have never been one to follow the herd and Lady Phoebe isna quite to my taste.' He moved closer to Kitty, angling his body to shield her from the view of others on the terrace, and lowered his voice, keen to provoke a reaction beyond that of social chit-chat. 'She is too young and too bold. I prefer my women more refined.'

'Your women...' Kitty spoke slowly, staring up at him, wide-eyed, as her chest rose.

'Aye.'

His voice deepened, turning husky. He succumbed to temptation, against all his better judgement. He reached out with his forefinger and traced her arm from shoulder to inner elbow, her skin warm and smooth, and he noticed her involuntary shiver at his touch. Kitty's teeth captured her full lower lip. He could still taste her, in his memory, and his blood surged. He leaned in to her, his cheek tantalisingly close to hers. Her breathing quickened, coming in little gasps and, encouraged, Adam turned his head to brush his lips over her satin-soft skin.

Tension flowed off Kitty in waves, the air between them charged with expectation, like the air before a thunderstorm. Adam fingered an errant curl, just behind her ear, then he took her lobe between his teeth and nipped gently. Just once.

She gasped and he sensed the shiver that racked her. She turned her face to his and their lips met, tantalisingly, fleetingly, and she gasped again as she jerked away from him.

'No!'

She seemed to fold into herself, wrapping her arms defensively around her waist. 'No. We cannot. We agreed to treat one another with civility. We cannot revive our old... friendship. I have no wish to travel that path again.'

Relief and regret clashed within him in a swirl of confusion, his heart still yearning for her even as his head rejected such romantic nonsense. Why on earth was he playing with fire? Why would he risk his heart again? How could he ever trust her? He dug deep to revive his anger and his hurt over the lies she had told him, both with her words and with her kisses.

'No more do I.'

He cursed himself silently for exposing himself—he couldn't bear for her to imagine he still harboured feelings for her when he could not even unravel his own tangled feelings.

Provoking her anger seemed the safest course, for both of them.

'Let us blame the darkness and us being out here alone together. It was easy...natural, even...for us to slip into old habits.'

Kitty stiffened. 'Old *habits*?'

Why, oh, why had she come out here alone? She had seen him watching her from across the ballroom and *still* she had ventured outside. Then, instead of joining another group, she had wandered alone to the edge of the terrace.

Did I, deep down, hope *he would follow me?*

Whatever her intention, she couldn't deny she had set a dangerous game in motion. She had been a hair's breadth from allowing him to kiss her, and he...her heart lurched... *he* had accepted her lack of refusal as an opportunity. She would end up hurt again.

Adam shrugged. 'You cannot blame me for forgetting our history when we were getting along so well,' he said. 'And you cannot deny we are both considerably less angry that we were last night.'

Stomach churning, Kitty took refuge in attack.

'I *thought* we had an agreement, my lord. Had I suspected you would take my civility as an invitation to intimacy, I would have been considerably less amiable. Allow me to explain. The reason for my conversing with you as I would *any* fellow guest is that, once the shock of meeting you again faded, I realised that anger is a waste of my energy. Such strong emotion about a person or an event can only make sense if my feelings are still engaged and they are not.'

Her emotions roiled and boiled within her, alongside a hefty dollop of shame, but she contained them all, desperate not to reveal how he affected her. Still. After all this time. After all his lies. *This* was why society had rules for young girls—rules to protect their virtue and their reputation. And because Kitty had been unwise enough—and naive enough—to welcome Adam's kisses all those years ago, he would naturally assume her present morals were equally lax.

'We have agreed that we are now as strangers and it surely follows that any feelings that once existed between us must be as though they had happened to two different people. Now, I shall return to the ballroom and I would appreciate it if you do not follow me. In fact, I think it might be for the best if we avoid one another as much as possible. Then, when we do meet again, as I am sure we will, we shall pretend this never happened.'

She pivoted on her heel and walked away, concentrating on keeping her head high and her pace slow, acting the society lady as she had never acted before.

Chapter Six

Two weeks later

Adam gazed gloomily around Almack's, wondering what the hell he was doing there. He had no interest in marrying anyone, yet it seemed that every person he met...well, those who were female, anyway...was convinced he was in the market for a bride. He stifled his snort of derision and sipped again at his glass of orgeat, an insipid light wine that passed for liquid refreshment in this godforsaken place. The choice, he had been loftily informed, was that or ratafia. What wouldn't he give for a wee dram right at this moment?

Lady Datchworth had taken it upon herself to instruct Adam as to the places a well-born gentleman simply *must* be seen and this place had been high on her list. She'd presented him with a voucher as though it were manna from heaven, impressing upon him how grateful he should be that the Patronesses had granted him permission to attend, and all his polite refusals to her request that he escort her tonight had met with the utter conviction that he did not mean it. And he *had* remained exceedingly polite, even in the face of extreme provocation.

And now he was here he could not for the life of him see what all the fuss was about and why so many people vied with one another for a voucher. The dress code was ludicrous—silk knee breeches, indeed—the refreshments wretched and the entire evening promised to be a bore.

'Well, Kelridge? Who takes your fancy?'

He glanced down at Lady Datchworth, seated on a chair, her gloved hands wrapped around the head of her cane which was planted firmly between her legs, spread apart in a very unladylike manner, albeit still covered by her skirts. The head of her cane, which accompanied her everywhere, was fashioned in the shape of a dog's head...a terrier...and that is exactly what she reminded him of. A terrier who, once it buries its teeth into something, refuses to give it up. And, it would appear, *he* was her latest obsession. And he... oh, hell and damnation...to be brutally honest, most of the time he found her company amusing, unlike many of the prattling idiots of the *ton* and despite her highhanded belief that she knew what was best for him—and for everyone else, for that matter.

He sighed. He had to face the fact that he *liked* the meddling auld woman. He would not willingly upset her, but he still had to refrain from throttling her every time she began to blather on about finding him a wife. And what made that worse was that her favoured candidate appeared to be Miss Mayfield, Kitty's stepdaughter, a circumstance that rendered him excessively uncomfortable given his history with Kitty and his renewed friendship with Robert. Talking of Robert, Adam had caught sight of him, his ex-

pression one of studied stoicism, not five minutes since—
which meant his womenfolk must also be here. So much for
Adam's attempts to avoid Kitty since Lady Charnwood's
ball. He had not spoken to her since, although he had seen
her at several events...had watched her, wondering about
that near kiss. But she had appeared utterly indifferent to
his presence and so he had continued to avoid her, as that
is what she appeared to want.

A sharp elbow nudged him. 'Well? You *cannot* attend
Almack's and not stand up for the dances. And, if you are
serious about making a match, you will do well to follow
my advice.' She looked around her. 'If Miss Mayfield isn't
to your taste, what about Miss Penhurst over there...?' She
flipped her cane up to point, almost spearing a passer-by.
'Oh! Catherine, my dear. My apologies. I did not see you
there. I was intent upon helping poor Kelridge here with
his marriage plans.'

A pair of startled grey eyes flew to Adam's face and, to
his intense irritation, he felt his skin heat as he blushed.
Blushed! What was he...a young girl still in the schoolroom?

'I have no marriage plans and Lady Datchworth is well
aware of that fact, for I have told her so many times,' he
growled, embarrassed both by the subject and by the rush
of pure desire through his body.

'Nonsense, Kelridge. You have a title and a fortune, you
are getting no younger and you need an heir. Of *course* you
must wed—it is your obligation as a peer of the realm. You
start at a disadvantage, it is true, but I am sure there are chits
here who would be prepared to overlook your unfortunate
upbringing if *only* you would wipe that black scowl from
your face and *apply* yourself to the task in hand.'

She looked him up and down, and he set his teeth. The woman had as much tact as a charging bull and was as impossible to deflect, but he was grateful for the spike of anger that helped to quell his desire.

'You have a fine figure,' Her Ladyship went on. 'Very manly. Of course, you will not display to advantage on the dance floor—unless you are lighter on your feet than you look—but there are chits who positively favour a man with a muscular frame such as yours. Do you not agree, Catherine, my dear?'

Adam caught Kitty's amused twinkle as she mimicked Lady Datchworth in looking him up and down. His teeth ground together.

'Oh, indeed, ma'am. A *fine* figure.'

The suppressed laughter in her voice wound his temper higher. How dare she mock him? How dare they both presume to treat him like...treat him like...?

As suddenly as it arose his anger subsided and he surprised himself by laughing.

'Now, now, ladies. Please do control yourselves. I must ask...is it entirely proper for ladies to discuss a gentleman's figure in quite so blatant a manner? And within his hearing, no less?'

Lady Datchworth, when she wasn't amusing herself by playing matchmaker, had helped Adam no end with learning and understanding the ways of this world.

She grinned up at him. 'I see you have taken in some of my lessons after all, Kelridge.'

'Lessons?' Kitty arched one brow. 'What, pray, has Lady Datchworth been teaching you, my lord?'

'Oh, this and that.' Lady Datchworth waved an airy hand. 'He is a receptive pupil when he has a mind to co-operate.

But he has proved himself remarkably stubborn in certain areas.' She fixed Adam with a darkling look. 'You will do well to heed my advice. You are already six-and-thirty... time is not on your side and, as your poor mother cannot be here to guide you, it falls to me as her oldest friend to step into her shoes.'

Kitty tucked her lips between her teeth, but the sparkle of her eyes gave her away.

Adam looked away, scanning the dancers. *I am pleased my situation is providing her with such enjoyment.*

'Perhaps I will—'

'No!' Lady Datchworth held up a peremptory hand. 'I understand your predicament better than you know, Kelridge, and I have the solution—dance with Lady Fenton here. That will ease you in gently and, in time, you may find the confidence to ask one of the younger, more eligible ladies to be your partner.' She sat back, satisfaction writ large on her face.

'I—'

'That is a splendid notion, ma'am.' Kitty tucked her hand through Adam's arm. 'Come, Lord Kelridge. We shall soon build your confidence.'

Adam found himself manoeuvred away from Lady Datchworth and out on to the dance floor where sets were starting to form. He planted his feet, giving Kitty no option but to stop.

'I have nae need of your charity.'

Her grip on his arm tightened. 'Is the prospect of dancing with me *really* so objectionable that you would prefer to endure yet more of Lady Datchworth's unique variety of persuasion?'

Her voice remained low; her words were forceful, with a

hint of anger, but her expression was serene—light-hearted, even—belying her tone.

'The last time we spoke ye could not wait to rid yourself of me. And yet, here you are, nigh on begging me to dance. I wish ye would make up your mind.'

'I have no more desire to dance with you than you do with me, my lord, but I took pity on you as I would on any other harried-looking gentleman suffering the undivided attentions of Lady Datchworth. I have no further agenda, I assure you, and what I said still holds true: what happened fifteen years ago happened to two different people and I have come to the conclusion that we cannot avoid one another for ever.'

'Verra well.' He walked on, leading her among the other couples forming sets. 'As you said before, after fifteen years we truly are little more than strangers. Blame my testiness on Lady D. The woman effortlessly stirs my ire. She is so...' He could think of many words to describe Her Ladyship, none of them suitable for a lady's ears '...exasperating. So, thank ye for rescuing me from her...um...*efforts* on my behalf.'

'No thanks are necessary. But...do not condemn Lady Datchworth too harshly, Adam. She actually has a heart of gold beneath her overbearing ways.'

His heart twitched at her seemingly unconscious use of his forename.

'I am aware of it, or I would not continue to tolerate her,' he said, then frowned at his own words. 'No. That is unfair. I admit she amuses me more frequently than she frustrates me.'

'That is at least one thing we have in common, then.'

'Indeed.' He glanced at Kitty. 'I confess I am surprised to find ye here. It does not appear the sort of place—'

She tensed. 'In the first place, my lord, you have precisely no idea of my current interests, likes or dislikes. In the second place, I am here as chaperon for my stepdaughter and this is precisely the sort of venue a young lady is expected to attend in her debut Season.'

My lord! Adam did not last long.

'Of course it is. I am still guilty of overlooking the passage of years, it seems. I wonder, though…'

Could he bury his hurt at her betrayal? He kept forgetting how young she had been and he could surely make allowances more easily for Kitty's behaviour than for his mother's lies. It was not Kitty's fault that she had mistaken a young girl's infatuation for love, but it *was* his mother's fault he'd wasted fifteen years of his life believing himself unworthy of an earl's daughter.

'…as we agree we are now strangers, might we also agree to get to know the people we are now a little better?'

Surely that would be preferable to this constant sniping at one another? Kitty slid him a sideways look and her expression softened infinitesimally.

'Yes. I think we might agree upon that. And I admit it is true that I have no great liking for this place but, as I said, I am here for Charis. Almack's is the perfect place for young, unmarried ladies to display their elegance and beauty.'

'It is known as the marriage mart, according to Lady D.' Adam couldn't resist the chance to tease her. 'I assume it is an equally suitable venue for young widows to attract a future husband?'

Kitty frowned. 'Not for this widow, I assure you, for I am resolved to never again marry.'

The dance began, Adam taking Kitty's hands as they circled one another. 'Why are you opposed to marrying again? Was your marriage to Fenton so very distasteful?'

He remembered that stubborn tilt of her chin. The action exposed the pale skin of her throat, and, without warning, a starburst of longing exploded within him. The memory... her skin, warm beneath his lips; the fresh scent of his lass, of crushed grass and the earthy smell of the woods where they held their trysts; the taste of those lush lips, as full and rosy now as when they tasted of the berries they picked.

But her lips were no longer stained with blackberry juice. His heart lurched as sorrow flowed through him. She was not his lass. His Kitty. She was Catherine, Lady Fenton. Fifteen years had changed them both and he still struggled to come to terms with it.

It was the strangest dichotomy: a girl he had known so well, a girl who had taken root in his heart and who had been a part of him—staying the same in his memory for fifteen long years—a girl he had loved, yet here she was...a woman who was a stranger to him. And his feelings for this stranger were...complicated. Undoubtedly, he felt physical desire for her. She was a graceful, beautiful woman and he...*he* was a man. How could he not want her?

They had agreed to get to know one another again, but could he truly move forward and view her afresh? Could he break those chains to the past, chains forged by the pain and the insult to his pride caused by that news of her hasty marriage? He could bury his hurt, yes. But it still existed and still coloured his reactions to her. It still confused him.

He clenched his jaw and dragged his thoughts into the present as Kitty replied.

'My marriage was far from distasteful, but I shall not

discuss it with you other than to say I miss my husband a great deal. I shall not remarry because I am perfectly happy remaining with my family at Fenton Hall and I have other interests that occupy me fully. I shall not remarry because I have no need. I shall not remarry because I have no desire to do so.'

Desire. That word on her lips stirred his own desire, even though she did not use the word in that context. Was it nostalgia that returned his thoughts to her and to their shared past so frequently? Or was it the growing conviction that there were still words unsaid between them? He wanted answers. He wanted to know how she had gone from a broken heart to marriage just two weeks after his departure. He wanted to understand how she had so speedily recovered from the anguish she had accused him of causing.

How he longed to sit down with her and talk about what had happened. Perhaps then he might untangle this mass of emotion that knotted his stomach.

But the opportunity to do so was unlikely to present itself here in London. Besides, was there any point when Kitty appeared to be utterly uninterested in him? He was a seething mass of contradictory emotions whereas she revealed no hint of any residual feelings for him.

Except...there *had* been that near kiss. That, surely, meant something?

The steps of the dance separated them, and he partnered others without really seeing them. No doubt he would be branded uncouth... Lady D. had told him often enough that a gentleman was expected to entertain the ladies with gay conversation and subtle compliments. Well, his tongue had never been silver. He veered more towards the unvarnished truth. His gaze roamed over the dancers until they found Kitty and, this time, his heart lodged in his throat.

All those months…all those *years*…he had suffered guilt over his treatment of her and she…*she*…had moved on without a second thought. All those years that his own attempts to find love had come to nothing because his heart had never been in it. Because they weren't her. They weren't Kitty.

They came together again in the dance and their hands met, but barely…her touch having no more substance than that of a feather lying in his palm.

And this is what we have come to. Two strangers, with an ocean of hurt and mistrust lying between us.

Did he want more from her? Or was he right in the first place and it was simple nostalgia swelling this lump in his throat and weighing down his spirits? But even if he did want more, she had made her position crystal clear.

The decision came from nowhere.

'I leave for Kelridge Place tomorrow.'

Her grey eyes regarded him. He could read nothing of her thoughts. His gaze dropped to her lips as they parted and he mentally swatted aside the sweet nip of desire and tamped down the swell of longing. He must use reason and logic to overcome her effect on him and keep reminding himself that she was a stranger, not the Kitty he had fallen in love with.

'The Season has another two weeks at least before families leave for the country.'

Adam shrugged. 'That holds no interest for me.'

'I thought…' She paused and frowned.

The music finished and Adam bowed.

'You thought?'

Kitty curtsied. 'The dance has ended.'

The tinge of relief in her voice stirred the pain that lurked ever ready in his depths, making him long to lash out at her. To make her feel the same hurt he suffered.

He proffered his arm.

'I shall escort you back to your family.'

Again, he barely registered her hand on his arm and was forced to glance down to assure himself it was there. She roused emotion within him like no other female ever had, but he was hard put to know if it was love or hate. Was it the past casting rainbows over the present that was keeping that sliver of hope alive deep inside him? He could not tell and neither could he tell if she, too, still felt this connection that hovered between them, binding them. She was so guarded, so difficult to understand, and he longed to provoke her into some show of the emotion she claimed was absent, but which he sensed—hoped?—was there, well hidden beneath her serene surface.

'You thought?' His voice harder this time—he would not allow her to wriggle out of explaining herself. He was confused enough, without her adding more questions to the list circling inside his head.

Again, that familiar lift of her chin.

'I thought you would wish to make the most of this time, while everyone is in town, to more fully establish your position.'

'To what purpose? These people mean nothing to me. They are not my friends. I have an interest in politics and I am happy to have my say in the Lords but, as to the rest…' He contemplated his surroundings and the people within. 'I miss the purpose of earning my living. This is not a way of life that I recognise or find fulfilling. I find no merit in lives lived in pursuit of idle pleasures.'

Kitty halted, releasing Adam's arm. Her mouth was tight and, when she spoke, so was her voice. 'You may leave me to find my own way to my companions, Lord Kelridge. I should thank you, I surmise, for your condescension in agreeing to so frivolous an activity as dancing. I trust you will find your estates in good repair when you go to Kelridge.'

'If they are not, I shall soon turn them around.'

Although he did not know quite how he would manage that when he had no clue about running an estate. The flick of her eyebrow before she stalked away suggested that Kitty, too, doubted his bold confidence. Let her think what she pleased. It would be a relief to leave London and its inhabitants behind him and, as for Kitty, maybe putting distance between them might help him to sort through the confusion of his feelings for her. At least he need no longer be burdened with guilt over the past, knowing now that she had not suffered after he left. He could now look to his future and plan his life free from the sentimental, romantic regrets that had plagued him for far too long, regrets over what might have been.

He returned to Lady Datchworth, who cast a glance at a nearby couple, deep in conversation with one another, before patting the empty chair by her side. As Adam sat, the couple moved away on to the dance floor and he recognised them as Miss Mayfield and Lord Sampford. Lady D. watched them go.

'What are those two up to?'

'Shush! Nothing. How should I know?' Lady D. tore her attention from the couple and turned it on to Adam. 'What did you say to upset Catherine? For two people who barely know one another you do seem to rub one another the wrong way.'

'I shared my opinion of high society and she took offence.'

Lady D. tapped his arm with her fan. 'You must learn to dissemble, Kelridge. Bluntness will win you no friends.'

'I do not need friends. I need to go to Kelridge and learn about my inheritance. And, to that end, I have decided I shall leave London in the morning.'

'Tomorrow?'

'Aye. It's time. I've told you many times I have no wish to marry in the foreseeable future. There is no need to stay here longer.'

'But…' Her Ladyship stared at Adam, her lips pursed. 'I need you to escort me to the Change tomorrow. At two o'clock.'

'Two o'clock? Why?'

'A shopkeeper there has a new cane for me. A very special cane.' Lady D. leaned towards him, putting her hand on his arm. 'Besides…you did express an interest in seeing the beasts in the menagerie…'twould be a pity to miss them.'

'I make no doubt they will still be there next time I visit London. Hertfordshire is not Scotland—it is a short enough journey. Only a couple of hours, so I am told.'

'Precisely! So it will not hurt you to delay your departure. Have you ever *seen* an elephant?'

'No.'

'Then you simply must go before you leave. I insist. You can set off for Kelridge Place *after* you have escorted me to the Change. As you rightly say, the journey is only a few hours so you will reach there long before dusk.' Her voice rang with satisfaction and she sat upright once again, clasping her hands over the top of her cane.

Adam raised his eyebrows and grinned. Really, she was totally impossible. He didn't for one minute believe her excuse of buying a new walking cane, but curiosity prevented him from arguing further.

'Very well. I shall escort you. But I shall not stay for long, so no lingering, mind.'

It would be amusing to discover the real reason for Her Ladyship's sudden desire to visit the Exeter Exchange. Leaving town a few hours later than planned wouldn't hurt him.

Chapter Seven

Kitty tamped down her rising irritation as she stalked
across the room, seeking Robert and Charis. How dare
Adam, with only a few short weeks' experience of this
world, be so judgemental of this life? *Her* life?

How she now wished she had not succumbed to that ridiculous impulse to rescue him from Lady Datchworth's
matchmaking mischief. In fact, she had regretted her impulse the second she had taken his arm—the play of muscle
and sinew under her fingers had roused long-suppressed
feelings within her, feelings that had only intensified as
they danced: a peculiar fluttery and yet clenching sensation deep inside her that she hadn't experienced since...

With a silent oath she diverted her thoughts from following that particular trail. They were physical feelings of no
use to a widow such as she and she had no intention of either encouraging them or, heaven forbid, indulging in them.

*But surely you want to know what it might be like. You
are fooling yourself—*

She ruthlessly quashed that taunting inner voice as she finally found Robert. She had learned her lesson and she *would* guard her heart from any such misery ever again. No matter how her treacherous body might react to the infuriating man.

Her stepson eyed her, then sighed.

'I recognise that martial light in your eye, Stepmama. Who has upset you?'

'I am *not* upset.'

Robert grinned. 'Let me hazard a guess. Was it the new Lord Kelridge? I saw you dancing.'

'Do not speak to me of Lord Kelridge! He had the utter gall to peer down his nose at us and our friends and acquaintances.'

'Did he, by Jove?' Robert scanned the room. 'Well, it appears he is also unimpressed by the entertainment and refreshments at Almack's, for it looks as though he is taking his leave. Clearly a man of impeccable taste. What did he say?'

'He finds, and I quote, "no merit in lives lived in pursuit of idle pleasures".'

'Ah.'

Robert stroked his chin, a mannerism that indicated he was secretly amused.

'You find that funny?'

'Well...might I point out to you, *dearest* Stepmama, that you have more than once uttered the same opinion?'

'That is entirely different.'

'How so?'

'This is *our* world. *Our* life. *I* am allowed to voice such criticism.'

'It is his world now, too. And he will see the absurdities

that, incidentally, both you and I know exist. He is entitled to his opinion, is he not?'

Kitty set her jaw, knowing she was being irrational but loath to back down. 'He may very well be entitled to his opinion, but I wish he would keep it to himself.'

Robert eyed her. 'Was that a metaphorical stamp of your foot?'

His lips quirked and Kitty felt her own quiver in response. Then she could no longer hold back her laugh and Robert laughed with her.

'There. I always was able to talk you down from the high boughs,' he said. 'I hope you weren't rude to poor Kelridge…it is a difficult time for him, you know.'

'I am never unmannerly, Rob. You know that.'

'No. But you can freeze a man with one look, as I know to my cost.'

'I am persuaded His Lordship is too thick-skinned to notice anything as subtle as a cool glance. Besides, he leaves for Kelridge Place tomorrow so we are unlikely to see him again for a long time.'

She shut her mind to a sensation that snaked through her…a sensation that felt very much like regret. She had no wish to explore that feeling further, afraid that if she allowed her thoughts to dwell too much on Adam and the feelings he aroused within her, the defences she had built around her heart would start to erode. And that she could not risk. Look at how he had tried to kiss her at Lady Charnwood's ball… an old habit, he had called her. Surely that was enough of a warning to avoid him—he had matured into an attractive man and it would be too easy to fall under his spell all over again. She must keep reminding herself of those lies, and of how he had let her down when she needed him. Like her father, he had used her for his own ends, then cast her aside.

'That is a pity. I had a mind to consult him on a matter concerning Fenton Hall.'

'The Hall? What matter?'

'Nothing much.' His hand rose to pull at his earlobe and Kitty watched him, puzzled. It was another habit of Rob's—this time when he felt uncomfortable, or guilty, over something. 'I've been pondering whether to have another wing built, to balance the one built after the fire. And, as Kelridge was involved at that time and as he is a trained architect, I thought to seek his advice.'

'Another *wing*? But… Rob…the Hall is surely sufficient for our needs? What do we need with more space?'

Robert shook his head. 'You may be right. It was merely a whim and this is not the place to discuss it.' He scanned the dancers. 'Charis is dancing with Sampford, I see. We need to keep an eye on that. I'm surprised the fellow even got a voucher for here.'

'The Patronesses must be lowering their standards. They allowed Kelridge in, too.'

Robert laughed. 'Poor Kelridge! He really has upset you, hasn't he?'

'Not at all.' She changed the subject. 'What is your objection to Sampford?'

'He is hanging out for a rich wife to reduce his debts.'

'Many peers are in similar financial straits. He *is* a little old for her, it is true, but Charis appears to be enjoying his company.'

'That,' said Robert grimly, 'is what I am afraid of. Charis enjoying his company, I mean. He is charm personified. On the surface.'

'Ah.'

Kitty did not ask Robert to elaborate. She had crossed paths with many such men and, in general, they shared the same selfish outlook on life. Charis deserved much better. Robert collected his sister as soon as the dance ended and the remainder of the evening passed uneventfully.

It was only later that night, as she prepared for bed, that Kitty realised Robert never did tell her why he was contemplating enlarging Fenton Hall and, by the morning, she had forgotten all about it.

'Stepmama?'

It was just past noon the following day and Kitty had hoped to make progress on her story, in which Arabella, her spirited and beautiful heroine, had just innocently interrupted the abduction of her six-year-old orphaned nephew, Arthur—the Duke of Northam—by his dastardly uncle, Lord Sidney Barmouth, whose intention was to gain control of young Arthur's fortune. The hero was about to step on to the page and she had just decided on Jason as the perfect name for him.

Her attention, however, had been wandering all morning—distracted by images of Adam. Last night was the first time they had spoken in the fortnight that had passed since Lady Charnwood's ball and Kitty's unwise foray on to the terrace. Until last night, Kitty had deliberately avoided him at society events and he, true to his word, had avoided her. But he had still regularly invaded her thoughts to the point where she suspected her preoccupation with him had strayed dangerously close to obsession.

How could she have guessed that he would turn up at Almack's of all places? What was Lady Datchworth thinking, dragging him there…unless, of course, she was still intent on throwing him and Charis together?

Kitty refused to examine quite why that idea made her feel so…so…*prickly*. He was unsuitable and too old. That was enough to warrant her objection. It was nothing whatsoever to do with that insistent voice in her head that mocked her for still being attracted to him, despite everything.

'Stepmama?'

Kitty started, rattled that she had, yet again, wandered deep into her own thoughts. She laid her quill aside before facing her stepdaughter with a smile, welcoming the interruption to the constant circling of her thoughts.

Besides, she thought with a despondent sigh, *my stories cannot hold a candle to those of Miss Austen. My first story was no doubt a fluke and I doubt I shall ever be good enough to be published again.*

Somehow, though, the more she told herself that, the more she felt driven to keep striving to improve. Her first published novel had barely caused a ripple of interest, but the drive to write and to have her stories published was a dream she could not quite set aside. She was fortunate that Robert regarded her 'little hobby' as harmless. He had been instrumental in achieving publication for her first novel, but only on condition her name was not known, even to the publisher, because female novelists were still regarded as racy and scandalous by many in society and he feared any notoriety might tarnish Charis by association.

'Yes, Charis?'

'Might we visit the Change today instead of paying morning calls?'

Kitty opened her mouth but, before she could speak, Charis rushed on, 'I know you will say we went there last week, but I am exceedingly eager to go and see the animals again.'

'But...the last time we visited the Menagerie you became distressed at how they are confined.'

'It is true I should rather see such creatures roam wild and free, but I know I shall never have that chance. We will return home soon and I *should* like to see them again.'

Kitty shook her head wonderingly. 'You really wish to spend time today staring at wild beasts at the Exeter Exchange rather than call upon your friends as we planned this afternoon?'

It was not that Kitty disliked the animals—she found them fascinating—but...surely a responsible stepmother should be able to channel her charge's interests in a more suitable direction?

Charis pouted. 'I shall see my friends tonight. Besides, Annabel can talk of little else other than her wedding and how utterly wonderful Talaton is. All one can do is nod and agree, and murmur "How fascinating" at suitable intervals.'

'It was only a few weeks ago you were in alt over their betrothal.'

'*That* was when it was news. We have surely said all there is to say on the subject by now and yet *still* Annabel and Mrs Blanchard prattle on and on, repeating themselves *ad infinitum* until I could happily close my eyes and go to sleep, I am so bored.'

Kitty eyed Charis, sensing there might be more to this than she was admitting.

'Charis...do you feel a little envious of Annabel?'

'No, I do not. She is welcome to Talaton. But I find it increasingly hard to keep smiling when I find myself the subject of pitying looks from both Annabel and her mama because *she* has found a husband and I have not. And there is nothing I can do about it—I cannot protest because they never *say* it, so they rob me of the chance to say I do not care. But it is exceedingly frustrating because I know precisely what they are thinking.'

Kitty took Charis's hand. 'Well, in my opinion, it is you who are the fortunate one. In her debut Season a young girl's head and heart should be filled with fun and frivolity, fashion and furbelows, dancing and dashing young men. There is plenty of time to find a husband.'

'But you married Papa when you were my age, Stepmama. And *you* never even had a Season.'

Adam once again hovered at the edges of Kitty's mind and she banished him with a silent growl of irritation.

'That is true. But my circumstances were very different from yours. And I never once regretted our marriage. How could I, when without it I would not have you and your brothers and sister?'

And even though I did not have the baby I so craved.

The sudden thickening of her throat and the sting in her eyes surprised her, for she had long ago accepted her childless state. Why did that thought upset her now? Then Adam's face materialised in her mind's eye and she scrambled to make sense of the connection until Lady Datchworth's words from last night, barely noticed at the time, echoed through her head: *I was intent upon helping poor Kelridge here with his marriage plans.*

But…that was just Lady Datchworth on one of her matchmaking quests. Was it not? Why should that trigger…? *Oh!* Her Ladyship's voice continued in Kitty's memory. *'You have a title and a fortune, and you need an heir. Of course you must wed—it is your obligation as a peer of the realm.'*

And the thought of Adam marrying…of him siring an heir…caused that tell-tale prickling behind her eyes once again and fear wrapped around Kitty's heart. Adam had reappeared in her life just over a fortnight ago and already, it seemed, he had begun to break through the barriers she had built around herself.

'And without it, we would not have you!' Charis hugged Kitty and kissed her cheek. 'Now *please* say we may go to the Change.'

Kitty forced her thoughts away from Adam. 'Very well. But you knew I would give way right from the start, didn't you?'

Charis kissed Kitty again. 'You usually do. Thank you.'

Two hours later, Kitty gloomily contemplated the elephant on the upper floor of the Exeter Exchange, marvelling at the sheer size of the beast, at his eyes—disproportionately tiny—and his huge ears as they flapped back and forth. His name, so a passing keeper had informed her on their first visit, was Chunee and he fanned his ears in order to cool himself down as his native land was India where the temperatures were very hot. As she turned from her study of Chunee—secretly agreeing with Charis that it seemed wrong to keep such an animal confined on its own in a small enclosure—she collided with a solid wall of male muscle.

'Oh! I *beg* your pardon.'

'Dinna fash yersel', lass. There's nae harm done.'

Kitty's head snapped up. Adam grinned down at her as he tipped his beaver hat and her heart leapt with what she feared was joy. She did *not* wish to feel like that at the mere sight of him. She gritted her teeth, battling both that visceral response and the near-overwhelming urge to reach out and touch him—his hand…his sleeve…it mattered not which part of him, it was simply a primal *need* to make physical contact. She curled her hands into fists at her sides, reminding herself that men could not be trusted and that Adam would only let her down, as he had before. As her father had.

'What are *you* doing here?' The war in her breast made her snappish.

His brows rose. 'I have come to view the animals. As have you, nae doubt.' His nose wrinkled. 'I confess I hadna anticipated the smell…it is a wee bit on the strong side, is it not?'

He held her gaze for a few minutes as Kitty scrambled for something to say, for normal conversation between two acquaintances. *He* managed it effortlessly. Why was it so difficult for her?

Adam turned to look at Chunee. 'And this is the elephant?' He shook his head wonderingly. 'I have seen drawings of such beasts—and of some of the others up here—but I had no idea of its sheer size.'

Kitty swallowed and forced a level tone. 'Indeed. And have you seen the lion and the tiger?'

'No. And I have nae desire to see them… Kitty…'

He paused and she waited for him to continue as he seemed to wrestle with himself.

'Why did you wed Fenton not two weeks after declaring undying love for me?'

She sucked in a breath at his unexpected question. She raised her chin.

'That, my lord, is none of your business.'

'Aye, it is. Ye owe it to me to tell me why.' His blue gaze burned into her, sending sizzles of awareness chasing across her skin.

'I owe you nothing.' She spoke through gritted teeth. 'When I would have told you the truth about my life, all those years ago, you refused to listen.'

The unfairness of that still festered deep inside and, although back then she had steeled herself to tell Adam about her father's cruel plan to sell her hand in marriage to settle his gambling debts, she was not prepared to expose her pain and shame to this near stranger. 'You did not want to know then and I do not believe dragging up old, forgotten feelings will serve any useful purpose.'

He searched her face and she fought to keep her anger in place as the intensity of his scrutiny aroused a swirl of conflicting emotions within her. She must protect herself, at all costs. Her heart was fickle...what if she fell for him again, despite the past? And if she did, there would only be more pain because even if, this time, Adam truly fell in love with her, it could never lead to marriage. Lady Datchworth was right... Adam *would* need an heir and Kitty could not give him one.

But his silence gave her time to regret her harsh words. 'Besides...' she indicated their surroundings '...this is hardly the place to discuss such a subject.'

He raised a brow. 'Indeed not. With ears that size, the elephant would nae doubt hear every word and trumpet our secrets far and wide.' He grinned, but then his brows twitched into a frown. 'When may we discuss it, Kitty? I think we must. Don't you?'

She could think of nothing more dangerous to her peace of mind. 'I can see no benefit in dredging up the past merely on some whim of yours.'

He sighed. 'Aye...well... I canna say I'm keen on being

labelled as a man with a tendency to whims, Kitty, but if it pleases you to think of me in such a way—'

'I would not waste my time labelling you as anything. You flatter yourself, sir.'

She hated hearing the words snapping from her mouth, but she could not help it, she was in such turmoil. Adam, however, merely chuckled, making her feel even more ashamed of her volatile moods.

'I was, believe it not, jesting with you. Have you lost your sense of humour as well as your charge, ma'am?'

'My charge?'

'Your stepdaughter.'

Charis! Kitty spun around, searching the room where the animals were housed. There were several people on the upper floor, but Charis was not among them. Kitty turned back to Adam.

'Have you seen her? Oh! Of course! You must have done, to know she is missing.'

In her agitation, she clutched his forearm, registering the sudden tension in his muscles at the same time as…something…some emotion…flared and died in those intensely blue eyes, triggering a response deep inside her: a tugging, yearning sensation.

'As I said before, dinna fash yersel'. She is downstairs with Lady D., who declined to come up here as she does not care for the menagerie. She says the monkeys give her nightmares. It was she who sent me to find you.'

'I must go to Charis. I do not understand why she went downstairs without telling me… I thought she was looking at the Arabian camel.'

Adam pursed his lips, his gaze wandering around the room before coming back to rest on Kitty's face. 'I passed her on the stairs. She appeared to be in company with a gentleman. Although…it could be I'm mistaken, but I did think you might wish to know that is a possibility.'

'Do you know who it was?'

'Sampford.'

'*Sampford?* But—' Kitty reeled with shock. That Charis should have met with Sampford here today after dancing with him last night could not be a coincidence.

'I did see them together at Almack's last evening,' Adam said. 'It made me question if there may be an attachment of some sort.'

Kitty could read nothing from his expression.

'You suspect they had an assignation?'

Adam shrugged. 'I thought it possible.'

'But she is only seventeen—far too young to form an attachment.'

His eyes narrowed. 'We both know how headstrong such young girls can be when they fancy they are in love.'

Chapter Eight

Kitty sucked in a breath at that jibe. 'Oh!'

She glared up at him, striving to project every single ounce of her outrage into that one look, then whirled around and marched to the stairs, battening down the swell of hurt his remark had provoked. A low blow, as Robert would describe it. How could she ever have imagined herself at risk of falling in love again with him? He was nothing but a boor and she hoped she never set eyes on him again. On that thought, she slammed to a halt and spun to face him.

'I *thought*, Lord Kelridge, you were to return to Hertfordshire this morning. Another lie?'

Proud at the icy tone she achieved and the fact her voice did not quiver, Kitty turned and hurried down the stairs to street level, where she could see Charis and Lady Datchworth at the far end of the Change, examining the wares displayed on one of the stalls set up outside the shops. Of Sampford there was no sign. She slowed her pace, relief flooding her at the sight of Her Ladyship.

'I enjoyed watching you flounce, Kitty.'

Her pulse rocketed as the low voice sounded in her ear and his warm breath raised the little hairs at her nape. Kitty halted.

'I do *not* flounce, my lord. And, if I did, it would be for neither your benefit nor your entertainment.'

Somehow, she knew not how, he manoeuvred her arm through his and they were again walking towards Lady Datchworth and Charis.

'You do not wish to give Her Ladyship the suspicion we have been squabbling, I hope?'

Put like that…no, she did not, so she accepted his escort with as good grace as she could muster.

'And, in answer to your…um—*accusation* might best describe your tone of voice—I am leaving for Hertfordshire later today. It is only a short journey and the evenings are light enough. I had a matter or two to tie up before leaving town and I wished to say my goodbyes to the few people I can regard as friends. Including Robert, of course.'

Oh, no! Robert wanted to speak to Adam…

'Have you seen Robert yet?'

'No. He was unavailable, unfortunately. May I impose on your good nature—you note I do not say goodwill as you appear to have a scant quantity of that towards myself—to pass on my good wishes and my farewell?'

'You may.'

'I thank you.'

Kitty breathed a little easier on learning Robert had not yet spoken to Adam about this new wing for the Hall. She would persuade him to consult a different architect, although she still couldn't fathom why he had suddenly formed this desire to refurbish the Hall. Unless…could he be contemplating matrimony? She frowned, racking her brains, but she could not recall him paying particular attention to any young lady during the Season—other than the Marquess of Patterdale's sister, Lady Phoebe Crawshaw. But Kitty could not believe Robert's attention to the Incomparable—as the gentlemen had dubbed Lady Phoebe, as they clustered around her like wasps around a ripe plum—was anything more than Robert following the latest fashion. Kitty prayed he had more sense than to view such a female as a suitable marriage prospect for, although the gentlemen were universally captivated by her beauty and her spirit, the ladies of the *ton* were divided upon the subject of Lady Phoebe. The younger ladies thought her fast but fascinating, the older matrons thought her fast and vulgar. Kitty's opinion lay somewhere between the two, but she had found the other woman intriguing as she observed her, drawing upon her antics and mannerisms for Minerva, a character in her novel and the flighty, avaricious betrothed of Arthur's villainous Uncle Sidney.

Kitty and Adam joined the others—Lady Datchworth's sharp gaze switching from Adam to Kitty and back again as Charis sent Kitty a look that managed to be both guilty and apologetic at the same time.

'I followed the keeper down here because I needed to ask him something.'

The rush of her stepdaughter's words did nothing to quell either Kitty's suspicions or her concern.

'And did you find out what you wished to know?'

'I… I could not catch him.'

'And you then met Lord Sampford, did you not, my dear,' said Lady Datchworth, 'which is why you did not *immediately* return to your stepmother.'

A blush lit Charis's cheeks. 'I did not wish to be thought unmannerly by not speaking to him.'

'Well, I thank you both for ensuring Charis's safety and for informing me of her whereabouts,' said Kitty, fighting to keep the disapproval and worry from her countenance. 'Charis, come. It is time we returned home.'

She would not discuss this with Charis in front of others, but she would have plenty to say to her on the journey home. She prayed poor Charis's heart was not engaged if that *had* been a clandestine plan to meet Lord Sampford because—following Robert's revelations about the man—Kitty had no doubt Charis deserved far better than a husband like him. He was utterly unsuitable and had proved he could not be trusted and was no gentleman by encouraging Charis to go downstairs with him, away from her chaperon. Thank goodness Lady Datchworth happened to be there at the right time. Charis was so young…only seventeen…far too young to fall in love.

Kitty sucked in a breath at the significance of Charis's age. Seventeen…the same age she had been when she had fallen in love with Adam. Not that she had truly been in love with him, of course. Infatuation. That was what it had been. He had been right, of course. She shot a glance at Adam and it collided with his knowing gaze. His lips twitched and a gleam lit his blue eyes, drat the man. It was as though he knew precisely what she was thinking—and it was no doubt the cause of his earlier comment about young girls.

'Lord Kelridge.' Lady Datchworth's crisp command brought both Kitty's and Adam's attention back to her. 'I desire a private word with Lady Fenton. Would you be so good as to escort Miss Mayfield to peruse the wares on that stall over there?' She waved her arm in the general direction of a stall displaying silver-plated trinkets such as snuff boxes and vinaigrettes.

Kitty frowned at Her Ladyship's blatant attempt to throw Adam and Charis together, in no mood to allow the Marchioness to interfere in Charis's future. As soon as Adam and Charis were out of earshot, she said, 'I intend to be straight with you, Lady Datchworth.'

'Oh. Please do.' A smile flickered on Her Ladyship's mouth. 'But, before you speak, allow me to explain that I overheard Sampford last night persuading your Charis to meet him here today, and I thought it my duty to circumvent any trouble.'

'You *knew* about their tryst? But why not just tell me last night? Why go through this charade?'

'Charade?' Her Ladyship's eyebrows shot skyward. 'Allow me to remind you that I have vastly more experience of life than you, my dear. Had you banned their meeting, all you would end up doing is cause resentment and a determination to be even more secretive. *This* way, Charis is both embarrassed and ashamed—and the lesson has been learned that she *will* be found out. Besides, it gave me an opportunity to throw her and Kelridge together.'

'Well, I wish you had not involved Kelridge. I told you before. I do *not* believe that would be a good match.'

'But you have still not furnished me with a good reason for your objection.'

Kitty's teeth ground together. 'I do not need to discuss my objections with you, ma'am. Suffice it to say that Lord Fenton would disapprove as well and that should be an end to it.'

Her Ladyship shrugged. 'Very well. If you do not wish my assistance, I shall say no more. Never let it be said that I interfere in others' lives even though, as I said, my experience does furnish me with a unique insight into my friends' well-being.'

Kitty swallowed down any further hot words as Lady Datchworth beckoned imperiously at Adam, who nodded and returned with Charis on his arm.

'It is time to return home, Charis.'

'Very well, Stepmama.'

Charis looked suitably chastened and Kitty allowed herself to imagine what her attitude might have been had Kitty been aware of her rendezvous with Sampford and flatly refused to come here today. Irritatingly, she realised Lady Datchworth might have a point about the best way to deal with Charis's clandestine meeting. She summoned up a smile for Her Ladyship even as she prayed Charis had not developed a *tendre* for Sampford, especially in light of Robert's revelations. She was aware it was impossible to protect Charis against heartache, but knowing she was powerless did not stop Kitty from wanting to do her utmost to protect her precious stepdaughter against any and every sorrow.

'I am grateful for your sage advice, ma'am.'

Lady Datchworth's lips stretched into an answering smile. 'You are most welcome, my dear.'

Adam bowed. 'Good afternoon, Lady Fenton, Miss Mayfield. It's been a pleasure to meet you both again.'

'Likewise, sir.' Kitty inclined her head as Charis curtsied. 'Good afternoon, Lady Datchworth, my lord.'

As they walked away she heard Lady Datchworth's peremptory tones float after them.

'How the devil did you contrive to provoke her this time, Kelridge?'

Kitty increased her pace to prevent any prospect of overhearing his reply.

* * *

'Hi! Adam!'

Adam paused with one booted foot on the carriage step as his cousin, Tolly, sprinted up the street, a valise in one hand. He waved and increased his pace. Adam lowered his foot and waited. That valise presented a strong clue that Tolly had decided to travel to Kelridge Place with him after all, although he had declined the offer last evening, when Adam had met him at Brooks's after he had escorted Lady Datchworth home from Almack's.

'Much obliged, Coz.'

Tolly dropped his case and bent forward, hands on knees, panting. Adam waited patiently.

'Thought I'd missed you!'

'Changed your mind?'

'I have.' Tolly straightened, his face red. He hauled in a breath and blew it out again. 'Phew! Not used to runnin'. Bit of a rush, by the time I got home and packed.' He picked up his valise. 'Given my man the day off, too. Never was much of a one for plannin' and so forth.'

Adam was surprised how pleased he was to have Tolly's company. If nothing else, it would stop him brooding about Kitty and obsessing over his ungentlemanly jibe at the Change. He had meant his comment about headstrong young girls to be humorous, but had realised his error as soon as it left his lips. And Kitty's reaction confirmed she had not found it amusing. He had no wish to squabble with her every time they met. Rather, he longed for the chance to question her properly, driven not only by the urge to understand why she had married Fenton, but also by this new burden of guilt over his refusal to listen to her explanation as to why she had been desperate to leave her father's home.

Somehow, he must find a way to have that conversation with her and he now regretted his impulsive announcement that he was leaving Town, admitting—if only to himself—that the heaviness currently weighing on his soul was entirely due to the fact he would not see Kitty again for the foreseeable future.

There was the consolation, however, that when she returned to Hertfordshire it would surely prove easier to find privacy there than in London. Until then, he must try to be patient. But that would be hard, especially since their meeting that afternoon. Her guard had slipped and he had glimpsed very real emotion in her eyes as they had sparred with one another. And that glimpse had given him hope that, maybe, they could work through the events of the past and reach a better understanding. And then...who knew?

He was still unsure exactly what he hoped for with regard to Kitty, but he did know he would rather be someone she trusted than someone she eyed with caution.

'Barlow—load Mr Trewin's luggage on the rack if you please.' The groom on the box jumped down and did as he was bid. 'In you get, then, Tolly, and you can tell me why the change of plans.'

Once the carriage was in motion, Tolly said, 'I just realised you might appreciate a friendly face there, to help ease you into your new role.'

He stopped speaking, his chest still heaving with the effort of his sprint.

Adam leaned back, stretching his legs out and folding his arms across his chest as he settled down for the journey.

'Well, I admit I shall be glad of both your company and your support. Plus, the journey will finally give you the chance to tell me all about my father.'

Adam had questioned Tolly about his father a few times since their first meeting, but Tolly had always fobbed him off—easily done when there had always been other people around. But now it was just the two of them and Adam burned to why his mother had run away from the man, depriving Adam of his father, and her husband of his son and heir.

'Ah. Yes.' A frown slashed between Tolly's eyebrows. 'It is...awkward.'

'As are so many things about this situation. Look... Tolly...my father was who he was. Telling me the truth about him will change nothing. I didn't know the man, so you will not be shattering dreams...' His mother had already destroyed those, when she admitted the soldier hero he had thought was his father was naught but a figment of her imagination. 'I just want to understand what he was like.'

And to know if he was really such a monster that his wife chose the life of a housekeeper rather than remain as his Countess.

'Well...if you put it like that, I can tell you he was quick-tempered and free with his fists, too. Your mother had already left him by the time my parents wed, but my mother did know yours and she told me she didn't blame Esther for running away, even though it created a huge scandal and most of society were unforgiving. Including my own father, I'm sorry to say.' He shook his head. 'Family loyalty, I suppose. I've even heard people say that a wife belongs to her husband and, if he has to beat her, then it's her own fault and she should mend her ways.'

Anger stirred at the thought of anyone beating his mother and Adam clenched his fists on his knees. No wonder she had always been quick to stop any signs of temper in her son. He stared down at his clenched fists and forced them to relax. He might be quick to anger, but he had *never* come close to hitting anyone.

'Did you know him? What did you make of him?'

'We saw very little of him when I was young as my mother disliked him but, after her death, Father sold his commission and moved back to Kelridge. I was in the cavalry myself by then, but I would visit him there whenever I had leave and I got to know Uncle Gerald better.' Tolly leaned forward, propping his forearms along his thighs. 'I saw more than I wished to: maidservants with black eyes and bruised faces. Staff didn't stay for long and the Place had fallen into disrepair, but my father gradually began to put things to rights.' He looked round at Adam. 'One of the estate men once told me your father used to make you drink brandy, as a punishment.'

'*Brandy?* But… I was only two years old when we left.'

'Quite.' Tolly sighed again and sat up. 'He wasn't punishing you…it was to punish your mother, if she dared to stand up to him. I tell you, Coz…you were better off brought up as a housekeeper's son than if your mother had stayed with that devil.'

Adam leaned his head back against the squabs and closed his eyes, regret coursing through him at his anger with Ma and that they did not part on better terms.

'Did your mother not tell you anything about your father?'

'Not a thing. She said she did not want to burden me with her view of my father. That I should discover the truth from people who knew him better than she did. She thought he might have changed in the years since she left.'

Tolly huffed a laugh. 'No. he didn't change. Your mother,

though…she could have chosen to fill your head with poison about your father, but she has allowed you to make up your own mind. She sounds a fair-minded woman.'

'She is. And she has been a good mother to me.'

And I miss her.

Adam felt even more guilty at his misjudgement. He had been too hasty to apportion blame…jumping to conclusions even though Ma had never given him cause to think her a vindictive woman who would keep father and son apart without good reason. That was a lesson he would do well to remember.

A few hours after leaving London, Adam recognised the turning that led to Fenton Hall, Kitty's home, although the house could not be seen from the road, shielded as it was by a belt of trees.

Half an hour later, the carriage turned on to a quiet, leafy lane and slowed.

'We are getting close now.' Tolly pointed between the trees at a distant Palladian mansion standing proud on the crest of a rise.

As the carriage bowled along the driveway, Adam took in the healthy cattle and sheep grazing the lush pastures. He had a lot to learn about this way of life and he hoped it would prove easier to establish a rapport with the estate workers than with the household staff, most of whom had travelled back to Kelridge that morning to prepare for his arrival. When the house came into view, Adam's first thought was how stark it looked…no wings to soften or extend the outline, just a solid block of a house with a central temple-like portico rising the height of the building. The severe lines were softened only by twin flights of steps rising to the entrance. It didn't look much like a home, but the windows sparkled and the forecourt was neatly raked.

'My uncle had done a good job in maintaining the house and park,' Adam remarked to Tolly. 'Everything looks in good repair.'

'It is. Your father enjoyed the high life and failed to invest much in the estate before he fell ill but, when my father took over, he made sure any neglect was made good. The rents provide a healthy living. You are a fortunate man, Coz.'

There was no edge to his voice, but Adam still found it hard to credit that Tolly did not feel even a little cheated by his reappearance.

'Are you certain you do not resent my turning up again, Tolly, when all this might have been yours one day?'

'Not I. My mother left me funds so I am quite comfortable, and all without the responsibility of running an estate this size. You are welcome to it, Coz.'

Tolly's comment was too breezily dismissive for Adam to believe him wholeheartedly but he kept his doubts to himself. If there were any bad feelings there, they would show themselves in time.

The carriage halted, and both men jumped down before the groom could let down the steps. Adam turned in a slow circle, taking everything in. He'd never felt more lonely and out of his depth in his life, and he was grateful Tolly had decided to accompany him.

'Come on. Let's find the old man and I'll introduce you.' Tolly bounded up the left-hand flight of steps to the door, which remained closed. He paused before opening it. 'Don't expect the fatted calf, Adam. M'father…as I said earlier… he's become accustomed to having the income from the estate at his disposal and he wouldn't be human if he didn't feel some bitterness towards you. He won't like having to return to his former, restricted way of life.'

His comment echoed the doubts Adam had just been having, but about Tolly. He didn't reply as Green opened the front door and bowed.

'Welcome to Kelridge Place, my lord.'

Inside, a soberly dressed man of around fifty was descending the stairs.

'Mr Bartholomew, sir. It's a pleasure to see you.' The man bowed.

'Thank you, Corbett. This is Lord Kelridge. Adam, Corbett is my father's valet. Is Father about?'

Corbett bowed to Adam. 'Welcome, milord.' He didn't quite meet Adam's eye before he turned to Tolly. 'Mr Trewin has just this minute gone up to change for dinner. Shall I have hot water sent up for you both? I dare say you will wish to refresh yourselves after the journey.'

The valet only spoke directly to Adam when he had no choice. 'The master's bedchamber is ready for you, milord, and Mr Bartholomew's chamber is always kept aired in case of a visit.'

'Thank you, Corbett. And, yes, please send up hot water. I shall meet my uncle later.'

Chapter Nine

'So. You're m'nephew?'

Adam nodded at his uncle's rhetorical question.

Uncle Grenville stood before the empty fireplace in the drawing room of Kelridge Place, his hands behind his back as he rocked up on his toes and back down again. He'd adopted the dominant stance the minute Adam joined him in the room to await the announcement of dinner. Adam allowed himself a wry smile and sat on a nearby chair, crossing his legs. He wouldn't take part in games of one-upmanship, if that was his uncle's aim. It mattered not how long Grenville had regarded himself as master of Kelridge Hall—that was now Adam's role.

'I realise my existence must be somewhat…difficult…for you to accept, Uncle, but we cannot change that. I should like to reassure you, however, that you may continue to regard Kelridge as your home for as long as you wish.'

Grenville nodded, his expression thoughtful. He was still a fine figure of a man despite nearing sixty years of age.

Tall, with an upright posture, and with steel-grey hair that showed no sign of receding, his shoulders were broad, his belly still flat and his features chiselled—no hint of a double chin above his neatly tied neckcloth. A legacy, maybe, of his years in the cavalry—as the younger son, that had been his chosen career.

'That is decent of you in the circumstances. And, as you have so generously made the offer, I have no hesitation in accepting it. While we are on the subject, have you a preference as to which bedchamber I use from now on? When my brother became too ill to climb the stairs, he moved into apartments on the ground floor and I moved into the master's suite of rooms. I have, of course, vacated them, since I learned that you...' His voice trailed into silence.

'That I am alive? It must have come as a...shock, after all these years.'

Adam had been going to say '*a blow*' but, at the last minute, dismissed the term as too provocative. He and his uncle must learn to rub along together. A flash of some strong emotion crossed the older man's features—gone in an instant.

'A *pleasant* shock, Nephew. I am delighted Gerald's bloodline has not died out.'

At least he *sounded* sincere.

'As to which bedchamber you should occupy, Uncle, ye may choose whichever ye please, other than the Countess's suite—well, that goes without saying, for I am sure you would have no desire to occupy those rooms—or the principal guest bedchamber, which I shall require for guests.'

Uncle Grenville's brows beetled. 'Guests? What guests? When do they arrive?'

'I have issued no invitations yet, but I shall require the

principal guest room for any guests I may choose to invite
in the future. You surely willna deny me the right to invite
friends to stay in my own house?'

After what Tolly had revealed of Adam's father's character—and now he understood better the reasons his mother
had fled his father—Adam hoped he could now persuade
Ma to come and make her home at Kelridge Place, where
she belonged. He did not, however, expect his uncle to welcome that news.

'Very well.' Uncle Grenville inclined his head. 'I shall
instruct my man to move my belongings *again*.' He paused,
his chest moving rapidly up and down as his jaw clenched.
Then he shook his head. 'I apologise if that sounded a touch
bitter, Ambrose.'

'Adam.'

'Adam. My apologies. Anyway, I find as I get older I do
not care for change. I have had sole responsibility for this
place for over five years since your father first fell ill and I
also shouldered much of the responsibility in the years before that. It is where I grew up and, although I have my own
house near Kelworth village, I have always regarded the
Place as my home. Yet now I am to be relegated to a minor
bedchamber to give way to *occasional* guests.'

Adam rose to his feet and strode over to the window, staring out unseeingly to give himself time to consider how best
to respond. He had learned over the years that was the best
way to control his sometimes fiery temper—words flung
out in the heat of the moment could do more damage than
intended. A temper—he was now aware, his stomach churning uneasily—he might have inherited from his father. His
mother's constant correction of his boyish outbursts made
sense now. Had she seen hints of his father's temperament

in Adam? The very thought made him shudder after what he'd learned from Tolly and he vowed to work doubly hard to keep his anger on a firm rein.

'I am sorry you find change uncomfortable—' he swung around to face his uncle, '—but you *have* had several weeks now in which to become accustomed to the fact I am still alive to claim my inheritance. And, as you have said, you do have a perfectly good house of your own near to the village.'

Grenville folded his arms, his expression stormy. 'It is hardly a fitting home for the son of an earl. Six bedrooms only and a mere thirty acres of land. Of what use is that? A gentleman is entitled to live in comfort. It is what I was born to.'

'It is more than most people have. It is far more than I ever had. And I, too, lest you forget, am the son of an earl.'

'*You* knew no better. Dragged up in a heathen country by that—'

'Take care!' Adam stalked back to face his uncle, but resisted the urge to grab him by the lapels and shake him, the spectre of his father looming large. '*Do not*, if you know what is good for you, insult my mother. Ever. I might have sympathy for your plight, hence my offer for you to continue to make Kelridge Place your home, but do not mistake my sympathy for weakness.'

He swallowed down his rage as his uncle's colour heightened.

'You—' Uncle Grenville broke off as the door opened.

'Good evening. Is this a private party, or may I join you?'

Tolly's amused tones floated into the charged atmosphere and Adam looked around to see his cousin had halted on the threshold, his eyebrows arched. A faint smile played around his lips, but his expression was watchful. He had donned a brown-leather eyepatch and that, coupled with his scrutiny, gave him a somewhat sinister appearance.

Adam forced a smile.

'Come on in, Tolly. Your father and I were just discussing the new arrangements to be made here at the Hall.'

Uncle Grenville's hand landed on Adam's shoulder. 'I spoke out of turn, my boy. This is a difficult adjustment for me…and for us all, you included. I confess I find it hard to forgive your mother for depriving my brother of his son and heir. Surely you can acknowledge how hard that is to stomach?'

Adam stared at his uncle. 'Nay. I canna acknowledge it, as it happens. My mother should have been safe in her own home and yet your brother…my *father*—' even saying that brought the sour taste of bile to his mouth, '—made her feel so *un*safe that she had no choice but to leave.'

Grenville's eyes glittered as he folded his arms. 'Gerald was *my brother* and, for all his faults, he was Esther's husband—the man she vowed to honour and obey. You were too young to know the truth of it. I—'

'Father.' Tolly stepped forward, his voice low and soothing. 'You cannot defend the indefensible. I witnessed my uncle's violence for myself and I can readily believe my aunt feared for her own life and for the safety of her child.'

'The law says—'

'Enough!' Adam paced the room in another attempt to calm himself. '*I* dinna care what the law might say. My heart tells me that no mother should fear for either her safety or that of her child. But what I do care about is that you continue to blame my mother for something that was clearly the fault of my father.'

Grenville shook his head. 'Neither of you understand what it was like, when Gerald and I were growing up.'

Adam sat down and gestured to Tolly to do the same. 'Tell us, then.'

'It was not Gerald's fault he was the way he was. Our father—your grandfather—he had a temper, too. But Gerald...he always protected me...took the beatings...distracted my father when he was drunk and in the mood to lash out. I...' Grenville looked from Adam to Tolly and back again, his eyes glittering with emotion '... I *owed* him. I know he had a nasty temper, especially when he'd been drinking, but he deserved my loyalty. Especially when your mother left him...the humiliation he suffered...his despair at never knowing what had become of you, Amb—Adam. It drove him to even greater excess. He was a bitter man.'

Adam sighed. Having learned the truth about his father's violence from Tolly, he did not now want to feel even a sliver of sympathy for the man. But Grenville's story did leave him with a touch more understanding of both his father's temperament and, more importantly, his uncle's loyalty to him.

'I am sorry for what you and your brother suffered as children,' he said. 'But that is no excuse for the way your brother treated my mother.'

'I accept that. Maybe I could have stopped him, had I been here, but I was away campaigning for much of the time in the early years of their marriage. And, once your mother had gone, all I could do was support him as best I could.'

Adam felt better to have cleared the air and the three men spent the evening together without further discord. By the time Adam retired to the master bedchamber, he felt more hopeful than he had at any time since his mother had told him the truth of his origins.

* * *

'I'll show you around the place after breakfast.' Uncle Grenville spoke through a mouthful of devilled kidneys the following morning. 'There's a decent hunter in the stables that'll be up to your weight. You'll be keen to get your bearings, I make no doubt.'

Adam picked up his coffee cup and drained it. 'I am.'

At that moment Tolly sauntered into the morning parlour, bleary-eyed.

'You look as though your night was as restless as mine, Cousin,' Adam said, with a grin.

Tolly yawned widely. 'I stayed up playing billiards after you both retired. Too accustomed to town hours.'

His yawn triggered Adam to yawn in his turn—he had lain awake for many hours in the night, pondering not only what he had learned about his father, but also dwelling on Kitty. And she was still on his mind this morning. Who had she danced with last night? What would she be doing today? Did she think of him at all? And, finally, how soon would she return to Fenton Hall, and when would he get that chance to ask her again about what had happened after he left her fifteen years ago? Learning how he had jumped to conclusions about his mother had prompted him to wonder if he had also made assumptions about Kitty's behaviour. And the only way to know that was to ask her...and keep asking until she told him.

Adam clenched his jaw as he scraped butter on his toast, pondering his contradictory attitude to Kitty. In London he had vowed not to go out of his way to meet her or to speak to her and it had been easy enough to stick to his resolve. But he'd seen her at a distance—in the Park, across a ball-

room, at the theatre, and there had always been the anticipation…the hope…that they might meet, even though he
had not recognised it as such. And, somehow, that had been
enough. Their meetings at Almack's and at the Change
had been all the sweeter for being unexpected, despite the
squabbles that had marred each occasion.

Now, though…now that there was no possibility whatsoever of catching sight of her and no possibility of bumping
into her in the street or at an event, it seemed as though a
little of the light had leached from his world.

He bit into his toast and chewed. This was ridiculous. He
knew the Fentons would not return to Hertfordshire until the
Season ended. He must banish Kitty from his thoughts and
concentrate instead on learning about his new life. Then,
when she came home to Fenton Hall, he would go and visit
her.

'I should like to meet with the steward today,' he said to
Uncle Grenville. 'Carter, isn't it? I'll send a message to him
to come up to the house at two o'clock.'

'Yes. Joseph Carter. He should be here at that time anyway. He's been working on the ledgers in the afternoons this
week to ready them for you. He's a good man and knows
the business inside out—he's been keeping the books ever
since your father took him on, not long before I sold my
commission and came home. Numbers have never been
my forte—I much prefer the practical side of running the
estates—and Gerald always had a haphazard approach to
the finances, so Carter's been a godsend.'

'Very well. Tolly? Will you join us this morning? Your
father has offered to show me around the estate.'

'With pleasure. But allow me to finish breaking my fast
first, or I shall likely fall off my horse and break my neck.'

* * *

As it happened, it was Adam who fell off his horse—a bay gelding by the name of Cracker—who reared up without warning as they rode along the lip of a steep-sided V-shaped river valley. Adam was taken by surprise, tumbling from the saddle and down the rock-strewn slope, and was only saved from a more severe bruising and a soaking in the River Kell by a clump of bushes a third of the way down the slope.

Tolly dismounted in a flash and scrambled down to Adam.

'Are you hurt, Coz?'

Adam sat up and touched his forehead, wincing. His fingers, though, showed no sign of blood. 'Only my pride. Although I dare say I shall sport some colourful bruises for the next few days.' He squinted back up the slope and winced again. This time at the number of rocks protruding from the surface. 'I dare say I should be grateful my skull is not broken.'

He scrambled to his feet and discovered, to his mortification, that his knees were like jelly.

'Here. Sling your arm around my shoulders. I'll help you to the top. What spooked your horse, I wonder? He is normally a steady sort.'

'I have no idea.'

They reached the top of the slope to find Grenville had been joined by two men, one of them holding both riderless horses.

'I am relieved to see you are not badly injured,' Grenville said. 'That could have been very nasty. This is Joseph Carter, by the way, and Eddings, one of the farmhands. They saw you fall and came running. And stopped your horses running off, incidentally. Left to me, they'd doubt-less be halfway home by now—I was more worried about you, Nephew.'

Adam eyed him, tamping down a rush of suspicion. His uncle sounded sincere, but Adam was conscious he would be unlikely to shed many tears should a fatal accident be-fall the new Earl of Kelridge.

After exchanging greetings, Carter—a stolid-looking man of around forty, with a ruddy complexion—said, 'I don't know what could have come over the horse, to rear up in such a way.'

'Likely them horse flies,' Eddings said. 'There's been a plague of 'em lately and that's a fact.'

'That could be it,' said Tolly. 'Nothing a horse hates more than a horse fly buzzing around its ears. Never fails to spook 'em.'

'True,' said Grenville. 'I was bitten by one once. Never forget it—I had a huge swelling on my arm. Must have been five inches across.'

Adam, his legs now steady, took Cracker's reins from Carter. Before mounting, however, he checked the horse over, finding only a trickle of blood on his chest to support the theory of a bite.

'I doubt we shall ever know for certain,' he said. 'Carter—are you coming up to the house later? I should like to go through the ledgers with you.'

'Very well, milord. But may I say I am happy to carry on with the bookkeeping on your behalf? If that suits you, of course?'

The man sounded anxious. Understandable, perhaps, if he thought his job might be in jeopardy.

'You may certainly continue as before, at least to begin with. Then we shall see how it goes, shall we?'

The man's expression was unreadable. 'Very good, milord.'

Carter and Eddings doffed their hats and walked off as Adam and Tolly remounted.

'I suggest you've seen enough for today, Adam,' said Grenville. 'Let us return to the house.'

The next few days were ones of discovery for Adam, not least of which was the gradually emerging realisation that he could not simply banish Kitty from his life. She was in his thoughts constantly and visited his dreams whenever he managed to snatch a few hours' sleep. More than ever, he felt the urgent need to talk to her. Properly. Not those whispered snatches of conversation they had managed in London, the result of which had been more questions to add to the list of things he did not understand.

How soon would the Fentons return from London? And when he called on them, how on earth could he get Kitty alone for long enough to get those answers he craved? He feared he was close to becoming obsessed not only by Kitty, but also by the need to *understand*.

His attempts to distract himself by learning more about the running of the estate were no more fruitful than his conjectures about Kitty. Uncle Grenville assured him he'd no need to worry his head over the day-to-day practicalities, insisting he had everything under control and that he would see the season through until harvest. Carter explained crop rotations and yields, and the basics of livestock husbandry, as well as showing Adam how the sales and purchase ledgers were kept but he, like Grenville, was reluctant to relinquish control. Conscious of his inexperience, Adam pored over the ledgers, but—between them and the figures thrown at him by Grenville and Carter, who often appeared to contradict one another—he made excruciatingly slow progress towards his aim of understanding the finer points of estate management.

The household staff stubbornly maintained a reserve in their dealings with Adam—deferring to Grenville and treating Tolly, clearly a great favourite, with more warmth than they ever showed Adam. The estate workers, no doubt sensing Adam's ignorance, always turned to Carter or to Grenville when they needed an answer to a question or were looking for instructions.

Adam remained the outsider. He really could not blame the staff for their loyalty to his uncle and he knew it was up to him to work hard to gain their trust. His own father had clearly been unpopular and it was understandable the staff would fear the son would be like the father. Adam knew it was his responsibility to convince them he was different, but he had to battle the urge to turn his back on everything and return to Scotland every single morning. The only thing stopping him was his pride. He refused to tuck his tail between his legs and run away like a cowardly cur. He counselled himself to have patience, with both himself and with the rest of the people who lived and worked at Kelridge Place.

One decision he did make, however, was to write to Ma. Since Tolly had told him about his father Adam felt a growing need to heal the rift with his mother, so he sat at his writing bureau in his library one day and wrote to her, telling her he now understood why she had run away from his father even though he still didn't quite understand why neither she nor Sir Angus had told him the truth once he reached adulthood. He begged her to visit him soon, reassuring her that he would not allow anyone—even Grenville—to be unwelcoming and he told her that Lady Datchworth—or Araminta Todmorden as Ma would remember her—was eager to be reacquainted with her and would she give her permission for him to pass on her address?

He wasn't confident Ma would accept his invitation but, if she did not, then he would damned well go up to Edinburgh himself and make sure he properly cleared the air between the two of them. He had just sealed the letter when Green entered.

'A letter has been delivered from Fenton Hall, my lord.'

His heart thudded with anticipation. 'Thank you, Green.'

Adam took the letter from the silver tray Green proffered, marvelling at the pomp required merely to hand a letter to a nobleman. But he remembered his vow not to be too hasty to change the way things were done. He was in an unfamiliar world and he must give himself more time to acclimatise to it before ploughing a furrow straight through their customs. But that didn't mean he wouldn't say thank you when the occasion warranted it, refusing to be deterred by the sourness of the butler's expression. Some of the lower servants were beginning to respond to his pleasantries with the odd smile, but only when Green was not around.

Adam broke the seal and read the letter, excitement stirring his blood. It was from Robert, who was now back at Fenton Hall, enquiring how Adam was settling into his new life and containing both an invitation for Adam to visit Fenton Hall, and a plea for a favour. Robert planned to build a second wing, to mirror the one built after the fire fifteen years before, and he begged Adam to advise him on the project…maybe, even, to draw up the plans for which, of course, he would suitably recompensed.

Robert's letter continued.

I realise you might view my request as an imposition, when you no doubt have a great many matters requiring your attention at Kelridge Place, and I appreciate that such a favour as I ask would necessitate you staying here at Fenton Hall for several days, but there is no one I would rather trust to steer me straight on a project such as this.

This was just the fillip Adam needed: a chance to escape the Place and its tensions for a few days; a chance to clear his head and order his thoughts; and, finally—and his heart squeezed at the thought—he would see Kitty again. He would be staying in the same house as her. He would get that chance to discover exactly why she had been so desperate to escape her father's house. More than that… he simply did not know, still not certain his interest in her was anything more than a nostalgic dream of the past, fuelled by a natural male interest in a beautiful woman. Still not confident that she would even entertain any revival of their youthful romance.

He sat back down at his desk and drew a fresh sheet of paper towards him.

Chapter Ten

In her cosy sitting room at Fenton Hall—where they had returned, on the orders of a furious Robert, within two days of Charis's clandestine meeting with Lord Sampford—Kitty read through the words she had spent the past hour painstakingly writing. She grabbed the sheets of paper and ripped them in half and then, for good measure, she ripped them in half again before casting them across her desk, watching as a couple of pieces skimmed over the polished wood to the edge and fluttered to the floor. She propped her elbows on the desk and buried her head in her hands. No matter how hard she tried, she simply *could* not lose herself in her story. Her thoughts kept sliding away from her heroine's dilemma and on to…

No! She shoved her chair back and stood up. This was nonsensical. A man she once knew, years ago, had reappeared in her life…but it was not even that, was it? For Adam was *not* in her life. He'd returned, but now he merely existed on the periphery of her life. Somewhere.

*It's not just somewhere, though, is it? It's Kelridge Hall.
It is not so very far away.*

She put her hands over her ears as if she could block out
that treacherous voice. But, of course, she could not. It was
inside her head. It was always inside her head, reminding
her, remembering. And, as time went on, she recalled more
of the good times she and Adam had shared, overshadowing
the one bad experience…the time he had walked away from
her, callously abandoning her to her heartless father, who
cared more about paying off his debts than he did about the
daughter he had never forgiven for not being a son.

Her heart ached at the memory. If only Father had been
an honourable man and acted as a father should, as a pro-
tector for his daughter, then she would never have had to
humiliate herself by begging Adam to take her with him.
Thank goodness Edgar—who had happened across her crying in the woods one day and had listened to the whole sorry
tale—had rescued her. She had often wondered, afterwards,
if she should have insisted on telling Adam about her father on that last day. On reflection, however, she was glad
she had not. He might well have felt obliged to 'rescue' her
and Kitty now understood the unbearable strain that would
have put on their relationship. Although it had broken her
heart, Adam's abandonment of her had been for the best
when his own heart had not been engaged.

His words came back to her, floating up from the depths
of her memory. *'I will still be an architect's apprentice and
you will still be an earl's daughter.'*

He had been right, however much she refused to believe
it at the time. The disparity in their positions in society had
been a chasm they would never have been able to bridge.
And it had all worked out for the best. Edgar had been a

decent husband and Kitty loved his children as she would her own, had she been blessed. She now barely noticed the dull ache at never having conceived a baby of her own. Neither prayers nor tears had ever produced the result she craved—a circumstance Edgar had never let her forget, with his monthly joke at her expense—and Kitty had eventually accepted the miracle she had longed for throughout her ten years of marriage would never happen.

She crossed to the window and gazed out across garden to the woodland in the distance. There, in those woods, she and Adam had met and, on the far side, lay her father's land, now occupied by the new Lord Whitlock—her distant cousin—and his family. She had cut all ties with her father as soon as she was safely wed to Edgar, not wanting anything more to do with the man who had caused her such anguish, and he had passed away around the same time as Edgar had died.

Restless, she turned from the window. She'd take a turn about the gardens…cut a few blooms for her room…and hope the solution for that scene in her story might come to her. She knew from experience that remaining at her desk when the words refused to flow merely resulted in more frustration and more stilted prose. She headed for her bedchamber to fetch her shawl and bonnet, then went downstairs.

In the entrance hall, as she paused to tie the bonnet ribbons under her chin, Robert emerged from his business room.

'Ah, well met, Stepmama. Are you going out?'

Kitty indicated her plain dress and faded shawl with a smile. 'Only as far as the garden, you will be pleased to hear.'

'Ah.' Robert's eyes danced. 'Is the writing not co-operating this morning?'

Kitty gave him a resigned smile and shrugged, raising her eyebrows.

Robert grinned. 'No need for words; I know what that look means. Never mind... I have good news for you.' He gestured to his office. 'Might you spare me a few moments of your time?'

Kitty walked ahead of Robert into the room and sat down, wondering if he'd received a communication from her publisher. Robert rounded his desk to sit opposite her and tapped a letter that lay on the surface of the desk.

'This is from Kelridge.'

Hearing his name sucked the breath from her lungs. *Good news?* She did not trust herself to speak, merely nodded for Robert to continue.

'Do you recall I spoke to you about building a new wing here at the Hall?'

Kitty frowned. 'Yes. But I did not imagine you were serious. We have no need for more room here. Do we?'

A frown knit Robert's forehead and he tugged at his earlobe. 'I thought it time to look to the future. The house is adequate for us, but...in time, I shall marry. And I should like the Hall to be suitable for entertaining. I wish to build a wing with a ballroom on the ground floor and additional bedchambers and a nursery suite above.'

'Well...' Kitty quashed down the pain that threatened. It was inevitable this time would come... Charis would marry and move out and Robert, of course, would want to secure the future of the earldom and the estates. She adopted a teasing tone. 'This is unlike you, Robert—planning ahead in such a serious way.'

She watched a blush rise to colour his cheeks and unease wormed through her stomach. Could she be wrong about Lady Phoebe? Surely Robert couldn't be serious about such a woman? And yet…who else could it be?

'Do you have a particular lady in mind?'

Robert's colour deepened. 'No. At least…no. Not really. I wish to prepare for the inevitable, that is all.'

Kitty bit back the questions she longed to throw at him. He was a grown man now. He would tell her when he was ready. But, one question she simply *had* to ask: 'What has this to do with Lord Kelridge?'

'I asked him to visit us, in order that I may pick his brains about my plans. You know…what is possible. What would not work.'

Kitty breathed easier. She might spend much of her time thinking about Adam, but that did not mean she wanted to meet him more than necessary. Kelridge Place was close enough to visit and return in a day, as that sneaky voice in her head persisted in reminding her. She would arrange to be out on the day Adam came to the Hall. It would be for the best. They seemed unable to meet without the past rearing its head and all *that* served was to stir anger and resentment in them both.

She closed her mind to the truth—that it also raised unbearable longing within her. *False* longing, as she had reminded herself ever since their last encounter at the Exeter Exchange. The Adam who was now Lord Kelridge was very different from the Adam she had known when she was seventeen and he was twenty-one. But her heart and her body could not be as easily directed as her mind. *They* remembered the Adam of old—the thrill of those clandestine meetings; the sublime pleasure of time spent in his arms; the heady rush of his lips on hers.

'And that is his reply?' she asked.

'It is…and more than merely advising me, he has agreed to draw up the plans. Is that not splendid? He writes that he will enjoy the challenge of such a project. Reading between the lines of his letter, I believe he is finding it difficult to settle at Kelridge. Hardly surprising, I dare say.'

'Why do you say that?'

'Oh, well, I doubt Grenville Trewin is thrilled to have him home when he has run the place for so long. And you know yourself how servants dislike change. I don't suppose the new Earl will have an easy time of it at all.'

'I see.' With any luck Adam would decide to return to his old life in Edinburgh. Then Kitty could return to normal and relegate him to the past once again. Where he belonged. 'Which day do you expect him?'

'Tomorrow. You do not mind? I know it is short notice.'

'Unfortunately, I have plans for tomorrow. I have already arranged to call upon Lady Datchworth.' Kitty latched upon the one excuse that Robert would accept that she could not possibly cancel, knowing Her Ladyship's imperious nature. 'I should be obliged if you will pass on my apologies for my absence to Lord Kelridge, but it cannot be helped, and I am sure I could add nothing of value to your discussions.'

Robert stood up, rounding the desk as he said, 'There will be no need for apologies, Stepmama. You misunderstand me…or, more likely, I have not made myself clear. Kelridge will not arrive until late afternoon—he will stay here a few days to give him sufficient time to reacquaint himself with the Hall before drawing up the plans.'

Kitty's stomach lurched as Robert took her hand and as-

sisted her to rise. 'He will be *staying* here?' She stared up
at her stepson. 'But…surely he has matters to attend to at
Kelridge?'

Robert gave her a puzzled smile. 'Have you an objection? I made sure you would not mind… I know you value
your quiet time while we are at home, in order to write, but
your path will only cross with Kelridge's at dinner and in
the evening.'

'No. I have no objection. I was merely surprised.'

Robert shrugged. 'I dare say his steward will ride over
if there is anything urgent that needs his attention. He will
draw up the plans while he is here.'

Kitty recalled Lady Datchworth's matchmaking between
Adam and Charis. 'Is he aware Charis is absent from home?'

Robert had packed Charis off to her sister Jennifer's home
as soon as they returned to the Hall from London.

'What has Charis to do with this?'

'Nothing really. Only Lady Datchworth seemed convinced that Charis would be a good match for Kelridge
and I wondered—'

'Well, don't! I'm very certain Kelridge's interests don't
lie in Charis's direction—she is far too young for him. Besides—' his brown gaze pierced Kitty '—have *you* ever noticed him pay any particular attention to my sister?'

'No. But—'

'There you are, then. He is not coming here to see Charis, but to help me.'

Relieved—surely only because of Adam's unsuitability
for Charis and not for any other more selfish reason?—Kitty
said, 'If Lord Kelridge arrives tomorrow, I must instruct
Mrs Kirk to prepare a bedchamber and consult Mrs Ainsley over the menus.'

Robert dropped a kiss on the top of Kitty's head. 'No need to trouble yourself over that for I've already informed Mrs Kirk and told her to warn the kitchen to prepare. You know as well as I that Mrs Ainsley will be in her element, devising dishes suitable for our guest.'

'How long will His Lordship stay?'

'Oh, a sennight at least, I should think.'

A whole week? Waves of heat rushed through Kitty. How on earth would she manage an entire week with him here? In her home? Could she maintain the façade of gracious hostess for that length of time or would that old hurt and resentment at his lies bubble to the surface? She could not face the humiliation should Robert discover what had happened in the past, nor the mortification should Adam ever realise exactly how much turmoil he still stirred within her.

'Now,' Robert continued, 'I have taken up enough of your time…be gone to the flower beds and allow those plot tangles to unravel in your head.'

Kitty walked away, her stomach tangled in as many knots as her plot and her throat clogged with emotion.

'What the devil is amiss with you, young lady?'

It was the following day and Kitty had called upon Lady Datchworth at her home, Peyton Park.

Her Ladyship raised her pince-nez and peered at Kitty, continuing, 'You call upon me without warning and then proceed to sit there, pale as uncooked pastry, and fidget your fingers in your lap. If you have no gossip with which to entertain me, you may as well go home.'

Kitty swallowed past the lump of dread that had taken up residence in her throat since yesterday and forced a smile.

'I apologise for my poor company, ma'am. I—I dare say

I am missing Charis—she has gone to Yorkshire to stay with her sister.'

'Then the solution is obvious.'

'It is?'

'Indeed. Invite a friend to stay with you. *That* will fill the gap in your life and provide the company you crave.'

Kitty could think of nothing worse. She would rather spend her days writing quietly than having to dance atten-dance upon guests. Her thoughts flew straight to Adam and his impending visit, and her stomach fluttered. She swal-lowed again.

Her Ladyship unexpectedly reached out and took Kitty's hand. 'You feel the same as any mother, my dear, whether or not Charis is your own child. You have raised her and you must face the prospect that she will at some time marry and move away from home, and grow away from you. But that is the natural order of things for we women—our fledg-lings must fly the nest and we must move on, finding new interests in our lives. At least, it is the natural order for *most* people. I could only wish that reprehensible son of mine would settle down. I have tried…heaven *knows* I have tried to find him a suitable bride, but he rejects every single one of them. But, there…we were not discussing my woes…' Her fingers tightened around Kitty's.

'Catherine, dear, I know you have always been adamant you will never remarry, but…mayhap it is time to recon-sider?'

Kitty started. 'Ma'am? You surely cannot mean Lord Datchworth?'

The Marquess was a dark, forbidding man with, as far as Kitty had ever been able to tell, no sense of humour at all. She had thought Adam brooding, but Datchworth was twice as bad and she could think of nobody who would make a worse husband, so much so that she'd modelled the villain in her novel, Lord Sidney Barmouth, on the man.

'Foolish girl! I care for you far too much to inflict my son upon you. I might be his mama, but I am not blind to his faults. No... I simply meant in general—is it not time for you to think about marrying again.'

Kitty shook her head. 'I cannot.'

'Cannot or will not?'

'It would be unfair on any husband who did not already have children, when I know I am barren.'

Just admitting that out loud brought a painful lump to Kitty's throat. How she would have loved a baby of her own...but that regret was another that lived in the past and that she tried hard not to dwell upon.

'Are you so sure you are, my dear?'

'I am. Edgar and I were married ten years and my four stepchildren are ample evidence of *his* prowess.'

'Then marry a man who has already produced his heir.'

Again, Kitty shook her head. 'I have no wish to raise a second stepfamily—I love the stepchildren I already have.'

'Then marry a man with older children, or an older man with no desire for children.'

Kitty shrugged helplessly. How had her missing Charis resulted in Her Ladyship deciding she must be ripe to re-marry?

Lady Datchworth released Kitty's hand and reached for a silver handbell on the table by the side of her chair. She shook it and the door opened in response to its tinkling sound. A maid entered and curtsied.

'Bring us a bottle of Madeira. Lady Fenton requires stron-

ger sustenance than another pot of tea. And a plate of sweetmeats would be welcome, I dare say?'

She gazed at Kitty, brows raised, and Kitty nodded,
knowing agreement was required of her rather than a polite refusal of the offer. Sweetmeats were Her Ladyship's
very favourite indulgence and the plate was really for her.

'So, let us think of ways around your predicament, my
dear. Which friend might you invite to stay with you?'

'No. I cannot invite anyone for the moment, ma'am. It
is impossible.'

'Impossible?'

Her Ladyship bent a look of astonishment upon Kitty but
said no more as the maid returned at that moment, carrying
a tray which she set on the table. She poured two glasses of
Madeira and then offered the plate of sweetmeats to Lady
Datchworth, who leaned forward, a line of concentration
etched between her eyebrows and rubbing her hands together as she examined the plate.

'Hmmm. Yes… I think…'

She reached out, selected a sugared almond and popped
it into her mouth before leaning back and closing her eyes,
chewing slowly, an expression of utter delight upon her face.
She waved her arm without opening her eyes and the maid
offered the plate to Kitty.

'Now. Where were we?' Lady Datchworth had finished
chewing and, despite a longing sideways look at the plate—
set within her reach on the side table—she turned her attention back to Kitty. 'Oh, yes. You claim having a friend
to stay would be impossible. How so?'

'W-we actually have a visitor arriving today…a visitor
for Robert…a man…they will be occupied all week—'

'Who is visiting you? Why did you not say earlier? A man, you say? Is he a gentleman?'

'Yes, but—'

'Then who? I demand to know his identity.'

'It is Lord Kelridge.'

'Kelridge? He has not informed *me* of his intention.'

'You have seen him, ma'am?'

'We have corresponded a time or two since he left London.'

'Well, his visit is only recently arranged and he arrives this afternoon, so he will not have had the time—'

'*This afternoon?* Why are you not at home to greet your guest?'

'Adam…' the sudden gleam in Lady Datchworth's eyes alerted Kitty to her error '…that is, *Lord Kelridge* is not *my* guest. Robert invited him, and he is to draw up architectural plans for a new wing at Fenton. Robert plans a ballroom and additional bedrooms for when he marries.'

'Fenton is to marry? I have seen him pay no particular attention to any lady. Whom is he to marry?'

Relieved to have diverted Her Ladyship away from the subject of Adam, Kitty said, 'He claims he has no one lady in mind. He claims he is planning ahead.'

'Hmm…well now, it will behove me to think carefully about this.' Lady Datchworth rubbed her hands together, a gleam in her eyes. 'I am sure I can come up with the perfect match for him.'

Kitty made a mental note to warn Robert to avoid Her Ladyship for the foreseeable future if he did not want one eligible bride after another—at least, eligible in Lady Datchworth's opinion—thrust under his nose. There was nothing Her Ladyship enjoyed more than a spot of matchmaking.

The Earl with the Secret Past

'Now. It is time you left for home, my dear, for you will want to be there to greet your guest.'

Lady Datchworth rang the bell and ordered Kitty's carriage, then she jumped to her feet with an energy that belied her years and escorted Kitty to the front door.

As Kitty paused at the open carriage door to say goodbye, Her Ladyship called, 'Look after Kelridge, Catherine. He is not nearly as tough as he likes to pretend.'

Chapter Eleven

Adam gazed around with interest as he drove his curricle along the tree-lined carriageway to Fenton Hall. Not much had changed in the fifteen years since his last visit. The lime trees flanking the carriageway were taller. More mature.

As am I.

Mature enough, surely, to persuade Kitty to confide in him without ruffling her feathers with his poor attempts to tease her as he had done the last time they met. He needed to understand if her marriage to Fenton was because she had been desperate to leave her father's house or was it as he'd initially thought—a young girl craving the adventure of being a wife, too naive to realise the implications of tying herself to a man so far beneath her own station in life? But if she had been in trouble, why had she not told him? She must have known he would never abandon her had she been in danger.

But I did stop her from confiding in me on that last day.

That guilt had been added to the other guilt that had tormented him for so long—the guilt of denying his love for her. But the past could not be changed, only the future, and here was his chance to uncover the truth as well as to untangle his feelings for present-day Kitty. Discovering the truth about what had driven his mother to take him from his father—and realising he had leapt to conclusions about her motives—had made him doubt what he initially thought about Kitty's hasty marriage. The Kitty he remembered had been spirited and bright and loving, not a girl who would cynically manipulate a man or lie about her feelings. He now believed he could have been wrong and he would listen to what she had to say.

Then, they would see. Could there possibly be a future for them, or was there too much hurt and suspicion between them now?

This was the perfect opportunity to discover what they *both* wanted while, at the same time, helping Robert with his plans. If nothing else, it would be good to feel useful once again, practising those skills he had learned and honed over many years.

The carriageway passed through the pair of familiar stone pillars that flanked the entrance to the forecourt and he steered his pair around the area, drawing them to a halt level with the front entrance. The front door opened and Robert bounded down the steps, reminding Adam of the young lad he had known.

'Adam! Welcome!' Robert leapt into the curricle. 'I'll ride with you round to the stables.'

'Thank you. It is good to be back… I shall look forward to getting reacquainted with the old place.'

'You'll find not much has changed. Hi! Gresham! Come and see to His Lordship's cattle, will you?'

The Fenton Hall head man emerged from the dim interior of the barn.

'Yes, milord.'

Gresham eyed Adam with the same mix of curiosity and caution Adam had recognised in his own staff at Kelridge Place. He did not begrudge Gresham his restraint—after all, he had known Adam as a simple architect's apprentice—but at least there was no hint of the resentment he detected in the Kelridge men. This time away from Kelridge and that odd, unsettling atmosphere would, he hoped, give him time to work out the best response to the underlying distrust and the hint of disrespect that threaded through much of his interactions with the men. Although reluctant to turn men off, he might have no choice if he could not win them over.

Anyway, he was here now and had a chance to clear his head and to help Robert design a new wing for the Hall. He couldn't wait to begin.

Adam saw nothing of Kitty until he came downstairs after changing for dinner. He made his way directly to the salon and there she was, standing with her back to the door, gazing out of the window. A gown the colour of periwinkles skimmed her curves in all the right places, her shining hair caught up with tortoiseshell combs, a few tendrils spiralling around her ears.

His heart leapt as he drank in the sight. Joy spread through him and his earlier confusion melted away with the certainty that he *did* still harbour feelings for her. But his uncertainty over what she felt about him...*for* him... remained.

'Ahem.'

She spun to face him, her face pale and her eyes wide.

'Lady Fenton, I am sorry to startle you.' He bowed. 'Good evening... I would have waited to be announced, but there was no one in the hall and Robert did say to consider myself one of the family and not to stand on ceremony.'

Kitty inclined her head and glided across to sit in one of the chairs near to the fireplace. 'Indeed, you must regard yourself at home while you are our guest.' She had swiftly recovered from her shock and now sat primly, her expression serene, with her hands folded upon her lap. 'Please, take a seat while we wait for Robert. I am sure he will be down soon.'

As he sat down, Adam recalled his poorly received joke about headstrong young girls and his other attempts at jesting that had also fallen flat.

'Before Rob joins us—might I apologise for my clumsy attempts to tease you when we last met? I fear I inadvertently upset ye. As I said, they were poor attempts.'

'It is forgotten, sir.'

Silence reigned.

'Do ye—?'

'How are—?'

They spoke simultaneously, and both paused. They laughed at the same time and the atmosphere lightened a fraction.

'Please, do go ahead,' Adam said, willing to take his cue from Kitty as to how they would treat one another.

'I was about to ask if you find the Hall much altered?'

'The house, from what I have seen, is much the same but, of course, the occupants have changed beyond recognition. Your late husband leaves a gaping hole where he stood and, with Edward in the army, Jennifer wed and residing in Yorkshire, and Miss Mayfield temporarily absent, the house seems strangely quiet.'

Kitty's lack of reaction, other than a faint wash of pink over her cheekbones, spurred him into trying to provoke a stronger response from her.

'But *you* are here now, of course. That is the greatest difference. And had our work lasted a mere couple of weeks longer, I should have known all about your marriage. It must have been hastily arranged, for I never heard even a whisper of His Lordship's plan to remarry during my time here.'

Adam fought back that old sense of betrayal that still simmered, driven by his uncertainty over *her* feelings, and despite his newly acknowledged feelings for her. If he continued to prod Kitty in an attempt to learn what she was truly thinking, she would never tell him the truth of what happened and, until she did, they would keep wandering in circles, stuck in the same fog of suspicion that had enveloped them since their meeting in London.

It was possible he had jumped to conclusions about the reason for Kitty's hasty marriage exactly as he had done with his mother and the reasons for her leaving his father. He was still determined to uncover the truth—if it was anyone but Kitty he would suspect she'd been with child, but he knew the marriage was not for that reason. It must have been because of her father.

'Kitty... Catherine...please, might we talk about what happened? We both have questions—'

'You are mistaken. I have no questions. You were very clear at the time and I accepted your decision long ago.'

'But—'

Adam bit back his protest as the door opened and Robert strolled in, looking from one to the other of them with a quizzical expression.

'I beg your pardon. Am I interrupting something?'

Kitty's chin lifted. 'Not at all, Robert. We were talking about the speed of my marriage to your papa. I was about to explain the reason for that to Lord Kelridge.' She switched her gaze to Adam. 'We met quite by chance and fell in love. There was no need to wait.'

The pain, sudden and sharp, stole his breath, but he caught a flash of guilt in those grey eyes of hers.

She was lying. She *must* be lying.

But he could not challenge her with Robert there. He must have patience. He would get his chance to coax the truth from her.

'Dinner is served, my lord.'

The butler, Vincent, stood at the open door, his announcement saving Adam from any further response.

The conversation between Adam and Robert flowed easily over dinner, with Kitty joining in only when applied to for her opinion. As soon as they finished eating, she rose to her feet and the men followed suit.

'I shall withdraw and leave you gentlemen to your port and your plans.'

'We shan't be long, Stepmama. You will still be in the drawing room when we've finished? Will you play for us?'

Adam was unsurprised when she shook her head.

'I regret I have the headache, Rob. If you do not object, I should prefer to retire early.'

'Then an early night is the best remedy.'

'Goodnight to you both. I apologise for abandoning you on your first evening here, my lord.'

'I hope your headache is speedily relieved, my lady.'

'It is little wonder she has the headache,' Robert said to

Adam as Kitty left the room. 'That woman would try the patient of a saint.'

'I...? Lady Fenton? But...?'

'Good Lord, no! I didn't mean my stepmother! She is a diamond!'

He paused as the butler came in with a bottle of port and poured two glasses. 'Thank you, Vincent.'

As soon as Adam and Robert were alone again, Robert continued, 'My comment was aimed at Lady Datchworth. Do you remember I told you my stepmother had visited her today?'

Adam grinned. 'Of course. And now I understand your cryptic comment. Lady D. in full sail could give anyone the headache. I experienced my share of that when in London, as ye know. But, still, I could not help but like her despite her inclination for matchmaking.'

Adam found himself the target of a searching look.

'Speaking of which, my stepmother is convinced Her La-dyship has earmarked you and my sister Charis as a likely match.' Robert's expression remained neutral.

'By no encouragement from me, Rob. Charis is a lovely girl, but much too young for my taste.'

Robert visibly relaxed. 'I am relieved to hear that. Lady Datchworth is convinced of her own shrewdness in match-ing couples and yet, to my knowledge, she has never yet met with success.'

'I shall be on my guard, but ye need have no fear, Rob—Charis is perfectly safe from me. Now, tell me your plans for this new wing.'

Adam spent most of the following day inspecting the Hall from top to bottom and taking measurements, paying particular attention to the wing Sir Angus had designed following that devastating fire. Robert assisted him with the measuring and they had a lively discussion about his requirements for the new wing, but once they were done Robert headed out on estate business, leaving Adam in the library, where he had been provided with a desk and a table to work on as he drew up the plans.

Of Kitty there had been no sign all day and, although he resolutely blocked her from his mind as he worked in the quiet of the afternoon, she hovered around the edges as a nagging presence, ready to pounce whenever his concentration wavered. Her announcement that she and the late Lord Fenton had fallen in love so swiftly still did not ring true and Adam was more determined than ever to discover the real reason behind their hasty marriage.

He found it liberating to lose himself in what he still thought of as his 'real life'—his occupation. And it was a relief to be away from Kelridge Place, even though he was aware his time would be better spent in establishing his position as master. It was good to feel he could breathe easily for the first time since coming down from London and so, as he settled down to the business of planning the new wing, not only did he block Kitty from his thoughts, but he also pushed aside his unease over Kelridge Place.

By mid-afternoon, however, his head felt stuffed full of wool. The weather had turned hot and humid, begging for the release of a thunderstorm to clear the air. Adam had already opened wide all the French doors that led outside on to the flagged terrace that wrapped around this wing of the house—the wing Sir Angus had designed—but there was little relief to be had and he had resorted to removing his jacket, discarding his neckcloth and working in his shirt sleeves and unbuttoned waistcoat.

Finally, craving the relief of a breath of fresh air, he pushed his damp hair off his forehead, laid down his pen and packed his instruments away before striding for the nearest open French door.

'Oh!'

He'd stepped outside without looking, only to collide with someone walking along the terrace. He reacted fast, his hands wrapping around Kitty's bare upper arms, even before he realised whom he had sent staggering backwards. He hauled her upright, her scent of warm woman mingling with that of the mass of blooms she carried as it coiled through his senses.

'Take care! You are crushing my flowers.'

Adam released her. The tingling caused by the satiny softness of her warm skin against his palms only registered with him when it ceased. He rubbed his palms against his breeches, conscious he had left his jacket hanging over the back of his chair and that his shirt sleeves were rolled up to his elbows. Their eyes locked—hers widening and darkening as a flush bloomed on her cheeks and her lips parted, giving every impression of a woman aroused. Adam's blood surged to his groin. Dare he hope she was mellowing towards him? Could they both let the past go? The tight knot that had lodged in his gut on arrival loosened a little.

'Rather a few crushed blooms than allow you to fall.'

She smiled and it appeared a more genuine smile than the strained efforts of last evening.

'That is true. I spoke out of turn. A few mangled flowers are as nothing compared to a bruised—' She bit her lip. 'That is, compared to a bruising tumble.'

Adam laughed. 'Indeed. I shall take especial care another time I exit the library. May I carry those for you?'

Her smile faltered. 'There is no need... I...that is...thank you.' She relinquished the flowers and indicated the open door. 'We may as well go through the library—I had intended to walk around to the back door to save disturbing you.'

She sent him an inscrutable look from beneath the sweep of her lashes. His gaze lowered to her lips as they parted and sparks of desire sizzled through him.

'You are our guest and I understand you have refused any payment from Robert for your services. While you are under this roof you may expect your comfort to be our highest priority.'

The perfect society hostess had returned and those sparks fizzled out. In his short time in this world, Adam had learned Kitty was renowned in the *ton* for her graciousness, her propriety and her charm. That knot tightened once more as they walked side by side through the library and the familiar uncertainty washed through him. He simply didn't know how to deal with this guarded woman who so rarely revealed any hint of her true thoughts or, more importantly, her true feelings.

'There is a storeroom near the kitchens where I dry herbs and mix remedies and salves, and that I also use for arranging flowers,' Kitty continued as she led the way. 'Are you making progress with the plans? I dare say they will not take long to complete.'

Is that a polite way of enquiring how long I shall stay?

'I haven't begun drawing them yet... I am sketching out a few ideas first and will get Robert's opinion before settling on a final layout. This will be a major investment for him and he needs to be aware of the options available before committing himself.' Her thoughtful expression prompted him to add, 'Do you have any preferences as to what is included?'

'Me? Oh, good heavens, no. This is Robert's home and, when he weds, I shall remove to the Dower House.'

'You will find that lonely after being a part of a family for so long.'

'I shan't be lonely. It is on the edge of the village, so there are neighbours all around. And I shall make it my business to pay regular, lengthy visits to all my stepchildren whether they invite me to stay or not.'

Her grey eyes twinkled as she looked straight ahead, her mind presumably on her family. Clearly there was a great deal of respect and love between them. She paused at a door and opened it.

'If you would kindly put the flowers in that bucket, sir—'

'Adam,' he said.

She was half-turned away from him and, to all intents and purposes, she did not react. But he caught the slight twitch in her jaw that suggested she had clenched it. He sucked in a deep breath, sensing now might be the time to broach the subject of the past and to hear Kitty's side of the story.

'We cannot ignore the fact we once knew one another,' he said. 'We were close. We called one another by name. I still think of you in my head as Kitty—'

'Catherine!' She pivoted to face him. 'In this family I have always been Catherine. Even my f-father always called me Catherine. I was only ever Kitty to you.'

'Well then. Catherine.' He frowned. Her voice had definitely hitched when she spoke of her father. 'I was sorry to learn of your father's death.'

'Spare me your condolences. I did not mourn his death—we were estranged long before he died.'

'Ah.'

Her expression suggested reluctance to continue the discussion and Adam recalled her long-ago reticence if he asked about her father or her home life. He did know her mother had died when she was a young child and now he also remembered the late Lord Fenton's dislike of his neighbour.

Kitty clasped her hands in front of her and faced Adam, with the look of a woman facing an ordeal. 'He disapproved of my marriage to Edgar.'

'Yet he must have given his consent for ye to wed Edgar.'

'He withheld his permission at first. But Edgar paid him handsomely and he was persuaded to grant his consent.'

'He paid him? That is an odd turn of phrase. What do ye mean?'

She turned abruptly and paced to the window where she stood gazing out, her arms wrapped around her waist. Adam took a step towards her, frowning as he realised she was trembling. He dropped the flowers into the bucket she'd indicated and followed her.

'What is it? You never would talk of your father and the subject obviously upsets you even now.'

Adam had always put her reluctance to talk about her father down to family loyalty, as well as to a daughter's natural wariness of a strict parent and the fear he might uncover their secret trysts.

He stood close enough behind her to feel the warmth radiating from her skin. Her scent weaved through his senses, and his blood quickened. Her hair was caught up with combs and pins, leaving short wisps curling at her hairline, from nape to ears. How he longed to press his lips to that sweet spot on the side of her neck where he could see her pulse thrumming in time with his.

She still hadn't answered him and his anger stirred at her silence.

'Well? What is it ye never told me about your father? Was he the reason ye were so determined to leave Whitlock Manor? And when I refused to help ye ruin yourself ye found yourself a convenient substitute! And do not tell me it was for love, for I didna believe ye last night and I shall not believe ye now.'

She spun around, her eyes flashing with fury. 'That is unfair. You do not know...' She shook her head before sucking in a deep breath. 'No. I am sorry. You are right and this is my fault for not telling you the truth when you first asked why I married Edgar so soon after you left.'

Adam listened, horrified, as Kitty told him of her father's plan to sell her hand in marriage in order to clear his gambling debts. He took her hand as she carried on with her tale.

'My father was still in London when you left and I continued to walk in the woods, dreading his return. I could see no way out of my dilemma. Then Edgar came upon me one day and saw my distress. Somehow, I ended up telling him about my father. As soon as my father returned, Edgar called upon him and offered to pay off his debts in return for my hand in marriage. We married by special licence...neither of us wanted a fuss. And we were happy,' she added, in a defiant voice.

His heart ached for her.

'If only I had known,' he said, reaching for her other hand. 'When we met again...when I found out how quickly you had married Lord Fenton…it made me so angry I couldna think straight. All I could see was your betrayal. I thought ye had lied about your feelings for me at first, but I did then wonder if I had been over-hasty.' He drew her closer, into his arms. 'I wish ye had told me the truth about your father, sweetheart.'

For a few glorious heartbeats Kitty melted into his embrace but, all too soon, she stiffened, jerking out of his reach with something very like fear in her eyes.

'Do not call me that. I have told you the truth because you deserve to know and I want your pity now even less than I wanted it then. I might have been young, but I did have some pride. And… I thought you felt the same for me as I did for you.'

Her chin tilted defiantly as she faced Adam.

'Thank you for your assistance, Lord Kelridge. Now, if you will excuse me, I have domestic matters to attend to.'

She stalked past him.

'Kitty…'

But she was gone.

Adam swept a hand through his hair, cursing himself for his clumsy assumption—or was it wishful thinking?— that her confession would smoothly lead to a rekindling of tender feelings between them. He cursed himself also for being all kinds of an idiot as he thought about the story she had just revealed—her fear of her father's despicable plan and her desperation to get away. And what had he done to that scared, lonely girl? He, who had professed his love for her so many times, had broken her heart. And her trust.

He stared at the open doorway through which Kitty had

vanished. They would have to talk again, but maybe not just yet.

He needed that fresh air more than ever. He headed out for a walk in the gardens.

Chapter Twelve

Kitty rushed from the house, hurrying through the gardens and into the meadow beyond before she slowed her pace. Her chest rose and fell rapidly as she caught her breath, memories flooding her thoughts—her father and his selfishness, and his disappointment that his only child was a girl; Edgar and his gentle fault-finding, leaving her convinced of her uselessness both as a wife and as a woman when she failed to get with child; Adam, the man she had loved with her entire being and the man who had lied about his love for her. The man who had broken her heart.

She had felt herself weaken when he'd pulled her into his arms. For a scant few moments she had thrust all doubts aside and relished the novelty of being held. But, all too soon, those memories had burst into her head, reminding her of her worthlessness and reviving her fear of getting hurt again. The fear of being let down. And she had run away.

Dear God, what must he think of me?

He would be their guest at the Hall for a week… She

could not avoid him, or Robert would surely notice and Kitty could not bear the humiliation of her stepson finding out what had happened between her and Adam. Plus, for all that Adam's lies still hurt, Kitty now accepted he had acted in both of their best interests by refusing to take her away with him. The strains would soon have killed off any tender feelings had he succumbed to her entreaties.

She walked on, her mind buzzing as she fanned her face with her hand. Goodness, it was hot. The chip straw hat she usually wore in the garden was still on her head, but she'd not had time to even think about fetching a parasol or a fan. The bodice of her gown was closely fitted with a high neckline, but there were buttons down the front of it and she unfastened the top two to allow a little more air to reach her skin. The woodland at the bottom of the meadow beckoned, with the promise of shade from the sun, although… she scanned the sky…clouds were massing on the horizon, promising a break in the weather and a welcome shower. She ought not to go too far.

She crossed the meadow, stepping high through the long grass which would soon be cut to make hay. Wild flowers were in bloom—meadowsweet, campion, purple loosestrife—and she admired their delicacy after the showier blooms she had cut in the garden.

She reached the welcome shade of the belt of trees. A brook trickled through it and she turned to follow its course towards the larger expanse of West Whitlock Wood, which reached almost as far as her old childhood home. She'd met her father only once after she married Edgar and that had been the year before both he and Edgar had died, when he had called at the Hall to beg for money to pay his debts. Ten years they had been neighbours, yet her father might as well have lived on the moon. He never mingled in local society. Was never seen in church. Never attended society events in London. Never went anywhere respectable as far as she knew. But, so Edgar had told her, he'd still visited those old haunts of his—the gaming hells in St James's and other, less salubrious, areas of London—and still mixed with the villains and reprobates who had brought him so low as to offer his only daughter in payment of his debts. He had never changed his ways.

Thunder growled, far in the distance, and Kitty turned her steps in the direction of home, up through those familiar woods, the woods where she had run to meet Adam whenever she could, breathless with excitement and the joy of seeing him again, of feeling his arms around her, his lips on hers. She dragged her mind away from those memories and the treacherous feelings they evoked. Whatever she had felt, he had not shared her feelings and it still hurt that such lies had fallen so easily from his lips. She had truly believed he loved her, but now she was wiser and would guard her heart against more pain, even though her pulse quickened at the sight of him and the scent of him and at the sound of his voice.

The thunder grumbled again—a long, drawn-out rumble—and she quickened her pace, taking a shortcut up a steep wooded slope that would bring her out close to the back lane that led around to the stable yard. As she neared the edge of the wood, however, she slammed to a halt at the sight of Adam seated under an oak, his back propped against the massive trunk, legs bent, arms resting on his knees. His head, hatless, was tilted back, his eyes closed. Her heart squeezed at the memories that again crowded her head—how many times had she found him waiting for her in just such a pose?

A sane woman would retreat. Quietly.

Kitty walked forward, making no attempt to hide her approach. Adam's eyes sprung open and he raised his head.

'Why are you here?' she demanded. 'Did you follow me?'

He huffed a laugh. 'I did no such thing. I was here first. Besides, ye told me ye had domestic matters to attend to.' He waved his arm. 'I shouldna call these surroundings *domestic*, precisely.'

Kitty pushed a fallen lock of hair back under her hat, aware her face must be pink and shiny with the effort of hurrying up the slope in the heat of the afternoon. Adam, on the other hand, was the epitome of cool and collected as he squinted up at her.

I cannot keep running away. I cannot allow my misreading of a young man's intentions all those years ago to continue to blight our every conversation.

'You're right. I am sorry I left so abruptly.' She clasped her hands together at her waist and inhaled. 'Please forgive my rudeness.'

'I shall forgive you on one condition.'

'Condition?'

'Aye.'

Adam rose to his feet in one smooth movement and Kitty stepped back. He followed, towering over her, but she had never felt intimidated by Adam and she still did not fear him. Not physically, at least. His temper was a touch more volatile than she recalled, but, if she were honest, so was hers. It seemed each sparked intense feelings in the other without effort. And, for all the local gossip that the apple never fell far from the tree, Kitty had never seen any sign of *uncontrollable* anger or any hint of violence in him.

He had been silent for too long, just staring into her eyes. She turned aside. 'Well? Will you enlighten me, or do you mean to make me guess?'

'Yes…sorry… I thought…my condition is that you call me Adam and I call you Catherine.'

She opened her mouth to refuse. Such intimacy would, surely, only encourage those long-ago memories; the memories she worked so hard to suppress. But…could she reasonably say no? Robert and Adam had lapsed into their old familiarity, from when Robert had been eleven and Adam just the architect's apprentice. Adam would remain at the Hall several more days and Rob would be curious if Kitty and Adam maintained a polite distance. He knew Kitty was often informal with her friends, both male and female, and that she called them by their given names. But it still moved her one step further along a path she had no wish to travel, still uncertain of her ability to guard her heart.

She took refuge in teasing to mask her unease. 'Not Ambrose?'

'No. Not Ambrose.' Adam's mouth twisted in distaste. 'I have always been Adam. I am in no mind to fit myself entirely into the mould of a stranger.'

His words, and the bitterness that tainted them, reached into Kitty's heart, beyond her own fear of being hurt again.

'Is it true you had no idea whatsoever of your beginnings?'

'None. My mother saw fit to keep the whole of her past— and, therefore, my past—to herself until she was forced to admit the truth by the fact of my father's death.'

She believed him, despite her initial suspicion he might be lying about that.

How hard that must be, to discover your own mother has lied to you your entire life.

Kitty allowed herself to study him more closely. The harsh lines drawn from nose to mouth…the crease between those dark brows, the etched line that never disappeared completely although it did soften from time to time…the latent anger she had sensed from their first meeting, anger that simmered just beneath the surface to erupt at the least provocation…all these began to make sense. She had been wrong to attribute his anger solely to her, but there was no doubt that some of it was, for she certainly seemed able to provoke an eruption with little effort, just by her presence. As he provoked *her* anger with ease. Their shared history had left its scars on both of them.

Unbidden, Lady Datchworth's final words of the day before whispered through her mind. *'Look after Kelridge, Catherine. He is not nearly as tough as he likes to pretend.'*

Was she right?

'Very well. I agree. Adam it is. And… I am sorry our meeting again has been difficult for us both. I hope we are truly able to put the past behind us now.'

'As do I.'

They were still standing, several feet apart, facing one another. Adam's gaze roved over Kitty's face, as gentle as a caress, and her pulse stuttered as she willed herself to remain still.

'And just so you know,' he added, softly, 'I *did* feel the same as you, fifteen years ago.'

Kitty stared at him, unsure how to react but, before she could speak, thunder cracked overhead. She started at the suddenness of it and cast an anxious glance up through the canopy of leaves to the ominous sky above.

'We must go back to the house or we are likely to get drenched.'

She took Adam's proffered arm, thankful for the reprieve, her stomach tightening at the warmth of bare, hair-dusted skin beneath her hand. They set off, emerging from the wood into a meadow where sheep huddled together, their backs to the rain which by now had started to spatter down in huge drops as the wind gusted.

The lane that led back to the Hall was across the meadow and it was not long before Kitty's gown was uncomfortably damp and clinging to her legs.

'Is there anywhere nearby we can shelter?'

Adam splayed one large hand to the small of her back, urging her to hurry, and Kitty found herself trotting to keep up with him.

'Yes! This way.' She tugged at his arm, turning him aside and heading for the hedgerow that edged the meadow. 'There. Look.' She pointed out the old gamekeeper's cottage behind the hedge. 'It is a bit rickety, but it still has a roof. Hurry!'

The rain worsened, soaking through Kitty's gown in seconds. Lightning split the sky, followed quickly by another crash of thunder, louder than before.

'There it is.'

They hurtled the last few paces to a gap in the hedge and slammed through the already ajar door into the stone building.

'Phew!'

Adam shook his head, scattering drops as the rain drummed on the slate roof, dripping through in several places. He returned to the door and shoved against it to push it shut. The hinges groaned in protest, but eventually the door closed against the downpour. Kitty, still panting from that mad dash through the rain, scanned the dim interior of the cottage, the sole source of light one grimy window. A pile of sacks in one corner—a corner free of leaks—caught her eye, and she approached gingerly to poke the pile with one foot, fully expecting to see mice scatter. None emerged and her breathing steadied. She discarded the uppermost sack and picked up the next one, conscious that her drenched muslin gown must be nigh-on transparent and would no doubt cling to her body in a scandalous fashion. She pulled off her sodden hat and draped the sack around her shoulders, banishing her distaste at the thought of the dust and dirt that would transfer to her clothing and of the likely former use for such sacking found in a gamekeeper's cottage.

She turned to Adam. His shirt, beneath his waistcoat, clung to the heavy muscles of his chest and she glimpsed a hint of dark curls at the open neck. Her pulse quickened again, the sound of her now ragged breaths thankfully drowned out by the drum of rain on the roof. She averted her gaze and thrust a sack in his direction. There was one rickety wooden chair and she stalked across to it and sat as another crack reverberated around the cottage. Lightning flashed simultaneously, illuminating the room with its ghostly glare.

'Thunderstorms usually pass quickly. We shall not be stuck here long.'

Her voice shook, irritatingly. She stared straight ahead, avoiding looking directly at Adam, but from the corner of her eye she saw his lips widen in a smile as one brow

quirked up. The dratted man was fully aware of her discomfort at being closeted with him in this tiny cottage, but at
least he made no move to approach her. Instead, he spread
his sack on an area of dry floor next to the cottage wall. He
sat down, adopting the same pose as he had against the tree
trunk earlier, as the lightning flashed again. After a short
delay, the thunder crashed, more distant this time.

Kitty wished she could be on her own to think about what
he'd said, but they were stuck there and she could not run
away this time. If he hadn't lied about loving her, if that was
what he meant, then why had he said those hateful words
fifteen years ago? Words that had haunted her for years.

*'I'm fond of ye, Kitty, but this was never more than a
pleasant way to pass the time when I had an hour to spare.
I thought ye understood that.'*

Words that had added to her feelings of worthlessness
all these years.

His eyes were on her, watching her, and she shivered.
If it was true…if he *had* loved her, all those years ago…
what then?

'Why did you say what you did? That last day?'

He heaved a sigh and gave her a rueful smile. 'I thought
it would make it easier for you. Better to think me a liar
and a scoundrel than to grieve over what might have been.'

She should feel mollified to hear that after all this time.
But fear wound around her heart as her anger drained away
for, without anger to cling on to, she felt…naked. Lost. *Vulnerable.* And she thought that, maybe, the awful truth was
that she had been holding on to that anger to shield her from
the feelings Adam had roused within her since his return.
Unwelcome feelings. *Frightening* feelings. To allow herself
to care for another man—and *this* man in particular—was

to risk more heartache. A risk that scared her more than she cared to admit.

'Thank you for telling me,' she said, striving to sound calm. 'I accept that I was naive...too young to realise the strain we would both have been under. You did the right thing.' Kitty stood, her heart a touch lighter now the air had been cleared between them. 'It sounds as though rain has stopped. Let us return to the Hall while we can.'

Adam leapt to his feet. He came to Kitty and took her hands in his. 'I still wish you had told me, Kitty.' His voice rasped with emotion and her heart leapt with joy. And with hope, even though it was far too late. 'We would have found a way. I—'

'No, Adam.' Kitty tamped down her whirling emotions and disentangled her hands from his. *This* roused fear in her heart. What good could come of them raking over coals grown cold, even if a tiny spark still lingered? Even if she was still drawn to him, as a moth to a flame, she could not risk getting burned again. 'Please, let us not rake it over again. We cannot alter the past and, as we have both said before, we must not mistake the people we were then for who we are now. The past fifteen years have changed us both. Please. Let it be.'

His eyes searched hers, and she concentrated on smoothing her expression. She'd sworn to never again allow any man the power to hurt her. Look forward. Not back. She'd been in danger of forgetting that one rule by which she lived her life. The rule that kept her sane.

She enjoyed her steady, unremarkable life. She could live vicariously through the characters in her stories—love, hate, quarrel, laugh—she could explore every emotion, all without risk to her peace of mind or to her heart. And that was how she wanted it to stay.

'Very well. If that is your wish, I shall respect it. For now. But I have never been a man to give up easily, Kitty.' A smile flickered on his lips. 'You remember that.'

Chapter Thirteen

What was Kitty afraid of? Not of him, Adam was certain—he hadn't mistaken that flash of joy when he took her hands, before she successfully masked her feelings. He longed to haul her into his arms and to kiss her, as he used to.

The last vestiges of anger and hurt had drained from him when she explained why she had married Edgar and hope had flowed in to fill the gaps those negative emotions left behind despite Kitty's assertion that the past could not be altered. Because—although both he and Kitty had changed on the surface—deep inside Adam was confident she was the same Kitty and he was the same Adam. His doubts about his own feelings for her had melted away as completely as his anger and his hurt, and he was as sure as he could be that Kitty was still the woman for him. They belonged together.

For whatever reason, though, she didn't fully trust him and had erected a barrier to keep him at bay. Was that to protect her feelings? He was not mistaken about her interest in him—her eyes, so guarded when they had first met again, now could not hide her response to him. The instinctive response of a woman to a man she desired.

So, she was afraid of getting hurt again. By him.

She had accepted that he had only denied his love for her in order to protect her, but that didn't change what he'd done. She'd had fifteen years of believing he hadn't cared and that he'd lied. It would take time to build her trust and the way to do that was to give her time to get to know him again. To start again, from the beginning.

This time, they were equals. This time, he was going nowhere. This time, he would court her as though they had only just met, as a gentleman would court a lady, and he would do everything he could to change her mind about remarrying.

He tugged open the cottage door and peered outside.

'You are quite right. The rain has stopped,' he said, 'and the thunder has moved away.'

He turned to Kitty, smiling as he spoke, then stepped aside and half-bowed as he swept his arm around, indicating she should leave. She picked up her discarded bonnet, squeezed it, then gave him a rueful smile.

'I think I shall just carry this.'

She stepped outside and they walked side by side across the meadow towards the lane that would take them back to the Hall. Adam deliberately did not offer her his arm to lean on, but clasped his hands behind his back to control his visceral urge to touch her. She, he noticed, retained her grip on that old piece of sacking, clutching it tight across her breasts.

'When we danced at Almack's you spoke of other interests, apart from your stepchildren.' Adam, alive to every nuance and change in Kitty's countenance, noticed delicate pink wash across her cheeks. 'Will you tell me of those? How do you occupy your time here at Fenton Hall?'

She slid him a sidelong look. 'You speak as though a house the size of the Hall can run like clockwork, with nothing more than a quick wind of a key from time to time.'

'I know that is not the case, but...' *But I hunger to know all there is to know about you.* 'I am curious as to what interests you have that occupy you fully, as you put it.'

When she did not reply, he continued, 'After all, as you said, we are as strangers now. And strangers who spend time together—as we shall, while I draw up those plans—can surely indulge in a little polite conversation in order to get to know one anoth—'

A loud retort interrupted him and his immediate thought was that the storm had returned but, even as that idea formed, another bang, followed by a searing pain in his arm, swept it away. He gasped, clutching his upper arm, and then Kitty grabbed him, tugging him to the ground.

'Stop shooting,' she screamed. 'There are people here.'

Adam, his heart thundering in his chest as he scrambled to make sense of what had happened, looked up at Kitty. She was on her knees, above him, staring back across the meadow towards the woods. Adam grabbed her, wincing at the pain in his arm as he tried to pull her lower.

'Get down!'

She struggled against his pull and he tugged harder until she overbalanced and landed on top of him, face to face. He wrapped his arms around her, holding her still even as she wriggled, trying to free herself.

'Stop fighting me, Kitty.'

She raised her head and captured his gaze, her grey eyes

wide with shock. 'That was a *gunshot*, Adam. Whoever it is needs to know we are here, or we might get hit.' She struggled to bring her hands between them and began to push against his chest, trying to free herself.

Adam tightened his grip, clenching his jaw against the pain. Kitty's eyes widened further.

'You're hurt! Adam!' She struggled again to free herself.

He forced his words between his gritted teeth. 'Be still, Kitty. Please.'

His arm burned and stung like the devil, but he was certain the bullet had just grazed him and had not lodged inside. Kitty lay still, breathing fast, her head on his chest, her hair tickling him under his chin.

At any other time...in different circumstances...

He swatted the thought aside. This was hardly the time to be lusting after her. Cautiously, he lifted his head and scanned the woods, about twenty yards distant. There was no sign of anyone, no movement, no sound. He frowned. Could it have been poachers? But why would poachers be out in a thunderstorm? Granted, there would be a lack of keepers or other estate workers around, but surely the wildlife would also take shelter at such a time.

'I can't see anyone. Or any movement,' he said. 'Hopefully your shout scared whoever it was away.'

'Robert will be furious about this…he *will* find who is responsible,' Kitty said. She had also raised her head and she captured Adam's gaze again. 'Where are you hit?'

'It's a scratch. Nothing more. It stings a bit, but I'll live.'

His brain ordered his arms to release Kitty, but the message was ignored. Now he had her in his embrace, he wanted to keep her there. For ever. His gaze moved to her mouth and, as her lips parted to release a faint gasp, he fought the urge to kiss her. He forced his gaze back to hers. Her eyes had darkened and his hand had started its glide up between her shoulder blades to cradle her head—to hold her ready for his kiss—by the time sanity returned. He halted that movement of his hand.

'It was most likely an accident, but we should not take any chances,' he said. He rolled her off him and instantly breathed easier. 'I will see if it is safe. Stay there. Do not under any circumstances move, or even raise your head.'

'But—'

'And do not argue!'

Kitty scowled. '*You* are the one who is injured! *You* should be the one to lie still while *I* see if it is safe.'

His heart melted. She had always been full of courage and spirit. It was one of the things he had loved about her. 'Kitty...allow me to do this. Please. Allow me to protect you this time.'

Her scowl smoothed over and she stilled. Then she nodded. Adam rolled on to his side, facing the woods where the shot had come from, then propped himself up on one elbow. Kitty grabbed his hand and he glanced back at her.

'Take care,' she whispered.

There was still nothing to be seen and no further shots. Adam sat up. Then stood. Nothing happened. He bent, holding out his hands to Kitty.

'I think he...they...have gone.'

He'd forgotten his injury in the tension of the moment and, as he pulled Kitty to her feet, his arm shrieked in protest and he could not disguise his wince. Kitty gasped.

'Adam! All that blood. You *said* it was a *scratch*.' Her small fist punched his other arm, punctuating her words.

'Steady, or I'll end up with both arms out of action.'

'Sorry.' Kitty stepped closer and, in one swift movement, she tore his bloodied shirt sleeve apart to expose the wound. 'We need to get you home and clean that up,' she said. She slipped one arm around his waist. 'Put your uninjured arm around my shoulders.'

'There's no need, Kitty. I'm quite capable of walking unaided.'

'Adam…' She fixed him with a stern look. 'You have suffered a shock and you have lost blood. Lean on me.'

It didn't take them long to reach the house. Kitty led the way to the same side room where they had taken the flowers and pushed Adam down on to a chair.

'Stay there. Take off your shirt while I fetch hot water.'

She hurried from the room. Adam stood up again to pull his shirt free from his breeches, then stripped it off over his head. It was ruined anyway—beyond repair, even if the bloodstains could be removed—so he dropped it on the flagged floor. Then he sat down again and examined his upper arm. He sucked in a sharp breath as he probed the groove gouged out by the bullet with the fingers of his left hand. His right hand gripped the edge of the chair seat as pain spiked through him.

'Don't touch it!'

Adam looked up as Kitty bustled into the room, carrying a bowl of water and with a linen towel draped over one arm. He straightened, his hand dropping away from his wound to grip the opposite edge of his seat, bracing himself for the pain he knew must come. But Kitty halted before she reached him, her eyes widening as her gaze travelled across his chest and his upper arms. Her tongue darted out to moisten her lips and heat flooded him as his blood quickened. Her eyes dropped lower and that blood surged to his groin. He shut his eyes, willing his body back under control, desperately forcing his thoughts on to the question of who had been shooting out in the woods in a thunderstorm and away from what he would like to do to Kitty...with Kitty... right here. Right now.

'Adam...?'

He opened his eyes at her soft enquiry. She'd set the bowl on the table and now stood close enough to touch...close enough for her scent to envelop him. Need overcame judgement and he reached for her, sliding one hand around her slender waist as he searched her expression.

Too soon, you fool. You'll scare her off.

But *she* was the one who acted, stepping even closer and cupping his cheek.

'I can't bear that you're hurt,' she whispered. 'I need... I just...' She sucked in a quick breath. 'You could have been *killed.*'

She stroked lightly down the side of his face and along his jaw until her fingers rested on his lips, which parted without volition. He closed his eyes once more, the soft sough of her breaths stirring his blood as her light citrus scent wove through his senses. One finger entered his mouth and he closed his teeth gently on it. The soft moan that escaped her had him hard, and hot, and heavy in an instant. He tightened his hold and pulled her on to his lap and their lips met in a fiery, urgent kiss, all hungry lips and duelling tongues as their quiet moans mingled.

She cradled his head, her fingers tangling in his hair as she pressed against him, her curves moulding to him, driving him wild. He shifted her, bending her back over his uninjured arm, allowing access to her breasts. His fingers explored her neckline, unbuttoning her bodice and gradually working her gown off one shoulder until he could release one breast from her stays.

Oh, God! His fingers closed around perfection, her skin satiny as the firm globe filled his hand, her nipple taut against his palm. Adam bent to her breast and drew that nipple into his mouth. Her hands fisted in his hair and she arched as he flicked that hard bud with his tongue, then suckled. Her soft moans drove him wild…he slowly tightened his embrace, raising her as he trailed open-mouthed kisses from her breast to her neck and again to her mouth, savouring the taste of those lush lips, holding her close to him, relishing the softness of her breasts as they pressed against his bare chest.

Then her hands were between them, palms flat against his chest, pushing him away, and he released her, the madness and urgency fading to be replaced by regret that he had so readily succumbed to temptation so soon after vowing to court Kitty slowly. From the beginning.

'Kitty?'

The look she cast him was stricken. Guilty. *Ashamed.* His heart clenched at the thought she was ashamed of her response to him. He began to wrap his arms around her again, until a searing pain reminded him of his injury. He gritted his teeth against making a sound, but Kitty had noticed, for she took hold of his forearms and gently moved them to release her. As soon as he released his hold again, she scrambled from his lap.

Chapter Fourteen

Shame flooded Kitty as she adjusted her neckline and made herself respectable. Adam was injured. She was meant to be caring for him but, instead, she had as good as ravished him.

The fear of what could have happened had that shot hit a more vital spot had overridden any other consideration. No. It had overridden *every* other consideration. Her only thought…no, not even a thought…her only *instinct* had been to assure herself that he was safe. Unhurt. And to be close to him, physically.

That fear still lurked, her heart still pounding as she hurried to the cupboard where she kept strips of clean cloth and grabbed a handful together with the flask of brandy she also kept in there and returned to the table. She soaked one strip in the still warm water and squeezed it out. Only then did she allow herself to look at Adam. His blue eyes—bright and direct—fused with hers and she swallowed at the heat banked in them—heat that confirmed he still found her attractive. But Adam had been attracted to her before, even

spoken words of love—which he now claimed he meant—
but that hadn't stopped him breaking her heart.

That unexpected surge of desire within her…that sudden
compulsion to touch Adam, to kiss him…had shaken her
to her core. What did this mean for them? Was she really
foolish enough to risk her heart again for the sake of physical desire? Better, surely, to continue to protect herself and
avoid any further hurt. She had learned the hard way that
men could not be trusted. Her father. Adam. Even Edgar—
kind, benign Edgar—had hurt her, without meaning to…
whittling away her confidence with his gentle comparisons
with the perfect Veronica. No. She had no wish to again
place her life in the power of any man so she would never
marry again. And she mustn't forget that Adam would need
an heir and she could not give him one. So any deeper relationship than friendship could never be permanent.

'That gash needs cleansing,' she said. 'It will hurt, I dare
say, but there is no other way.'

He shrugged his broad shoulders, causing the muscles in
his chest to ripple in a most fascinating way. Kitty set her
jaw and dragged her attention to the wound in his upper
arm. She frowned, bending to peer closer.

'There are fibres stuck in there, from your shirt.'

His hand came up as if to probe the gash again and, without thinking, she grabbed it.

'I *said* do not touch.'

Adam's fingers closed around hers, sending sparks tingling up her arm, and Kitty abruptly straightened, catching her breath, her heart racing as he raised her hand to his
mouth and pressed a kiss to it.

'I'll behave.' His voice a husky murmur that sent heat
washing through her body in waves. 'Do your worst.'

Kitty swallowed again, her knees jittery, and she prayed her hand wouldn't shake. With her left hand on his shoulder, she bent again so she could see what she was doing.

'Wait!'

Adam stood up, so close the heat emanating from his bare chest did nothing to cool Kitty's blood, and neither did the close-up view of those crisply curling hairs that spread across his chest like outspread wings, then arrowed in towards the waist of his breeches. She dragged in a breath to calm herself, but only succeeded in flooding her senses with his scent: musky, spicy, manly. She stepped back, almost stumbling in her haste, and his hands shot out to grip her shoulders.

'I am sorry. I startled you.'

His voice and words were so matter of fact they steadied her and she looked up at him. Their gazes fused again...but he appeared unaware of her visceral reaction. There was no knowing gleam in his eyes, no raised eyebrow, no quirk of those sensual lips to ruffle her anger and help her maintain her guard. He, unlike her, appeared totally unaffected.

'It will be easier if I sit on the table. You will not have to bend and there will be better light from the window on to my arm.'

'Yes. I...yes, of course. That is a good plan.'

Adam rounded the table and hoisted himself up to sit on it, the muscles in his arms bulging as he raised his body.

Without volition, Kitty licked her lips. 'That is an improvement.'

And it was, as far as cleansing the gash was concerned, but it also put that chest on a level with Kitty's eyes and mouth. His nipples—and their flat, dusky areolae surrounded by whorls of hair—proved yet another distraction.

Resolutely, Kitty tore her attention from the expanse of bare male skin and directed it at that gouge caused by the bullet. And the very thought of the bullet quashed any further lustful thoughts. Someone had *shot* at Adam. Her heart stuttered and her mouth dried. Who could it have been? And why? Her mind tumbling with conjecture, Kitty steadied Adam's arm with her free hand as she bathed the wound, sluicing water through it to wash it clean of dirt and fibres.

'Do you think it was deliberate?' she asked as she worked. Adam sucked in a sharp breath. 'Sorry. I am trying to be gentle.'

'I know you are. And...'

Kitty paused her ministrations when Adam failed to continue, her gaze flicking to his frowning face. 'Well? Do you?'

Adam's brows rose. 'Yes. I do. It makes no sense otherwise. No poacher would be out in a thunderstorm—he would know the animals have more sense than to be out and about in such weather. And the same goes for gamekeepers. I dinna wish to alarm ye, but I can think of no explanation other than one of us was the target. And, of the two of us, I would say that I am the more likely, would you not?'

Kitty bit her lip, considering, pleased that he had answered her honestly.

'Ye have to think about that?' Adam tipped his head to one side. 'Why on earth would anyone wish to shoot at you?'

'Oh! No! That is not what I was thinking about. It is... I was thinking how refreshing that you have admitted that to me. Most other gentlemen would try to hide the truth...they believe that ladies ought to be protected from the harsh realities of life, that their sensibilities are too delicate to cope with being told the truth. But you...you answered my question with a direct answer. Thank you.'

Adam's eyes narrowed as he studied Kitty and her face heated at his scrutiny. But she held his gaze. She made her mind up there and then. She would keep strong those barriers surrounding her heart, so that he could never hurt her again, but she *would* be his friend and be honest with him, as long as he treated her as an intelligent being and not as a grown-up child to be sheltered and humoured.

Adam smiled then and Kitty's heart leapt even though she silently scolded herself for her foolishness. But he was so handsome. So masculine. He stirred her blood in a way that no one had since...*no*. She must be honest with herself as well. *No one* had ever stirred her blood like this, not even Adam when they had known each other fifteen years before. She had been too young, maybe, to fully understand the full depth of the sensual attraction that could exist between a man and a woman. Her marriage to Edgar had never been one of passion and it was only now—at the age of two-and-thirty—that her body was awakening to the full potential of sexual attraction between a man and a woman. Lust and the promise of physical fulfilment. And far from being shocked at herself, as she had been mere moments before, she was now intrigued.

She turned away, to give herself time to compose her features now that this new understanding of herself—not to mention these new, hitherto unsuspected feelings thrumming through her—had seemingly sprung from nowhere. Was she strong enough...brazen enough?...to explore physical desire without risking her heart? Men managed to keep the two separate—look at Adam just now. Utterly unaffected while she was a jittery mess. Many women, both wid-

owed and unhappily married, indulged in *affaires*. But…
could she? Uncertainty swept through her. Now the idea
had occurred to her, however…did she not owe it to herself
to at least consider it?

She took her time, picking up the flask and unscrewing
the top before she faced Adam again. He still watched her,
his eyes alert. Intent. A faint crease between his brows.

'This will sting,' she said.

He took the flask from her hand and raised it to his
mouth, taking a swig. 'For fortification,' he said. 'And it
is good for shock.'

She stepped closer, her skirts brushing his leg, his musky
scent creating strange sensations within her as it coiled into
her depths, awakening all her senses.

'Keep still,' she whispered and placed one hand on his
shoulder as she trickled the spirit on to his wound. He stiffened, but made no sound, and she glanced up at him, capturing his gaze. She caught her lower lip between her teeth
and his gaze lowered to her mouth. Then, and only then, a
low groan emerged, seemingly wrenched from deep within
his chest.

'Kitty…'

His throaty growl reached deep inside her, grabbing and
squeezing. She gasped as heat spiralled through her and
an aching need gathered in the feminine folds between her
thighs.

This is desire. This is lust.

All thought of guarding her heart fled. Excitement
thrummed through her as she moved between his legs and
pressed close, tilting her face to his, aware of every tiny
change in his expression—the flare of his nostrils; the un-
mistakeable craving in those dark eyes; the slight compres-

sion of those sensual lips before they relaxed, parting as he hauled in a ragged breath.

Long fingers curled behind her head, taking a fistful of hair as he angled her face to his.

'May I kiss you, Kitty?' A tortured whisper.

'Yes. Please.'

He lowered his face to hers, until their lips met. Not a kiss of uncontrolled passion—not the frantic onslaught she craved...a kiss like before, a kiss she could lose herself in—but a gentle caress as his lips glided over hers. And she lost herself anyway, her eyes closing as every nerve in her body homed in on the meeting of their mouths. Then his tongue traced the seam of her lips and she opened to him. Adam gave a groan and his tongue swept inside.

Possessive. Assured. Masterful.

Her arms wound around his neck and she gave herself up to these wonderful new sensations, her entire body tingling...coming alive. His tongue plunged, mimicking the timeless rhythm that she recalled from her marriage, but now...this time...with this kiss...it felt as though an invisible thread ran straight through her, connecting her mouth with her breasts—full and heavy, and *aching*—and with her womb, which wanted...needed...*craved*...in a way she had never felt before.

Boots ringing in the stone-flagged passage outside wrenched her back into the present and she tore her lips from Adam's and stepped away, feeling the heat burning in her cheeks, her knees trembling. Adam looked no less discomposed as their eyes met. He could do nothing, sitting on the table as he was, so—as the door opened—Kitty began to sort through the strips of linen lying on the table. She selected the longest.

'I think this will suffice.' She held it aloft, then spun to face the door, pasting a look of surprise on her face as though she had missed their visitor's approach.

'Adam! What is this I hear? You have been hurt?' Robert strode into the room, his eyes filled with angry concern and fixed on Adam. 'Is it true?'

'It is. As you may see, Lady Fen—Catherine is about to bandage my wound, having cleaned it thoroughly. And painfully.'

'What happened? A shot, Vincent said.' Robert grabbed Adam's elbow and moved his arm to get a better look at the wound. 'It looks painful.'

'Someone,' said Kitty, nudging Robert aside so she could bandage Adam's arm, 'was shooting out in the woods. We had each gone for a walk to get some air and met quite by chance in the woods. Then we were caught in that thunder shower and took shelter in the old keeper's cottage until the rain stopped. We had just started on our way home again when we heard the shot.'

'And, as you can see, he missed.'

Robert frowned at Adam's sardonic comment. 'Are you saying it was deliberate?'

Adam shrugged. Robert's frown deepened. 'We've had some trouble with poachers, but as long as they are local and restrict themselves to taking the odd rabbit, I turn a blind eye. But they usually use snares, not guns.'

'You're forgetting the thunderstorm,' said Kitty. 'The animals can sense such a change in the weather and they normally take cover long before the storm strikes. Any countryman worth his salt would know *that*.'

Robert stared at her, still frowning. 'That is true.' Then he started, as though seeing her for the first time. 'You will catch your death of cold, Stepmama. Look at the state of you.'

Kitty glanced down at her wet, muddy gown. 'We were already wet through before we were forced to dive to the ground.' She shook her head. 'A muddy gown is the least of my worries.'

'Your stepmother is too modest, Rob. It was her quick thinking that saved us—she dived to the ground and took me with her even as I was still trying to work out what had happened.' Adam smiled ruefully.

'I had no idea whether that shot was an accident or by design, but I wasn't prepared to take the chance it was a deliberate act.' Kitty shivered then, as the reality of what had happened hit her again. 'Who knows what might have happened had whoever it was shot at us again?'

Her stomach churned and she wrapped her arms around her torso as though she might contain the tumult of emotions that erupted from nowhere. Adam muttered something beneath his breath and jumped down from his perch on the table.

'Thank you for your help, Catherine. You need to go and change out of your wet clothing. In fact... Rob, I think your stepmother would benefit from a warm bath.'

Robert wrapped his arm around Kitty's shoulders and, grateful for the support, she sagged against him even as she castigated herself for her weakness. She hadn't noticed the chill of her damp gown before and the fear about what had happened—and what *might* have happened—only now seemed to have caught up with her.

Still, even though she longed to do as Adam suggested, she felt she must protest. 'It is you who have been injured, Adam. Not I. And you are equally as wet.'

'And Adam will no doubt go and change into dry clothing now his arm has been bandaged,' said Robert, steering Kitty towards the door. 'Come on. I shall help you upstairs.'

'I can manage, Robert. There is no need for all this fuss.'

'Caring is not fuss. Now do as you're told.' Robert paused as they reached the door. 'I'll have hot water sent up to your bedchamber, Adam,' he said, 'and I will send my man up to assist you.'

Kitty, glancing back, saw Adam's attention on her, his eyes brimming with concern. She forced a smile and was rewarded by a smile in return.

'Come, now, Stepmama.' Robert tightened his grip as they stepped into the passage. 'You know Charis will never forgive me should you succumb to a chill on my watch. Let me help you upstairs.'

Chapter Fifteen

When Adam, freshly washed and clad in clean clothes, descended the stairs a short while later, Vincent awaited him in the hall.

'Where might I find His Lordship?'

'He is out riding, my lord. With some of the men.'

Adam's brows rose. 'Out in the woods?'

'I believe so. He desired me to tell you on no account were you to follow him and he will come to see you the minute he returns.'

Adam's instinct was, indeed, to follow, but common sense warned him he was unlikely to be much use and his arm had stiffened up enough to make him reluctant to attempt to ride.

'Very well. You may consider your duty discharged, Vincent. I shall continue my work in the library, so that is where I shall be when His Lordship returns.'

The plans he had been working on had completely slipped his mind in among everything that had happened that afternoon and, although his wound might render fine draughtsmanship as tricky as horse riding, he could use the time to sketch out rough ideas and plans. That would help to distract him from that shot and from what Robert might discover.

Nothing, however, could distract him from Kitty.

'How fares Lady Fenton?'

'I believe Her Ladyship is resting in her room, my lord. Might I bring you refreshments to the library?'

'Thank you, Vincent.' What he really wanted was a dram of whisky, but Robert did not keep that *heathen spirit* in the house. 'A glass of brandy would be most welcome.'

He strolled to the library, his heart full of fear and his head full of images of Kitty.

She could have been killed.

He'd been aware of that ever since the shot rang out, but so much had been happening that the full horror of it had been kept at bay. Now, though, alone with his thoughts as he entered the library, that knowledge hit him with force. It would be impossible to concentrate on work, so he swerved away from the desk and, instead, headed for a wingback chair by the centre window. Vincent appeared a moment later, carrying a tray with a decanter and two glasses, and set them on a table within reach of the chair.

'Two glasses?'

'For if His Lordship wishes to join you in a glass upon his return, my lord.'

Vincent poured brandy into one glass, bowed, and then left the library, closing the door softly behind him.

Adam reached for the glass, drained it in one and then refilled it. He closed his eyes, tilting his head to rest on the back of the chair, and willed away the utter terror that now paralysed him at the thought of what could have happened.

She could have been killed!

Images again filled his brain.

Kitty... I've only just found her. I could have lost her again.

Had it been deliberate? Aimed at him? If it was...there was only one culprit he could think of.

'Uncle Grenville.'

The rustle of fabric reached his ears seconds before the scent of flowers with a top note of citrus registered. 'My thoughts precisely.'

His eyes flew open. He sat up straight and glared at Kitty. 'Ye should be resting.'

'As should you.'

'I am.'

A brief smile flickered on her lips. She gestured, indicating the chair in which she was now sitting. 'As am I.'

He scowled. 'Will ye please stop humouring me? Ye should be in bed.'

With me. A new, mouth-watering picture now filled his head... Kitty, in bed, the covers rumpled, her hair loose around her shoulders, her eyes heavy-lidded with desire. He thrust aside that image.

'But I am too restless. I want to talk about what happened. Or, more to the point, talk about who might have been responsible. And it would seem we have reached the same conclusion.'

'I was thinking aloud,' Adam growled. *God, I just want to hold her. Protect her always.* 'Ye weren't meant to hear that.'

Her brows arched. 'Of course I was not, because I am a lady and must therefore be shielded from the brutal reality of this world.'

That was close to what she had said before. She had been so happy he had told her the truth...and he could not disagree with her point. She was—and he could verify it—no child.

'What you mean,' she continued, 'is that you would not say such a thing to me because I am female. I should be prostrate upon my bed because I am female. We spoke about this earlier—I need neither protection nor cossetting. It happened. I was there. Someone shot at us...with you as the most likely target...yet I am expected to quash any conjecture or curiosity because of my sex?'

'Put like that, no. Of course not. But ye *were* in a state of shock when I last set eyes upon ye.'

Her eyes narrowed. 'As. Were. You. And yet...' again, she gestured '...here you are and here am I.'

Adam sighed and shook his head. 'Ye're just as stubborn as I recall.'

Her smile lit her face. 'And, you will find, just as opinionated. So...may we discuss your uncle and his possible involvement as adults or is it your intention to exclude me entirely from what you and Robert will surely talk about upon his return?'

How could he deny her? She was beautiful and charming and graceful: the most desirable woman he had ever known—and he included her younger self in that—but, more than that...so much more...she fascinated him. Now they had cleared the air between them, he felt he could talk with her for hours and never grow tired of listening to her, watching her. He wanted her, physically. But that could wait. For now, what she was asking him was that he treat her as an equal...as though he were talking with another man. And so that is what he would do. And he would always strive to respect her wishes.

'Let us talk, then.' He cocked his head to one side. 'Would ye care for refreshments? Shall I ring for Vincent?'

'You may pour me a brandy, if you will,' said Kitty.

'There is no need to disturb Vincent when there is a spare glass just begging to be filled.'

'Is there no end to your rebellion? Brandy in the afternoon? Quite shocking!'

She grinned and, for the first time since they had met again, those beloved dimples made an appearance. 'It is good for shock. You said so yourself.'

Adam poured the brandy and handed her the glass. She grew serious then, staring reflectively into the amber liquid as she swirled it gently.

'Seriously, Adam…do you truly suspect your uncle?'

He didn't want to think it, but what other explanation could there be? *If* it had been a deliberate act.

'I think we are agreed it was unlikely to be a stray shot from poachers,' he said, still pondering, 'and *someone* pulled that trigger. Twice.'

'So…you do not believe it was accidental?'

'No. And, as I can think of no one I have angered enough to cause him to wish for my death, I fail to see we can reach any other conclusion.'

'Or her.'

'Her? No!'

'Because a female would never kill?'

He huffed a laugh. 'Not a bit of it. Women, I am sure, nurse grievances and think murderous thoughts just as men do. I meant I can think of no female I have angered enough for her to wish to end my life.'

'No other young ladies you have wooed and then abandoned?'

He started at her question.

'I apologise.' She looked contrite. 'Now it is my turn to squirm at an attempted jest that has fallen flat.'

Adam did wonder how much truth lay behind that question. He'd known she'd be upset when he left, but… He raised his brows. 'Tell me ye never hated me enough to wish me dead, Kitty.'

'No. Of course not. I cannot imagine hating *anyone* as much as that.'

'I am relieved to hear it. And, in answer to your question—no.'

'Which leaves your uncle. Or…' A frown knit her brow. 'Or?'

'Your cousin. Bartholomew Trewin. Your uncle is your heir and, after him, your cousin.'

'Tolly? No…surely not. He is…that is…he seems a good man. And he is a friend of Robert's, is he not?'

He felt his colour rise under her scrutiny. 'Do you believe that good men cannot be driven to do bad things, given desperate circumstances?'

'Why, of course not. But… Tolly…what circumstances? He gave nae hint of debts or such.'

He desperately did not want to suspect his cousin but, now the notion had been put into his head, he could not deny Tolly would probably have more cause to wish Adam dead than Uncle Grenville. Tolly was still at Kelridge on the day Adam left, so either man could have ridden over to Fenton Hall and stalked the woods. But…to what purpose?

'As a plan, it left much to be desired,' he said. 'What if I had been more conscientious and remained working at my desk? How long would my assailant wait, hoping to take a pot shot at me?'

'Hmmm.' Kitty tapped her lips with one forefinger, frowning. 'Tell me…did you establish a routine of any sort while you were at Kelridge?'

Adam eyed her with admiration. He hadn't even considered that, but it was logical. 'I did ride out most afternoons.
It became something of a habit.'

It had become a necessity, if he was honest. Anything to
get away from that stifling atmosphere in which he'd felt
more and more of an interloper. Maybe he should air his
concerns, especially as they pointed more definitely at his
uncle as the culprit.

'To be honest, I found it difficult to settle at Kelridge.
There was this…oh, I don't know… I suppose you'd call it
an undercurrent. And not a pleasant one.'

'I am sorry to hear that, but you must have expected it
to be a difficult period of adjustment. Not only for you, but
for everyone at Kelridge Place.' Kitty frowned. 'Was your
father popular among the staff? I had heard he could be…
difficult.'

'He was, without doubt, *un*popular.' And that was an un-
derstatement. 'Did you never meet him?'

'No. Edgar knew him, of course, but our paths never
crossed. I *have* heard that your uncle has improved the estate a great deal since he took over running it, though.'

'So I have been told. Many times.'

'It makes sense, therefore, that the servants and other
workers will view him favourably.'

'Without doubt. That message was made clear in numerous subtle and not-so-subtle ways by many senior members
of my staff. Grenville Trewin is still regarded as the true
master of Kelridge Hall, no matter what the laws on pri-
mogeniture and entails might decree.'

And he was beginning to wish he had never learned the
truth. That his mother had kept her secret to her grave. Ex-

cept…he would not then have met Kitty again. And that
was unthinkable.

'Hopefully that will all change once I have an heir of my
own.' An image of Kitty with a babe in her arms appeared
in his mind's eye, filling him with hope and contentment.
The future looked rosier than it had for many, many years.
But he was rushing ahead of himself. He must keep to the
topic at hand. '*That* would soon quash any random hopes
that my uncle will ever fully control the reins again.'

Adam emptied his brandy glass. Without a word, Kitty
leaned forward and refilled both his glass and her own. She
sat back and sipped as she stared at the window, her fine
brows drawn together.

'Maybe,' she said, after a few minutes' reflection, 'they
fear you are your father's son? If he was a cruel master, they
will fear a return to that regime.'

'But I have given them no reason to suppose I am like
my father. In fact, I have been at pains to be friendly in my
dealings with them.'

Kitty tucked her lips between her teeth. Adam scowled
at her. 'What is so funny?'

'Servants, my dear Adam, do *not* appreciate their masters
trying to make friends with them. They want to serve a man
they can look up to and respect. A master who can make
them feel superior to servants in the neighbouring houses.
You must understand that they have their pride, too. And a
nobleman is expected to behave as such.'

'I do not wish to live in that manner of household. I want
a more relaxed feeling, like when I was growing up. I canna
believe they wouldn't appreciate that.'

Kitty smiled at him. The tenderness in her look evoked
a swell of longing, but a longing tinged with a sadness he

couldn't place until Ma's face materialised in his mind's eye. Sadness and guilt, that was it. He thrust his fingers through his hair, sweeping it back from his face.

'Anyway. We are straying from the point. Yes, I established a routine of sorts, but why would my uncle or anyone else suppose I would continue that routine at Fenton Hall?'

'That is true, and the theory has been disproved because you did *not* ride out. You went for a walk.'

'And we are no nearer to finding out who might wish me dead.'

Kitty shuddered. 'It is a horrid feeling. It may not, of course, be about the money. It might be the lure of the title. I heard Tolly was hanging out for Lady Sarah Bamford—a duke's daughter might lower herself to wed an earl, but I doubt either she or her father would countenance an offer from plain Mr Trewin.'

Adam laughed. 'You have a lurid imagination there, Kitty. You believe Tolly might commit murder for love? You should write novels!'

She stared at him blankly for a moment. 'Now there is a thought. I take it you disapprove of such mindless drivel?'

'I neither approve nor disapprove. I have never read one and I have no wish to waste my time on such an activity. Do I take it ye are an avid reader of novels?'

'I am. I particularly enjoy the work of the late Miss Austen—she has a sharp wit and holds a mirror up to society with all its faults and contradictions. Her books are amusing, but also interesting in their insight into human behaviour.'

'Well, I have no objection to others indulging in such a pastime if they wish to waste their time. It is not for me, however.'

'And you can state that without ever having read a novel?'

Kitty shook her head, leaving Adam feeling he had somehow disappointed her. 'Anyway…to return to the matter in hand, I do not say Tolly would kill for the sake of love, but I would urge you to keep an open mind. People *do* kill for love…there was a case recently where a man poisoned his wife in order that he might be free to marry his mistress. I agree to the *feeling* that Mr Grenville Trewin is the more likely culprit, but that is illogical. My instinct is simply because I *like* your cousin and I really do not know your uncle very well. However, being less likeable does not make a man guilty.'

'Ye're right. I'll keep an open mind. I hope Robert might discover something in his search of the woods.'

Kitty started up from her chair. 'Robert is searching the woods? Adam…why did you not stop him?'

Adam surged to his feet and caught Kitty's arm as she headed for the door. 'I didna know until after he had gone. But ye need have no fear. He has taken men with him. He will be in no danger.'

'Oh! Of course. How silly of me. I did not think… I dare say I am still more rattled than I thought.'

'Ye're trembling.' Adam wrapped his arms around Kitty. 'There's nothing to be afraid of. I promise.'

She leaned into him and he tightened his embrace as he breathed in her scent…the scent he now recognised as Kitty. This Kitty, not the girl he had loved, but the woman she was now. He tipped up her chin and lost himself in their kiss as her arms encircled his waist and she hugged him close.

The sound of the door opening sent Adam's heart leaping into his throat as he and Kitty sprang apart. His face burned as he turned to face Robert, who sauntered into the room, his expression innocent of even a hint of suspicion.

Adam's pounding heart slowed as his breathing eased—he needed all the friends he could get at the moment and he had no wish for his feelings for Kitty to drive a wedge between himself and Robert.

'Robert! You are back!' Kitty's voice was too high-pitched and even though Robert appeared not to have seen their embrace, Kitty still managed to look and sound panicky as she launched into speech. 'I... Lord Kelridge and I were discussing what happened. I was so afraid you might be shot at too. I...we...'

Her words petered out. She looked helplessly at Adam and he sent her a look of reassurance.

'Did you see anyone, Rob?'

'No one. And you, Stepmama, should be in bed.' Robert eyed the table and the two half-drunk glasses. He quirked a brow at Adam. 'So...not content with failing to ensure my stepmother gets the rest she needs, you have encouraged her to partake of spirits.'

He strode back across the library, opened the door and stuck his head around it. Adam heard him request another glass and he took advantage of Robert's distraction to catch Kitty's eye.

'He did not see us.'

'I know. But I still find it hard to believe he didn't notice anything amiss,' Kitty whispered. 'I could not help but panic... Edgar was his father and—'

Kitty fell silent as Robert returned.

'As I was saying,' he said, 'we saw no one, but we did find fresh hoofprints entering and leaving the wood from the road.'

He dragged a third chair to join the other two and then gestured for Kitty to sit. Once she was settled the two men both sat. Vincent brought in a third glass and Robert poured himself a generous measure of brandy and topped up Adam's glass. When Kitty wordlessly held out her own glass for a refill, he obliged with only a slight flick of one brow in Adam's direction. But Adam could settle for that. Better he blame Adam for leading Kitty astray with brandy than he should suspect what Adam really wanted to do with his stepmother.

'Did ye glean anything from those prints?'

'Nothing. I am afraid we are no closer to knowing who was responsible than we were before.'

Adam told Robert briefly what he and Kitty had been discussing.

'Tolly? Well… I should not like to think…but if that *was* an attempt to kill you, Adam, it makes sense it must be by someone who stands to benefit. And that can only lead to either your Uncle Grenville, or to Tolly.'

'Do ye doubt it was an attempt on my life, Rob?'

'No, but…' Robert frowned. 'Why wait until now? If it was your uncle or your cousin, they had ample opportunity while you were at Kelridge Place.'

'Could they think they're less likely to fall under suspicion if Adam is attacked away from Kelridge?'

'They could. But the timing makes no sense. Why now? Why not wait several months when it would be less obvious?'

'Or, for that matter—if it was Tolly, why didn't he try something in London?' Robert rubbed his jaw. 'That would make far more sense and it would surely have been easier to dismiss as a random attack by thieves, or an accident even. A spill off Westminster Bridge into the Thames has claimed many poor souls over the years. And I still cannot believe Tolly is capable of cold-blooded murder despite your theory he might be driven to drastic measures in the cause of love, Stepmama. I always said your imagination is too vivid for words.'

'Which leaves my uncle as the main suspect. Or a complete stranger, for reasons unknown. Or...it was, after all, an accident.'

Chapter Sixteen

Kitty arose early the following morning after a restless night. The sky held the promise of a summer's day, azure blue dotted with fluffy clouds, and her heart…her foolish heart…swelled with joy at the promise of time to spend with Adam. She steadied herself on the windowsill as she leaned towards the glass, gazing mindlessly at the garden below and the parkland beyond. What should she do? She knew Adam. At least, she knew the young man he had been. And the fire that now kindled openly in his blue eyes whenever he looked her way suggested he felt as passionately about her as he had back then. They'd not had a moment alone together yesterday after Robert returned from his search and, if she was honest, her main feeling had been one of relief. It had given her the whole of the night to think about what she wanted. About how she would react when Adam kissed her again, as he inevitably would.

Her skin prickled as a shiver chased over her. She wanted his kiss. Even more after yesterday. That kiss had been an entrée and had only whetted her appetite for more. More kisses. More caresses. More…*everything.*

But how much *everything* did she mean? That was the question that had her tossing and turning throughout the night. Her only certainty was that, whatever everything meant, it must be purely physical.

The door opened behind her and Effie entered, carrying a gently steaming pitcher.

'You're awake early, milady.' She crossed to the wash-stand and poured the water into the basin. 'Which gown shall I lay out for you?'

'Oh, any of them will—no. Actually, I shall wear my blue muslin.'

'Very well.'

'Effie, are the gentlemen up and about yet?'

'Yes'm.' The maid's voice was muffled as she rummaged in the clothes press. 'I saw Lord Kelridge going downstairs just now and His Lordship has been up for hours.' She straightened, the blue sprigged muslin draped across her arms. She shook the gown out and held it up, examining it with a critical eye. 'I don't *think* this needs pressing, milady, but maybe I should, just in case.' She turned for the door.

'Effie…no. The gown is barely creased and what there is will soon drop out.'

By the time she had washed and dressed and was alone again, Kitty was no nearer a decision on that all-important question. She would not…*could* not…risk opening her heart to the pain she had suffered before, yet she did not wish to deny the cravings of her own body. Cravings she had never before experienced…or, at least, not with such intensity. Before, in her marriage, there had been the odd fleeting hint of greater pleasure in the marital act. Nothing more than a glimpse of something more exotic, more intoxicating, that quickly evaporated, like the fast-fading memory of a dream upon waking. Now, her curiosity had been piqued.

Could she satisfy that curiosity without risking her heart? Men did it all the time—satisfied the lusts of their bodies without their emotions being involved.

But this is Adam. Your emotions are already involved, whether you like it or not.

She acknowledged the truth of it. So, the question became…was her curiosity, and that deep-down hum of need, strong enough for her to take the risk of heartache if she followed her desires? At least, this time, she knew there would be no fairy-tale ending. Not when Adam would need an heir. This time, she would not expect a pot of anything at the end of the rainbow.

She went downstairs and into the parlour where breakfast was laid out on the sideboard.

'Good morning. How is your arm today?'

Adam paused in the act of raising his coffee cup. The table before him was bare of crockery or food, suggesting he had finished eating. As Kitty helped herself to a boiled egg and a slice of toast, he returned her greeting, adding, 'It is still sore to the touch but, otherwise, much better, thank you. I trust you slept well?'

'Very well, thank you. And you?'

'Well enough. Well—if I'm honest, I was restless.'

Kitty sat opposite him. 'I am not surprised. Being shot would have that effect.'

He captured her gaze, and that same fire in his eyes— banked low for now—quickened her pulse and fractured her breathing. Heavens! Did she have any choice but to explore this further? If he could heat her blood with one look, what more might he do with a kiss? A touch? The memory of the day before—those feelings—shivered through her.

'Coffee, milady?'

She jumped at Vincent's quiet murmur close behind her. The coffee pot appeared next to her. He filled her cup and his arm withdrew. The interruption had allowed her to bring her emotions back under control. She scraped butter on to her toast and bit into it. Behind her, she heard Vincent leave the room.

'It was not being shot that disturbed my sleep.' Adam's comment was no less forceful for being so quiet. 'It was you, Kitty. *You* were on my mind.' His eyes burned into her. 'I—' He broke off as Robert's voice rang out from outside the room. 'We need to talk, Kitty. Come to the library later, after Rob goes out. Please?'

Kitty nodded her head as Robert—full of cheer and early morning energy—breezed into the room.

It was almost eleven before Robert left the house, intending to visit his bank. Kitty—her nerves winding ever tighter at the thought of a tête-à-tête with Adam—suggested she might accompany Robert and pay a visit to her dressmaker, but Robert fobbed her off, saying he intended to be in and out of the bank in a flash and there was far too much demanding his attention back here at the Hall for him to have time to waste while Kitty shopped. Kitty recoiled at his brusqueness, so unlike Robert.

'My apologies, Stepmama. I had no right to snap at you. This business with Adam is bothering me...he told me this morning he intends to ride out this afternoon. I cannot stop him, I know, but I cannot help but worry there may be another attempt on him. I need to be back in time to accompany him.'

'But...you will then put yourself at risk, Rob. You must not.'

And neither must Adam.

He gave her a brief hug. 'Don't you worry about me! Besides, why are you not hard at work writing? I thought you would relish the opportunity to spend more time on it while Charis is away.'

'I am not in the mood for it today.' She was far too distracted to even try to lose herself in her story. Her heroine must wait patiently until Kitty was in the right frame of mind to rescue her from that cliff face she clung to, praying that hero Jason would find her before the evil Lord Sidney—desperate to stop her revealing his plan to kill young Arthur—spotted her hiding place and hurled her into the foaming seas far below.

Robert smiled down at her. 'That is understandable. We are all of us unsettled. Give me a few days, until we have a clearer idea of what happened, and then I will gladly escort you to town to visit your modiste and to shop to your heart's content.'

Kitty thanked him, knowing she would not accept his offer. She had no wish to shop...she had, like a coward, impulsively seized upon the idea as an excuse to delay the forthcoming talk with Adam. She was still no more certain of what she would say or do.

She approached the library with dragging feet.

But when Adam looked up and saw her...when he jumped up and rounded the desk...when he strode towards her... all indecision fled. She stepped into his arms. They folded around her and she leaned into his strength, breathing in his spicy maleness, her head against his chest. The steady thump-thump-thump of his heart reassured her; the heat of his body relaxed her. It felt like coming home.

Kitty thrust her hands between them and pushed against his chest, only the fabric of his shirt separating her palms and his skin. As yesterday, he had discarded his jacket and was dressed in shirt sleeves and unbuttoned waistcoat. When his embrace loosened, she stepped away. She folded her arms.

'Robert tells me you intend to ride out this afternoon. Are you mad?'

She hadn't meant her first words to be so confrontational, but she couldn't bear to see him put himself into danger.

Adam quirked a brow. He crossed to the place where he had been working, then turned to face her, hitching one hip up to perch on the desk, and folded his own arms.

'I will not skulk indoors shivering in my shoes.'

Of course he would not.

'He...they...might try again.'

'Then that will give me the opportunity to discover who he is. Or who they are.' His lips quirked in a smile. 'Kitty... I will not be alone. Robert and two grooms will be with me. And I will be on my guard. Yesterday, neither of us had any notion that someone might mean mischief. I don't know about you, but I was giving none of *my* attention to our surroundings.'

His smiled faded. His gaze heated. His voice deepened. 'I was far too interested in my companion.'

Awareness coiled deep in her belly and her pulse leapt.

'You wanted to talk?' The question emerged as a squeak.

'I did.' He stood. 'I do.'

He beckoned and Kitty moved towards him. All at once

it no longer mattered that she still had no plan about what to say or what to do. This, she realised, was about instinct. It was about feelings. It was about spontaneity. It was about doing what was right for her in *this* moment. She had lived her life looking forward, not back. But this need not be about the future. That would happen come what may. This was about now.

She paused an arm's length from him. 'What did you want to say?'

Alive to every nuance in his expression, she saw his eyes narrow infinitesimally before creasing in a smile.

'I want to say…words are overrated.' He took her hands, his thumbs circling her palms as he held her gaze. Her breath grew short. 'Actions. Now they have more…value.'

He moved then, walking backwards, still holding her hands, thumbs still caressing. She followed. Not coerced. Not pulled in his wake. She followed willingly as he backed around the painted screen that shielded the reading corner from the rest of the room. He released her hands and she raised them to his shoulders as waves of longing heated her blood and sweet anticipation coursed through her.

Strong fingers flexed at her waist as his mouth swooped on hers, crushing her lips in a fiery kiss. She pressed close, her hands tangling in his hair, her fingers curving around the solid shape of his skull. That distant thrum of need strengthened, growing ever more insistent as her insides melted and her body moulded to his.

He tore his lips from hers. 'Kitty.'

His groan lingered in the air as he trailed hot kisses across her jaw and down her throat. Her head fell back, her eyes drifting shut as everything faded away. Everything but Adam and the feelings conjured up by the magic of his lips on her skin and the caress of his hands as they swept her body, stroking, fondling. She savoured the sheer joy of all that latent power, harnessed and controlled, as Adam skimmed her skin with the finest and tenderest of touches. His fingers released the buttons fastening the bodice of her gown and he opened it, spreading it wide to allow him to release both of her breasts from her corset. He kneaded them, his thumbs rubbing her nipples before he dipped his head and tasted her, sucking one hardened bud deep into his mouth, flicking it with his tongue as his fingers played with the other.

Need climbed within her and she thrust her fingers through his hair as pressure built inside…a craving for more. And more. How had she never felt this before?

She pressed her hips closer to him and the hard ridge of his arousal pressed against her belly aroused an urgency she'd never experienced, and she slipped a hand between them to stroke his length. His groan vibrated against the bare skin of her shoulder, where he'd pulled aside her gown to press hot kisses, as her other hand reached for his breeches' buttons. She released him, wrapping her fingers around him—all silken skin sheathed over hard, hot iron—following her instinct as she squeezed and stroked, and caressed the rounded tip with the pad of her thumb. Never had she held her husband in such a way.

'Kiss me,' she whispered and hungry lips seized hers. Tongues tangling, they moved as one to the wing-backed chair, set with its back to the window. Adam sat, his hands on Kitty's waist. He looked up at her.

'Tell me you want this, Kitty. Tell me you want me.'

'Oh, yes,' she breathed.

She could not tear her gaze from his erection as it jutted proud through the open placket of his breeches. Adam grasped her skirts and gathered them high, then pulled her between his splayed legs to press his mouth to the soft curls at the juncture of her thighs. She jerked as his tongue probed her secret, feminine lips, clutching his hair as her womb clenched and something hot and fierce leapt within her. He slid forward, nudging her back until he sat on the front edge of the seat, his hands on her hips, still holding her raised skirts clear. Then he pushed his legs between hers, forcing hers apart, and leaned back until his body stretched out before her. Beneath her.

Her intimate folds were swollen and wet and ready and aching with need. Her heart hammered. Her chest rose and fell ever faster. She was wanton; desirable; *glorious*. The tip of his shaft touched her entrance. Adam's eyes were on her, watching, the flames leaping. His tongue snaked out to moisten his lips.

'Just lower yourself,' his voice rasped.

She did, her eyes locked on to his.

She sank down until he filled her. Stretching her. *Fulfilling* her.

She closed her eyes. And she closed her mind against the warnings clamouring to make themselves heard. At this moment, she did not care. For this moment, *any* risk was a risk worth taking. For now, her heart filled with joy as she began to move and as the sensations began to build within her. She propped her hands on his shoulders, feeling the edge of the bandage beneath her fingertips, reminding her not to grab at his arm. Her movements quickened and excitement bloomed and spread within her as she strained to reach the wonderful reward that she knew instinctively lay before her.

For now...*this* was everything.

Adam moved beneath her, thrusting up again and again in time with her own movements. His lips closed around her nipple and he sucked hard, then nipped. Her gasp feathered through the quiet of the library and her fingers clenched, grabbing folds of his shirt. Higher and higher she climbed, but that pinnacle stayed just out of reach until he reached between her legs and stroked that secret nub of flesh she hadn't even known existed.

She reached the edge and took flight, sucking in a huge lungful of air. Then his mouth covered hers, swallowing her cry as ecstasy pulsed through her, turning her entire body into a quivering, fluid mass. She collapsed against him, tearing her mouth from his as she panted, her energy spent as those ripples slowed, the spaces between them lengthened, and her brain scrambled to make sense of the conflicting emotions tumbling through her.

It was wonderful...she wanted to experience that all over again. And again.

And that scared her. No. It petrified her. Had she truly believed she could satisfy her curiosity and her lust so easily? As she steadied and those tumbling emotions quieted, the realisation growing that this was not enough, would never be enough...that she would always crave him, as long as he was near... *that* was what petrified her.

Could she cope with occasional liaisons until he decided to marry? Would that ever be enough for her? Could she still protect her heart?

She could no longer deny her love for Adam, but even if he had marriage in mind for their future—and even if she could find the courage to marry again—she could never accept him because she could not give him the heir he would need.

And though she loathed self-pity, the burn of tears at the back of her eyes told her she was in danger of wallowing in it. It seemed so unfair. She had always longed for a child of her own and now her barrenness would rob her of any chance of a future with Adam, doubling the torment of her failure as a woman as she added the loss of the man she loved to her childlessness.

But she must find the courage from somewhere to protect them both—her from the future agony that was now inevitable and him from the self-sacrifice of marrying a barren woman and living to regret it.

She lay still, snuggled into Adam's strong chest, safe for now in his embrace, reluctant to move and to face reality.

Chapter Seventeen

Adam hugged Kitty close, tucking her head into his shoulder as his chest heaved.

God! Dear God! Never...

He tightened his arms. He never wanted to let her go. She fit him so perfectly. He could stay like this for ever.

Gradually, though, the fear that someone might enter the library and catch them urged him to move. Even though they were hidden from the door by the screen it would be obvious what had taken place and Kitty did not deserve the gossip that would surely follow. Adam pressed his lips to her hair, breathing in the scent of her.

'We must move, my sweet.'

She snuggled closer for a minute, with a soft moan of protest, then pushed herself upright.

'Yes.'

Her obvious reluctance to move pleased him. She slid from his knee and rose to her feet, smoothing her skirts before adjusting her clothing and making herself decent.

Adam, too, stood. He buttoned the placket of his breeches as Kitty began to tidy her hair, gathering the scattered pins.

When she was decent, he took her hand and led her back to the table where the plans he had already drawn were spread out.

'I am sorry I did not withdraw, my darling,' he said. 'But, after all, it will not matter if there should be consequences... I can think of nothing more delightful than you, holding our baby in your arms.'

Kitty's face paled. 'I... Adam... I—'

She broke off as the door opened. Adam gave her a reassuring smile as he realised he had said nothing about marriage. He would soon remedy that, however, with a proper proposal such as she deserved. Although...he recalled her claim that she would never remarry and a voice of caution whispered that she might take some convincing that marriage was the right solution for them both.

'My apologies for the interruption, my lord.' Vincent entered, carrying a silver salver on which lay two letters. 'These have just been delivered from Kelridge Place.'

Adam frowned as he took the letters from Vincent and perused the direction on each of them.

'Who brought them? Is he still here?'

'He is, my lord. He gave his name as Carter. Your steward. He brought them himself in case you have any instructions for him. He is in the entrance hall.'

'Thank you. I shall read these and then speak to him.'

Vincent bowed and withdrew. Adam examined the letters again.

'This one is from my mother, but the other is an unfamiliar hand.'

He broke the seal on Ma's letter and read it quickly, then reread it, giving himself more time to digest her words.

My dearest Adam,

Thank you for your letter. You cannot know what it means to me to have this chance to properly heal the rift between us. Since you left I have tortured myself, wondering if I did the right thing in not fully explaining my actions over all these years.

But, as I said before you left Edinburgh, I could not know if Kelridge had changed and I did not want to compound the harm I had already done by further damaging your opinion of your father. I am happy Bartholomew told you something of your father's character and, from what you wrote, it seems that even Grenville now accepts that Gerald was a violent man!

You ask why I settled for the life of a housekeeper when I was a lady. Well, at first I was terrified Kelridge would find us—because, of course, he had the legal right to take you from me and he would have done so, make no mistake. I could not allow that to happen. Not when his violence towards me had already spilled over into violence towards you. So, rather than keep house as Angus's widowed cousin, as he originally offered, I masqueraded as his housekeeper.

But, whatever my title, what I do is no more than I would do if I was Angus's unwed sister—I run his household and oversee the servants.

My experience of marriage killed any appetite for knowing any other man and Angus was and has always been a godsend to me—the brother I never had. I have been most content, I assure you. I have never

*been comfortable socialising—it was my father's ambi-
tion to see me marry into the aristocracy, not mine—
and I am happy with my own company, as you know.*

*Thank you for your invitation to visit you at Kelridge
Place. Not without some qualms, I accept. I thought
to come next month and I am looking forward to seeing how you are settled into your new role, although
I am also a little apprehensive at meeting again with
those people I knew from before.*

*I must also say, yes, of course you may pass on my
address to Araminta—or Lady Datchworth I should
say, I suppose. I remember her with some fondness,
despite her outspokenness! It was useful to have a
friend so full of confidence when I felt so awkward
and diffident in my first and only Season. I shall look
forward to meeting her again.*

*Adam—Angus would like to accompany me, if you
are agreeable? I know you blame him as well for not
telling you the truth, but you need to know that it was
my decision to keep silent and that Angus had no
choice but to respect my wishes.*

*I still feared your father, you see, even when you
were a grown man. I feared his power to corrupt you.
And, from the tales Angus heard about your father
when you both worked on that job at Fenton Hall fifteen years ago, I was right to hold that secret.*

I look forward to seeing you next month, Son.

Your proud and loving,
Mother

After Adam's second reading he looked up to find Kitty
watching him, concern writ large on her face. She had re-

gained her colour and he made a mental note to find out soon what she had been about to say when Vincent interrupted them.

'All is well,' he said and she smiled. 'My mother has accepted my invitation to come to Kelridge Place. Both she and Sir Angus will come next month and she writes that she hopes I have had enough time to settle into my new role.'

He huffed a laugh, shaking his head. 'I've made a poor job of that so far. I ought to have stayed and stamped my authority on the place and my staff.'

Instead of which, at the first opportunity I ran away.

He knew he ought to go back and begin work on setting things straight, but he couldn't leave Kitty. Not yet. It was too soon. He was certain in his own mind now that he wanted to marry her and, until that was settled, he would stay. He laid aside Ma's letter and broke the seal on the other. He quickly scanned the writing.

'Oh. It is from Tolly. He writes that he and my uncle are leaving Kelridge Place.' He read the date. 'It was written yesterday. Their intention was to leave before noon and to stay in London for a few days before travelling on to Brighton.'

Kitty frowned. 'Did he give a reason? Surely he does not mean they are leaving for good?'

'No, it is not permanent. He writes that he has persuaded my uncle that a breath of sea air would do them both good. And that it will give me the opportunity to take the reins at Kelridge Place.' He thrust his fingers through his hair, the news raising conflicting emotions. 'If they left on time, then neither of them could have shot at me.' Which was both a relief and a worry, for if it was not Grenville or Tolly, who could it have been? 'Of course, we cannae know that they *did* leave on schedule. And we also cannae know they did not divert their route to stop by here.'

'No. You are right. But, if they did so, then it must mean they were in it together.'

Adam prayed that would not prove to be the case. The news that his uncle and cousin were no longer at Kelridge Place presented him with a further dilemma, however, as he realised that now he *really* should go back. But he didn't want to. He wanted to stay with Kitty.

'I must complete these plans before I leave.'

Kitty half-turned from him, her shoulders tense. 'I am sure Robert will not object to a delay. Or you could take them with you and work on them at Kelridge Place.'

'I dinna want to leave ye,' he said. 'Not yet.'

Not ever!

Kitty faced him again. 'Do not fear I shall accuse you of seduction and abandonment, Adam.'

Her amused, slightly mocking tone brought a frown to his face. The Kitty, full of passion, who had writhed on his lap not fifteen minutes ago was now concealed behind a cool, distant mask and she was once again the Kitty he had met in London, but he had no idea why she had re-treated behind her barrier. He'd thought it well and truly demolished, but here they were again with, seemingly, not a brick out of place.

'I did not imagine ye would,' he said, matching her light tone. 'If you will excuse me, I shall go now and speak to Carter.'

His skin heated under the cool appraisal of her grey gaze and his doubts and uncertainties about her...about what she truly thought and felt...intensified.

'Do not forget to ask what time your uncle and cousin left yesterday,' she said.

Adam strode from the room, his thoughts in turmoil.

Joseph Carter waited in entrance hall, his hat in his hands, under the watchful eye of Vincent.

'Might we use Lord Fenton's study, please?'

He could have bitten his tongue as he registered the hint of contempt in Vincent's tone as he replied, 'Of course, my lord.'

How many times had Lady Datchworth warned him it was not done to speak to servants as though one was asking a favour, or to thank them for merely carrying out their duties? But being unmannerly to *anyone* simply wasn't in his nature.

'Carter. This way.'

The steward followed him to the study.

'I was surprised to learn my uncle and cousin have left Kelridge Place. Was it a sudden decision?'

'I believe so, milord.'

'What time did they leave?'

Carter's lips pursed as he pondered the question. Adam waited.

'About noon, I should say. I didn't take note of the exact time.'

'And I presume they travelled in the carriage?' At Carter's nod, Adam continued, 'My cousin made no mention of when they might return. Did they say anything to you, or to Green?'

'Not to me. Have you any instructions for me to convey back to the Place, milord?'

'Aye. I do. Please advise Mrs Ford that my mother and her cousin, Sir Angus McAvoy, will visit next month, so the work to refurbish the guest bedchambers needs to be completed as soon as possible.'

'Very good, milord.'

Adam frowned. 'Why is it you chose to deliver the letters yourself, Carter? Surely a groom could have ridden over with them?'

'With the mast—that is, with Mr Trewin away, I thought I ought to report to you direct, milord. We lost some sheep yesterday. To poachers.'

'*Poachers?* How many sheep? When?'

'We can't be certain exactly when, milord, but Eddings found the remains of three beasts at the far edge of South Kell Wood. Soon after Mr Trewin and Mr Tolly left, it was. That was why the letters weren't delivered yesterday—we were looking for tracks and tryin' to work out what happened. It looks like they'd been shot, then butchered where they fell. The meat and fleeces were taken away. We found hoofprints.'

'No one heard the shots?'

He shook his head. 'If anyone heard them, they were far enough away for them to take no notice. They'd have been muffled by the woods, too.'

Adam frowned, his mind whirling. 'Was that before the thunderstorm yesterday?'

'It was, milord. Though me and Eddings got wet through riding back afterwards.'

'Very well. You were right to report this in person, Carter. Thank ye. You may get back now and please tell the men to keep a sharp lookout for any strangers hanging around.' Adam strode to the study door and out into the hall, leaving Carter to follow. 'I shall return to Kelridge Place in a day or so.'

Carter bowed. As he exited the front door, Robert entered.
'Who was that?'

'My steward.'

Adam filled Robert in on both Tolly's news and the report of poachers as they walked to the library. Kitty was no longer there and Adam found himself unsurprised. Putting aside the fact that she desired him physically, she clearly still had reservations about him. He didn't fully understand why, though. He'd explained his reasoning in not agreeing to elope with her all those years ago and she had agreed he had done the right thing. If she had told him of her father's plan for her...well...yes, he probably would have found a way to rescue her. But she had not confided in him and he'd made his decision based on what he knew.

He'd find her. Try to talk to her. He needed to understand what was going on in her head.

'Poachers...' Robert frowned. 'That might put a different interpretation on what happened here yesterday, but let us concentrate on your uncle and Tolly first. They left Kelridge at noon, driving south, and their route to London would bring them close to Fenton Hall. But you were not attacked until much later.'

'They could have waited. In fact, whoever it was who shot me—if it was his *intention* to shoot me—must have hung around for some time.'

'But...the Kelridge carriage standing at the side of the road for that length of time...would they take such a risk? No. I cannot believe it.'

Adam sighed. 'Nor I. Plus, the culprit was on horseback. *If* those hoofprints you found belonged to him. Although— and I'm reluctant to even think this—if Grenville and Tolly *were* in it together, it is possible that one of them made the

journey in the carriage while the other switched to horseback and rode on to Fenton land with the sole purpose of
trying to kill me.'

His words repeated in his head, souring his stomach. 'I
cannot credit that but, if there is any chance my uncle and
cousin were to blame, that is the only scenario that fits the
facts. Surely it must make more sense for it to be poachers after all. The argument that wildlife would take shelter
with a thunderstorm approaching does not apply to sheep.
They cannot take refuge in the undergrowth or in burrows
and there *were* sheep in the meadow next to the woods, all
huddled together with their backs to the rain.'

Robert paced the room. 'I'll be happier if we can fully
eliminate Grenville and Tolly before we hang the blame
entirely on poachers. I confess, I have never experienced
poaching on that scale—it sounds more like an organised
gang than the work of a local poacher wanting a bit of meat
for the pot.'

'Could ye send a man to make enquiries?' Adam said. 'I
assume Grenville and Tolly are well known in the area—
someone must have seen them pass and will be able to confirm at what time.'

'I'll do better than that,' Robert said. 'I shall go myself.
I'll ride south and enquire at the toll houses. The carriage
has the Kelridge crest on its doors, as I recall, so I'm sure
they will be remembered. Hopefully the gatekeepers will
remember the time they saw the carriage as well as confirm both men were inside.'

'I shall come with you.'

'No. Please do not. It will not take two of us and, although
I know you must now feel obliged to return to the Place as

soon as possible, I really do hope you can finish those plans first, Adam. It is important to me.'

Adam puzzled over that. Kitty had mentioned Robert had ideas of matrimony but, in consideration of the time it would take to build that new wing, what difference would a few extra days—or even weeks—make?

'Very well,' he said.

As it happened, Robert's words suited Adam, for his conscience demanded his immediate return to Kelridge Place and here was the perfect excuse to stay at Fenton Hall, the perfect excuse to stay near to Kitty and to use the time to persuade her to change her mind about remarrying. And if spending more time with Kitty meant those plans would take even longer to finish, then, so be it.

'I shall leave immediately,' Robert said. 'In fact, rather than ride, I shall drive my curricle. There is no time to lose… the sooner I leave, the more likely it is that the gatekeepers will recall Tolly and your uncle passing through. May I leave you to inform my stepmother? And do not worry should I fail to return tonight. I intend to make damned sure they did not leave a false trail and double back.'

'It sounds as though you are enjoying this, Rob.'

Robert grinned. 'Oh, I am. I love a mystery to solve. And if, as I hope, we find that Grenville and Tolly could *not* have shot you, then I am sure we will all breathe a sigh of relief.'

He strode from the library, calling to his valet to pack an overnight bag. Adam—furnished with the perfect excuse—asked Vincent where he might find Lady Fenton.

'She is in her sitting room, my lord. But she asked most particularly not to be disturbed.'

Adam wanted to see her now. Right away. But a sly inner voice reminded him that if he told her too soon, before Robert left, she might very well persuade her stepson he must return that evening. The prospect of dinner with just Kitty for company, not to mention the entire evening together, was simply too enticing. He could wait to see Kitty until Robert had safely left the Hall—there was no need to disturb her rest.

'Very well, Vincent. I shall be in the library. Please let me know when Lady Fenton is available.'

He lasted half an hour after Robert left the house. The Hall was quiet, the silence weighing down on him as he quit the library. He knew where Kitty's sitting room was…and there was no sign of Vincent to disapprove of or prevent Adam disturbing his mistress. He climbed the stairs, then hesitated outside the sitting-room door. It was quiet within. He wondered if she was sleeping, but he convinced himself Kitty would want to know of Robert's plan. He put his ear to the door and heard a faint scratching noise. He pressed the door handle down and eased the door open until the gap was wide enough for his head. Just one peep.

Kitty sat at a table in front of the window, her back to the door. Not asleep, then, but writing. Letters, he presumed. He tapped on the door. She started. Glanced over her shoulder, her eyes somehow vague, shadowed by low, bunched brows. Then her expression cleared. She coloured, pushed her chair back and leapt to her feet. She stood with her back to the table, which he could now see was littered with dozens of sheets of paper covered in writing.

Adam frowned. 'What are ye doing?'

Her nostrils flared. 'Waiting for you to tell me why you are here. I left strict instructions I was not to be disturbed.'

'I am aware of it. I assumed you were resting and, had that been the case, I would have quietly withdrawn.'

'What can I do for you, Lord Kelridge?'

Adam's brows shot up. 'Kitty? What is it? Why am I suddenly Lord Kelridge once again? Do ye…are ye…?' He stopped. Sucked in a deep breath as he recalled her earlier coolness. 'Kitty. Do ye regret what we did?'

She stared at him silently for several moments. Then she gave him a rueful smile. 'I have no regrets.'

Adam waited for her to elaborate, wondering what was going through her head. What it would mean for him.

'I am sorry for my reaction,' she went on. 'You startled me. My mind was…elsewhere.' She walked towards him. He grabbed the opportunity to look at her table again, but he was no clearer about what she was up to. If she was writing letters, there were a great many of them. Unless…

'Kitty. Are ye writing a novel?'

'And if I am?'

Adam shook his head. 'Well…nothing, really. You are entitled to do as ye please. Does Robert know?'

'He does.'

'And he approves?'

'He does not disapprove.' Her tone suggested that she would not care even if he did.

'Will ye tell me about it?'

She glanced back at the table, then looked at him. 'No. I would rather not.'

She sounded defensive and he recalled their conversation about novels. What had he said? He could not remember, but he hoped he had not given the impression he disapproved of such books. Even though, if he were honest, he thought them a waste of valuable time.

'Now, if you will excuse me, Adam... I have reached a critical point of the story and I do not wish to lose the thread of my narrative. Did you come here for a particular reason?'

'Ah. Yes.' He hesitated. 'But it will wait until you have finished writing. I'm sorry to have disturbed ye.'

Her eyes softened. 'And—again—I am sorry for my reaction. I tend to get over-involved in my story and my characters are currently in the middle of an argument. The mood can spill over into real life at times, until I have adjusted from my fictional world to the actual world.'

She tucked her bottom lip between her teeth, looking contrite and far younger than her thirty-two years. Tenderness, spiced with lust, welled up inside Adam. He reached for her hand and raised it to his lips.

'I shall leave you in peace.'

'No. Wait. You wanted to talk to me...have there been any developments?'

Adam smiled at her. 'It will wait. We will talk later.'

Chapter Eighteen

The door clicked shut behind Adam, leaving Kitty staring abstractedly at the space where he had been. Her mind whirled, but she found no solution to her conundrum. Their relationship had changed and, whether she willed it or no, she had opened her heart to more pain. It was inevitable. Adam had spoken no words of love. Neither had he mentioned marriage, but the implication had been there, cutting her to the quick.

She loved him. She could no longer lie to herself. And that terrified her because nothing could ever come of it. There was Charis to consider. And Robert. And...

She growled low in her throat as she acknowledged the real reason there could *never* be a happy ever after for her and Adam. Children. Babies. *An heir.* She was barren and Adam was now Earl of Kelridge, and all noblemen needed an heir to follow them, to care for their estates and provide security and a living for their tenants and for the many local craftsmen who depended upon a thriving 'big house' in their neighbourhood.

I can think of nothing more delightful than you holding our baby in your arms.

Those words had flayed her, bringing harsh reality to the fore after she had successfully banished all thought of the future from her mind. And if he were to ask her to marry him, what reason could she give for a refusal? How could she tell him the truth—speak out loud those brutal, final words *I am barren*—without falling apart in front of him? How could she bear his sympathy or, worse, his pity? And what if he *still* felt obliged to urge her to marry him, even when he knew the truth? A man such as he might see it as a matter of honour. He might break down her resistance. And he would be stuck in a childless marriage and would come to resent her...blame her.

And that she could not bear.

Feeling sick, she turned back to the table. She would lose herself in her work once again and worry about Adam later. But, mere minutes later, she slammed down the quill in frustration, causing ink to fly and speckle the nearby sheets of paper. The magic was lost. Her head was full of Adam. And her heart was full of that pain she had so carefully protected herself from all these years. She pushed back her chair and went in search of Adam.

'He has gone to the stables, milady.'

She recalled his plan to ride out that afternoon. 'Is Lord Fenton with him?'

'No, milady. His Lordship is driving to...well, he is driving *towards* London.'

'London?'

Vincent lowered his voice. 'His Lordship did confide in me before he left, milady. After the occurrence yester-

day, and the letter Lord Kelridge received, His Lordship is
determined to track the movement of the Messrs Trewin
yesterday. Gresham has gone with him and they hope to as-
certain at what times the Kelridge carriage passed through
the toll gates. His Lordship did say he may not return tonight and Lord Kelridge would have informed you immediately but—as you instructed me no one was to disturb
you—I asked him to wait.'

'I see.' But Adam had come anyway, knowing she
would want to know Robert's plans. And she'd given him
no chance to tell her. 'Thank you. And Lord Kelridge has
gone to the stables, you say? With the intention of riding
out, even after what happened yesterday?'

'I did try to reason with him, milady. But he was in no
mood to listen.'

And that is my fault.

Her first reaction had been dazed, as it always was when
she was interrupted in the middle of a scene in which she
was fully immersed. But afterwards…she ought to have insisted on knowing why he had interrupted her.

'Very well. Send word to the stables to saddle Herald,
will you please? And if His Lordship has not already left,
ask him to wait for me to join him. I shall change into my
riding clothes right away.'

'Milady… I do not think—'

Kitty, already on the fourth stair, paused. 'Vincent. You
are not paid to think. Now do as I ask without further ado.
Please.'

The butler executed his stiffest bow before stalking towards the back of the house. Kitty ran upstairs and to her
bedchamber to change into her riding gown, her heart
pounding with fear.

* * *

Within ten minutes, she was clattering down the stairs again. She grabbed her leather riding gloves and crop from a stony-faced Vincent and hurried out of the already open front door. Davey, one of the grooms, waited outside, holding the reins of both Herald, Kitty's chestnut gelding, and a brown gelding that went by the uninspiring name of Brownie.

'His Lordship left word that one of us must accompany you if you go out, milady.' Davey touched his cap. 'On fear of dismissal if we don't follow his order *to the letter.*'

'Very well, Davey. I understand.'

Normally she insisted on riding alone—it gave her imagination the perfect opportunity to wander. But normally there was absolutely no danger. She remained on Fenton land and Robert trusted her to do so. She couldn't fault such an order after yesterday and it would be unfair to blame Davey for following his master's instructions.

The groom cupped his hands to help her mount. As she gathered the reins and settled into the saddle, she said, 'Had Lord Kelridge already ridden out when my message reached the stables?'

'Yes, milady. About quarter of an hour since.'

'And did anyone accompany him?'

'Yes, milady.'

Kitty breathed a little easier.

'He told us he would head up to Fenton Edge.'

'Then let us go.'

They rode at a fast trot, breaking into a canter where they could, and before long they saw two riders ahead of them, heading up a track over the heathland that led to the Edge, an escarpment with views over the relatively flatter land to the north—a view that included Kelridge Place and its parkland. Before long, Adam halted and looked back, presumably alerted by the thud of horses coming up at speed behind him. His hand had already withdrawn a pistol from his pocket and more relief flooded Kitty that he had at least come prepared.

When they drew to a halt, Adam's expression was as menacing as yesterday's thunderclouds. His horse—a piebald gelding called Jester—danced sideways, made skittish by his rider's clear annoyance.

'Why are ye here?'

Kitty, somewhat breathless from their fast pace, ignored him to speak to Dexter—Adam's companion and second in rank to Gresham in the hierarchy of the stable yard.

'Kindly drop back with Davey, will you, Dexter? And stay alert for anyone else in the area.'

Dexter, a man of few words, nodded and touched his cap. The two grooms held their horses still as Kitty nudged Herald into a walk. Adam, audibly grumbling—although she couldn't make out his words—followed, ranging his mount alongside hers.

'Why are ye here?' His demand was quiet, but no less forceful. 'He could be out there anywhere.'

'Precisely! And *I* am not his target. Or so we agreed yesterday. Why are you putting yourself at such risk? What do you hope to achieve by this…this act of stu—bravado?'

'Ye shouldna have come.' His tone milder now. 'I can look after myself, but you…'

She glanced up at him. His stern profile as he stared straight ahead. The tightness of his lips and the frown that creased his forehead.

'But I…?'

His lips quirked then, in a brief smile, and he flicked a sideways look at her before turning his attention once again to their surroundings.

'Ye're a terrible distraction and ye ken it. How am I meant to concentrate when your scent is weaving through ma senses, firing ma blood?'

Her heart thumped at his words. As if she wasn't already hot enough after that ride. 'Why, Lord Kelridge...' she strove to keep her tone light '... I never imagined that gruff exterior concealed such a poetic soul. You kept that well hidden.'

He smiled at her. Such a sweet smile. 'I canna help it, lass. You have that effect on me...ye're a woman to turn any man inside out.'

The track they were following up the gentle southern slope of the Edge petered out as they reached the open land at the top. Kitty reined in and twisted to look all around. There was no sign of life other than a few sheep grazing the sparse, coarse grassland on the top. Adam pointed.

'There. That is Kelridge Place. My new home—' he pointed at a speck in the distance, a light-coloured cube that perched on a rise in the land '—and that is the boundary—that woodland. South Kell Wood.'

Kitty had never been to Kelridge Place even though there was only six miles between it and Fenton Hall.

'Ye canna see it very well at this distance, I ken, but after what Carter told me I felt the need tae come and see it for myself.'

'What did Carter tell you?'

She'd never even thought to ask him earlier about the steward's visit and now she listened as Adam told her about the sheep that had been shot and butchered.

'But…is that not good news? Oh, not for the poor sheep, or that they have been stolen from you. But does it not support the theory that poachers shot you by mistake? And is that not better than believing the worst of your uncle and cousin?'

'Well, aye. Of course it is.'

'But I do not understand why Robert has gone haring off after Mr Trewin and Tolly.'

'We need to be certain, Kitty. It is no use our lowering our guard on a supposition. Rob will, I hope, find the evidence to confirm it was impossible for either my uncle or my cousin to have fired that gun. And, in the meantime, he has ordered the men to keep watch and even to patrol the outer reaches of the estate to look out for strangers or for further attempts to steal sheep.'

'That makes sense, I suppose.'

Kitty stared across to the distant Kelridge Place, the knot of fear in her stomach easing for the first time since the shooting. But she was still burdened—not by fear, but by anxiety. There was still the conundrum of what the future held for her and Adam. She had made matters worse by succumbing to her desires and was unsure how to handle what their relationship was now and what it might become.

'Are you pleased with the turn your life has taken, Adam? Is it what you want?'

'I wasna happy. At first. I admit it.' He shifted restlessly in the saddle, then dismounted. 'Will you walk with me?'

He lifted his arms to Kitty. She put her hands on his shoulders as he grasped her waist and lifted her from the saddle.

'Dexter. You and Davey hold these two, will you?' she called. 'His Lordship and I wish to stretch our legs.'

The grooms rode over and dismounted, taking control of Herald and Jester.

'Lord Fenton said—'

'Have no fear, Dexter,' Kitty interrupted the groom's concern. 'We will not go out of your sight. I promise. And we will remain alert.'

She laid her hand on Adam's arm and they strolled across to the edge of the escarpment.

'I adore this view,' Kitty said. 'I love that you can see for miles. It is worth the climb just to enjoy it.'

Adam tipped his head to one side and eyed her as he laughed.

'Why is that so funny?'

'It is clear you havena travelled over-much, Kitty, my love.'

Her heart clenched at the endearment. She could never be his love—not fully, not legitimately—even if he meant it.

'I have been to London. I know that must seem nothing to you, but I love my home and my family. I have never looked to travel away from them.'

'I didna mean that. I laughed at your calling this a climb. This, dearest Kitty, is but a pimple compared with the hills and mountains of the north.' He paused. 'And of bonnie Scotland,' he added in a wistful tone.

'So you do have regrets about the change in your life?'

'Some.' His arm flexed, squeezing her hand into his side. 'But they become less important by the day.'

He halted, capturing her gaze with his, raising a quiver of awareness as she recognised the fire smouldering in his blue eyes. She tugged his arm to keep him moving. 'Do not forget we are being watched.'

They strolled on, their pace slow, their eyes on the view, their attention on one another.

'I should like you to see Scotland, Kitty. The rugged mountains and glens of the Highlands. Edinburgh, with its castle towering over the city. The rolling hills and lochs of the Lowlands and the border country.'

'I have seen paintings and illustrations. It does look magnificent.'

'Aye, it is. But ye canna fully comprehend just how magnificent without seeing it with your own eyes, breathing the scent of the heather and feeling the caress of the air over your skin.'

That wistfulness was even more evident. Robert had speculated that Adam might not be content to make Kelridge Place his permanent home...that he had spoken of returning to Edinburgh and leaving his steward in charge of his estates. But Kitty had no wish to remind him of that, so she resolved to lead his thoughts away from Scotland and any homesickness. There might be no chance of marriage between them but, if he made his home at Kelridge Place, she would at least still meet him on occasion.

They might even have an *affaire*. They would have to be discreet. No one could know. She could not risk any hint of scandal tainting either Charis or Rob, but she was a widow, after all, and widows were allowed a certain amount of licence. A thrill ran through her, raising gooseflesh.

'Vincent said Robert might not return home tonight.'

'That is true. It depends, I would think, on how quickly he can establish whether or not my kinsmen could have been at Fenton Hall yesterday afternoon at the time I was shot.'

Is it so wrong that I hope Rob will be forced to spend the night away from home?

She ought to feel ashamed...*shocked*...by such a hope. But she did not.

'I suppose,' Adam said, slowly, 'we shall have to amuse ourselves if he does not come home.'

Their gazes fused again. Kitty swallowed. 'I suppose we will.'

Robert was not home by the time dinner was served. Kitty had never felt so on edge. She ate her meal, but she took no notice of the food as she chewed and swallowed. She did not look at her plate to see what she was eating and paid no attention to taste.

She could not tear her attention from Adam, seated opposite her.

Every mouthful, every look, every word spoken fuelled the fire that smouldered deep in her belly. Every sip of wine, as their eyes locked over the rim of their glasses, sent sparks sizzling through her veins. Finally it was over, and they rose from their chairs.

'Would you care to bring your brandy to the salon, my lord? There is no need to sit here alone.' Her voice, somehow, sounded utterly normal.

'Thank you, my lady. I will do that.'

'I shall not stay up late,' she continued as they left the dining room, for the benefit of Vincent and the other servants within earshot. They headed towards the salon, side by side. 'I find I am tired after a restless sleep last night. And you, I make no doubt, must also be weary.'

'I am.'

'Vincent, have the tea tray brought in as soon as it can be arranged, please.'

'Yes, milady.'

Somehow, as they walked towards the salon, side by side, Adam's hand found Kitty's. Strong fingers stroked her inner wrist, her palm and the length of her fingers. She stifled her gasp, but closed her fingers around his for the briefest caress before he moved his hand away.

'I doubt Robert will return at this late hour,' Adam continued. 'I will keep ye company while ye drink your tea, then I shall retire.'

Less than an hour later, Kitty was ready for bed. She dismissed Effie and then, after a moment's thought, she stripped off her plain cotton nightgown. In her chest of drawers, she found what she sought—a white silk nightgown, trimmed with lace, its neckline threaded with green ribbon. She pulled it on and regarded her reflection in the cheval mirror. She had bought it shortly after she'd married Edgar. It had never been worn. She had quickly realised that although there was affection and regard within their marriage, there was no romance. And little lust. The marital act had been perfunctory and had, invariably, taken place in the dark. And she had failed in her duty as a wife. Failed to get with child. But thank God—as Edgar had reminded her on a monthly basis—he already had his heir and spare in Robert and Edward.

Resolutely, Kitty cast Edgar from her thoughts and considered the lit candle by her bedside. Although it was still twilight outside, the curtains were drawn and the room was dark. Would he come to her? She thought he would and, when he did, she wanted to be prepared. She took her bed candle and used it to light the pair of candles standing on the narrow mantelshelf over the unlit fireplace, and another on her dressing table, its flame reflected by the mirror hung on the wall behind. Then she replaced her bed candle and climbed into bed to wait, ruthlessly quashing all thought of the future, all doubt, any whisper of heartache. For now, she would simply enjoy Adam and allow nothing to spoil this time together.

Before long there was a tap at the door and it opened a crack. Adam just looked at her, raising his brows. Kitty smiled and nodded. He came in, closing the door behind him, then turned the key in the lock.

They needed no words.

Touch, smell and taste dominated as they learned one another without haste and as they discovered how to give—and how to receive—pleasure.

As dawn broke, Adam embraced Kitty, stroking her hair back from her face as he peppered kisses over her forehead, eyebrows, eyelids, nose and cheeks, finally taking her lips in a long, slow dreamy kiss.

'Sleep now,' he whispered. 'I shall see you later.'

Chapter Nineteen

'Good morning, Adam. I hope you slept well?'

Kitty entered the parlour as Adam broke his fast the following morning, a smile stretching her lips. Adam's pulse quickened at the memory of those lips and their exploration of his body, and blood rushed to his groin. He cleared his throat.

'I had a wonderful night, thank ye, Ki—Catherine. And a very good morning to ye, too.'

Kitty sat opposite Adam and the footman in attendance filled her coffee cup.

'May I serve you with some food, my lady?'

'Not now, Terence. But I shall want more coffee—is there enough in the pot?'

'I shall go and fetch more, milady.'

The footman left the parlour, closing the door behind him. Adam caught Kitty's gaze.

'Are ye not hungry?'

She sipped from her cup and then set it down on the saucer before replying.

'I was,' she said. 'But I satisfied my appetite in bed.'
Those fascinating dimples appeared, squeezing his heart.
'Effie brought me chocolate and rolls this morning before
I arose.'

'Tease!' Adam had emptied his plate and pushed it aside.

Kitty raised a brow. 'Do I take it you are now replete?'

'Oh, indeed. Fully satisfied, in fact.'

The door opened and Terrence returned, carrying the
coffeepot.

'Until the next meal,' Adam continued, allowing his gaze
to lower to Kitty's breasts before returning to her mischief-
filled eyes. 'I find my…um…appetite somewhat stimulated
recently.' He patted his stomach. 'I shall have to ensure I
do not gain too much weight.'

'Oh, you ought not to be overconcerned.' Kitty's lips
pressed together, suppressing her smile. 'My advice, if you
are concerned about your weight, is to take plenty of exercise. You may then indulge your appetite to your heart's
content.'

Adam drained his coffee cup and gestured to Terence
for a refill.

'Thank ye,' he said. He didn't bother to notice if Terence
responded adversely to his thanks. He'd made his mind up
he would no longer strive to be something he was not and he
would start now. And when he returned to Kelridge Place,
if his staff disapproved, then he would employ men and
women who were more amenable to his ways.

'Thank ye for your advice, Catherine. And, to demonstrate my attention to your sage advice, I intend to take a
walk around the gardens after breakfast, before I continue

working on the drawings for the new wing. Would ye care to accompany me?'

'Why, thank you, Adam. I accept.'

The presence of gardeners prevented anything other than the most innocuous of conversations as they strolled, but it felt good to have Kitty on his arm.

'How soon will you complete the plans for the Hall?'

'Is that a subtle way of enquiring how soon I will leave?'

She lightly pinched his arm. 'You *know* that is not what I meant. I wondered how much longer we shall have the pleasure of your company, that is all.'

'I should think they will be finished in a couple of days.'

It was a fib. He *could* finish them today if he pushed himself. But reluctance to leave Kitty made him inclined to drag the job out. Except...

'I do know I *ought* to return to the Place as soon as possible, especially after those sheep were poached. But, also, I have a lot to learn and now would be the ideal time, with Grenville absent. The servants will have no choice but to refer matters to me first, rather than through ma uncle.'

'Would you rather complete the drawings at Kelridge Place? That way you can return sooner, if you think you should.'

But...he wanted to stay with Kitty. His hopes were high...he was *almost* sure she felt the same for him as he did for her. And yet...there was still a caution there...a reserve. Odd, after yesterday and after the night they had just spent together. Her body expressed love, but her mind... she still seemed reluctant to allow that breakthrough. She was holding back, reining in her emotions. And he didn't understand why. They were both adults. Both single. Did she think Robert might object? Or her other stepchildren?

No, he would not rush to complete his work. He needed to stay here and try to finally breach that barrier surrounding her heart.

It was early afternoon by the time Robert returned.

'Well, you may clear your uncle and cousin of any wrongdoing,' he said without preamble as he strode into the library.

Adam put down his pencil as Robert pulled a chair up to the table where he was working on the plans.

'What did ye find out?'

Robert shook his head. 'Wait a moment. I have asked Stepmama to join us—it will save me repeating myself.' He grinned at Adam and raised his brows. 'I trust you contrived to entertain yourselves last night without my scintillating repartee to make the evening fly?'

'You were sorely missed, my friend.'

Robert laughed. 'Very droll.'

Puzzled, Adam ran the conversation through his head again. Was Robert hinting that he was aware of the attraction that had simmered between Adam and Kitty ever since they met again in London, or was that merely an innocent quip? It was hardly something he could ask him—do you mean did your stepmother and I take advantage of your absence to indulge in bed sport? He was relieved when Kitty came in, saving him from trying to bluster his way through an awkward moment.

'Rob!' Kitty hurried across the room and embraced her stepson. 'What happened?'

'It was not them. It could not possibly have been them.

We tracked them all the way to Highgate and the gatekeeper confirmed they passed and kept going towards London. Both Grenville and Tolly were present at each tollgate and there were no unexplained delays in their journey. They are innocent.'

Adam had been unaware of the tension that gripped him until it dissolved.

'I am verra relieved,' he said. 'And it surely now points to poachers such as those who struck at Kelridge Place. I wonder if there have been any other incidences in the area.'

'I did enquire at a few inns we passed—and we passed Datchworth on the road as we drove home, and I asked him, too—but no one has heard stories of an increase in poachers in the district. Nor is there any whisper of organised gangs. I think that is the most likely explanation, however. What is your opinion?'

'I think the same. And I am mightily relieved. I have nae wish to spend my life looking over my shoulder.'

'The men have reported no suspicious sightings around the estate,' Robert went on, 'but I have ordered them to stay on the alert.'

'But...what about when you return to the Place, Adam?' Kitty said. 'It might not be poachers. Just because your uncle cannot have pulled the trigger himself does not mean he did not give the order.'

'Nae. It is one thing for a man to attempt to kill another for his own sake. I canna credit that any man would do so at the bidding of another.'

'You would be surprised what many men will do for money, Adam,' said Robert. 'But... I know Grenville Trewin. He was a cavalryman—he has killed before, albeit during battle. But if he wanted something done, he would do it himself. He is no sneaksby.'

'I am inclined to agree with ye, Rob. If it were my uncle, he would more likely do it to my face.'

'Well, we have done all we can for now. Tell me, how are those plans coming along?' Robert slid one around until it faced him and bent over it. 'This looks complete.'

Adam cursed silently. He had told Kitty a couple of days and now he could feel her eyes on him. He looked at her, noting the crease between her brows. With Robert's return he would not have the luxury of time to court her and to persuade her to rethink her objection to remarrying. Her reasons for not marrying again—the ones she had listed during their dance at Almacks—well...if Robert intended to wed, and if Charis found a husband, she had already told him she would remove to the Dower House. Her other interests—she must have referred to her writing. Well, he would not interfere with that. And her final objections— neither need nor desire to remarry...surely last night must have given her reason to think again?

'If you will excuse me, gentlemen, I shall leave you to it,' Kitty said and left the library.

Adam sighed in resignation as he suppressed his urge to follow her. He switched his attention to the plans.

'We do need to discuss some of the finishing touches still.'

'Ah. That sounds as though you will need me here. In which case, might we leave it until tomorrow? My bed was so lumpy last night I barely slept a wink and my brain is far too foggy to pay proper attention to detail.'

'Of course it can wait until tomorrow.'

Robert grinned and slapped Adam on the back. 'Good

man! I'll see you at dinner. I'm off out to attend to estate matters.'

He strode to the door leaving Adam wondering what had prompted Robert to lie, for he appeared nothing like a man who had missed a night's sleep and, until that very moment, had been perfectly alert.

Still…grateful for the reprieve, he went in search of Kitty. She was nowhere in the house or the gardens. At the stable yard, however, he learned from Dexter that she had ridden out. Alone.

'She refused to allow anyone to accompany her, my lord,' the groom said when Adam questioned him. 'And being as it was you that was shot at and she has always ridden alone on Fenton land… Well.' He shrugged. 'What could we do?'

'Did she say where she was heading?'

'No, milord, but she went in that direction.' He pointed. It was the same direction Adam had taken yesterday. Towards Fenton Edge.

'Saddle Jester, will ye please, Dexter?'

'Very well, milord.'

It was the reverse of the day before. Adam set off at a fast trot, heading for the heath and Fenton Edge. This time, it was he chasing Kitty and his doubts about her feelings for him eased as he recalled her anger when she had caught him up yesterday—anger that had been fuelled by her worry for his safety. Anger that proved she cared for him. Hell, her every touch, every caress proved she cared. She was not the sort of female who would give her body without having *some* feelings for her lover.

They reached the beginning of the heath and he urged Jester into a canter. The horse's stride lengthened willingly and he soon flattened into a gallop. Of course, Adam couldn't be certain Kitty would head for the Edge, but instinct told him she would. If she felt anything like he did, she would yearn for the chance to gallop up that long, gentle slope that led to the top.

Jester slowed as they reached the top and the ground levelled. There was Herald, tied to a bush. And there was Kitty, her back to Adam as she gazed north. She hadn't noticed their approach and his worry gave way to anger of his own. He leapt from the saddle, tied Jester to the same bush and strode across the open ground to where Kitty stood.

'Kitty.'

He spoke before he reached her, not wanting to startle her, but she jumped anyway and spun around, her cheeks pale.

'Oh! You frightened me!'

Adam's chest swelled as he held in his temper. 'I did not mean to, but it proves how vulnerable ye are up here alone. I could have been anyone.'

She shook her head. 'Yes. You could have been. But you are not. I have been riding up here alone for fifteen years, Adam. There is no danger.' She tipped her head to one side. 'Why have you followed me?'

'We need to talk.'

Her grey eyes searched his and then a smile of resignation curved her lips. As though she knew what he would say and was solidly certain of her own reply. That smile gave Adam pause…what if he waited? If he didn't give voice to his hopes…his heart's desire…then she could not refuse him. His feelings had grown steadily since they met again and he now knew with absolute certainty that what he felt for Kitty was love…he had loved her fifteen years ago and he loved her now and he wanted her in his future. To keep silent about his feelings was the coward's way and so, even though his confidence balanced on a knife's edge, he hauled in a deep breath and took a leap of faith.

'Kitty...ye must ken how I feel about you. I love you.'

Her eyes closed, as though she were in pain, and she shook her head slowly from side to side. Adam gathered her hands in his, squeezing, as though to impress his words upon her.

'I know you have feelings for me. Ye canna disguise them, ye know, even though you try. I *love* you, Kitty, my darling. I want to spend the rest of my life with you.

'Kitty...will ye marry me?'

She shook her head again. 'No, Adam.' She opened her eyes. 'I do not have feelings for you. Not in the way you mean. I cannot marry you.'

Cannot...not will not.

He gazed into her eyes, chasing after hope, clinging to belief. 'You are as stubborn as ever. And as...adorable.'

Her eyes sheened.

'What have I said? I thought... Kitty... I dinna understand ye. Tell me why not—ye canna deny you were as eager as me last night.'

Kitty sighed. 'No. I cannot deny that.'

His heart leapt.

She gave a helpless shrug before gently disentangling her hands from his. 'When I cannot deny I was eager, Adam, I am speaking of lust. Pure and simple. A physical need that we both felt...a natural urge for adults such as we are now. It does not mean I have any wish to rekindle a...a... an *emotional* relationship. That is not on offer.'

He stilled. 'Not on offer?' He thrust his hand through his hair. 'Then let us understand one another. You were willing to give your body to me, but ye willna give me your hand in marriage? No!' The word burst from his lips. Disbelief battled with pain. 'I canna believe…ye will truly refuse me, after last night? And dinna tell me ye have no emotional feelings for me, for I shall not believe you!'

'It is for the best.'

Regret shone in her eyes, contradicting her words, leaving him even more confused. How could she expect him to believe she did not love him? Her body could not lie so convincingly. Could it?

'Adam. I *told* you I have sworn never to marry again. I have never pretended that is what I wanted from you.'

He stared at her in disbelief as her words ripped his heart. Tears burned behind his eyes and he blinked to keep them at bay.

'Adam… I cannot admit to a desire for you other than physical, but… I am a widow. If we are discreet, surely we may indulge our passions from time to time?' Her hands clutched his and then, just as quickly, released them. 'Think about it. Please. Before you, I have been intimate with no man other than my late husband and your touch has awoken a strange force in me…an urge that I long to explore.' Her hands gripped one another before her, her knuckles white. Her chin rose as she sucked in a deep breath. 'If my offer is unacceptable to you, however, then we shall forget this conversation ever took place and we may each get on with our own lives.'

Adam's throat ached with the effort of holding tears back, his heart leaden even though her offer—her body with no strings attached—would surely be most men's idea of heaven. But it was not enough for him. He wanted all of her, mind and body and soul. He wanted the essence of her. To live with her and to see her every day of his life.

'I canna accept such an offer, Kitty. I shall never be content with the occasional loan of your body...how can I bear to live so close to ye and yet not see ye every day? How can I bear not to have the right to hold ye in my arms every night?'

Her grey eyes were stricken. 'You will not return to Scotland, though?' Her voice was little more than a whisper.

'I dinna ken.' Again, he thrust his hand through his hair, holding his emotions in check by a mere thread. 'In a straight choice between you and Scotland, ye win every time. But now...if I canna have ye...' His voice cracked and he cleared his throat to add, 'I still canna believe ye truly mean it, Kitty.'

He trusted himself to say no more. He pivoted on his heel and strode away from Kitty, his vision blurred by tears and his only thought to return to Kelridge Place as soon as he could.

Chapter Twenty

Kitty swallowed desperately as the pressure of tears built in her throat. She bit back the near-overwhelming urge to call Adam back, to reassure him of her love for him, to ease some of his pain. But she did not, for she must still refuse to marry him.

What choice do I have?

Even if she could find the courage to speak of her barrenness, Adam would no doubt claim it made no difference—and maybe it would not, at first. But it would. Eventually. She was convinced of it. Every peer of her acquaintance was obsessed with one thing and that was to sire a son to continue his line and to succeed him to his title. And Adam had already spoken of the joy of their own baby.

Her way was surely better. Once Adam calmed down, he would see they could enjoy one another's company discreetly and no one need ever know. It would be safer for her to continue with her contented life with Robert and Charis, and her writing. If she allowed Adam to persuade her to wed him, she could not bear to see his regard for her slowly turn to resentment as her failure to conceive eroded his love for her and he grew to realise exactly what that meant to him and to the earldom.

Adam had not hesitated in his stride. Kitty watched with heaviness in her heart and tears in her eyes as he reached the horses, untied Jester, leapt into the saddle and raced off down the slope.

When she had arrived home, Vincent had informed her that Lord Kelridge was at work in the library and, that evening, Kitty and Robert were both seated at the dining table before Adam put in an appearance.

'My apologies for my tardiness,' he said. 'I became engrossed in my work and lost track of the time. Rob... I have finished the plans. I would appreciate it if we might meet early tomorrow to go over them. After the news Carter brought, I have decided I must no longer neglect my duty and must return to the Place as soon as possible.'

'Of course,' said Rob.

He caught Kitty's eye and frowned at her. Unable to interpret what that frown signified, Kitty did not respond and instead she began to drink the white soup placed before her. Although she and Robert did their best, the conversation that evening was strained, and it was with some relief that Kitty rose to withdraw. When Robert joined her in the salon only ten minutes later, he said that Adam was feeling unwell and had gone to bed early.

'Do you know what has upset him?'

Kitty started at Robert's bald question and she wilfully misunderstood his meaning.

'I have not the slightest idea—it cannot be anything he

ate, for neither you nor I are unwell. I am sure he will be recovered by morning.' She stood. 'However, I am also very tired and, if you will excuse me, I, too, will retire early.'

She willed herself not to blush at Robert's quizzical stare and, after Effie had left her, she wondered if Adam might come to her room, if only to talk. But he did not, and she had too much pride to go to him uninvited.

The next morning, Adam had gone by the time Kitty went downstairs and, although the news was no surprise, she none the less had to blink back the tears that he had not even said goodbye.

But what did I expect? He has his pride. And I had no choice—this has to be for the best.

She had repeated that refrain countless times through the night, reminding herself of Adam's words, just two days ago. *'I can think of nothing more delightful than you holding our baby in your arms.'*

That could never happen. But her heart was breaking. What if he went back to Scotland? She might never see him again...could she bear that? *Should* she have told him the truth?

'Stepmama?' Robert popped his head around the parlour door where Kitty lingered over her coffee. 'Would you come to my study when you are finished here, please?'

It had taken Kitty some time to get her emotions under control. When she felt more secure, she went to Robert's study, where he sat at his desk, and sat opposite him.

'May I tell you a story, Stepmama?'

'Of course.' She tried a joke. 'Does it begin with once upon a time?'

'As it happens, it does.' Robert stood then and stared out of the window, his back to Kitty, arms folded. 'There once was a boy who had lost his mother in the worst way imaginable.' His voice quivered a little, confirming he spoke of himself. Kitty knew the story, from both him and from Edgar. How they had battled to save Robert's mother from the fire. 'And he felt lost. Then a young man came to stay and he was kind to the boy, who looked up to him as his hero, because he took him fishing but, mainly, because he spent time talking to the lad—unlike the boy's father who had withdrawn into himself. But, sometimes, the young man would disappear and the boy felt hurt. Abandoned. So, one day, the boy followed the young man into the woods.'

Kitty gasped. Robert turned to face her.

'You saw us?'

Robert nodded.

'Why did you never say anything?'

'What would I say?' He shrugged. 'At the time, I felt guilty for spying on you both. I knew what I was doing was wrong. And I didn't want to risk losing Adam's friendship. I guess I didn't really think ahead to when he left. And one day, he was gone. And I saw you crying. So I...'

He paused. He sat again at the desk. Kitty narrowed her eyes at the sympathy and the guilt in his.

'So you told your father?'

He nodded again.

'I always wondered what made him walk through that part of the woods. He never said.'

'I didn't tell him about Adam. I just...it sounds naive now, but I saw my father, so sad and withdrawn, and I saw you with your heart breaking, and I hoped you might help each other.'

'And we did, so your plan worked.' Kitty swallowed past the painful lump that had thickened her throat. 'Why are you telling me this now?'

'Because I was hoping you and Adam might end up together after all.'

'A happy ever after?'

He smiled. 'Like in your novels.'

'Real life isn't as neat as fiction, Robert.'

To her horror, a sob began to build up in her chest. In a flash, Robert was round her side of the desk and handing her a handkerchief. He waited until she had herself under control.

'Tell me... I could never work out why Adam was so angry with you. When you and he first met again, in London.'

'He was hurt that I'd married your father so soon after he left.'

'But...he knew you had to escape your father's plans.'

'I never told him the truth. I was too ashamed that my own father would do such a thing and I didn't want Adam to take me out of pity. So I just begged him to take me— he'd said he loved me and I thought, naively, that would be enough. And when, on that last day, I tried to tell him why, he wouldn't listen. He didn't want to know. He said it would make no difference, our positions in society were too far apart and I would be ruined. As if I cared for that.'

'And why has he gone now? What happened? I've seen the way you look at each other... I've felt the tension in the air whenever you are together...what went wrong?'

She had no pride left to lose. Robert, it seemed, already knew her heart was breaking, as it had fifteen years ago. What was a bit more humiliation? So she told him.

'He proposed to you and you refused? In the name of God, why?'

'I cannot leave you and Charis.'

'Nonsense! You have raised us all selflessly. It is time to put your own happiness first. Charis will be quite happy home here with me and it is not as though you would be far away at Kelridge Place, is it?'

A thought occurred to Kitty. '*Are* you looking for a wife, Rob?'

'Ah.' He had the grace to blush. 'No. That was a bit of subterfuge to bring you and Adam together.' He scowled at her. 'Without success as it turns out.'

'So I have no need to worry about you and Lady Phoebe Crawshaw?'

'Lady *Phoebe*?' Robert shouted with laughter. 'Is that what you feared? As if The Incomparable would look twice at a mere viscount!' He raised his brows at her. 'And do not think to divert me on to the subject of *my* matrimonial plans, Stepmama, for they are non-existent. We've established you cannot use Charis and me as an excuse, so what is now to stop you accepting Adam?'

She really did not want to discuss such personal matters with Robert, but she could see no way out of admitting the truth.

'Adam will want an heir.'

Robert shrugged. 'I should think he will, now he has something worth handing down. What of it?'

Kitty cringed inwardly. 'Have you never wondered why your father and I never had any children, Rob?'

She watched a tide of red rise up his neck to flood his cheeks. 'Er...no. I assumed... I thought, maybe, you did not...that is...'

She took pity on him. 'Your father sired four children in his first marriage. None in his second.'

'And what did Adam say?'

'I did not tell him. It is personal.'

'So he doesn't know the real reason you refused him.' Robert frowned. 'You do realise you are in danger of re-peating history? You are concealing the truth from him, just as you did before, and denying him the chance to make his decision based on the facts.'

Kitty hunched her shoulders as if against a blow. He was right and part of her had known it ever since Adam had stormed away from her up on Fenton Edge.

'Do you love him?'

She nodded, wordlessly.

'And I am certain he loves you. So, is it not *Adam's* deci-sion as to whether having an heir is more important to him than his love for you?'

Kitty slumped, dropping her face into her hands at Rob-ert's accusation.

'He would feel obliged to claim it did not matter,' she mumbled. Then she looked up, 'But it would, Rob. In time. He will want an heir and he will resent being tied to a woman who cannot give him one.'

Robert shook his head, his expression grim. 'Well, I can-not force you to be honest with him and you need not fear I shall interfere any more than I have already but, if you will take my advice, you will tell him the truth. He is a grown man. He is perfectly able to understand the implications and deserves the chance to decide for himself whether or not he can accept never being a father.'

Kitty's thoughts whirled, seeing her dilemma more clearly after hearing Robert's opinion.

If I am honest with Adam...if he understands precisely why I refused him then, even if he decides siring an heir is more important to him, maybe he will accept my offer of an affaire?

At least he might not then disappear back to Scotland because, if he did, how could she bear never seeing again?

'Very well,' she said. 'And thank you for the advice. I shall write to Adam and ask him to meet me. I shall tell him the truth and he can make his decision in possession of all the facts.'

Her heart felt immeasurably lighter as she penned her letter. She sent it to Kelridge Place, via a groom, with the instruction he must hand it direct to Lord Kelridge himself.

Adam found it strange to return to Kelridge Place when neither his uncle nor his cousin were in residence. He felt like an intruder, as though he could be challenged at any moment and thrown out, and it was an effort to portray a confidence he did not feel in front of the servants. As a distraction from Kitty's rejection, he immediately settled down to educate himself about the management of the estate. By one o'clock in the afternoon, however, his eyes were already sore from deciphering Carter's miniscule letters and numbers in the stock records and ledgers, and his notebook was full of questions to which he needed answers. He sent for Joseph Carter.

While he waited, Adam leaned back in his chair and rubbed his eyes, for the first time allowing himself to properly think about what Kitty had said and, more importantly, *why* she had refused his offer of marriage. No matter what words came out of her mouth, he knew—viscerally and wholeheartedly—that she loved him. Some women might fake their responses during intimacies such as they had en-joyed, but not Kitty. She was too honest.

Yesterday…his anger and pain had roiled inside him, threatening to erupt, and he'd acted on instinct with the des-perate need to get away from Kitty amid all those churning emotions…the need to give himself time to calm down and to recover his pride. Such a volatile situation demanded si-lence, yet accusations had been clambering over one another in his head, battling to be spoken out loud. All he'd been ca-pable of thinking was what a fool he had been to believe he and Kitty could ever truly put the past behind them. There was too much past hurt and he'd been convinced she would never forgive him for abandoning her, no matter how good his motives at the time.

Now, though…the question still remained unanswered. Why in God's name would a respectable widow like Kitty be prepared to be his lover, but not his wife? It made no sense.

He propped his elbows on the desk and dropped his face into his hands.

I will put this right. Somehow.

But he had no idea how.

He straightened up at a knock on the door. 'Come in.'

'You sent for me, my lord?' Carter waited just inside the door.

'Ah. Yes. Good afternoon, Carter. Do sit down.' Adam wrenched his thoughts back to estate matters and ledgers. 'I have several questions about the estate records and, from what Mr Trewin said, I understand you have been keeping the books for the past several years?'

The steward's brow puckered. 'Is there aught amiss, my lord?' His defensive tone caught Adam's interest and he studied the man opposite, who avoided making eye contact but sat back and folded his arms across his chest. 'I do my utmost to ensure accurate records are kept, I can assure you. Neither your father nor Mr Trewin ever found reason to complain about my work.'

'This is not a complaint, Carter.' Adam spoke calmly. There was no point in antagonising the steward if there was indeed anything wrong with the books. But his interest was piqued and he determined to examine them with even more thoroughness as soon as Carter left. 'I merely require clarification upon a few points as I am unfamiliar with the running of an estate.'

Carter visibly relaxed. 'Of course, it must be difficult for you to decipher such records, my lord, being as you are unused to country matters and to estate business. I shall be glad to answer any questions you might have.'

'Thank you. Now…first…crop yields. Wheat, barley and oats are, I think, all grown here?'

'They are.'

'As I know nothing about yields, I looked back over the records for the past five years.' Carter's expression stayed open. Unconcerned.

Perhaps I am wrong?

Adam ploughed on. 'Even non-country folk like myself were aware of the disastrous harvest in 1816 and that it was hardly better in 1817.' The entire country had suffered through a summer when the sun simply did not shine— all the result of a volcano that erupted the year before on the other side of the world, so it was said. There had been widespread failure of crops up and down the country, and much starvation as the price of corn rocketed. 'And yet…' Adam indicated the notebook where the crop yields were recorded, then swivelled it around to face Carter '...the last three years' yields at Kelridge Place are barely better than they were in 1817. I found that strange.'

'Our yields in '16 and '17 did not drop as much as they did elsewhere so they would not show as much recovery, would they?'

'Where are the records for the years prior to 1816?'

'They are in my room, my lord.'

'Will you please fetch them?'

'It may take some time to lay my hands on them. Were there any other queries first? In case I need to look out more old records for you.'

'Very well. Yes. I have a question about stock numbers. There is an anomaly in the record of sheep numbers at the start of the year, the number of lambs born and the current flock size. What is the explanation for that?'

'Sheep die all the time, my lord. They are notorious for it.'

'Deaths are recorded. There is still a difference in numbers.'

'Poachers and thieves, my lord. We lost three just the other day, as I told you when I spoke to you at Fenton Hall.'

'Indeed ye did. Well, I suppose that explains it. What steps have ye taken to protect the flock?'

'I have ordered the men to—'

He broke off at a knock on the door. It opened and Green entered.

'I am sorry to interrupt you, my lord. A groom from Fenton Hall has arrived with a letter and he refuses to leave. He says he is under strict instruction to deliver it direct to you.'

Adam's heart leapt with hope. Kitty. Surely it must be from Kitty. Could she have had a change of heart?

'Please send him in.'

Green's lip curled. 'He is a *groom*, my lord.'

'I do not care if he is the night soil man. Send him in.'

Green bowed and walked ramrod straight from the room. He soon returned, and stood aside for Davey to enter, cap in hand.

'Beg pardon, milord, but milady said most particular that I was to hand it to no one but you.' He slid a defiant glance at Green. 'No one.'

'Thank you, Davey. You may bring it to me.'

With hands that, of a sudden, shook, Adam took the letter and opened it, his gaze quickly picking out Kitty's signature at the end of the brief message.

> *Dear Adam,*
> *I am aware I did not properly explain the reason behind my decision yesterday and would appreciate an opportunity to do so, if you will allow.*
> *I shall be on Fenton Edge at three this afternoon. I hope you will meet me there.*
> *Your friend,*
> *Kitty Fenton*

It did not say she'd changed her mind, but Adam would grab this chance with both hands. Whatever her reason, he would persuade her she was wrong. He must.

He took out his pocket watch. He must make haste. The Edge was a good four miles from Kelridge Place and he must find the best route to the top from this side. He looked at the three men waiting patiently. He grabbed a clean sheet of paper, scribbled a note to Kitty—simply, *I will be there*—and blotted it before folding and sealing. He addressed it to Lady Fenton and held it out to Davey.

'Make sure ye give this to Her Ladyship the minute ye

arrive home, Davey. Thank you.' The boy bowed, then hurried out.

'Green?' The butler bowed. 'Please send word to the stables to saddle a horse for me. I am going out.'

He still didn't know the horses in the stables well enough to have a favourite. That was another matter requiring his attention—it would give him great satisfaction to buy his own horse, and a pair for his curricle, rather than keep using his uncle's pick of animals.

Adam pushed away from his desk and stood. 'I am sorry, Carter. We will have to finish our discussion another time. In the meantime, though, perhaps you can locate that old crop-yield notebook and leave it on my desk?'

Carter had already risen to his feet. He inclined his head. 'Of course, my lord. If I might… I will just check the exact number of that book to ensure I find the correct one.'

'By all means.' Adam gestured at his desk and Carter reached across, moving Kitty's letter aside to find the crop book. 'I will be gone a few hours so I will speak to you again tomorrow.'

They left the study together—Carter back to his work and Adam to the most important meeting of his life, his head full of hope and fear and doubt and dreams.

Chapter Twenty-One

Kitty's stomach fluttered with nerves as she set Herald's head up the long sweeping slope to Fenton Edge. There was no hurry, so she held the horse to a steady trot. She had come early deliberately. Adam had said he would come in the note Davey had brought back from Kelridge Place, so she would get there early and watch his approach—at least until he disappeared into the trees at the base of the Edge. He would have to ride around to the south side before he found a way up and that would give her time to prepare herself and to plan what she wanted to say. Not that she hadn't already planned it, and practised it, *ad infinitum*. But she needed to make sure she missed nothing out. She had all her logical answers ready and must make sure she didn't allow emotion to cloud her judgement. And she would pray that her honesty would tempt him to stay at Kelridge Place where they could at least see one another from time to time.

She would stand firm. She would refuse to be swayed, even though she loved him to distraction and believed that he loved her. And it was because she loved him she must let him go. She would not...could not...trap him in a childless marriage. He would say it did not matter to him, but it did. It should. He had many others relying on him now... his workers, his tenants. It was Adam's duty to sire an heir to take on that responsibility.

She reached the top and dismounted, tethering Herald to the same bush she had used before. She stripped off her riding gloves, removed her hat and unbuttoned her jacket—she had dressed with such care in her best riding dress, with her midnight-blue spencer and matching hat, but now, with the sun still high in the sky and not a breath of wind, she was close to being uncomfortably hot. She hurried across to the edge of the escarpment, eager to catch her first glimpse of Adam.

There he was—and her heart leapt to see him—astride a grey horse, cantering along a track that crossed a field far below. Kitty squinted, trying to make out his expression even though he was clearly still too far away. She estimated he had ridden three of the four miles that separated Kelridge Place from Fenton Edge, which meant she had plenty of time before he joined her, so she sat on the grass and watched his steady progress as she rehearsed her arguments in her head. He disappeared from view as he reached a tree-lined lane that edged the field. Kitty watched, waiting for him to reappear. And waited. She frowned.

Where is he?

He should have turned to his left once out in the lane. After about a quarter of a mile, there was a junction, where he would turn right on to the road that curved around the base of Fenton Edge, bringing him round to the gentler slopes to the west and south. Kitty jumped to her feet, her heart suddenly thundering.

What has happened?

She moved closer to the steep drop, peering down, trying without success to penetrate the canopy of the trees. Then, she spied a movement. Her heart leapt but, within seconds, her stomach lurched, filling her mouth and throat with the sourness of bile. The grey horse was there, yes. But he was tied to the back of a carriage drawn by two brown horses. A man—she could only see the top of his cap, but he was all dressed in black—drove and...she squinted again...she could just make out another figure through the carriage window. Although she couldn't quite make him out, she would swear he was not Adam.

She whirled around and ran for Herald, tore his reins free and mounted, using a nearby rock. She urged him into a canter and sent him careening down the slope, angling him to the left as they descended. He seemed confused, wanting to head for home, but Kitty insisted. As the terrain levelled out, she urged him even faster, bending low over his neck, his mane whipping her face. There was no time for thought. Or to plan. If she was wrong, if for some reason Adam had met friends and accepted a ride in their carriage, then she would laugh at her own stupidity later. Once she knew he was safe. But the image in her head, as she headed for that road that would lead her around to the other side of the Edge, was of Adam, his arm bleeding after he had been shot.

Stupid. Stupid. Stupid. Why did we all so easily dismiss the threat?

Too late to regret it. She thrust aside the pointless recriminations that threatened to engulf her. They would slow her down too much. All she could do now was concentrate on catching that carriage. After that…no point in even thinking about it. She would catch it and then she would do whatever she could.

They reached the road at last and she reined Herald to the north. They did not slow until they reached the junction with the lane the carriage had been on. No sign of anything or anyone. She listened, but heard nothing other than her own heaving breaths. But there was only one direction they could have taken. She set Herald to a ground-eating trot, sitting erect in the saddle, craning her neck to try to see…anything.

Ten minutes later, she slowed. A roadside gate afforded her a view across a paddock and, on the far side, she spied a small, enclosed carriage with a pair of brown horses hitched to it—their steaming coats glistening with sweat—next to a ramshackle wooden-sided barn. The barn stood in a yard behind an abandoned cottage, its thatched roof long caved in and its window glass shattered, which was set back from the road and fronted by a large garden enclosed by stone walls. Kitty could see no sign of the grey horse, or of Adam or the men she had seen earlier.

Kitty slid from Herald's back and tied him to the gate before running along the road until she reached the track that led up to the side of and behind the cottage, only to find the barn and the carriage were now hidden from her sight. A flash of white further along the road caught her attention, however, and she looked in time to see a riderless grey horse disappear from view. Her insides curdled with fear and she looked around her helplessly. She had no weapon. What could she do? She eyed a nearby hedgerow.

A stick? Hopeless. What use a stick against two men? A rock? The broken-down stone wall that edged the cottage's garden would provide plenty, but what would she do with one? Or even a hundred? Never had she felt her own sex and its lack of strength so keenly.

She hesitated at the end of that short track, ideas darting into her head, only to be dismissed almost immediately. Then her nose twitched and she fought a sudden urge to sneeze, squeezing her nose between two fingers, as the creak and rumble of carriage wheels reached her. She jerked her head up in time to see the horses' heads emerge from behind the cottage and, beyond them...her heart bounded into her throat as she took in the lazy spiral of smoke above the cottage roof, rising and spreading in the still, summer air.

Oh, dear God! Adam! Then... *Don't panic! Don't freeze.*

She could do nothing to help if she was seen. A glance up the track confirmed she still had time to hide before the driver spotted her, so she scrambled over the wall and crouched low, her heart beating so loudly she was afraid they would hear it. As the carriage drew level with her, she risked a quick look through a chink between the stones and caught one fleeting glimpse of two men on the box of the carriage. Her blood chilled and her insides turned liquid as she saw they were masked, with mufflers drawn up to cover their lower features. Sick with fear, she realised they would see Herald if they turned back towards Fenton Edge, but luck was on her side. The carriage turned north, away from the Edge and towards the village of Kelworth, beyond which lay Kelridge Place. She risked lifting her head high enough to peer into the carriage window as it passed her by, but there was nothing, and nobody, to be seen.

She didn't bother clambering out into the road again, but

sprinted through the abandoned garden, brambles catching and tearing the skirt of her gown. She reached the cottage and raced around to the back, terrified at what might await her. She skidded to a halt, taking in the three fires spaced out along the base of the front of the barn, including one at the bottom of the big double doors that had been firmly wedged shut by two large poles, one end against each of the doors and the other ends jammed into the dry earth in front of them.

'Adam!' Her scream reverberated and she both longed to hear him answer and dreaded hearing him, still clinging to the hope she had misunderstood everything and that he was even now waiting impatiently for her on top of Fenton Edge.

She started at a loud crack from the far side of the building and peered up to see thicker smoke rising, pluming black above the ridge of the barn roof. The sight jolted her into action and she fell to her knees, scrabbling at the bare dry earth in front of the doors and throwing it on the fire set there. It took time…too much time…to smother it. The other two fires had taken hold of the tinder-dry grass and brambles that grew right up to the side of the barn. There was no dry earth close by either fire and a quick scan of the yard revealed no shovel to help her douse them in time to stop the flames that even now licked up the side of the barn.

She leapt to her feet and lunged at the nearest pole, tugging at it for all she was worth, but it was wedged too tightly and wouldn't budge. Sobbing with frustration, she tried the other pole but, like the first, it was wedged solidly into the earth. Then, with a flash of inspiration, she moved to stand underneath it, allowing her to push it upright instead of trying to pull it. She shoved at it with all her might until the top end lifted away from the barn door. She didn't have the strength to topple it right over, but she had loosened it sufficiently for it to slip sideways down the barn door until the entire pole lay on the ground. Grunting with the effort, Kitty rolled it, bit by bit, until she could open the door wide enough to slip inside the barn.

Smoke had fingered its way inside, roiling and curling up to the roof and escaping through the many gaps in the tiles. It immediately caught in Kitty's lungs and she coughed, her eyes smarting. Remembering Edgar's nightmares about his frantic, futile efforts to save his first wife from the blazing wing at the Hall, and the things he blamed himself for not knowing—that he should have covered his nose and mouth, he should have kept close to the floor where the air would stay clearer of smoke—Kitty dropped to her knees and screamed Adam's name again.

She ripped off her spencer and held it to her nose and mouth, her eyes darting all around the dim interior of the barn. She could see further, down here at floor level, and she could see a man, lying on his side. Unmoving.

'Adam?'

A pathetic, choking sob, muffled by her jacket. She crawled to the huddled figure, grabbed its shoulder and heaved with all her might until it toppled over on to its back. He groaned and his arm flailed.

Oh, thank God!

Sobs of relief swelled her chest and choked her throat, but there was no time for emotion. If they were to get out of the barn, she must rouse Adam. Somehow. A glance overhead confirmed the flames had not yet reached the roof beams, but it was surely only a matter of time.

She shook Adam. He groaned again, his eyes screwed shut. She put her lips to his ear.

'Adam.' She fought to keep her voice steady and low, but the tremor was there nevertheless. 'It's Kitty. You have to help me. I can't move you by myself.' She slipped her hand behind his head, feeling the sticky warmth of blood. 'Adam.' It was an effort not to scream at him...shriek at him to *wake up*...but she needed him to come back to her, not to retreat back into oblivion, driven away by shrill pleas that would serve no purpose. 'Come. You can do this. Adam... I love you. I cannot *bear* to lose you again.'

A sob broke free. She grabbed his shoulders and shook him. *'Please...'*

She was sure he was coming around. His breathing was erratic, his forehead puckered and his eyes were still screwed shut. If he were unconscious, surely all his muscles would be limp? She didn't really know, but she took them as good signs. She twisted to look at the door. So near. When she again glanced up at the roof a thrill of fear leapt through her as she spied flames licking along the heavy beams.

She scrambled to her feet. She grabbed Adam's hands, stretching his arms over his head, straight out behind him. She leaned back and pulled with all her might. He didn't budge. Worse, he snatched his hands from hers and she was powerless to stop him. But that must mean he had some idea of what was happening to him.

'Adam Monroe!' she bellowed at him before bending double as she was seized by a paroxysm of coughing. She dropped again to her knees by his head. 'Fire! Fire! Fire!'

He stirred, mumbling.

'Move, Adam. Fire! You have to move because, as God is my witness, I will *not* leave you. If you choose to stay here and burn, then I will burn right alongside you.' She cradled his face and lowered her mouth to his, kissing him. 'I *love* you, Adam. Help me. We can only do this together.'

One eye slitted open and his hand went to his head. 'Hurts,' he whispered.

She shook him again. 'It will be better soon. We have to get you—'

Again, she was overtaken by a spasm of coughs, but she saw Adam's other eye open and a look of horror suffuse his features as his gaze swept their surroundings. She put her lips to his ear.

'Adam. If you do not help me, we will both die.'

She didn't waste her breath with more words. She shuffled around on her knees and thrust her arm behind his neck, straining to lift him into a sitting position. His groan was almost smothered by the crackle of flames. She glanced behind them again. The doors were still untouched by the fire, but for how much longer?

'Adam! Stay awake! When I pull you *must* help me.'

She scrambled to her feet and stood behind him, then stooped to push her hands under his armpits.

'Bend your knees. When I pull you must dig your heels into the floor and push with your legs.'

His head was still upright, so he was awake. She prayed he was aware enough to understand what she wanted him to do.

'*Now!*' She pulled back and could have sobbed when she saw him bend his knees up, just a little, and then straighten his legs, using his feet to shuffle himself backwards.

'Again!'

Little by little, they neared the door.

'Hie! Is there anyone in there?'

Her blood turned to ice, despite the heat that had slowly

built inside the barn. The sweat trickling down her back raised gooseflesh and she shivered. Those men. Had they come back? She didn't even have a clue what they looked like. Then an ominous, low roar grabbed her attention and, with horror, she saw the main roof beam engulfed in fire— the flames almost alive as they danced across the inner surface of the roof, greedy and gleeful as they hunted more fuel.

She had no choice. 'Help!' It was barely a croak. She took the two steps to the door and thrust her arm out, waving frantically. She could have gone outside, but she would not leave Adam. The air was fresher there, however, and she filled her lungs, which just made her cough even more. She crouched down, waiting for the fit to pass. Then tried again. 'Help!' This time, it emerged as a shriek. She waved again, then returned to Adam, who was again flat on his back.

'Push with your feet or, heaven help me, I will *never* speak to you ever again,' she growled into his ear.

He moaned, but he did as she demanded, and they continued to inch towards the door.

Then everything happened with a whoosh. Literally. As the doors were flung open, the fire leapt with life, the walls all around the barn alive with flames. Strong hands grabbed Adam, and Kitty found herself swung up into the arms of someone who ran out of the barn, cradling her. Dazed, she stared over his shoulder at the burning barn and she winced as, with a loud crack, the roof caved in. Tears leaked from her eyes. She raised them to her rescuer's face.

Grenville Trewin.

She gasped and the energy she had lacked a moment ago now surged through her. She struggled.

'You! Let go of me! Put me down!'

Chapter Twenty-Two

'Steady, Lady Fenton. You are safe. Stop struggling or I'll drop you. We need to get you away from the barn.'

Pain racked Kitty's chest, her lungs burning and throat burning as she was seized by another bout of coughing. That surge of energy had drained away, leaving her limp and close to tears. Mr Trewin carried her from the yard and then lowered her to a grass verge, a rough stone wall at her back. In front of her was the track that led to that abandoned cottage and on that track stood a carriage. Fear flooded her. They'd come back to make sure Adam was dead.

'Where's Adam?'

'Safe. Tolly has him.'

'But you…'

She put her hand to her chest, pressing, incapable of more words. Her breathing was shallow and fast, but she willed herself not to pass out. Not until she knew for certain Adam was safe. Mr Trewin went to the carriage and rummaged about inside, emerging with a water canteen such as soldiers carry.

'Here. Drink this.' Mr Trewin held the flask to her lips. 'Lucky I always carry water,' he said. 'A result of all my years on campaign…water can mean the difference between life and death.'

Water had never tasted so sweet. Kitty gulped it and promptly brought it back up.

'Sorry.'

'Do not worry about it. Just sip this time.'

She did.

'Better?'

She nodded.

'Shout if you need anything. I'll not be long.'

Mr Trewin stood up and walked away. Kitty grabbed the opportunity to look around. She could see Adam, lying on the ground, through the legs of men clustered around him. She frowned. Where had they come from? What was Grenville Trewin doing here? He was supposed to be in London, as was Tolly, who she could see barking orders at men who had formed a line between the barn and a well. She ought to object…she ought to warn somebody that Mr Trewin had tried to kill Adam…she ought to…

Her roving gaze stilled at the carriage that Grenville Trewin had, without doubt, arrived in, as it had the Kelridge crest upon the door. It looked…big. Her eyes travelled slowly to the horses. Four, not two. Black, not brown.

Tears welled again, this time of relief.

This time, when Adam woke up, his brain felt…clearer. More normal. He was able to string thoughts together to make some sense. He was only vaguely aware of other times he had surfaced...people tending to him. Urging him to drink. His eyelids so heavy...

But, this time...his thoughts froze. Kitty. His nightmare...she had been there right alongside him. Burning...

Gritting his teeth, he levered himself up on his elbows. 'Adam.'

She was there, cool hand on his forehead. Smiling. He flopped back to his pillow, and pain shafted through him. He raised his hand to his head and fingered the bandages. His eyes sought hers. Grey. Brimming with love. That hope he'd felt when he rode to meet her...

'Masked,' he muttered.

'Don't worry about that now. It is all under control. Your uncle—'

'Not uncle. Voices...'

'No, it was not your uncle,' she soothed. 'But he has everything under control. We'll talk about it when you feel a bit better. Sleep for now.'

She brushed his forehead with warm, soft lips and Adam closed his eyes, calmed by her presence. Her words echoed in his memory: *I love you. I cannot bear to lose you again.* He forced one eye open and sought her beloved face.

'D'ye really love me?'

Cool fingers caressed his cheek. 'I do.'

Now he could sleep.

Kitty was still there when he woke again. She helped him to sit up and to drink some water.

'There is someone to see you,' she said and Adam's gaze moved past her to the end of the bed.

'Tolly.' His voice still rasped in his throat and he sipped more water. 'You here?'

Tolly moved around the bed, to the opposite side from Kitty.

'I am,' he said. 'And happy you are on the way to recovery.'

Adam frowned as hazy images jostled each other in his head, his recollection of the day before still muddled. He only had a vague memory of what happened after a masked man had tackled him from his horse and he'd been knocked out by a blow to the head. But he did remember Kitty's sweet voice in his ear telling him she loved him and threatening to stay there and burn with him if he did not help her get him out of the barn. And his own pathetic efforts to help—pushing with legs as weak as a baby's.

Horror filled him at what she had risked. For him. He reached out, groping for her hand, and gripped it when she put it in his.

'Ye put yourself in danger, Kitty. Ye saved me. How can I ever thank ye?'

Kitty shook her head as she perched on the edge of the mattress. 'It was Tolly who saved you, not I. He saved us both.'

'You are far too modest, my lady,' said Tolly. 'Adam... believe me when I say that without Lady Fenton, you would not be here now. Had you been further from the door when we arrived, we would not have had time to get *either* of you out. She'd managed to coax you to move until you were both right by the door, even though you were barely conscious. My father grabbed Her Ladyship and I managed to drag you clear just before the roof collapsed.'

Adam raised Kitty's hand to his lips and pressed a kiss to

her soft, sweet-smelling skin. 'Thank ye.' Her warm smile enveloped him. He tore his gaze from hers to focus on Tolly. 'How did you and my uncle come to be at the barn? I thought you were gone to Brighton.'

'We hadn't left London when we heard the news you'd been shot.' Tolly looked grim. 'Father worried one of us might be thought responsible, so we came straight home.'

'Who told you about the shooting?'

'It was Lord Datchworth,' Kitty said. 'You haven't met him, of course, but he is Lady Datchworth's son.'

'And how did Datchworth know?'

Kitty huffed a laugh. 'Robert did, if you remember. He met Lord Datchworth on the London road after making his enquiries at the tollgates.'

'Ah. Yes. That.' Adam felt his face burn. 'Sorry, Tolly... but we had to be sure it couldn't be either my uncle or you.'

Tolly shrugged. 'I'd have done the same. We were the most likely suspects, I can see that.'

'Anyway,' Kitty continued, 'Robert asked His Lordship if he'd noticed any increase in poaching and told him about you being shot so, when he met Tolly in town, he told him.'

'And we headed for home right away,' Tolly said. 'And, as we passed the cottage, we saw the smoke. We might not have thought much of it, but I'd noticed a horse tethered to a gate we'd just passed and so we decided to investigate. And, of course, as the smoke rose higher, it was visible from the village, so other helpers soon arrived.'

'And ye got us both out in time.' This time, Adam reached for Tolly's hand and gripped it. Hard. 'I canna thank you enough. You *and* my uncle.'

'Nor I,' said Kitty.

'So...did ye find out who attacked me? And why?'

'Oh, yes. We found out almost immediately,' said Tolly. 'It was Carter and Eddings.'

Adam sat bolt upright. *'Carter?* The steward?'

'Yep. And we caught them red-handed, thanks to Lady Fenton here,' said Tolly. 'If she hadn't remembered the details of the carriage, and the pair that drew it, I'm not sure we'd have found the evidence we needed to implicate them.'

'I was petrified when your uncle carried me out of the barn,' Kitty said, 'and I was convinced that he and Tolly were the masked men I'd seen for, otherwise, why were they there when they were meant to be in London? And they had a carriage…but when I calmed down a little, I realised the carriage was bigger than the one I'd seen earlier, and it was drawn by a team, not a pair. So, I soon realised your uncle and Tolly hadn't been involved and so I told them all I knew. Your uncle suspected right away that the brown pair of horses I'd seen were Kelridge horses.'

'We went to the stables immediately,' Tolly continued, 'and sure enough, there were the horses, which had clearly been worked. One of the grooms confirmed that Carter and Eddings had taken the small carriage out and had only recently returned.'

Adam shook his head, aghast to discover Carter's villainy. 'Where does Eddings fit in?'

'He is the brother of Carter's wife,' said Tolly. 'It transpires that Carter has been stealing from the estate for years by falsifying the accounts. The abduction was a last desperate attempt to stop you uncovering the truth. All three of them have been benefitting from the extra money Carter swindled and Eddings helped by reporting livestock deaths and thefts that never actually happened. Father is mortified he never noticed what was going on and that he allowed

Carter such freedom in keeping the estate books. He thought he could trust him.'

'I had found some irregularities in the record books,' said Adam, 'but I had not even begun to imagine that anyone was deliberately falsifying the entries. Poor Uncle Grenville. But I can hardly blame him…he really *does* have no head for figures. At first, I thought he was deliberately trying to confuse me when he answered my questions so inconsistently, but I believe he genuinely does mix numbers up. No wonder he left the bookkeeping to Carter.'

'That is true,' Tolly said. 'He has always been the same… absolutely no head for numbers. But he does have his uses… he was so furious about all this that he…er…*persuaded* Carter to admit to everything before the constable came to arrest him.'

'Yes,' said Kitty. 'He admitted it was he who shot at you that day at Fenton Hall. He had ridden over to deliver Tolly's letter—choosing to do so himself in case he saw an opportunity to kill you…' her voice hitched and she swallowed before continuing '…and then, when his shot failed, he returned to Kelridge Place, taking the letter with him, knowing you might be suspicious if he turned up that same afternoon.'

'So…' Adam frowned. 'Was that story about the poachers and the three sheep even true?'

'No. He concocted it to divert us all from believing someone was targeting you. And he succeeded.' Kitty stroked Adam's hand.

'He got the idea of killing you after your horse threw you when you first arrived at Kelridge Place,' said Tolly.

'So that incident was not down to him?'

'No.'

Adam shook his head again. 'Well, at least they are safely locked up now and can do no more harm. I guess I shall have to start looking for a new steward.'

'Not right away, though, Coz,' said Tolly. 'You look done in. I'll leave you in peace.'

He squeezed Adam's shoulder and left the room. Adam leaned his head back and closed his eyes. What a sorry tale... He forced his eyes open and looked at Kitty, clad in a soft green gown, drinking in her lush curves and her beautiful face with her clear grey eyes and pink, full lips. How he loved her...

'Here,' she whispered, 'allow me to help you lie down.'

With her help he wriggled down into the bed. She adjusted his pillows and pulled the covers up as exhaustion rolled over him and his eyelids drooped.

'Kitty...we need to talk...' It took great effort to get his words out.

'Hush.' Kitty soothed his forehead. 'Sleep now. I will still be here when you wake and we will talk then.'

The next time Adam roused it was morning and she was still there, in the chair by his bed, her eyes closed, her long dark lashes a crescent on her cheeks. Her chest rose and fell gently as she breathed peacefully. He watched her silently, all the while taking stock of how he felt after his ordeal. He was pleased to find his headache had all but gone, his throat no longer felt scratchy when he swallowed and his mind felt as sharp as before.

Adam's heart swelled with contentment. All was right with his world.

Well. Nearly all.

'Kitty.'

Her eyes snapped open, as though she had not been sleeping, merely resting. She reached out to feel his forehead and smiled. A smile so full of love his pulse raced and his spirits dance with joy.

'How do you feel?'

'I feel fine.' He pushed himself into a sitting position and began to swing his legs from the bed.

'No.' Kitty grabbed his shoulders, preventing him from rising. 'You must not...the doctor said you must rest.'

But Adam was in no mood for more sleep.

'I wish tae get up. I have been confined to this bed for days,' he grumbled.

Kitty shook her head. 'You have not. You are exaggerating. The fire was just two days ago, and it is only ten o'clock in the morning now.'

Adam scowled. 'We need to talk, Kitty, and it is not a talk I wish to have while lying in bed. I want tae get up and I want tae get dressed. I have waited two days to hear why you refused me and I willna wait any longer.'

He recalled all too clearly his stomach roiling with a mix of conflicting emotions as he rode to meet her: doubts and hopes; fear and joy. She'd told him in the barn, time after time, that she loved him, but did that mean their problems were resolved and that she would agree to marry him?

'I need to understand, Kitty. I need to know. I cannae rest with these vexatious questions nipping at me.'

She bit into her bottom lip, and desire surged through him. That decided him—if he was well enough to want to drag her into the bed and kiss her senseless, he was damned well fit enough to get dressed and sit in a chair to talk. He threw back the bedcovers.

'Ye have two choices, Kitty, my love. Ye can wait there

and watch me while I wash and dress myself, or ye can ring the bell for Corbett to come and help me and then ye can wait downstairs.'

Wordlessly, Kitty went to pull the bell. 'I shall await you in the drawing room.' She stuck her nose in the air—making Adam grin—and then she left the room.

Corbett—Uncle Grenville's valet, who had been attending to Adam's needs while he was confined to bed—had soon appeared and helped Adam with his ablutions before assisting him to dress. By the time Adam was fully clothed he felt more human, and more than ready to discuss their future with Kitty. Apart from a slight tenderness from the bump on his head, he appeared to be suffering no residual effects from the attack.

He went downstairs and to the drawing room where Kitty was sitting, waiting. She watched him through narrowed eyes as he entered the room and crossed to sit in the matching chair to hers.

'I am not an invalid,' he said. 'Ye need not watch my every move.'

'If you say so,' Kitty said, with a sweet smile. 'I ordered a tea tray. Shall I pour you a cup?'

I'd rather something stronger.

He needed fortification, but tea would have to suffice. He could bear no further delays. His gaze grazed over Kitty, finding comfort in her presence as he drank in her creamy skin and her clear grey eyes. Those full, pink lips. The craving to taste them again filled him, but he put it aside for the time.

Kitty had promised him the reason behind her refusal of him and the need to know...the need to understand...

overshadowed any number of cravings for a kiss. She had stayed at Kelridge Place since the fire and, as far as Adam was concerned, she could stay for ever. He could not bear for her not to be here, with him, near him. This was where she belonged, but he was aware that if Kitty had refused his offer of marriage despite loving him as she claimed, her reason must be a powerful one. And this would be his best, and possibly only, chance to persuade her to change her mind.

His nerves wound tight and he hauled in a breath.

'Why did you say no, Kitty?'

Chapter Twenty-Three

Kitty's hand jerked at the suddenness of Adam's question, slopping tea into the saucer of the cup she was pouring. Her gaze snapped to his and she saw a tumult of emotions in his blue eyes: pain; fear; hope. Her heart cracked.

She was the cause of all those feelings. Her main reason for refusing his proposal might have been a selfless one, but at what cost?

There had been several reasons—or maybe they had been excuses—why she had shied away from getting too close to Adam after meeting him again. Some of those reasons had dropped away as time passed and no longer could she fear opening her heart to love again, for it was too late. The barriers she had erected had tumbled. She already loved Adam; her heart was open and vulnerable and already hurting.

But the main reason remained. Insurmountable.

If only she could make him understand how her inability to have a baby would risk blighting their love in the future. She feared he would be reluctant to listen to her reasoning, but she hoped his pain would be less, knowing she refused him out of love.

The silence stretched as tight as Kitty's nerves and, as she handed the teacup and saucer to Adam, her hand was shaking. Adam took the cup and frowned.

'Ye asked to meet me yesterday to tell me the truth as to why ye said no even though ye say ye love me. Please…tell me now. And tell me what I can do to change your mind.'

She rubbed her hands over her cheeks, searching for the words to help him understand.

'Kitty…' Adam put his cup down and slid to the floor, kneeling before her. 'I *love* you.' He cradled her face between his hands. His blue eyes pierced her, searching. 'I have loved you for fifteen long years… I fell in love with ye then and I have loved you ever since. Ye know now that I only denied my love for you to stop ye throwing yourself away on an architect's apprentice, fearing that, in time, ye'd grow to resent being tied to a man of my lowly status.'

Kitty laid her hand over his as it cupped her cheek. His words had struck a chord with her. It was the same message she had been telling herself…the same reason she had refused his offer of marriage without explanation…the fear that, in time, he would come to resent being tied to a woman who could not give him a child.

But there would be no magical reprieve for her: Adam had found himself to be the son of an earl; Kitty would still be unable to conceive a child and give him the heir he would need.

'Adam…' She turned her face into his palm and pressed her lips to his warm skin, swallowing past the painful lump that constricted her throat. She had almost lost him yesterday and now she must risk losing him for good. 'I know you were shocked when I refused to marry you, but was willing to have an *affaire* with you, but I had…*have*…a very good reason for that offer.'

She paused, willing her emotions under control. This reason…this reality of her life…had caused her so much pain in the past and now it was to cost her the man she loved if she could not persuade him to accept her offer.

'Adam, I am barren. I was married to Edgar for ten years without getting with child.'

Adam's dark eyebrows bunched as his eyes searched hers.

'Kitty, ye cannot think that matters to me.' His hands slid from her face to clasp her shoulders. 'I want you as my wife and that is far more important to me than whether we have children. I love you. I want to have ye in my life for ever. Till death us do part.'

She saw by his puzzled expression that he had not appreciated the full implications of her bald confession. She quelled the misery and the pain that the subject cost her, knowing she must make him understand.

'Adam, this is not just about whether or not you become a father. You are now a peer of the realm. You have a duty to secure the lineage of your family and of the earldom, quite apart from your responsibilities to your workers and your tenants. You must at least give yourself a chance to sire an heir.'

Adam's frown deepened. His hands slipped from her shoulders to the arms of her chair, which he used to push himself to his feet. He sat back down on the companion chair, his blue eyes never once straying from her face, while she fought to keep her expression from revealing the full depth of her misery.

'Kitty…my darling…do you really…?' He stopped, and

swiped one hand through his hair, pushing it back from his face. His chest expanded and he shook his head. 'You speak of duty and of responsibility. I think only of love. Of need. Of making my life, and yours, as happy as I can humanly make them. Kitty…my love…a few months ago I had no notion of titles or estates. I did not ask for them. I will go so far as to say I did not *want* them. If not for you…' His voice trembled and he cleared his throat. 'If not for you, Kitty, I should have returned to Scotland within a fortnight and left the lot in my uncle's hands.'

She searched his expression, hope rising despite her best efforts to deny it. Could it be that easy, after all her anguish and heart-searching? Did he really not care who might succeed him? The notion was utterly foreign to her…never had she ever known a nobleman who did not care whether or not he had a son capable of continuing his bloodline.

Adam leaned towards her, reaching out, and she placed her hands in his. With one powerful tug he pulled her across to his lap and wrapped his arms around her waist. He nuzzled her neck, kissing her.

'I never expected any of this, Kitty, and I do not care who might inherit it when I am gone.'

'You cannot mean that, Adam. You—'

He pressed his fingers to her lips. 'I do mean it. Every word of it. I am sorry for your sake you cannot have a child, but you must believe me when I tell you that what is important to me is *you*.'

She shook her head, still trying to deny that swell of hope. 'You do not mean it. You have not thought properly about it.'

He gripped her chin and turned her face to his, capturing her gaze.

'Who is my heir now, Kitty?'

'Your Uncle Grenville.'

'And after him?'

'Tolly.'

'And Tolly…he is a good man, is he not?'

Kitty nodded, that sense of hope burgeoning as she gave up the fight to suppress it.

'Then tell me again why I must sire an heir when there are two good men ready to take on the mantle of the earldom. Although I confess I would rather live long enough to deprive my uncle of that honour.'

'But—'

'But nothing, my sweet. I have no need to think about it. Tolly will make a fine earl—let *him* worry about siring an heir and perpetuating our line. *Our* marriage will be no different to countless other couples who get married every day. They wed, and they face the possibility they may not be blessed with children. It is a gamble. Some married couples produce one child. Some produce a dozen, or even more. But nobody knows, when they make their vows to one another, what their destiny will be.'

Kitty gasped. 'I never thought of it like that.'

Adam kissed her, tiny kisses peppered all over her face.

'I promise you, my dearest love, that is *exactly* how I will view our union—if you will have me. The fate of the title and the estates simply do not feature in my plans for the future.'

Emotion welled up, blurring her vision. So much wasted time. So much pain. Adam gently passed his thumb beneath her eyes, one after the other.

'Don't cry, sweeting,' he whispered. 'Don't cry, or you will have me in tears, too.'

Her throat ached as she summoned up a smile. 'A big brave man like you, in tears?' she teased.

'I am brave enough to admit I have cried,' he whispered, his voice raw. 'I cried when I left ye fifteen years ago and I cried when ye turned me down.'

His fingers curled around her scalp, urging her face to his. She opened her mouth as his lips covered hers, pouring every ounce of her love for him into her kiss.

Too soon, he pulled back and captured her gaze again.

'Kitty...' His eyes glowed with love, tinged with uncertainty. 'Will ye *please* put me out of my misery? Please say ye will have me. Say ye will marry me.'

Her heart bloomed with love for him.

'Oh, yes, my darling Adam. Yes, I will marry you.'

The doubts that had plagued Adam ever since they met again vanished and he finally...*finally*...could allow himself to believe in a happy ever after for him and for Kitty. He seized her lips in a searing kiss that lasted a long time. A *very* long time.

When he eventually drew back, he tipped his head to one side. 'Will I have to ask Robert his permission?'

Kitty gave him a puzzled smile, then laughed. 'He is my step*son*, not my step*father*,' she said, giving his shoulder a light slap. 'Of course we do not need his permission, as you well know. Besides...he already knows, more or less.'

She told him how Robert had followed Adam into the woods and seen their trysts. Adam laughed.

'I suppose we must be grateful we did nothing more scandalous than kiss in those days. I should hate to have corrupted such a young lad.'

He took her lips in another long, dreamy kiss. This time it

was Kitty who ended it, leaning back against his encircling arms to search his face with suddenly serious grey eyes.

'You will still permit me to write my novels, Adam? My new one is almost complete now and I have had the most splendid idea for an exciting finish.'

He shook his head, then concealed his smile at her suddenly crestfallen expression.

'Kitty...you goose! I will not permit you because you do not—and will never—need my permission for anything you wish to do. Unless, of course, ye decide to run inside a burning building again. For that, my dearest love, ye will *never* have my permission. No more heroics. Are we quite clear about that?'

'Crystal clear, my darling.'

She kissed him, her smooth lips caressing his as the tip of her tongue teased his mouth to open. He needed little encouragement, tightening his arms around her waist again as he tasted her sweetness. Then she straightened.

'But,' she said, 'the fire *was* a valuable experience. Just think how real it will be when I write it—it will be truly authentic.'

'Authen—? *Kitty!* Is *that* the exciting ending you have planned?'

'Well...' She hung her head, then peeped at him from the corner of her eye. Adam bit back a laugh, keeping a frown on his face.

'But, Adam, my darling...it will be truly marvellous. The heroine rescues the hero, who then realises how very much he loves her and—'

'But I already knew how much I loved you. It was *you* who was hiding her true feelings.'

Kitty waved a hand dismissively. 'Details,' she said. 'I

am sure my readers will prefer the hero to be the one who refuses to submit to his true feelings.'

He couldn't help it. He laughed.

Trust his Kitty. And, at last, *this* was the Kitty he remembered.

* * * * *

THE RAGS-TO-RICHES GOVERNESS

Lady Tregowan's Will

An unexpected inheritance. A year to wed.

When Lady Tregowan dies, she leaves an unexpected will. Her estate is to be divided between the three illegitimate, penniless daughters of her late husband—complete strangers until now. The terms? They must live together in London for a year and find themselves husbands or forfeit their inheritance!

The Rags-to-Riches Governess

Available now

And coming soon from Janice Preston:

The Cinderella Heiress

Beatrice Fothergill is determined to make a marriage of convenience on her own terms—she doesn't expect to fall for her suitor's brother!

The Penniless Debutante

Left destitute when her parents die, Aurelia Croome doesn't trust men—especially aristocratic ones. Until she meets James, Lord Tregowan...

Author Note

Sometimes an idea comes to you as a writer and you dismiss it as too complicated to write. And so it was with Lady Tregowan's Will. I loved the idea of three young women—all strangers and down on their luck—who inherit a share in a fortune out of the blue, and who discover at the same time that they are half sisters. But I couldn't quite see how it would work, given that—inevitably—the three women's stories would be closely intertwined.

But the idea wouldn't go away, and so I explored how I could make it work without too many overlaps, given that each book must be able to be read as a stand-alone story. And I'm pleased I persevered, as I've thoroughly enjoyed writing this first book in the trilogy, all the while with one eye on the other two stories to come.

I hope you'll enjoy this first part of the trilogy as governess Leah earns her happy-ever-after with Lord Dolphinstone. Watch out for Beatrice's story next (*The Cinderella Heiress*) followed by Aurelia's tale (*The Penniless Debutante*).

With grateful thanks to my good friends and
fellow authors Lynn Forth and Elizabeth Hanbury,
who gave up a morning of their time to
brainstorm the Lady Tregowan's Will trilogy.

Chapter One

Miss Leah Thame stepped down from the post-chaise sent to convey her from Dolphin Court on the Somerset coast into the centre of Bristol and peered up at the office of Henshaw and Dent. The letter she'd received two days ago had been most insistent she attend a meeting here today, hinting she would miss out on the opportunity of a lifetime if she ignored its summons. Leah did not entirely believe in the idea that good fortune might strike one out of the blue, but even she, with her practical nature, could not quite bring herself to ignore the possibility of good news.

She surveyed the building in front of her—no different from the neighbouring houses in this terrace, except for the brass wall plaque next to the door—and bit her lip. Henshaw and Dent, Solicitors. Her hand slipped inside her cloak and she traced the shape of Mama's wedding ring, which she always wore suspended from a ribbon around her neck. Normally it remained hidden beneath the serviceable brown or grey gowns she wore day-to-day in her post as a governess at Dolphin Court, but today both ribbon and ring were on display, adding a touch of decoration to her old royal-blue carriage gown.

She rummaged in her reticule for Papa's pocket watch and opened the cover. Twelve minutes still to noon, the time of her appointment. It had been fifteen years since Mama's death and seven since Papa's, but the ring and the watch still conjured their memories and left Leah feeling slightly less alone in this world. A sudden, craven impulse to flee was quashed. She had come this far and, besides, she must rely upon Mr Henshaw for her transport home to Dolphin Court, for she had little money of her own to squander upon luxuries such as the hire of a post-chaise-and-four.

The clip-clop of hooves and the rattle of a carriage down the street behind her shook her from her thoughts, and she shivered as the brisk chill of the air on this, the last day of January, fingered beneath her cloak. It was time to find out why she had been summoned; she set her jaw, straightened her shoulders and rapped on the door.

'Miss Leah Thame,' she said to the sallow-faced, stooped clerk who opened it. 'I have been summoned to a meeting with Mr Arthur Henshaw at noon.'

'Follow me, miss.'

Leah stepped past the clerk, who closed the door, plunging the hallway into gloom. The building smelled of damp and dust, and her throat itched as she followed the clerk up a steep flight of stairs to the first floor. He knocked on a door and waited. Not once did he look at her or catch her eye, and although she was not a nervous type of woman— governesses could not indulge themselves in a surfeit of sensibility—Leah nevertheless identified the subtle tightening of her stomach muscles as being caused by unease.

'Enter.'

The clerk flung open the door and gestured for Leah to enter.

'Miss Thame, sir.' The door clicked shut behind her.

The office was lined with shelves crammed with books. A fire smouldered sullenly in the fireplace, emitting little warmth, and an ornate bracket clock sat on the mantel shelf above. Seated at the far side of a large mahogany desk was a middle-aged, bespectacled man with a receding hairline, who now rose to his feet and rounded the desk to bow.

'Arthur Henshaw, at your service, Miss Thame. May I take your cloak?'

Leah removed it, and he hung it on a coat stand in the corner of the room.

'Please, take a seat.' He indicated a row of three wooden chairs facing the desk. 'I am sure the others will arrive very soon.'

Leah frowned. 'Others?'

'All will soon be revealed.'

Henshaw returned to his chair at the far side of the desk, which was bare apart from a low stack of legal-looking documents, a silver and cut-glass inkstand and a silver wax jack, and immediately selected one of the documents and began to read, his high, narrow forehead furrowing. Leah chose the middle of the three chairs and sat down. The ticking of the clock was loud in the silence.

Her thoughts touched upon her employer, the Earl of Dolphinstone, and the news he was back in England after more than sixteen months away. He was expected back in Somerset soon—although he had not yet confirmed the date of his arrival—and Leah quailed as she imagined his reaction if he were to discover she had left his two young sons in the care of the local vicar's daughter, even though this was the first time she had left them, despite being entitled to one day off per month.

Leah adored both her job and her charges, but she was apprehensive about His Lordship's return. Since being forced to earn her living as a governess—following her father's death when she was nineteen—this was the first time she had felt settled, happy and at home. She couldn't help but worry her employer's return would herald change.

A mental image of His Lordship—appealingly masculine and ruggedly handsome—materialised in her mind's eye. She had met him just the once, at her interview for the post of governess, and he had seemed harsh and remote but she'd made allowances at the time, knowing he had been recently widowed. By the time she took up her post, however, Lord Dolphinstone had already left for the continent and had been away ever since. For him to leave his children so soon after the death of their mother, and to stay away so long, beggared belief, and she still struggled to understand such a lack of fatherly concern. Leah had since done everything in her power to give the boys the stability they needed.

The clock suddenly chimed the hour, jolting Leah from her worries about the Earl's return. Henshaw looked expectantly at the door. Within seconds, a knock sounded.

'Enter.'

'Miss Fothergill, sir.'

Henshaw, once again, rounded the desk and greeted the newcomer before taking her coat. Leah fought the urge to peer over her shoulder at Miss Fothergill—she would see the other woman when Henshaw introduced them. The newcomer sat to Leah's right, but Henshaw remained out of sight behind them, tapping his foot on the polished floorboards and emitting the occasional sigh rather than perform any introduction.

Leah succumbed to her curiosity and glanced sideways. Miss Fothergill's eyes were downcast as she chewed her bottom lip. Light brown curls peeped from beneath her brown bonnet and her fingers fidgeted in her lap, prompting the governess in Leah to want to reach out and cover her hand to conceal both her restlessness and her emotions, as befitted a lady.

Before long there was another knock at the door and the previous performance was repeated as someone called Miss Croome arrived. This time, Leah did not look sideways at the newcomer but directed her attention onto the solicitor as he returned to his chair.

'Allow me to make the introductions,' he said. 'Miss Aurelia Croome.'

Leah inclined her head to acknowledge the woman to her left, summing her up with a sweeping glance—petite, and pretty enough, although she looked a little gaunt, as though a square meal wouldn't go amiss. Her dove-grey gown was well made but ill-fitting and shabby, much the same as the bonnet covering her hair, which was fair, if her eyebrows and lashes were any indication.

'Miss Leah Thame.' Leah became the object of attention from the other two women, and she acknowledged each of them with a nod.

'And Miss Beatrice Fothergill.'

Miss Fothergill—also petite and pretty but pleasantly plump—looked nervous, her smile hesitant. That knot of unease inside Leah tightened. Should she be anxious too? She glanced again at Miss Croome, who looked irritated, if anything, and she felt reassured.

'Well,' said Henshaw, leaning back in his chair. 'This is quite unprecedented.'

He removed his spectacles and peered down his nose at each of them in turn, then removed a handkerchief from his pocket and wiped his brow, the only sound in the room the ticking of the clock. Henshaw stuffed his handkerchief back in his pocket.

'Yes.' He shook his head as his gaze once again passed from woman to woman. '*Quite* unprecedented, not to mention perplexing. You ladies must appreciate it has given me a real dilemma as to how best to proceed.'

Miss Croome stirred. 'Perhaps if you enlightened us as to the purpose of this meeting, Mr Henshaw, we might shed some light on your...er...dilemma.'

She was well spoken; clearly a gentlewoman down on her luck.

'Yes. Well...'

The solicitor again paused, and again he fished his handkerchief out of his pocket, polished his spectacles and placed them back on his nose.

'Yes...the terms of the will are quite clear, of course. I just... I simply...' He looked at each woman in turn, his eyes, magnified through the lenses, perplexed. 'Lord Tregowan—the *current* Lord Tregowan—will be unhappy, you may be sure of that. I have written to him again, to clarify matters. Bad tidings for him, but *I* did not draw up *this* will, you understand. I thought I had her latest will and testament—drawn up by me and signed and witnessed three years ago in this very office.'

A will? Leah frowned. She had no family left to lose, unless one counted Papa's Weston connections on his mother's side, and she doubted any of them even knew of her existence. They had never shown the slightest interest in Papa, the connection far too distant. And what did it have to do with Lord Tregowan?

'This…' Mr Henshaw picked up a document, pinching one corner of it between his forefinger and thumb as though it might contaminate him, his nose wrinkling in unconscious distaste '…*this* arrived last week. And yet I cannot refute its authenticity. I'd recognise Her Ladyship's signature anywhere, and it is witnessed by the partners of a legal firm in Bath, although quite why she went to them I have no notion. No. I am afraid it is authentic. There can be no doubt of it.'

The dratted man was talking in riddles.

'*Mis*ter Henshaw. *If* you would be good enough to proceed…?'

'Patience, Miss Thame. Patience.'

Patronising wretch. Leah glared at the solicitor. 'The three of us have been sitting in this office for twelve minutes now, and in my case, considerably longer, and all we have learned is that the reason for this meeting—which *you* arranged, requiring the presence, I presume, of all three of us—meets with your disapproval. I have taken leave from my post to attend here today, and I should appreciate your expedition of the matter in order that I may return to my duties as soon as possible.'

Henshaw straightened, looking affronted. '*Miss* Thame—'

'You spoke of a will, Mr Henshaw?' Miss Croome interjected.

'Indeed, Miss Croome,' the solicitor said. 'The will of Lady Tregowan, late of Falconfield Hall, near Keynsham in the County of Somersetshire.'

Miss Fothergill stirred. 'My…my mother worked at Falconfield Hall.' Her voice quavered, as though it had taken courage to speak. 'She was companion to Lady Tregowan. Before I was born.'

'Quite.' Mr Henshaw levelled a censorious look at each of the three in turn. 'Your mothers each had a connection with Falconfield. And with Lord Tregowan.' His upper lip curled.

Leah elevated her chin. '*My* mother did not work there. She and her parents were neighbours of the Earl and Countess.'

She would not have this shoddy little lawyer look down his nose at her. She might be forced to earn her living as a governess, but her mother—who had died of consumption when Leah was eleven—had been born to the gentry and her father came from aristocratic bloodlines, descended from the Fifth Earl of Baverstock.

Henshaw levelled a disdainful, but pitying look at her. Leah's teeth clenched, her pulse picking up a beat. She looked at Miss Croome, who had yet to react.

'I know of no connection between my mother and Falconfield Hall,' she said, 'but Lady Tregowan did once visit my mother's milliner's shop in Bath.'

Mr Henshaw consulted the will again. 'Miss Aurelia Croome, born October the fourth 1792 to Mr Augustus Croome and Mrs Amelia Croome?'

Pink tinged Miss Croome's cheeks. 'Yes.'

'Then there is no mistake. I am convinced it is the three of you who are to benefit from Her Ladyship's largesse.'

'What is the connection between the three of us?' The other women looked as confused as Leah felt. 'It is clearly through our mothers, but how?'

Henshaw's lip again curled. 'The connection is not through your mother, but through your sire. You are half-sisters.'

Chapter Two

Leah stiffened, staring at Mr Henshaw. 'But...that is not possible. Papa...he would never... He was a man of the Church! He would *never*...'

Words failed her. She did not dare look at either of the other two, although she had heard their gasps at his pronouncement.

Sisters? No! It was impossible.

Mr Henshaw's lips pursed, and Leah's courage surged at his clear disdain for the three of them.

'My father,' she said, enunciating clearly and precisely, 'would *never* have played my mother false.'

'Well, I would believe almost anything of *my* father.' Miss Croome shot a sideways look at Leah. 'And, as for yours, I believe what Mr Henshaw is implying is that Lord Tregowan fathered each of us—presumably, in your case, before your mother married Mr Thame.'

'That is correct,' said Henshaw. 'It was Lord Tregowan who arranged the marriage of each of your parents, once your mothers'…errr…*conditions* were made known to him. And, from what I gather, each marriage was to a gentleman in need of funds, and none of your mothers suffered a lowering in their status after their indecorous behaviour.'

Shock sizzled through Leah. No wonder Henshaw viewed the three of them with condescension. She knew enough about the law, however, to understand that Mama's marriage to Papa before Leah was born meant she was not illegitimate. A shudder racked her at the thought—at least she did not have that stigma to blight her life.

'This…' Miss Fothergill sucked in an audible breath, and when she spoke again, she sounded close to tears. 'If this is true, it changes everything. I do not know what I shall do.' Her distress was palpable and, again, Leah resisted the urge to pat her hand.

'You mentioned the *current* Lord Tregowan earlier,' said Miss Croome. 'Does that mean our father is dead?'

'He died eight years ago, and the title and the Tregowan estates—which were entailed—passed to his heir. Falconfield and the London house were brought to the marriage by Lady Tregowan and he left them to her. He'd fallen out with the current Lord Tregowan's father years before, and so refused to leave his heir any more property than he was forced to under the entail.'

'Have you proof of this?' Every principle she held dear urged Leah to reject the solicitor's words. Her darling mama, fallen from grace? Her beloved papa, not even her true father? Nausea rose to block her throat.

'I have had copies made of Her Ladyship's will, which you may take with you when you leave,' Henshaw said. 'It confirms your paternity.'

'Would you kindly get to the point swiftly, Mr Henshaw?'

Miss Croome's eyes narrowed as she stared at the solicitor. 'Clearly you are unhappy, and I, for one, will be pleased to leave this fusty old office behind. You mentioned bequests, so please say why you have summoned us and be done.'

'Very well. Lady Tregowan of Falconfield Hall has passed away, and it is my duty to advise you that she left the three of you her entire estate, to be divided equally between you, subject to certain conditions.'

Leah froze, barely able to comprehend his words. *Her entire estate?*

Miss Croome leaned forward. 'How much is it worth?'

'It is substantial. It comprises Falconfield Hall and its land, which, as I said, is near to the village of Keynsham on the Bath Road, plus a town house in London, and various funds, the income from which, in the past year, amounted to over fifteen thousand pounds. You are now three very wealthy young ladies.'

Miss Fothergill gasped and swayed in her seat. Leah, still reeling herself, opened her reticule and handed her smelling salts to Miss Fothergill. Beatrice. Her *half-sister*.

Excitement exploded through her. She had family. She would be wealthy. She would no longer have to earn her living as a put-upon governess. Except…as quickly as it had risen, her elation subsided. Her current post was not drudgery—she loved her life at Dolphin Court, and she adored Steven and Nicholas, as well as baby Matilda, and the boys adored and relied upon her in their turn. How could she turn her back on them? The very thought dismayed her.

And what about Papa? Her stomach churned. He wasn't her father. Worse, he had known it. But he had been the best, most loving father she could ever have wished for—to take pleasure in this news of unexpected riches seemed disloyal, almost as though she would be rejecting Papa in favour of a man who had seduced her beloved mama.

A sharp prickling in her nose warned of imminent tears and she surreptitiously pinched the bridge between thumb and forefinger.

Oh, God! I have sisters! How often as a child had she prayed for a sister or a brother, prayers that had gone unanswered? Until now. And, of a sudden, she had two of them. But they were complete strangers. Her mind whirled as violently as her stomach, but she strove to keep her inner turmoil hidden.

Beatrice handed back the smelling salts, smiling shyly. As Leah tucked the bottle back into her reticule she wondered where the other two women lived and if they would ever meet again. That thought triggered another. She frowned.

'You mentioned conditions?'

'Ah. Yes. They are quite straightforward. For a full twelve months from today the three of you will have the joint use of the two properties, and your living expenses will be met out of the income from the funds as mentioned. After that year, providing you have met the further conditions of the will, you will inherit your share of Her Ladyship's estate outright.'

'What further conditions?' Miss Croome... Aurelia... demanded.

'I am getting to that, Miss Croome. The conditions specified in the will are that you will reside in London for the entirety of the coming Season and you will remain under the chaperonage of Mrs Butterby, who was Lady Tregowan's live-in companion, until you marry. After the Season ends you will have the choice of whether to reside in London or at Falconfield Hall, but you must each of you marry within the year.'

'*Marry?*' Miss Croome's upper lip curled. 'Why?'

'As Lady Tregowan failed to consult me in drawing up this final will, I am not privy to her reasoning.' Henshaw's lips thinned. 'I dare say Mrs Butterby will be able to enlighten you.'

Leah raised her brows, exchanging mystified looks with the other two—her half-sisters. 'And if we do not marry within the year?'

'If you fail to wed, Miss Thame, you will forfeit the major portion of your share of the inheritance, which will then be divided between the other two sisters. You will be required to return any purchases made during the twelvemonth period, other than purely personal items such as clothing. So, jewellery, for instance, or carriages, or even houses, will be forfeit. A cottage on the Falconfield estate will be provided for you to live in, and you will receive a lifetime annual allowance of two hundred pounds so you are not left entirely destitute. Plus, there are two final stipulations. If any of you wish to sell your share of Falconfield Hall, the others—or, strictly, their husbands—will get first refusal. And, finally, you must not marry your father's—that is, the late Lord Tregowan's—successor, the current Lord Tregowan, who is a distant cousin.'

Leah frowned at the final condition. The aristocracy were usually keen to keep their land and estates together. 'Why?'

'As I said, Lady Tregowan sought neither my services nor my advice.'

An uneasy silence fell in the room and Leah used the time to attempt to collect her thoughts. Uppermost was the news she would have to marry, but she had long ago dismissed any likelihood of marriage. If she ever wed, she would want...*need*...a marriage like that of her parents: warm, loving, respectful, happy. She would never settle for putting her life and now her fortune—*how strange that sounds*—in the hands of a husband who did not love her. She had seen too many examples of such unions in her time as a governess, and she had no desire to be trapped in such a marriage herself.

She harboured no illusions about her prospects—she was already six-and-twenty, and she saw herself in the mirror every day, with her sharp nose, high cheekbones and pointed chin; her tall, lanky figure; her red hair and freckles. She had learned from bitter experience she was not a woman to stir romantic feelings in any man. The only two men who had ever shown any interest in her had both seen her merely as a means to an end.

Her father's curate, Peter Bennett, had courted her, but she'd learned too late he'd only done so in order to curry favour with Papa. When Papa died and Leah—with no prospects other than having to earn her own living—was forced to vacate the vicarage, Peter quickly revealed his true colours by turning his back on their informal understanding. Instead, he'd immediately set out to win the favour of the new vicar, who possessed two daughters.

And then there had been that dreadful Christmas when she had been working for Lord and Lady Petherton. Their eldest son and heir, Viscount Usk, had come home with two friends for the festive season and had promptly set out to charm Leah. She had been wary and had resisted him until, on Christmas Eve, he had captured her under the mistletoe and pleaded for a kiss. His single-minded pursuit of her had lulled her instincts... She had fallen for his protests that he adored red hair and freckles, and she had allowed the kiss. Even returned it. Whereupon Usk had pushed her aside and crowed to his friends, 'Got her! Told you I'd do it. Five pounds from each of you!'

She would never forget that humiliation, nor the shock of being turned away before the New Year after Usk's parents had learned of that wager. They had been painful lessons, and she had learned to be cautious where gentlemen were concerned. She had little doubt her half-sisters—both of them younger and far prettier than Leah—would have more chance of finding husbands.

'Ahem!' Henshaw broke the silence with a cough, then shuffled through the stack of papers on his desk. He handed one document to each woman. 'As I said, I have had copies made of the will—' he rummaged in his desk drawer and withdrew three small leather pouches '—and here is a purse of money for each of you, to offset any interim expenses before you arrive in London. You will no doubt need a little time to prepare for the change in your circumstances and to leave your old lives in good order, but I would urge you to allow time in London for your new wardrobes to be made before the Season proper begins after Eastertide.'

Leah stowed her copy of the will and the purse in her reticule, her mouth dry as uncertainty flooded her all over again. What would this mean for her future? She'd become accustomed to changes in her life since Papa's death, but each change had become harder and her soul yearned for safety and stability. Her chest squeezed with pain. *Papa.* He wasn't even her real father, but he'd been all that was kind and loving, all that she could have wanted in a father.

'All I require is your signatures to this declaration, confirming you have been advised as to the contents of the will and the conditions attached to your inheritance, and then you may leave,' Henshaw said.

Each woman signed the document in turn and Leah was appalled to find her hand was shaking. Surreptitiously eyeing both Aurelia and Beatrice, she identified signs of their own stress as they avoided making eye contact.

'Three post-chaises will be waiting outside to transport you home,' Henshaw continued. 'You must arrive at the London house—the address is in the will—at the very latest on the day after Easter Sunday, that is, by the fifteenth of April, or your share will be forfeit. Mrs Butterby is already in residence and preparations to accommodate you are under way. Do you have any questions before you leave?'

'I do.' Aurelia's voice faltered, her face bright red. Leah was alarmed to see her eyes sheen with tears. 'Might I… *may* I go to London immediately? Will I be allowed to live in the town house straight away?'

For the first time Leah spotted a glimpse of compassion in Henshaw's expression.

'Yes, Miss Croome, you may.' He scribbled a note. 'Here is a note for Mrs Butterby. Shall you need to return to Bath first?' Aurelia shook her head. 'Then I advise you to travel on the mail coach. It leaves the Bush Tavern on Corn Street at four every afternoon. It is not far from here; I shall send my clerk to purchase a ticket on your behalf and instruct him to dismiss your post-chaise.' He looked at Leah and Beatrice. 'Would either of you care to go immediately to London with Miss Croome?'

'Oh, no! My brother… I will be expected home,' said Beatrice breathlessly.

'No, thank you,' said Leah.

Henshaw crossed to the door and opened it, and she could hear the murmur of voices.

On his return, he said, 'I shall bid you all good day now. Miss Croome, you may wait downstairs in the general office until my clerk returns with your ticket.'

As Henshaw assisted Aurelia with her coat, Leah frowned, realising it made no sense.

'Why would Lady Tregowan concern herself with us?'

'I know nothing more than I have told you, but I dare say Mrs Butterby will provide you with more detail. She was Her Ladyship's companion for the last twenty years or so. I suggest you ask her when you convene at the town house.'

If I go to the town house. I need not accept the terms of the will.

The idea of a London Season—filled with beautiful, elegant young ladies, all vying for a husband—filled Leah with horror.

But two hundred pounds per annum is a substantial sum, and I would have a roof over my head.

True independence, even on a limited income, was enticing. But...how lonely it would be. For that, she would have to leave the boys—the very thought wrenched at her heartstrings and reminded her she must get back to them. Of a sudden, Leah could not wait to be in the solitude of the post-chaise with the chance to get her thoughts in order. She led the way down the dingy staircase and out into the fresh air, where two post-chaises waited at the kerb, each with a post boy stationed by its door. The third vehicle was driving away.

She turned to the other women. Her sisters. And had no idea what to say.

'We cannot discuss this here on the pavement,' Aurelia

said. 'But… I am happy to meet you both. I always wanted a sister.'

Her smile glowed, and Leah could see the potential for beauty, once her skin bloomed with health, her hair shone and her face filled out. There was no doubt this news made Aurelia happy.

'As have I,' said Leah.

'And I,' said Beatrice, 'and now I have two.'

'Well, I hope you will both join me in London very soon, and we can get to know one another properly.'

'Ladies?' The nearest post boy interrupted them. 'Transport for Miss Thame? We must be leaving, or we won't get back before dark.'

'Thank you. I will come now.' Leah smiled at her sisters. 'If you wish to write to me, I live at Dolphin Court, Westcliff, Somerset. I know where you will be, Aurelia. And you, Beatrice?'

'Oh.' Beatrice appeared to shrink away from the others. 'I am not sure… That is…my brother…he will disapprove. I *shall* come to London, though, no matter what he—' She bit off her words with a gasp. 'I shall see you both then.' She hurried to the second post-chaise. 'Is this one for Miss Fothergill?'

The post boy nodded, and she stepped up into the vehicle. As the chaise pulled away from the kerb, she lowered the window and waved, her smile doing nothing to alleviate the anxiety of her expression.

'Well,' said Aurelia. 'I already dislike her brother intensely.'

'As do I.' Leah looked at her sister, mentally scrabbling for a friendly comment. 'Aurelia is such a pretty name.' She stepped up into her waiting post-chaise. 'I hope I shall see you soon. Have a safe journey.'

The horses moved off sharply, jolting her off balance. She sat down with a bump, and by the time she looked through the window, the post-chaise was turning out of the street and Aurelia was lost to sight.

Chapter Three

Piers Duval, Lord Dolphinstone—Dolph to his friends—
leaned his head against the glass of the carriage window,
straining to catch his first glimpse of Dolphin Court. Home.
As the familiar building came into view across the valley,
his throat thickened with a mix of guilt, dread and joy.

He had missed home and his three children more than
he'd ever thought possible during the long months away.
Within that churning mix of emotions, guilt gained the
upper hand—he should never have stayed away so long, not
when the children had just lost their mother. The guilt intensified. When the request had come for him to join Lord Castlereagh, the Foreign Secretary, in Vienna, he had grabbed
the excuse of duty with both hands and had rushed off to
Europe rather than face the bewilderment of two young
boys whose mother was there one day and gone the next.
Matilda had thankfully been too young to grasp the cata-
strophic change in all their lives. Dolph had selfishly fled
his own guilt and grief, unable to cope with reliving each

and every day that had led up to Rebecca's death, wondering in despair what he could have said or done differently. Wondering what signals he overlooked. Wondering how he could have stopped her.

He'd thought Rebecca was content with her life. Theirs had been an arranged marriage—they'd rubbed along together well enough, but they'd never been in love. Whatever that meant. Maybe he was incapable of loving anyone? After they'd wed, Dolph's life had continued much as before, with extended stays in London due to his interest in politics and government, and, when he *was* home, with the estates. Rebecca disliked London and had seemed happy to remain in Somerset. Looking back, he realised they had never really talked in depth about their lives or their feelings or their expectations of the other.

And his wife had been more unhappy than he had ever imagined.

Swamped by guilt, he'd been incapable of comforting his children after Rebecca died. Hell, he'd barely been able to look at them, knowing how badly he'd let down his entire family. So, he'd appointed a governess for the boys and he had left, convinced they'd all be better off without him.

'You're quiet, old fellow.'

Dolph straightened, pushing away from the window and from his inner turmoil, and eyed his travelling companion, George, Lord Hinckley, in whose carriage they travelled and who had been quick to accept Dolph's invitation to convalesce at the Court after a duel left him fighting a life-threatening infection.

'You must be eager to see the children again after all this time,' George continued. 'I can only apologise once more for further delaying your return.'

Dolph huffed a laugh. 'It was not entirely your fault—Tamworth has always been a hothead, but it was lunacy for him to challenge you over one waltz with Miss Andrews.'

'And lunacy for me to accept his challenge?' George's left arm rested in a sling to protect the shoulder pierced by Tamworth's sword. 'I did attempt to appease him, but he was spoiling for a fight and there's only so many insults a fellow can take.'

Dolph refrained from pointing out Tamworth would not have taken such exception had George refrained from flirting quite so outrageously with Miss Andrews. That comment would achieve nothing. George was a known flirt who fell in and out of love with alarming regularity, but his flirtations were never serious, and Tamworth, had he been thinking straight, knew it. Dolph had arrived back in London in time to act as George's second and had then felt obliged to remain with his old friend until his life was out of danger.

'I wonder if the children will recognise you,' George continued, reviving Dolph's fear the boys would never forgive him for abandoning them. 'How long is it since you've seen them?'

Too long. 'Sixteen months.'

It had been a long haul. Dolph had joined the British delegation in Vienna in October. He had been just one member of the delegation assisting firstly Castlereagh and then the Duke of Wellington in their endeavours to negotiate a long-term peace plan for Europe after twenty-three years of almost continuous war. And then had come the news of Napoleon's escape, and the appalling carnage at Waterloo, followed by weeks and months in Paris to negotiate a definitive peace treaty between France and the four Allied powers of Great Britain, Austria, Prussia and Russia.

'The boys will recognise me, but Matilda was only three months old when—' He swallowed down the pain. *When Rebecca died.* 'When I left.'

Guilt stabbed him again. If only he had noticed the depths her moods had sunk to...the implications of her state of mind...he might have been able to stop her. To save her. He thrust that thought away. Officially, it had been an accident, and she had lost her footing as she walked on Dolphin Point.

Only Dolph knew the truth that Rebecca had taken her own life just three short months after giving birth to the daughter she had always longed for. He had destroyed the incoherent, rambling letter she had left him, aghast at how low she had sunk without him even noticing, her words seared into his brain. She had not blamed him. She had, heartbreakingly, blamed herself. Convinced herself he and the children would all be better off without her.

But he *was* to blame. If he had spent much less time away in London and more time with his young family when at home—and less time preoccupied with estate business— then surely he *would* have noticed. He *could* have stopped her. And it seemed he had learned nothing, for, rather than stay at home with the children after Rebecca's suicide, he had run away like a coward.

The call to go to Vienna had appeared to come at exactly the right time, allowing him to escape the tragedy. He now saw, however, that it had come at the very worst time, giving him the perfect excuse—patriotic duty—to avoid the difficult and painful aftermath of Rebecca's death.

He had, eventually, dealt with his grief, but his guilt at abandoning his children remained—hence the mix of joy at the prospect of seeing them again and the dread they would never forgive him. But at least—according to Mr Pople, his estate steward, who wrote regularly to update Dolph on all matters pertaining to Dolphin Court—the boys were thriving in the care of Miss Thame, the governess he'd appointed before he left. So at least he'd got that right.

After the Paris Treaty had been signed in November, Dolph had hoped to be home for Christmastide, but a bout of influenza had delayed his journey, and then bad weather— with winds whipping up such a fury that ships lay hunkered in port rather than risk the English Channel—had delayed it some more. Once he'd reached London, George's escapade had delayed him still further, and here they were, already at the end of January.

Now was his chance to make amends, however. He intended to sacrifice his interest in politics and stay in Somerset for the sake of the children. Henceforth, they and they alone would be his priority.

He turned to George. 'We're almost there. How's your shoulder?'

'Still a bit stiff and sore, but I should soon be able to discard this sling. It has helped cushion my shoulder during the journey, however; the roads down here are shockingly full of potholes, my friend. I wonder you don't repair 'em.'

Dolph laughed. 'You cannot hold me responsible for the state of the entire road from Bristol to Westcliff.'

His laugh disturbed the third occupant of the carriage. Wolf lifted his great, shaggy head and gazed worshipfully at Dolph while his tail thumped gently on the floor. Dolph scratched Wolf's ear, and the dog's head lowered back to his paws as he heaved a sigh. He'd first met Wolf—full name

Wolfgang—in the Augarten in Vienna, where his owner, Herr Friedrich Lueger, walked him every day.

The two men had struck up a friendship, enjoying many and varied discussions about the world, life and their place in it. It had been Herr Lueger who helped Dolph understand that burying his emotions beneath the business of the day was merely delaying the time when he must come to terms with Rebecca's suicide. By then, however, he had been fully embroiled in the Congress, and his patriotic urge to do his duty for his country had prevented him leaving until he was no longer needed to help navigate a diplomatic route through the turmoil Napoleon had left through vast swathes of the continent.

His heart ached at the memory of Herr Lueger, who, one day, had missed his daily constitutional in the park. After he'd failed to turn up for several days running, Dolph had gone to the building where Herr Lueger had rooms to discover he had died. The landlady had informed him, tersely, that the dog wasn't her responsibility, and she had turned him out. Several hours' searching had found Wolf, and Dolph had adopted him as his own.

The carriage rocked to a halt and Dolph yawned and stretched, thankful to reach the end of the journey. He gazed up at the Court. Home. He flung the door wide and leapt down onto the gravelled forecourt, followed by Wolf, before lowering the carriage steps for George, and then turned again to the house, the front door still firmly shut. Maybe he should have written to inform them of the exact day of his arrival, but he had wanted to surprise the children. All was quiet and still—hardly surprising at four o'clock when the light was fading... The children were no doubt indoors with their governess, maybe listening to a story by the fire.

Then a whoop split the air, and a young lad hurtled around the far corner of the house, closely followed by a younger boy shouting, 'Wait, Stevie. Wait for me.'

Dolph's heart leapt. Steven and Nicholas. His sons.

Dear God, how they have grown.

Dolph watched, enthralled, as his eldest son turned at his brother's plea and waited for him to catch up. He grabbed Nicholas's hand, and then, without looking up, he set off at a run, tugging Nicholas behind him, straight towards Dolph, who dropped his hand to Wolf's collar in case the dog should become too excited.

It was Nicholas who noticed the carriage, men and dog first, and he stopped, pulling Steven to a halt, pointing ahead, his eyes big with wonder. At that moment, a woman carrying another child puffed around the corner. Matilda. Love exploded through Dolph. His three children. Safe and well. He frowned. The woman…she looked familiar, but she was not Miss Thame and neither was she one of his servants. He could not fully recall the governess's features—they had only met the once, at her interview—but she had been uncommonly tall for a woman, and slender. The woman carrying Matilda was short and plump, and as she spotted Dolph, she jerked to a halt, her expression a picture of dismay. Dolph's eyes narrowed in recognition of Philippa Strong, daughter of the local vicar.

What the Devil is she doing here, and where is Miss Thame? And why does she have Matilda as well as the boys?

He employed a nursemaid to care for the baby so the governess could concentrate on Steven and Nicholas. Perhaps she was ill?

Dolph released Wolf and strode forward. 'Hold him, will you, George?' he snapped over his shoulder. But almost at once, he slowed. To reach Miss Strong and demand answers, he must pass his sons, who clung together, their eyes wide.

He reined in his exasperation and paused next to them. 'Well, Steven? Well, Nicholas? Do you recognise your papa?'

'Yes, F-Father. W-welcome home.' Steven, trying to be grown up at seven years of age. Let down by the quiver of his lower lip.

The urge to drop to his knees and to gather his sons to him in a hug was constrained by a surge of awkwardness. He'd been a somewhat distant father before he'd gone away, in the same way he'd been a distant husband. Uncertainty wound through him. What if he scared them? What if they didn't want to be hugged? What if he made them cry? Instead of following his instinct, he patted each boy on the head.

'Thank you, Steven. I am happy to be here.' His heart ached at the wariness in both boys' expressions. Miss Strong reached them at that moment.

'Lord Dolphinstone,' she puffed. 'Good afternoon. And welcome home. Leah…that is, Miss Thame…did not say you would arrive home today.'

Dolph bowed. This was not Miss Strong's fault. At least *she* was looking after his children, unlike the women he paid to care for them.

'Good afternoon, Miss Strong. I do not deny I am surprised to find you here. Would you care to explain?'

As he spoke, he reached out a tentative hand to touch Matilda's cheek with his forefinger. So soft. So pretty, with a mop of fair curls just like her mother's. Matilda jerked away from Dolph's touch and hid her face against Miss Strong's shoulder. She was a year and seven months now, and he was a stranger to her. He did not even know if she was walking yet. He glanced back at the boys, still clutching one another where they had stopped.

'I...um...well...'

Miss Strong's voice faded as a yellow bounder bowled up the carriageway at a reckless pace and swung into the forecourt. The postilions reined their mounts to a steaming halt. Dolph frowned. A glance at Miss Strong revealed her relief. Before either of the postilions dismounted, Dolph strode to the door of the post-chaise and flung it wide. He recognised Miss Thame in an instant, with her scraped-back red hair, her pale, freckled skin and her large, wide-set eyes, although he recalled neither the brilliance of those same eyes nor the soft curve of her lips, parted in a gasp of surprise before they firmed. In that first moment their gazes collided, her eyes darkened until her pupils were ringed by the narrowest band of turquoise and Dolph's breath caught in his lungs.

'My Lord! I... I did not know you were expected home today.' Guilt danced across her expression as her cheeks flushed.

'That, Miss Thame, is patently obvious.' He held out his hand to assist her from the vehicle, ruthlessly quashing an inexplicable urge to close his fingers around hers. 'We will discuss this inside.'

By the time he closed the door and turned, Miss Thame had crouched down and Steven and Nicholas had run to her, clinging to her. Pain pierced Dolph as he took in the tableau—the scene he had wanted to create with his sons played out before his eyes with their governess.

'We *missed* you, Miss Thame,' Steven said. 'Miss Strong made me read the Bible!'

'Stevie…you know very well we study the Bible every Wednesday morning.'

Morning? She's been gone all day?

Dolph frowned. How often did she leave the boys like this? And why?

'Miss Strong was following *my* instructions,' Miss Thame said, before addressing the vicar's daughter. 'Miss Strong… I have arranged with the post boys to drop you at the vicarage on their way back to Bristol, as they pass through the village.'

She rose gracefully to her feet. She was as tall and as slender as Dolph remembered, even clad in that dull cloak, which parted at the front to reveal a gown in a becoming shade of blue. Willowy, that was how he would describe her if ever called upon to do so. He tore his gaze from her, confused. What the Devil was wrong with him, noticing such things about his sons' governess?

I'm weary from the journey. I'm confused…seeing the children again… I am not myself.

'Thank you so much for standing in my stead,' Miss Thame was saying as she took Matilda from Miss Strong. 'I shall see you at church on Sunday.'

She took charge effortlessly, while he stood there, mute, like a visitor to his own home. Dolph shook himself, mentally, and stepped forward.

'Thank you, Miss Strong.' He handed her into the postchaise.

'Thank you, my lord. And welcome home again.' She smiled shyly, and her gaze slid past him. 'I do hope your friend's arm is soon better.'

George! He'd forgotten all about him. Dolph glanced around, to find George—his hand still on Wolf's collar—

smiling engagingly at Miss Strong, his eyes bright. Dolph's heart sank, knowing it only took a shapely ankle, a pair of fine eyes or a tinkling laugh to turn George's head, and he made a mental note to warn George off Miss Strong—a country vicar's daughter would be unprepared for the kind of flirtations a more worldly girl would take in her stride.

He turned again to Miss Thame, who stood quietly waiting for his attention, Matilda hugged close and the boys clinging to her cloak. Irritation that he understood none of this made him brusque.

'I suggest you resume your duties by taking charge of the children, Miss Thame, and allow my guest and I the chance to go indoors and recover from our journey. We will talk later about where you have been and why you saw fit to leave my children with a woman not in my employ.'

Her cheeks flushed. 'As you wish, my lord. Come, boys.'

He watched her walk to the front door and stop to speak to Palmer, the butler, who was now waiting at the open front door. A groom, alerted by the arrivals, had appeared to direct George's coachman, Winters, to the stables.

'Well!' George broke the silence. 'I am exceedingly happy I accepted your invitation, Dolph. Miss Strong is a gem, is she not? No chance of me getting bored now.'

He grinned happily and Dolph heaved an inner sigh; George was truly irrepressible.

'Come. Let us go inside.'

He shivered, suddenly aware of how the temperature had dropped while they had been standing there. The wind had picked up, bringing with it the salty tang of the nearby Bristol Channel, and he shivered again. Not, this time, at the cold but at the memories. He thrust them aside, greeting Palmer as they went indoors. The butler closed the front door behind them.

The entrance hall looked the same. Palmer looked and sounded the same. Everything was familiar, and yet unfamiliar because Rebecca was not there. The reality of her loss rose closer to the surface than at any time during the past sixteen months—his grief might have eased, but guilt still hovered like a black spectre at the edges of his mind. He still woke up in a cold sweat some nights, haunted by how unhappy and confused Rebecca had been and tormented by his own failure to see it.

The sound of Palmer clearing his throat interrupted his thoughts, and Dolph realised he had omitted to inform his household, not only of his arrival today, but also that George would be accompanying him.

'Please prepare a bedchamber for Lord Hinckley, Palmer. He will be staying with us until he returns to London for the start of the Season.'

George would be fully recovered by then and would be loath to miss the balls and parties and other entertainments. Dolph, however, had no interest in such frivolity and had barely looked at a woman since Rebecca's death. Indeed, the very notion of marrying again made him shudder. How could he face that responsibility? Look how he had neglected Rebecca. What if he was incapable of making any woman happy? Guilt continued to haunt him. Had he driven her to such a drastic solution? Had life with him been such a trial?

It was too late now to compensate for his inadequacy as a husband, other than to vow never to risk destroying any other woman's life. All that mattered now was his determination to redress his failings as a father.

Palmer bowed. 'Mrs Frampton is already preparing the guest room with the maids, my lord. We saw you arrive. And there is hot water upstairs already for you both.'

'Thank you, Palmer.'

'And the dog, my lord?' Palmer's tone made his opinion of Wolf absolutely clear.

Dolph bit back a grin as he ruffled Wolf's head. 'Get used to him, Palmer. He is here to stay.'

'Very well, my lord.'

Dolph could feel peace and contentment hovering. Tentative feelings as yet, maybe—he might feel awkward with his children and he might still have his guilt to cope with, but it was good to be home.

Chapter Four

An hour later, having bathed and changed his travel-soiled clothes, Dolph made his way downstairs, Wolf close behind him. Palmer greeted him in the hallway.

'Lord Hinckley is resting,' he said, 'and Mr Pople is waiting in your study, as he wanted a word before he leaves.'

Roger Pople had been steward at Dolphin Court since Dolph's father's time.

'Thank you, Palmer. Be so good as to advise Miss Thame I wish to speak to her in the drawing room in half an hour.'

No need to be formal, with an interview in his study—he would listen to the reason for the governess's absence before judging her.

'Very good, my lord.'

Thirty minutes later Dolph—Wolf padding at his heels—headed for the drawing room after Mr Pople had updated him on the latest news about the estate. Now to face Miss Thame and find out what on earth she had been playing at. He deliberately hadn't questioned either Palmer or Mr Pople

328   *The Rags-to-Riches Governess*

about her absence, and neither had he asked how frequently she left his sons in the care of others. He was interested to hear what she had to say for herself first.

He strode into the room and slammed to a halt, a peculiar hollow feeling in his chest among the emotions that erupted at the sight before him—Miss Thame sitting on the sofa with a sleepy-looking Matilda on her lap as she read aloud to Steven and Nicholas, who were snuggled either side of her. The governess fell silent and her impassive appraisal of Dolph swiftly dispersed that odd flood of nostalgic nonsense as well as the lingering memory of his visceral response to her as he handed her down from the post-chaise. No longer did he attribute a magnetic quality to those wide-set eyes, which now considered him coolly and somewhat haughtily. Her lips were far from luscious, as he'd earlier thought, but were now firmly pursed above her surprisingly delicate chin. And she found him wanting, he realised, with a start of temper that very quickly morphed into amusement. If one look had that effect on *him*, what effect must it have upon two small impressionable lads?

Relief spread through him as he realised that earlier inexplicable tug of attraction had been an illusion, born out of a combination of his own weariness and a trick of the late afternoon light. Her features looked almost severe, with her high, sharp cheekbones and her compressed lips and her red hair severely scraped back from her face with the aid of numerous hairpins. She had changed out of the blue gown he had glimpsed beneath her cloak and was now attired in a plain, dull brown gown. *This* was the woman he had hired. A governess with enough backbone to raise two boys without accepting any nonsense from them.

'Good evening, my lord. I brought the children down to

say goodnight, as you did not have much time with them earlier. I make no doubt you will be happy to see them before they go to bed.'

He detected a note of warning in her tone but, although he would take heed and do nothing to upset the children, Miss Thame need not imagine the children's presence would do anything other than delay his questioning her over her absence and neglect of duty.

'I am. Thank you for the thought.' He advanced into the room. 'What book are you reading?'

Her smile was cool. '*The History of Little Goody Two-Shoes* by John Newbery. Have you read it?'

He frowned. 'No.'

'It was in your library,' she said. 'The only children's book I could find. The boys enjoy it, although I do not believe they fully understand it all.'

'What is it about?'

She glanced down, and he saw her suck in one cheek before releasing it again as her lips twitched. But when she looked up at him again, that hint of amusement in her expression had smoothed away.

'It is the story of Margery, a poor orphan who makes a career for herself as a teacher before she marries the local landowner, having won his heart through her honesty, hard work and good sense.'

Her gaze held a hint of challenge, as if daring him to object, and he could hardly fail to see the irony even though there was no chance of fiction turning to real life in their case, despite that ridiculous emotional reaction to seeing her there, on his sofa, with his children surrounding her. Two could play at blanking expressions, however. He'd developed that trick during his diplomatic role in Europe, as well as the ability to understand people beyond what their words might reveal, by observing their unconscious mannerisms and behaviour.

'I see. It sounds an innocent enough fairy story. Now, Miss Thame, I still wish to speak with you about today. I suggest, therefore, it is time the children went to bed.'

'Of course.'

Steven clutched Miss Thame's sleeve and whispered urgently in her ear.

'I am sure he won't harm you, Stevie. My lord…is your dog safe?'

'You cannot think I would bring a dangerous beast into the house where my children live?'

'I know not what to think, my lord, as I barely know you.'

Dolph narrowed his eyes, suspecting her of insolence, but her open expression and slightly raised eyebrows belied that thought, and when he examined her words, he could not fault them.

'*I* am not afraid of it,' announced Nicholas, with a slightly scornful look at his brother.

Steven leaned across Miss Thame's lap and punched Nicholas on his arm. 'Nor am I! Don't you say I'm scared!'

'Boys! Enough!' Miss Thame stopped any further physical contact by the simple expedient of standing up, still holding Matilda, and taking Steven by the arm, obliging him to stand too. She kept her own body between the brothers as Nicholas, too, scrambled off the sofa. 'What *will* your father think of such behaviour?'

Dolph hesitated and then knelt down on the Aubusson carpet. Wolf immediately sat on his haunches next to him. 'Their father thinks they should come here and meet Wolf and then go up to bed.'

He caught Miss Thame's flash of approval, but he felt absurdly awkward considering they were his own children. He was more nervous facing them than he ever felt while negotiating between high-powered military men and politicians. If only he'd made more effort to spend time with them when they were younger, but it had never occurred to him. During his own childhood, he and his sister had been brought up by servants, his parents remaining remote for much of the time.

Miss Thame urged the boys towards Dolph and Wolf, whose head reached as high as Steven's waist.

'Lie down,' Dolph ordered, and Wolf shuffled his front paws forward. He laid his head on his outstretched legs and sighed.

The boys crept closer. Nicholas appeared the bolder of the two, even though he was the younger. He was the first to touch Wolf's head, and then he stroked, getting braver as the great dog just lay there and suffered his attention. Steven, after hanging back looking worried, finally followed suit. He then beamed with delight as he patted Wolf. Miss Thame crouched down to show Wolf to Matilda, but Dolph's daughter was having none of the dog, or of Dolph, as she clung to the governess like a little monkey, hiding her face.

'She is tired,' said Miss Thame. 'She will be better in the morning if you visit the nursery. The boys will be at their lessons, too, if you care to come to the schoolroom?'

'I shall try,' said Dolph.

He reached out to stroke Matilda's soft curls. He ached to hold her in his arms, but he feared making her cry, so he made no attempt to take her from Miss Thame. He stared hungrily at Steven and Nicholas but, as with earlier, he could not quite bring himself to hug them. Partly because he did not want to frighten them but mostly, he realised with a lurch of sudden understanding, because he was afraid of rejection.

But I am their father and they are just children. And so young. It is my responsibility to bridge this divide.

'Steven? Nicholas? Will you hug your papa goodnight?'

The boys came to him, eyes downcast, and allowed Dolph to enfold their stiff little bodies in his embrace. Dolph closed his eyes, lowering his face to their hair, breathing in their scents as his heart cracked. He had felt it his duty to stay in Europe all these months, but now...oh, how he regretted it. He'd missed over a year of their lives, a year he could never get back. How abandoned they must have felt, so soon after losing their mother. How on earth had he made such a colossal error in judgement in leaving as he did?

Remorse swirled through him and he silently swore he would make it up to his family, whatever it took.

Leah watched Lord Dolphinstone with Stevie and Nicky, her throat tight with emotion. How many times had she cursed this man for leaving the boys when they were already hurt and bewildered by their mother's sudden disappearance? Every day of the sixteen months she had lived here at Dolphin Court, that was how many times. Although the other servants had spoken well of His Lordship, Leah's opinion had been formed by the brusque—albeit handsome—man who had interviewed her. She had been shocked he would leave his sons immediately after their mother's funeral and disgusted by his prolonged absence, and she'd worked hard to give the boys the love and approval they needed in their lives to try to compensate them for the loss of *both* their parents.

And yet, seeing him now with his sons, he seemed truly remorseful. She knew from working as a governess in other households how little love many gentlemen showed towards their own children. She did not doubt they loved their children but, somehow, they appeared unable or unwilling to show it. She had been so fortunate with her own papa... She dragged her thoughts from the man she had called Papa. The news was too recent and the emotions it aroused still too agonisingly raw.

She crossed to the door. Cassie, the nursemaid who cared for Tilly, was waiting in the hall to take all three children up to bed—Leah had not wished to further anger His Lordship by taking them upstairs herself while he kicked his heels waiting for her in the drawing room.

It had been a calculated risk, bringing the children down to say goodnight to their father after he had ordered Leah to wait for him in the drawing room. She no doubt faced a reprimand for her absence that day, but the boys were already wary of their father. She had noticed Dolphinstone's discomfort in that short first meeting with his sons, and so she had followed her instinct that the sooner they began to rebuild their relationship, the better.

After Cassie left with the children, Leah remained standing while Dolphinstone paced the room. She had already decided to tell no one about Lady Tregowan's will and her unexpected inheritance. Not yet. The journey home had given her time to think, and she had not only decided she must, for her own sake, accept this opportunity, but she had also decided to delay leaving Dolphin Court for as long as possible. Partly for selfish reasons—just the thought of leaving the children shredded her heart—but also because the boys were already so unsettled by their father's imminent return.

And now Dolphinstone was here, and the boys' reaction to his arrival confirmed she had made the right decision. Both father and children needed time to overcome their understandable awkwardness, and it would surely be easier if they were unaware Leah would be gone before Eastertide.

Her initial reaction that to accept the inheritance would be disloyal to Papa had soon been dismissed by her usual logic. A woman in her circumstances had little choice but to be practical, and she could almost hear Papa's voice in her head saying, *'Leah. Will you really cut off your nose to spite your face? Accept this chance to improve your life, and I will be looking down on you and cheering you on.'*

Only a fool would reject such a change in fortune, and she was not a fool, but…marriage? Nerves coiled in her stomach. Her parents' marriage had always been her ideal. She had been wrong to believe it was a love match from the start, but the truth—that it had been arranged, and her parents' love had developed *after* they wed—gave her hope that, even if she didn't marry for love, she might at least meet a decent man she could respect.

And if not, at least she would have somewhere to call home and a guaranteed income of two hundred pounds per annum. No longer would she fear losing her job or falling ill and being unable to work. She might be lonely, of course, but one could also be lonely in the wrong marriage, and she loathed the idea of putting her life in the hands of a man who was only interested in her for her money. If only she could meet a good man, as Mama had done. A man like Papa.

Oh, Papa… The grief she had suffered when he died

now reared up to engulf her anew. She had lost him all over again, for he was not her father at all.

'*Miss Thame!*'

Lord Dolphinstone's exasperation dragged Leah from her thoughts. Her cheeks burned as he glared down at her, his dark brows bunched. He was so close she noticed his newly shaved cheeks and the glint of silver hairs at his temples. His close-cropped dark brown hair curled a little at his hairline, softening his male ruggedness, and she once again felt that unwelcome flare of attraction she'd experienced earlier when he had wrenched open the door of the post-chaise and their eyes had met.

His gaze pierced her again now, and she lowered her eyes. 'My apologies, my lord. I'm afraid I was wool-gathering.'

'Still dreaming up excuses for your absence?'

Leah stiffened, her emotions on a tight rein as grief over Papa still simmered.

'I have no need to dream up excuses, my lord. Today is the very first day I have left the boys for more than an hour since you employed me sixteen months ago. Employed me with the promise, might I add, of one day off per month. A day off I have *never* taken.'

His eyes narrowed. 'Until today.'

'Until today.' She dug deep inside herself for a measure of calm. 'I am sorry I left the children, but they are already familiar with Miss Strong, which is why I asked her to come and look after them, knowing the rest of the staff have been busy preparing for your return. Cassie would have been run ragged had she been required to watch the boys as well as care for Tilly for the entire day.'

'Tilly? Her name is Matilda.'

Petty...inconsequential...

'She is a little girl. Let her be Matilda when she grows up. Which she will…faster than you can possibly imagine.'

'I am aware of it.'

She barely heard his muttered words. Might they signify regret at how much of his children's lives he had missed? The sigh that sounded next, however, was loud. And still exasperated.

'Sit down, Miss Thame.'

Leah perched on the sofa, plaited her fingers together on her lap and braced herself for his questions, for the first time realising her plans might be in jeopardy. Her nerves fluttered as she watched Dolphinstone cross to the fireplace and lean down to poke the fire into life.

The decision was in this man's hands. This *stranger's* hands.

Although she had decided to leave, she needed time to grow used to this change in her life. Dolphin Court was her fifth post since she had been forced to earn her own living, and it was the only one where she had felt loved and valued. She liked the rest of the staff, without exception; in Philippa she had a close friend who lived nearby, but, above all, she adored the children and she was not yet ready for the wrench of leaving them. Besides, after all they had suffered, she was determined to help them adjust to their father's return before she went.

His Lordship threw a log onto the fire and, despite her preoccupation, she was struck by his powerful frame as he filled the shoulders of his coat. His features were somewhat harsh in repose, as though he smiled seldom—frown lines rather than laughter lines were etched into his face—but he'd had little to smile about after losing his wife in such a tragic accident. He sat opposite Leah, on the matching sofa, and leaned back, crossing one leg over the other and folding his arms across his chest. In his evening clothes and meticulously tied neckcloth, he looked every inch the wealthy aristocrat as his penetrating grey gaze raked Leah.

Like my real father: entitled; powerful; privileged.

Leah's unease faded to be replaced by icy control at the thought of her real father and his despicable actions.

'Well, Miss Thame? Would you care to enlighten me as to your whereabouts today?'

'It was a personal matter requiring my presence in Bristol, my lord.'

His brows lowered. 'And is that your entire explanation?'

What would he do if she told him the truth—that the man she thought to be her father was not? That, technically if not legally, she was illegitimate? That she was some dissolute nobleman's by-blow? Would he turn her off immediately?

She could not risk it. She would keep her secret for a few weeks, at least, before going to London and getting to know her new half-sisters. Her heart leapt with anticipation. Would Aurelia and Beatrice become friends as well as sisters? Leaving Dolphin Court would be a dreadful wrench, but knowing she was no longer entirely alone in the world, that she now had a family... That thought was a huge comfort, like being wrapped in a warm blanket.

'Wool-gathering again, Miss Thame?'

Her gaze flew to his and, again, her cheeks heated.

'This meeting you attended today... Forgive me if I have misread you, but it appears to have left you with a dilemma of sorts.'

She stared at him. 'What makes you say that?'

His eyebrows flicked high. 'Reading people is a skill I have developed over many months of complex negotiations in Europe. You are undoubtedly distracted, and it is reasonable to assume your preoccupation stems from your meeting.'

She swallowed. 'I do not deny there is some truth in both of those statements.' She would stick as close to the truth as possible. 'And I have been wondering how much I must reveal, for, as I said, it was a *private* matter. I received a letter from a firm of solicitors in Bristol requesting I attend a meeting today. I did so and I am sure you will understand my reluctance to reveal the details of that meeting.'

He frowned and she sensed his desire to probe further, so she elaborated, 'The meeting involved other individuals and therefore I am not at liberty to divulge any further information.'

His jaw bunched, before he said, 'I do not like secrets, Miss Thame. Do you anticipate further attendance at such meetings?'

'I do not.'

'And will any of this affect your employment here?'

'Not at this present time,' she said, carefully.

He held her gaze, his own expression revealing nothing. 'I do not appreciate such a veiled threat hanging over me, Miss Thame.'

'Threat?'

'The possibility you may—for whatever reason connected to this clandestine meeting with your solicitor—leave your post here. That *is* what I am to gather from your answer, is it not?'

Leah considered her clasped hands. 'Lord Dolphinstone,' she said when she looked up again. 'Do you concede my employment in your household is by mutual agreement?'

His brows shot up again, but this time a smile hovered

around his mouth. His assessing gaze elicited a strange tingling sensation deep in the pit of her stomach.

'I cannot deny it.' His voice deepened and he sounded warmer, somehow. Or, maybe, amused.

'Then you must also concede that I—or, indeed, you— have the right to terminate my employment whenever we might choose. My comment was not a threat, my lord. It was a simple statement of fact. All I am in a position to say is that I intend to remain in my post in the immediate future. More than that, I am unable to promise.'

Chapter Five

Dolphinstone stood up and strode to the window. As he tweaked the curtains aside and peered out into the darkness, Leah stared at the fire. A log settled into place with a soft sound, followed by the hiss of sap evaporating, and a cold, wet nudge at her hand brought her gaze back into the room. The dog—Wolf—stood by her, looking at her with his yellowish-brown eyes. When he saw he had her attention, he waved his tail and nudged first his broad muzzle and then his domed head under her hand. Remembering his gentleness and patience with the children, Leah stroked his thick, soft, black-tipped, tawny fur in a soothing rhythm. He leaned into her leg, his body solid and warm.

'Wolf! Where are your manners?'

Leah's head snapped up. She had been lulled by the repetitive action of stroking...the sense of peace it induced... and had failed to notice Dolphinstone's return. He towered over both her and Wolf, who turned his head to gaze up at his master adoringly, his tongue lolling from the side of his mouth. Leah shivered as she glimpsed his teeth—if she had noticed them earlier she doubted she would have drifted into that state of unawareness while stroking him. But she was glad she had not. He seemed sweet-natured, despite his size.

'Please do not reprimand him. I do not mind.'

Dolphinstone's smile relieved the harshness of his face. 'Most ladies are too afraid to be anywhere near him,' he said. 'And plenty of gentlemen too. But he really is a gentle giant.'

'Then why do you call him Wolf? Is it *meant* to give people a fear of him?'

'No. Of course it is not.'

Dolphinstone flung himself down on the opposite sofa, surprising Leah, as this was the first time he had appeared relaxed.

'Wolf is short for Wolfgang.'

'Oh! That is an unusual name for a dog. Is he named for Mozart?'

'He was, yes. But not by me. His former owner died, and I adopted him. In Vienna. Wolfgang—or *Volfgang*, as Herr Lueger pronounced it—is, in my opinion, too much the mouthful for a dog. So I shortened it. Didn't I, old lad?'

Wolf padded across to Dolphinstone and laid his head on his knee, grunting his pleasure as his master fondled his ears. Dolphinstone appeared much more at his ease with the dog than with his own children and he appeared to forget Leah's presence as he stroked. A frown marred his brow, and the urge to soothe it—to soothe *him*—crept over Leah as she watched and waited. Finally, his hypnotic stroking, the silence and that inexplicable urge became too much, and Leah cleared her throat. His gaze snapped to her face.

'My apologies, Miss Thame. I am afraid it was my turn

for wool-gathering.' His frown deepened. 'I admit I am un-comfortable with the idea of someone in my employ who is keeping secrets from me, but I cannot fault you when you declare it is your private business that also involves other people.' He smiled at her, and her heart gave a funny little leap. 'Your point of view was cleverly argued, by the way... I suspect you would make a good solicitor yourself!' He so-bered again. 'I cannot force you to confide in me but...' He paused, his gaze roaming her face, and she felt her colour rise, yet again, under his scrutiny. 'If I am correct that what you learned today has left you with a conflict of emotions, and if you wish to discuss the matter—in general terms, without compromising the others involved—please know I shall be happy to oblige.'

A conflict of emotions. That perfectly described her feel-ings. But she would not confide in anyone until she had helped Dolphinstone rebuild his relationship with his chil-dren.

'Thank you. I shall bear that in mind.'

'Very well. You may go.' He stood, and Leah did like-wise. 'Miss Thame...' He hesitated, and she sensed a tussle going on inside him, although he gave little outward sign. 'I wonder...would you care to join myself and Lord Hinckley for dinner? I am aware in some households the governess dines *en famille* and, due to my absence, that is a custom we have yet to establish.'

Leah could think of nothing worse, especially tonight when she had so much on her mind and she craved time and peace and quiet to think. On the other hand, it would be foolish to miss this opportunity to practise her social skills when she would no doubt be invited out to dine when she moved to London.

'Thank you, my lord. I appreciate your thoughtfulness and I shall be delighted to accept, although I should prefer to dine in my parlour tonight, as usual. I am weary after today and I fear I might nod off over the soup.' She smiled at him, hoping not to sound too ungrateful.

'As you wish. I shall bid you goodnight, Miss Thame.'

Leah bobbed a curtsy. 'Goodnight, my lord.'

Dolph scratched his jaw as the door closed quietly behind Miss Thame. That final smile was strained, and he did not believe it was solely due to weariness. She might believe herself to be unreadable but, as they had talked, he had picked up on her unconscious signals that she was troubled. Her reluctance to confide in him was understandable but, although he had accepted her silence, he had an instinctive dislike of secrets and mysteries, especially within his own household. If Rebecca had not so successfully concealed her inner torment, he felt certain she would not have reached the stage where she could see no solution other than to take her own life.

Why could she not confide in me?

Guilt and regret swelled yet again. He sat down, fondling Wolf's ears when the great head again settled on his lap, and his tension slowly seeped away as his mind cleared. The sound of the door opening eventually interrupted what had slipped perilously close to a doze.

'Dolph! This house is amazing!' George strode into the room, waving his good arm. 'Palmer has been telling me all about the secret passages and hidden doorways.'

Dolph straightened, his friend's enthusiasm jerking him fully awake. George was only four years younger than

Dolph but, at times, it seemed more like a fourteen-year age gap. 'I know... I did grow up here, after all.'

George's excitement was undaunted. 'Well, of course you did. But why did you never tell me you live in such an intriguing place? My country estate is modern and utterly boring—but now I plan to build a folly in the park, and to have a secret passage dug.'

'A passage leading to where?'

George waved his hand dismissively. 'Does it matter? Just think, when I have sons, we will have such fun.'

Dolph flinched at his words. When had he ever considered simply *having fun* with his sons, even before Rebecca died? His family had been a copy of the family he had grown up in and he had modelled himself on his father— stern and remote, his word law. Rebecca had been raised in a similar family, although she had been closer to the children. Dolph's experience of childhood fun had come from his sister and, later, from his school friends.

'I was fortunate, I suppose.' He was referring to the house rather than his family life. 'You can imagine the thrill of exploring it as a young boy. My sister and I loved to play tricks on our governess when we were young.'

'I am thrilled enough as a grown man—I'd have been in my element as a schoolboy. Have I your permission to explore tomorrow?'

'Of course. There are no secrets here. There is even a tunnel that supposedly once led to the church. I suspect it was used to transport smuggled goods in days gone by, but no one knows for certain.'

'The church, you say?' George said, with a telling smile. 'Now, *that* will be worth exploring.'

'Well, you will be out of luck, George, for that tunnel has been blocked up for as long as I can remember.'

'That is a pity. How far is the church from here, did you say?'

Dolph eyed his friend. 'George…'

George raised an innocent brow at Dolph's warning tone. 'Dolph?'

'Miss Strong is the vicar's daughter. She has lived in the village her entire life. Do not, I beg of you, raise expectations with one of your flirtations—she is far too innocent to understand *that* sort of game.'

'What do you take me for?' George laughed. 'I shall be as discreet as…well, as discreet as I can possibly be.'

'That,' said Dolph, 'is what I am afraid of.'

It was late when the two men retired for the night after a few hands of speculation and a game of billiards. Dolph bid goodnight to George on the first landing and, with Wolf at his heels, he headed to his bedchamber, where his valet awaited. After settling in bed, however, he found sleep elusive and, after a good half-hour of tossing and turning, he threw aside the bedcovers and reached for his banyan and slippers. He paced to the window and pulled back the curtain, but there was only a black void beyond the windowpanes. He leaned his forehead against the cold glass and closed his eyes, a jumble of images and snatches of conversation whirling through his thoughts. He made no attempt to pluck any one of those fragments from the spinning mass to examine it more closely but allowed them to come and go as they pleased.

A distant noise tweaked his attention. A noise from *inside* the house—the creak of a floorboard and the click of a latch. He turned and saw Wolf, too, had been alerted. The dog still lay on the rug before the hearth, but his head was up, his ears pricked. All the occupants of the house *ought* to be asleep. Even George had been yawning widely as they came upstairs. So, who was awake, and what were they doing creeping around in the dead of night?

Dolph lit his bedside candle with a taper from the smouldering remains of the fire before walking softly to the door and easing it open. He strained his ears. He could hear nothing and see nothing, the landing and stairs swallowed by the dark shadows beyond the halo of light cast by his candle. Wolf pushed past him and trotted across the landing to stand, head cocked, at the foot of the upper staircase, which led up to the second floor, where there were a couple of smaller guest rooms and the children's rooms.

The children!

He ought to have thought of them first, not last. Dolph strode to the stairs, protecting the flickering flame with his cupped hand, and ran up them, before pausing to listen. Again, he could hear nothing, but Wolf did. His attention was fixed on the boys' bedchamber door, standing slightly ajar, his ears pricked as he whined low. Dolph trod quietly now. If the boys were asleep, he had no wish to frighten them by startling them awake. He put his ear to the door. Silence. And it was dark within. He reached to push the door open but, as he touched it, it suddenly opened.

To give her credit, Miss Thame quickly stifled her squeak of alarm, her hand clapped around her mouth. Her eyes, though…they were huge, his candle flame glittering in those dark, dark pupils, the irises a deep green-blue, like the sea on a bright day. Dolph felt his heart turn over in his chest as his breath caught. He tore his gaze from hers. And his pulse rocketed. Her hair was no longer severely scraped back, but lightly caught in a thick plait draping over one shoulder. Loose, glimmering strands—russet and gold, the colours of autumn—framed her freckled face.

Her gaze dropped to his chest and then snapped up again, a telltale blush washing her pale cheeks and her forehead puckering, jolting Dolph out of his sudden paralysis.

'I—'

His jaw snapped shut as Miss Thame sucked in a breath, placed one hand squarely on his chest and pushed him, gently but firmly, back. She exited the bedchamber and turned to quietly ease the door shut.

'What—?'

'Shhh.'

Her long, slim forefinger pressed to her lips in a hushing motion, and his mouth watered as he focussed on her full lips. No longer pursed in disapproval, they were lush and tempting.

For God's sake, man. She is your sons' governess. You're lusting after her as though she were a comely barmaid.

Not that he had lusted after any woman, let alone a barmaid, for more years than he cared to recall. He beckoned to her to follow him, pivoted on his heel and strode for the stairs.

'Wait!'

He halted mid-stride at her command and pivoted to face her. He raised his brows, remaining silent as she glided towards him. A blue and gold paisley shawl enveloped her from neck to…almost…foot. Both shawl and nightgown fell a few inches short of her feet, which were bare and thrust into embroidered slippers that had seen better days. Her ankles were as fine and as well turned as any he had ever seen. Again, he wrenched his gaze away, but there was no-where to look other than at her, and every part of her enticed and intrigued. He fought to keep any hint of his feelings from his face as she halted in front of him, telling himself he was simply unsettled by his return to his marital home.

'We will not wake Stevie if we talk in my sitting room. Nicky—' her smile flashed '—will sleep through almost anything. No fear of waking him.'

Stevie! Nicky! As if Tilly is not bad enough.

Poking at his irritation as though it were a fire in need of rekindling, Dolph strode to the door she indicated, thrust it open and stood aside as she preceded him into the room. He noticed her shiver and draw her shawl tighter around her shoulders, but a glance at the grate revealed a bed of cold grey ashes. He closed the door—after Wolf padded in—and took a stance by the fireplace, one elbow resting on the mantelshelf. Miss Thame sat on a wooden chair next to a table by the window, ignoring the solitary wingback chair next to the hearth. He noticed she avoided looking directly at him.

He came straight to the point. 'What happened? I heard movement and thought we had an intruder.'

Rattled by his visceral reaction to the governess, he knew he must control this conversation, get the business done and remove himself from her presence before the unthinkable happened. She was not even particularly beautiful but, somehow, he found it hard to tear his eyes from her as his body responded in entirely inappropriate ways.

'Stevie...that is, Steven—' she spoke to the fireplace, flags of colour still highlighting her sculpted cheekbones '—suffers from occasional nightmares. If I hear him cry out, I go to him. I can usually soothe him straight back to sleep, but if he awakens fully he becomes distressed, and it's much harder to settle him back down. And then Nicky is more likely to wake as well.'

Her voice and her expression were exactly those of a governess reporting to her employer, but her failure to meet his eyes suggested she was embarrassed, or maybe even offended, by his state of undress. Shame washed through him as he accepted his earlier irritation with her was totally unfair. Any anger ought to be directed at the person he was actually angry with—himself, for his inappropriate response to her.

And Rebecca.

The whispered thought rocked him to his core. *Was* he angry with Rebecca? The thought had never occurred to him. It seemed heartless but, yes...there was anger there. Deep inside. He would think about that later.

'I see. Yes, of course,' he said to Miss Thame. 'I understand now.' He tried a smile. 'I dare say I must accustom myself to having children in my life again.'

'Indeed.' She finally looked at him, her voice frosty.

'You disapprove of my having been away all this time?'

Her chin tilted. 'I believe it was not the wisest...' She hesitated, her fine eyes narrowing. She shook her head slightly, and her chest rose as she inhaled. 'I believe it was neither the wisest nor the kindest decision for your children's sake.'

The fact she was right hurt more than if she'd accused him unfairly. 'What about for *my* sake?'

She eyed him in silence, before shaking her head again. 'It is not for me to say.'

'Oh, come, Miss Thame. You have given your opinion most freely. Do not hesitate to speak your mind now.'

He read the doubt in her eyes before she bent her head.

He softened his voice. 'Do not think I shall hold it against you. I am not so petty as to dismiss an employee because they dare to voice a criticism of me. Please believe me when I say that, from now on, my sole purpose is to do what is best for my children. If my absence has injured them, then I need to know before I can begin to make amends.'

'Very well. Since you ask, I shall tell you my opinion. I make no doubt your wife's death was painful and shocking for you and I understand your need to get away from the place where painful memories dwell. But you were not only a husband. You are a father, too. And the children were— and still are—too young to fully comprehend death. All they knew was their mother left them, and then their father disappeared, leaving them with a houseful of servants and a new governess. A stranger to them. I could have been a dreadful governess—and a monstrous person—for all you knew. You did not even wait to find out.' Her voice rose, shaking with strength of feeling. 'You ran away and you did not return for sixteen months! Your daughter has already spoken her first words, and she has started to walk.'

Her words stung, even though they were no different from the words with which he had castigated himself. Many times.

'I had my duty to do for my country.'

'That, with the greatest respect, is a weak excuse. There are plenty of other men who could have taken over your role, and you must know that. There was no other man to fill your shoes here at Dolphin Court. Those children only have one f-f-father.'

Her voice cracked over her final word, her eyes sheening over.

'What is it, Miss Thame? What is wrong?'

She flicked her hand in a dismissive gesture.

'It is nothing. I am tired, that is all.'

She was lying but, as she'd pointed out earlier, everyone was entitled to a certain amount of privacy. As long as it did not interfere with his children's well-being, he would not pry.

Dolph pushed away from the mantelshelf. 'In that case, I shall bid you goodnight, Miss Thame. Come, Wolf.'

He went down the stairs to his bedchamber, shrugged out of his banyan, kicked off his slippers and climbed into his now cold bed. Shivering, he huddled under the covers, but sleep continued to elude him as he pondered Miss Thame.

When had he last experienced such a physical desire for a woman? Certainly not since long before Rebecca's death…in fact, since she had known she was with child again. Maybe that was his trouble—it had been over two years since he'd enjoyed intimacy, and returning to Dolphin Court had revived his natural male desire for a woman. His marriage to Rebecca might have been arranged—the result of a long understanding between both their families—but he had remained faithful to her throughout their marriage. Somehow, his subconscious linked home with lovemaking, and poor Miss Thame had become the unwitting object of his reawakened sexual urges.

Satisfied he had logically explained away his uncharacteristic and odd fascination with his sons' governess, Dolph rolled onto his side and slept.

Chapter Six

'Not too close to the water, boys, or you will get wet feet.'

The following day Leah watched, smiling, as Stevie and Nicky played with Wolf on rock-strewn Dolphin Beach—a small, secluded cove on the Bristol Channel, sheltered by low sandstone cliffs with angled faces—the eastern cliff rising a touch higher towards Dolphin Point at its head. It was from here that poor Lady Dolphinstone had slipped to her death. The thought always made Leah shudder, but the boys—unaware of the location of their mother's tragic accident—loved to run around the beach and release their pent-up energy after suffering an entire morning of lessons.

At least here on the beach there was no danger of disturbing anyone, unlike if they ran whooping and shrieking around the house and gardens. Here, the breeze soon carried away the sounds of their exuberance, and Leah was a great believer in the efficacious effects of sea air. Today, the boys had the added bonus of Wolf to play with, and Leah's legs were saved from taking part in their game of chase.

It had been a frustrating morning. After their encounter last night, Leah had fully expected His Lordship to look in on the boys' lessons. Truthfully, she had eagerly anticipated his visit even as she assured herself she merely wished to show him how well the boys had progressed with their lessons.

Last night, upon opening Stevie's door to find Lord Dolphinstone looming there—clad in a deep red dressing gown, the neck of his nightshirt agape, revealing a tantalising glimpse of dark chest hair—heat had scorched her skin as she'd struggled to hide her instinctive response to the sight of him. He was so...*commanding.* Tall, upright and ruggedly handsome with penetrating grey eyes. She couldn't help but be physically attracted to him, even though she scolded herself for reacting like an infatuated schoolgirl.

But today, for all his fine words, he had not visited the schoolroom as promised. When she and the boys were preparing for their customary walk before luncheon, she had learned the reason for his absence—His Lordship was showing Lord Hinckley around the estate and the surrounding area.

So much for making his children his priority.

The boys had asked after their father, and Leah told herself any disappointment was purely on their behalf and nothing to do with her own wish to see him again. She knew words meant nothing, from past experience—it was a person's actions that revealed their true character. So far, Dolphinstone's actions had done nothing to persuade Leah of his worth as a man. Men such as he felt entitled to do as they pleased, concerned only with their own needs and pleasures without consideration of the consequences for others.

Men like her real father, Lord Tregowan. Men like Peter, Papa's curate. Men like Lord Usk.

His Lordship had left Wolf behind when he and Lord Hinckley had set off on their tour, and feeling sorry for the dog, Leah had suggested to the boys he might join them on their walk. Although both boys had been wary at first, Nicky had soon gained his confidence, and Stevie, determined not to be outdone by his little brother, had soon joined in and was now happily haring around the beach with Wolf, dodging the boulders that dotted the patches of shingle and sand.

Leah closed her eyes and tilted her head back, breathing in the bracing air, trying, without much success, to quiet her conflicting emotions: nervous excitement at the change and opportunity coming her way; eagerness at the prospect of getting to know Aurelia and Beatrice; anxiety as to what the future held; dread at the prospect of leaving this place and the children.

She spun around at the crunch of shingle behind her, her heart leaping into her throat, to see Lord Dolphinstone and his friend Lord Hinckley—both well wrapped up against the cold weather in greatcoats, scarves and gloves—approaching.

'Oh! You startled me.' She put her hand to her chest, which heaved as though she had run the length of the beach. 'I did not hear you approach.'

As her fear subsided she felt her cheeks scorch and a curious swooping pull deep in her belly as her gaze met that of Lord Dolphinstone, in spite of her earlier annoyance that he hadn't visited the schoolroom. Heavens! What a ridiculous state of affairs—a twenty-six-year-old spinster governess reacting like a breathless girl of eighteen at the mere sight of her employer. An earl, no less. But, surely, that had been an answering blaze in those hard grey eyes of his... just as there had been last night. Or had that been a trick of the candlelight?

Or the product of a too-vivid imagination! You are seeing what you want to see. Did you learn nothing from that episode with Viscount Usk?

One thing was certain—she could not put *this* reaction down to the magic of the night and their state of undress, as she had last night. Her face burned even hotter. She put her gloved hands to her face, praying Dolphinstone would attribute her flushed cheeks to the sea breeze. She never could blush a pretty pink, but always turned a fiery red that clashed with her hair.

'I am not surprised with all the racket the boys are making,' Dolphinstone said dryly as he turned his attention to the boys.

Lord Hinckley, however, grinned at Leah in a friendly manner. 'What a splendid place to grow up. I wish I'd had this when I was a lad. You don't know how lucky you are, Dolph. *My* place, Miss Thame, is in the Midlands—as far from the coast as it is possible to be in this country.'

Leah smiled back at him, grateful for any distraction from the brooding figure by his side.

'Dolph has been showing me around the place this morning, so I have my bearings,' Hinckley continued. 'Good of you, old man—' he slapped Lord Dolphinstone's back '—when I know you were eager to visit the children at their lessons. Do you know, Miss Thame, upon our return, Dolph was so disappointed he had missed them, he insisted on coming straight down here to find you all.'

Leah's earlier irritation with Dolphinstone faded. At least

he'd been thinking about the boys…and Lord Hinckley *was* his guest, so he did have a duty as his host. Mayhap she'd been a bit harsh in her condemnation—it was only his first morning home, after all.

Hinckley continued, 'Look at your fine, healthy lads, Dolph. They're a sight for sore eyes, sure enough.'

'They are indeed.'

Leah noticed a touch of strain in Dolphinstone's voice, and she caught his sideways glance up towards Dolphin Point. A muscle bunched visibly in his jaw, and he looked away. Leah sympathised. This beach must revive tragic memories for him. The cliff might not be high, but the mounds of rock at its base would prove lethal to anyone who fell, even when the tide was high. She suppressed another shudder, thoughts of the late Lady Dolphinstone close to the surface.

'Anyway, I have my bearings now,' Hinckley went on, 'and I promise not to monopolise so much of your time in future. I am afraid you will have to bear my company for a few weeks yet, Miss Thame. I cannot face another long, bruising journey until this wretched shoulder heals, so I shall remain until it is time to return to London for the Season.'

Leah frowned. Did that mean Dolphinstone, too, would be leaving the children to go to London again? And how would these two aristocrats react if they saw her—Dolphinstone's former governess—at Society events? She thrust aside those questions for now.

'How did you come by your injury, my lord?'

Hinckley reddened. 'A misunderstanding, that is all. Nothing too serious, you understand, but I am grateful for the opportunity to rusticate.' He surveyed the beach and the surrounding cliffs. 'I wonder...do you see much of your friend Miss Strong? I was sorry she had to rush away yesterday.'

'You forget, my lord—I am here to work. My days are taken up with teaching the boys.'

'Teaching?' Dolphinstone dragged his attention from his sons and stared at Leah. 'What is it they are learning here, other than to run wild?'

Leah stiffened, wounded by such unfairness. 'They are hardly running wild, my lord.' She kept her tone even and polite, but the knowledge she would soon be leaving gave her the courage to defend the boys. 'They have worked diligently all morning, and they are now benefitting from much-needed fresh air and exercise. Young boys, in case you have forgotten, have a surfeit of energy that needs release on a daily basis.'

'You cannot argue with that, Dolph. You were one yourself, once. Allegedly.' Hinckley grinned at Leah, waggling his eyebrows. 'Now...where is that cave you told me about?' Dolphinstone, his lips tight, pointed to the western cliff. 'Ah, yes. I see it. I must take a closer look. Do either of you care to accompany me?'

'I must stay and watch the boys,' Leah said, when Dolphinstone remained silent, even though the question was clearly not meant for her.

'I will stay here too,' said Dolphinstone. 'I outgrew my fascination with caves long ago and that one is hardly worthy of the name. It is disappointingly shallow.'

'But I have never been inside a cave before. You cannot expect me to pass up such an opportunity, Dolph.'

Dolphinstone grinned, shaking his head at Hinckley. 'You never cease to amaze me, George.'

Hinckley strode away across the beach, leaving Dolphinstone with Leah, who wondered if he would deliver another reprimand following that jibe about the boys' noisiness and excitement. In the ensuing silence, she reflected that if Dolphinstone should prove a harsh father it would make leaving the boys even more distressing for her, although at least it would counteract any physical attraction she felt for him.

It had been many years since that part of her nature had stirred, not since she had fallen for Viscount Usk's silver-tongued compliments and cajolery. That, as well as Peter Bennett's false courtship to gain favour with Papa, had been a harsh lesson to learn, but she had learned it well.

'I apologise for my earlier remark, about Steven and Nicholas running wild.' Dolphinstone's voice broke into her thoughts, sounding strained, his expression, in profile, somewhat grim. A gust of wind caught his hat, and as he grabbed it, one end of his scarf was blown from around his neck. He rammed his hat back on his head and held it secure with one gloved hand. 'I can see they are not. They have clearly thrived under your care.'

'There is no need to apologise to me, my lord.'

'There is. I… I do not care for this place, but that is no reason to take it out on you.'

Leah gripped her hands together against her natural instinct to touch him in sympathy. To offer comfort. As she would do for anyone, male or female, in distress. But she had already succumbed to an inexplicable urge to touch him, last night…so tempted by that glimpse of hair at the open neck of his nightshirt that she had laid her hand against his chest to propel him away from the boys' door. Her fingertips tingled at the memory. That was a boundary she would not cross again.

She would be leaving here within the next few weeks, however, and she was emboldened to touch upon subjects she might otherwise avoid.

'I understand,' she said. 'It must bring back painful memories.'

His gaze raked her, his expression inscrutable. 'It does. Tell me, do the boys ever talk about their mother?'

'They do. Especially Stevie. Being that bit older, he remembers more, and he still misses her a great deal.'

'Remembers…? He does not know about…about…what happened?'

'He knows she had an accident, but he knows no details. That is why this beach is still a happy place for the boys to come and play—I did not think there would be any benefit in them knowing the location.'

'No. That is true. I should have thought…' He folded his arms across his chest as his words faded. He stared out across the water. Then he visibly swallowed. 'I was not thinking rationally when I left. But I should have thought of that and left instructions. You made the right choice in not telling them more. Thank you. I count myself fortunate it was you who answered my advertisement—Mr Pople has told me how good you have been. As you said last night, I did not even wait to ensure you were capable, let alone kind. I should never have left as I did.'

He fell silent. His claim of not thinking rationally echoed what Philippa had said to Leah several times, in defence of Dolphinstone's abandonment of his children. Leah had still found his behaviour hard to excuse, however. The wind had dropped a little, and Dolphinstone used the lull to wrap his scarf securely around his neck again. 'This wind is chilly. But, then, it *is* the first day of February. It is to be expected.'

Leah deduced from the change of subject that the confidences—and the apology—were over.

'Do not blame yourself too much, my lord. You were distraught. But it is in the past now. They—' she gestured to Steven and Nicholas, who were trudging back up the beach, while Wolf investigated the rocks at the base of the cliff '—are what is important now. Them and Matilda.'

Dolphinstone's lips quirked. 'You may continue to call her Tilly. And I shall even endure Stevie and Nicky for my sons. For the time being. I have no doubt they will be called far worse things when they go to school.'

The thought of either boy being sent away to school was unbearable, even though Leah would be long gone by then. The fact of her imminent departure from this place and from the children she loved hit her all over again, as it had done at unexpected times throughout the morning even though she tried to ignore any thoughts about her future while she was with the boys. At those times she felt herself gripped by the fear and uncertainty of giving up her life here, and the worry she would fail to find a man who might fall in love with her...a man with whom she could be happy. Whenever she thought of the Season to come, her stomach tied into knots, for she would be competing in the marriage stakes not only against all the young ladies making their debuts this year, but also against Aurelia and Beatrice, both of whom would match her fortune and both of whom were far prettier, and younger, than Leah.

And now she had the worry of meeting Lord Hinckley— let alone, God forbid, Lord Dolphinstone—in London to add to her fear of seeing that rat Lord Usk again.

'Miss Thame?'

Leah came to with a start.

'Wool-gathering again?' His Lordship asked, dryly. 'Is this a habit of yours…a quirk I must become accustomed to?'

She was spared from reply by Nicky, who reached them ahead of Stevie and now held out his hand to show them something.

'Miss Thame! Look what I found. It's sea glass like you showed us before. The sea's made it all smooth. Here.' He handed it to Leah. 'It is a present.'

'Why, thank you, Nicky. It is beautiful. I shall treasure it.' Her throat thickened with emotion.

'Good afternoon, Father.' Stevie halted about three paces from Dolphinstone and bowed.

So solemn and correct… Leah's heart went out to him. He'd taken his position as the oldest—he was now seven, to Nicky's five—so seriously in the time she had been here, and now he stood before his father, unsmiling, like a little soldier presenting himself for inspection. She willed Dolphinstone to do, or say, something to help the boy relax, but a glance at the man revealed his indecision, and she recalled his awkwardness with his sons yesterday. But how could she help them when this was a moment strictly between father and son?

As it happened, she was saved from having to intervene by Wolf, who, unlike Stevie, was absolutely convinced of his welcome. He barrelled up to them, tongue lolling, tail wagging furiously. He stopped midway between Stevie and Dolphinstone and shook himself vigorously.

Dolph flinched as ice-cold drops of sea water showered over him. Stevie and Nicky both shrieked with laughter, dancing away from Wolf, and the strained atmosphere eased. Suddenly, it seemed easier to know how to act with his sons. He knew what he didn't want—he didn't want his son to bow to him or to be stiffly formal. Despite his jibe at Miss Thame earlier, he preferred to see them as they had been on his arrival at the beach. Running around, playing, having fun. She was right—they had worked hard, and they deserved a chance to run off their excess energy. And he wanted them both to feel as relaxed with him as they were with their governess, who, at this moment, was laughing with the boys as she attempted to restrain an overexcited Wolf. Her unfettered laugh was musical. The joy on her face warmed him. And that she could have fun with the boys as well as teach them effectively was a definite bonus. The affection between them all was clear to see.

'Here. Allow me.' Dolph reached around Miss Thame to take hold of the dog's collar. His gloved hand closed over hers. He heard her sharp intake of breath, and he loosened his grip. 'Sorry,' he muttered. 'I hope I didn't hurt you. I know how strong Wolf is… I have difficulty in holding him myself if he is determined to go.'

She turned her face to him. She was close. Too close. Her deep turquoise eyes fathomless like the ocean, framed by thick, auburn lashes and straight, no-nonsense eyebrows. Countless light brown freckles danced across her nose. Freckles that seemed far too frivolous for such a straight nose and for a prim, proper and practical governess. Her scent mingled with the sea breeze—soap, with the merest hint of lavender. Her lips were parted in surprise, and the urge to kiss her grabbed him. It took hold of him deep inside, squeezing until he felt breathless.

Chapter Seven

Dolph jerked back, noticing a fiery blush colouring Miss Thame's cheeks as her lashes swept low to conceal her innermost thoughts. The entire interlude had lasted a second… less than a second…but had seemed endless.

'You did not hurt me,' she said. Then her eyes opened, and she was visibly back in control of her feelings, once again the archetypal governess, any hint of a sensual being ruthlessly quashed. 'You are right. He is exceedingly strong. Thank you for your help. But…' She lowered her voice to a whisper and leaned closer. His breath seized all over again, with the anticipation of her touch, but that touch never came. 'Please…tell Stevie to call you Papa. He usually does when he speaks of you. He is unsure of himself, and of you, and he is desperate to please you.'

Then she moved away, leaving Dolph to silently rebuke himself for his uncharacteristic… He struggled to come up with a word. Lust? But, no, that did not fit. And when the word eventually came to him, it was need. Hardly flattering and not at all as he would normally view himself, but it perfectly described how he had been overcome with the sudden desire for someone to be close to…someone to share his innermost feelings.

Maybe returning to Dolphin Court had been a mistake? He'd had no choice, however. He must think of the children, which meant he must come to terms with his guilt over his failure as a husband, and he must get used to the ghostly re-minders of Rebecca. Time might have helped him over the worst of his grief, but he was no closer to forgiving himself for his failure to recognise how mentally disturbed she had become in her final months.

But those feelings, unexpectedly awakened by his return to Dolphin Court, were no excuse for him not to maintain a proper professional relationship with his sons' governess, no matter his sudden craving for intimacy.

He wrenched his thoughts away from Rebecca and onto his sons and Miss Thame, who was saying in a laughing voice, 'Did Wolf get you all wet? Come…it is time we went home, and you can change out of your damp clothes.' She looked towards the cave and then back at Dolph. 'I see Lord Hinckley is returning—shall you wait here for him?'

Dolph read the unspoken plea on both boys' faces. 'No. George will soon catch us up, and I would prefer to walk with you three, if you have no objection?'

Nicky whooped and ran ahead. Stevie, on the other hand, smiled—a touch hesitantly—and said, 'Of course we do not object, Father.'

'I do have one condition, though, Steven… Stevie.'

The small solemn face tugged at his heartstrings. 'Yes, Father?'

'My condition is that you call me Papa, as you used to.

When you call me Father it feels as though you are cross with me.'

Those grey eyes...so like his own...searched Dolph's face. He smiled encouragingly, noticing Miss Thame put her hand on Stevie's shoulder and give him a gentle squeeze. Then Stevie smiled and the solemn little man transformed into the small boy he should be.

'Very well. Papa.' He gave a little skip, then shouted, 'Come on, Wolf, let's catch Nicky,' and hared off after his brother.

Dolph watched his son scamper away with a smile and a sigh. 'Thank you,' he said to Miss Thame. 'That was a timely reminder.'

He waved to George and pointed up the beach before he and Miss Thame started to stroll in the direction of home. Off to their left, George altered his direction to intersect with them at the top of the beach.

'You are welcome, my lord. And I am pleased you do not object to my...um...*interference*, some might say.'

He was pleased to note she seemed to have put that instant of... What had it been? A frisson of awareness? A spark of some current between them? Well, she appeared to have put it behind her, and he would do likewise. No good could come of him lusting after a governess. Or even needing her. She was a gently bred lady in his employ and his own honour would not allow him to take advantage of her.

'Interference? Have you been accused of such in previous posts?'

He knew Miss Thame had been governess to other families before she came to Dolphin Court.

'Once or twice.' She was unsmiling, but her voice revealed hidden amusement. 'I cannot help myself, it seems.

It is often easier for an outsider to detect strains within a family and how they…er…mismanage those strains, thus worsening them. And, in those circumstances, I confess I find it difficult to keep my opinion to myself. Not everybody is open to advice, however, and previous employers have raised objections to my *getting above my station*. Understandably, perhaps, for we none of us enjoy criticism, do we? Even if, deep down, we know it to be justified.'

'That is true. At least I am forewarned, and I shall now brace myself for more of your *interference*.'

'Oh, I try to keep my advice to a maximum of once per day, so you are quite safe until this time tomorrow.'

Dolph roared with laughter. George joined them at that moment and said, 'What is the joke? Do share.'

'Miss Thame is managing my expectations about our future working relationship,' Dolph said, still chuckling. 'She has just warned me she will have no compunction in educating me, should she deem it necessary.'

'Oh. I say…that *is* a bold manoeuvre, Miss Thame, if I might say so. And what sort of education did you—?'

'George…' Dolph put as much warning as he could into his tone, realising his guest had mistaken his meaning. 'Miss Thame has promised to help me rebuild my relationship with the children and will tell me if I make mistakes. *That* is all I meant.'

'Ah. Yes. I see.' George executed a bow to the governess. 'My apologies—I assumed you were to teach Dolph decent penmanship at long last, Miss Thame. His handwriting is quite abysmal, you know.'

Smoothly recovered, my friend. Fortunately, Miss Thame appeared innocently oblivious of the end of the stick George had initially grasped, much to Dolph's relief after that earlier frisson between them.

'Now, then.' George rubbed his gloved hands briskly together. 'I understand from Dolph you are to dine with us tonight, Miss Thame?'

'Oh! I…' Her gaze flew to Dolph's. 'I was unsure if that was something of a spur-of-the-moment suggestion, my lord? If you would rather—'

'Nonsense!' George grinned at Dolph. 'No offence, Dolph, but a third to vary the conversation would be welcome, would it not?'

'Yes, without a doubt. And no offence taken, George. Your presence, Miss Thame, will hopefully lead to more civilised subjects of discussion at the table.'

George guffawed. 'Are you suggesting my conversation is uncivilised, old fellow?'

Dolph bit back a grin. 'I cast no such aspersion, *old fellow*. I was merely expressing a general desire. Well, Miss Thame? What do you say? Are you prepared to lend your calming influence at the dining table each night?'

'As you put it like that, my lord, the answer is yes.' A smile curved Miss Thame's lips, her eyes crinkling with silent laughter. 'After all, I have garnered plenty of experience in directing and diverting the attention and conversation of small boys, and that skill will no doubt prove valuable.'

They had reached the track that led to the Court. Steven, Nicholas and Wolf had ranged far ahead of the adults and were currently tussling over a fallen branch in a tug of war, the boys at one end and Wolf at the other. Shrieks of laughter rent the air.

'Evidently,' said Dolph.

'My lord…one of the most important lessons with children is to learn which battles to fight.'

Miss Thame's smile turned wistful as she watched the boys, and Dolph once again realised how lucky he had been it was she who had replied to his advertisement. Her fondness for his sons was clear, and she had undoubtedly helped them to recover from their mother's death.

'I do have one request, though, as we are on the subject of evenings,' said Miss Thame, her attention still on the boys. 'During your absence, I have been accustomed to play the piano for a short time after the boys are asleep. I wonder if I might continue the practice—mayhap while you gentlemen indulge in your after-dinner port?'

'Of course, Miss Thame, and we would also be delighted if you would play for us on the occasional evening as well.'

'I should say so,' exclaimed George. 'Unfortunate there are no ladies with whom to dance, though, eh, Dolph?'

Dolph just smiled. He, for one, had no desire to dance with anyone. But some light piano music to soothe the soul? That would be most welcome.

Dolph spent the afternoon visiting his tenants with Roger Pople, followed by catching up with his correspondence while George—claiming to be in need of exercise—set out to walk the half-mile to the village. He returned two hours later with a smug smile on his face and a twinkle in his eyes that put Dolph immediately upon the alert.

'And what delights did you discover in the village?' he asked his friend, somewhat dryly. 'I am surprised you were away so long, unless you dawdled at a snail's pace all the way there and back.'

'I called at the church and the Reverend Strong told me

all about its fascinating history and showed me its interesting architectural features.'

'Such as?'

'Eh?'

'I wondered which architectural features in particular?'

'Oh…you know…columns and stained-glass windows. The altar. The bell tower—you know, Dolph. The usual churchy type stuff.'

'It must have been a thorough examination of the building. As I recall, it is not that extensive.'

'Oh, well, we got chatting and he very kindly invited me to the vicarage for a glass of Madeira. Well, I could hardly refuse, could I? Not after he had been so attentive.'

'And was Miss Strong at home, perchance?'

'Why, yes. She was. I was delighted to be properly introduced to her. A charming girl.'

'George…please do not forget these people are my neighbours. And Miss Strong is an innocent.'

George's eyes opened wide. 'Dolph! You wound me! I am not Bluebeard, you know. And what is a little harmless flirtation? Miss Strong blushes most delightfully—she reminds me of a plump little chicken.'

He sighed, his expression dreamy.

'I have never yet seen a chicken blush, George. Do, please, take care. Miss Strong is young and not at all worldly-wise. You ought not to raise her expectations.'

'So you said before, old chap. And I shall watch my words, believe me. I have no wish to be sued for breach of promise.' He winked. '*I* am too worldly-wise to fall into *that* trap.'

Later, Leah stared at her reflection in her mirror. It had taken no time to choose a gown to wear to dinner, as she only had two suitable dresses from which to choose—a green sprigged muslin round gown, more suited to day wear, and an evening dress of light blue net over a white satin slip that she used to wear on the odd occasion Papa invited guests to the vicarage to dine. Both were somewhat outmoded, but neither of the gentlemen would expect a governess to wear the latest fashions. Besides, she was not dressing to impress—although that did not stop her spending an inordinate length of time styling her hair. For once, rather than scraping it back from her face, she pinned it more loosely and teased out a few tendrils to frame her face. She hesitated over whether to wear the necklace she had made out of Mama's wedding ring but, in the end, she decided in favour of it, simply because her upper chest looked horribly bare without it and it detracted from the horrid freckles that marred her skin.

Finally, it was time to go downstairs. The boys had been in bed for a while—they were both early risers—and Cassie had agreed to listen out for them as well as for Tilly. Leah's nervousness had killed her appetite and, as she descended the staircase and heard male voices drifting from the drawing room, her hands grew clammy and her pulse raced. Never had she dined in such exalted company and she prayed she would do nothing to disgrace herself.

'Miss Thame!'

Lord Hinckley leapt to his feet as Leah entered the room while Lord Dolphinstone was already standing next to the fireplace in a similar pose to that he had struck in her sitting room last night. That memory did nothing to quell her nerves but sent more heat spiralling through her as her mind's eye conjured up that intriguing glimpse of dark chest hair and her hand twitched in memory of that solid wall of muscle beneath her palm. Her unruly imagination painted a picture of his entire chest and she felt another of her wretched blushes rise up her neck to flood her cheeks.

Hinckley ushered her across the room, while Dolphinstone looked on, his expression—as it often was—inscrutable as his gaze roved over her, appraising her. As their eyes met, without volition that moment on the beach sprang into her consciousness—the moment when they had been so close, and time appeared frozen, and he had looked deep into her eyes and she had seen...what? Heat? Desire?...flare in the depths of his, triggering that same tug of attraction she had experienced before.

Her mouth dried, and she licked her lips. His Lordship's grey gaze dropped to her mouth, causing her pulse to leap. She lowered her own gaze, resolutely quashing her growing fascination with her employer.

'Good evening, my lords.' She bobbed a curtsy.

'Welcome, Miss Thame.' Dolphinstone pushed away from the mantel and nodded to her. 'Might we dispense with the "my lord" appellation? Sir will be sufficient. If that is agreeable to you, George?'

'Yes, indeed. Or Hinckley, should you prefer, Miss Thame. After all, you're almost one of the family, ain't that right, Dolph?'

Her employer's grey eyes gleamed with amusement, and he bowed again—this time, Leah felt sure, somewhat ironically. 'Indeed. But Dolphinstone is such a mouthful, so perhaps you would prefer to stick to "sir"?' He clearly did not intend Leah to reply as he continued, 'Shall we make our way to the dining room?'

Leah was surprised when Hinckley proffered his arm—it was a courtesy she had not anticipated, with them both

372 *The Rags-to-Riches Governess*

being earls and her a mere governess. She supposed gentlemanly behaviour came naturally to men of their ilk—although that had not been her experience in the past—but she still felt a fraud as she placed her hand on Hinckley's forearm. As they entered the dining room, however, she reminded herself this was an excellent opportunity for her to practise the etiquette expected in Society.

In the dining room, Dolphinstone himself held her chair as she sat, and she began to feel less of an interloper. A glass of wine served with the meal helped her relax, but she took little part in the conversation other than to reply when directly applied to for an opinion, which was seldom. Lord Hinckley proved to be an entertaining guest with a ready supply of stories, many of them self-deprecating. He clearly enjoyed being the centre of attention, and he recounted many anecdotes about London—in which Leah had no need to feign interest—before embarking on conjecture about the forthcoming Season.

'I hope I am not boring you, Miss Thame, with all this talk of people you have not met. I did not mean to rattle on so.'

'Not at all, sir. I am interested to hear about lives and places so far removed from my own experience.'

'Have you ever been to London?'

It was the first time Dolphinstone had directed a question to Leah, and she noticed his gaze lingered somewhere around the crown of her head as he avoided meeting her eyes.

'No. I have never visited, but I should like to.'

'Oh, you must! You would enjoy it. I have told Miss Strong the same thing.'

It was easy for Hinckley to say. He clearly had no clue

how impossible it was for a woman in Leah's position to simply go to a big city like London upon a whim. Although now, of course, she had precisely that opportunity—but she could not admit it. Fortunately, Hinckley did not wait for her to answer.

'I am eager for the start of the Season. Are you not, Dolph?'

'No, I have no intention of going away again so soon, as I told you before we left London.'

'But...' Hinckley's brow puckered. 'I made sure you would change your mind. After all, you missed the Season last year when you were overseas. Although, come to think of it, last year would have been too soon after Rebecca's death, would it not?'

Leah cringed at Hinckley touching on such a personal subject in front of her, and a glance at Dolphinstone saw his brow darken. Hinckley, however, appeared not to notice as he forked roast beef into his mouth, chewed and swallowed before continuing.

'Really, Dolph...you must reconsider. You ought to marry again, for the children's sake if not your own.'

'George. I have no intention of marrying again. Ever.'

Dolphinstone's growled words brought Hinckley up short.

'Ah. Yes. Of course. I apologise. None of my business. I quite see that.'

A strained silence prevailed. Leah wished the ground could swallow her up, even though it was Hinckley who was at fault, with his glib chatter. She raised her wine glass and sipped as the two men applied themselves to their food, casting around for a subject to ease the strained atmosphere.

'My lord...sir...' Dolphinstone looked up, his grey eyes hard. Leah's spirit reared up in response—she would not be cowed by that look. 'Might you visit the boys at their lessons tomorrow? They would be delighted to show you what progress they have made. Stevie, in particular, has made great strides in his reading and writing. Although that is not to decry Nicky's ability but, being younger, he is, of course, behind.'

'Yes. I will come in the afternoon, if that will fit in with your plans, Miss Thame.'

Embarrassment that she'd witnessed his reprimand of his guest gave way to nervous but pleasurable anticipation of him visiting the schoolroom the next day. Dolphinstone continued to stare at her, his features rigid. Then his expression softened.

His chest inflated as he inhaled. 'I apologise for barking at you, George. I know you only meant well. And I am sorry you had to witness that lapse in manners, Miss Thame. I cannot excuse myself.'

Leah experienced a satisfying sense of accomplishment. *She* had successfully soothed Dolphinstone's temper and rescued a fraught situation. She eyed His Lordship surreptitiously as she sipped her wine. He looked so very splendid in his evening clothes, radiating masculinity. He drew her attention like a magnet and, before she could help herself, she found regret coursing through her that he was so far out of her reach. Not only due to his status in Society but also because he was clearly still in love with his dead wife.

You fool! Did you learn nothing from Peter and Usk? Do not allow a handsome face to draw you in again. You will end up hurt.

'It's quite all right, old chap,' Hinckley was saying. 'I didn't think… I know returning here has been something of a trial for you. You will settle in time, I'm sure.'

Dolphinstone's lips quirked in a brief smile. 'I know.'

Leah sat awkwardly for a few minutes before realising she was expected to withdraw now they had finished eating. That was one of the stories with which Papa used to regale her and Mama about life in Society, for, as the younger son of a gentleman, he had travelled well in his youth and had spent some time in London during the Season, even though he had always been destined for the Church. She pushed back her chair and rose to her feet.

'If you will excuse me, I shall withdraw now. Is it still acceptable to you I practise on the pianoforte, sir?'

'It is. It will be a pleasure to hear music in the house again.'

Chapter Eight

❦

The next afternoon Dolph hesitated outside the schoolroom door. His palms, ridiculously, were damp, and his stomach roiled uneasily. He sucked in a calming breath. How absurd was this…a grown man nervous of talking to his own sons? They were only children. But maybe that was the trouble. If they were older, closer to manhood, he would not be so anxious about saying or doing something to upset them. Or even frighten them. What did *he* know about how to talk to children?

He rubbed his palms down his coat and steeled himself to push open the door.

The minute he was inside the room his nerves subsided when he saw the delight shining on the two little faces turned to him. He might still worry the boys would hate him for leaving them the way he did, but it seemed his sons were more forgiving than he deserved. A little of the guilt he had carried for the past sixteen months slipped from his shoulders.

'Greet your father, boys.'

Miss Thame's murmured instruction drew his attention. She was once again clad in her governess garb, as he thought of it. Every inch the respectable governess. She had appeared a different woman last evening—alluring in a way that captured his interest—with her hair pinned in a much softer style and wearing a blue gown that accentuated her porcelain skin and revealed the upper slopes of her breasts. The only adornment had been a simple blue ribbon from which a gold ring was suspended. His gaze had returned to her décolletage time and again—drawn as though to a magnet—as he'd speculated about whose ring it was. Her mother's, perhaps? It was too small to fit a man's finger. A memory from last evening formed in his mind's eye, of Leah at the pianoforte, her slender, sensitive fingers dancing across the keys, the pale vulnerability of her nape and the long lines of her back... He jerked his thoughts away from those mental images before his body could respond.

'Good afternoon, Papa,' the boys chorused obediently across the width of the room.

'Good afternoon, Stevie. Good afternoon, Nicky.'

'Would you care to hear the boys read to you, sir?' Leah—as he had begun to think of her inside his head—approached him, and her fresh scent filled his senses. She lowered her voice, smiling a conspirator's smile. 'Would you ask Nicky to read first, as he is a little less sure of himself in the schoolroom than he is outside it? If Stevie reads first, it will make him more anxious.'

'Whatever you think best,' Dolph murmured, then raised his voice. 'Nicky, will you read to me first?'

His younger son's face fell, but he nodded stoically.

Miss Thame returned to sit with Stevie and redirected his

attention to the map they had been studying when Dolph came in. As he listened to Nicky laboriously reading aloud the words chalked on his slate, Dolph also eavesdropped on the way Leah tested Stevie upon his understanding of the world. She teased out Stevie's knowledge, and his admiration and respect for her grew as she seemed instinctively to understand when the boy reached his limit, never pushing him too far beyond his capabilities, so he didn't get discouraged and give up. Dolph attempted to adopt the same tactic with Nicky, although he soon realised all his younger son needed was a huge amount of patient repetition to try to imprint the letters and the sounds they made into his brain.

He had vowed to concentrate solely on the boys during his visit to the schoolroom, but it proved impossible to completely ignore his growing fascination with Leah. That unexpected frisson between them on the beach when their gazes had locked, kindling the slow burn of desire deep inside him—for the first time in a very long time—had unsettled him enough. As a consequence, he had found himself uncharacteristically tongue-tied at the dining table, wary of revealing any hint of his inappropriate interest in her, and she, too, had been clearly ill at ease. He was glad she had agreed to dine with them, however, and she had impressed him with her skill in defusing the tension after George's crass remark about Rebecca.

When the time came to swap over, he was impressed with Stevie's quick mind and his confidence with reading—he was reading from a text rather than from a slate—and he noticed Leah completely changed her approach to help Nicky, who was clearly struggling with the concept of maps and countries.

But, still, only half his attention remained on his son and

his schoolwork. Still, it proved impossible to keep his eyes from straying to Leah, eyeing her tightly pinned hair and imagining how it would look, and feel, if let loose to flow over her shoulders and down her back.

And those freckles... Where else did they dot her pale, translucent skin?

As the days passed, such improper thoughts made him careful to avoid being alone with Leah. When they spoke, their conversation—as if by mutual, unspoken agreement—focussed on the children and their progress, and when Dolph visited the schoolroom, Leah's attention remained steadfastly on her pupils. Dolph would watch them with an aching hollow in his chest, envying their closeness, hoping he might soon achieve that same, easy relationship with his sons.

The evenings became less fraught, with George as entertaining a raconteur as ever and proving the perfect foil. It was then, at dinner and afterwards, that Dolph noticed more of those telltale signs Leah was still troubled. At odd moments her thoughts seemed to turn inward, and a vertical line would score the pale skin between her brows while her teeth worried at her lower lip, sending Dolph's pulse rocketing.

The relative intimacy of those evenings bothered him. What would happen when George left? He could hardly insult Leah by not dining with her, but what if this unexpected lustful interest continued? He had never before considered taking a mistress, but that might be the only solution if his physical needs continued to plague him... Surely there must be a local widow who would be happy to— That line

of thought slammed to a halt as every fibre of his being re-
belled against the very idea of a mistress.

The weather turned colder over the next few weeks, with
brisk winds bringing daily showers of hail or sleet. Every-
day life fell into a pattern: every afternoon, George rode
or walked into the village—rendering Dolph uneasy as he
wondered about George's intentions towards Miss Strong—
and Dolph would visit the schoolroom for half an hour. The
deteriorating weather increasingly confined the boys to the
house and, on those days, instead of their daily brisk walk,
they were set free to play as soon as morning lessons were
over. The house would shake to the din of thundering feet,
shrieks of laughter and excitable barks from Wolf, who, increasingly, had abandoned Dolph's company in favour of
spending time with the boys. Later, after afternoon lessons,
there would be more outdoor exercise or a quieter session of
indoor play, when the boys would fight battles with their toy
soldiers or play a game of hide-and-seek, with occasional
bursts of excitement as someone was found.

On the first day Dolph had experienced the phenomenon
of what Leah called *indoor play*, he had emerged from his
study ready to restore the peace but, at that precise moment,
the noise had suddenly abated and order had been restored.
Later that afternoon, when Leah had brought the boys and
Tilly to the drawing room to say goodnight—another habit
that had become a routine—she had turned to him, saying
with a smile that reached deep inside him and tweaked his
heartstrings, 'Do you now appreciate why I take the boys
outside for exercise whenever possible?'

It had taken him a moment or two to identify the emotion triggered by her smile. Loneliness. That was how he felt. And, without warning, resentment—aimed squarely at Rebecca—spiralled through him. How could she have left him...left her *children*...in such a cruel way? As quickly as it arose, his anger with his dead wife subsided and he was consumed once again with guilt.

My fault. I should have noticed. I let her down.

He had retreated to his study without answering Leah, headed straight for the decanter and poured himself a glass of claret, downing it in one, mentally shoving those feelings into a box and slamming the lid. He didn't *want* to feel, dammit. Nothing could change what had happened.

On the twenty-third day of February, which had so far lived up to its reputation as the worst winter month weather-wise, Dolph came downstairs dressed for dinner to discover a message from George had been delivered, along with a letter for Leah.

'Have that taken up to Miss Thame, Palmer,' he said to the butler as he opened the seal on George's note.

My dear Dolph
Reverend Strong has kindly invited me to dine tonight.
I know you will not object and, as it has been a rare
dry day, I shall walk back later by the light of a lantern
so you need have no fears for my safe return.
Your friend
Hinckley

Dolph's first reaction was dread at the prospect of dining *à deux* with Leah, but he soon realised there was no point avoiding it—George would not be at the Court for ever, and Dolph must learn to behave normally around his sons' governess whether they were alone or not. He went to the drawing room to await Leah, positioning himself by the fireside and staring mindlessly into the flames until he heard her enter.

He turned. She was dressed tonight in her green muslin gown, her shawl around her shoulders, and that wedding ring around her neck, tonight suspended on a green ribbon. Her cheeks were flushed, and her eyes sparkled, prompting him to wonder who her letter had been from. She was clearly happy with the news it contained. For a split second his imagination conjured up an image of her dressed in a fashionable evening gown, with sapphires or pearls around her neck, but he batted that picture aside with a surge of self-loathing.

I pay her wages. She is powerless. If I do not control these lustful urges for the poor woman, it will be her who suffers. Not me.

'I'm afraid it is just the two of us for dinner this evening, Miss Thame.' He would make no big thing of them dining alone together. She, he knew, would follow his lead. 'George sent word that he is invited to dine at the vicarage.'

'The vicarage?' She frowned. 'He visits the Reverend Strong almost daily, does he not? Or is Miss Strong the magnet that draws him to the village so frequently?'

'George enjoys the Reverend's conversation, but I won't deny he also takes pleasure in Miss Strong's company—he is a man who enjoys the society of women probably more than that of other men.' Dolph resolved to warn George once again about not raising Miss Strong's expectations. 'He means nothing by it… He likes to flirt and pay compliments.'

Leah's eyes narrowed.

'It's just his way,' Dolph added. 'Now, shall we go to dinner?'

Once seated, with bowls of soup in front of them, Dolph said, 'I see you received a letter today.'

Her cheeks coloured. He adored the way she blushed so readily—an unexpected trait in a woman who was ordinarily so sensible and unemotional.

'I did.' She raised a spoonful of soup to her mouth.

'And...?' he prompted.

She fixed him with a steady look and a lift of her brows.

'Did you have time to read it before you came down to dinner?'

'I did, thank you.'

Dolph rubbed his jaw, stubble rasping his fingers. 'Will you tell me who it was from?'

He caught the twitch of her lips before she raised her wine glass and sipped.

'Am I obliged to?'

'Of course not.' Dolph sipped from his own glass. 'But I thought you might like to share your news. I recall from your interview you have no immediate family.' Her gaze slid from his and sought her plate. A thought struck him. 'Was it from your solicitor? Does that explain your reluctance to speak of it?'

'No.' She still studied her plate but had ceased to eat. 'It was from someone I met at that meeting, though.'

It was Dolph's turn to raise his brows. A man, perhaps? Did that account for her secrecy?

The servants came in with the main course and dessert then, and the conversation paused as they helped themselves to game pie, creamed leeks, boiled potatoes and carrots, and more wine was poured.

'It was not from a man,' Leah said when they were alone again. It was as though she'd read his mind. 'It was from another lady. But that is all I can say, I'm afraid.'

He could pry no further without being rude, but the exchange left him feeling unsettled. He truly did dislike the idea of her keeping secrets from him, not least because she was in charge of his sons, but he could not force the truth from her. Thinking of Stevie and Nicky, though...

'Do you think the boys have forgiven me yet?'

She shot him a puzzled look. 'Forgiven you?'

'Yes. For abandoning them.'

'Children are very forgiving... They will judge you on how you behave with them now and henceforth. They are not like adults, forever looking back and regretting this thing they said or that way they behaved.'

Her words comforted him. 'I hope you are right. When I returned, I feared they would never be able to forgive me, but they have never given me reason to believe they resent the way I left them. I am immensely proud of them...and I do thank you because I know that is due to you and your care for them. They are lucky to have you. As am I.'

Her gaze lowered again, and her hand rose to cover the ring suspended around her neck.

'Did that ring belong to someone special? I have noticed you wear it every evening, albeit with a change of ribbon.'

'It was my mother's wedding band.' She sipped more wine. 'I wear it all day, too, beneath my gown.'

Hidden beneath her awful, drab governess garb.

She shrugged, appearing almost embarrassed. 'It keeps the memory of my parents close. Mama's ring and Papa's fob watch.'

'Ah...the watch I have seen on your desk in the schoolroom?'

She nodded. 'I have Papa's old writing slope too. I always feel him near whenever I use it. I do not need wealth...' she appeared to have forgotten he was there; it was as though she was talking to herself '...not when I have such treasures and such precious memories. And I don't...' She paused, and he saw her throat ripple as she swallowed. Then she shook her head and sat a little straighter. When she looked at him her eyes were bright with emotion. 'I didn't feel as alone as long as I had them with me.'

'You must miss them very much, but it seems you have happy memories of your childhood.'

'Oh, indeed. My parents...they were very much in love. I always hoped—' Her cheeks turned fiery red.

'You hoped...?'

She shrugged and gave him a rueful smile. 'You will think me a fool. It was never more than a forlorn hope, really, but my ideal if I ever married was for a love match, like my parents. I should not talk like this, I know, but I fear the wine has loosened my tongue and I am feeling somewhat nostalgic.'

His heart went out to her. 'It must have been difficult for you—a woman alone—when your father died.' She had told him at interview that she'd been nineteen years old. 'You must have felt very alone.' Her words sounded again in his head. 'You changed from *you don't* to *you didn't*. May I hope that means you feel more at home here than you have in previous households?'

Her smile was sad. Reflective. 'Yes. Everyone here is so friendly. And the children are an absolute joy.'

Her voice cracked on her final words. Her hand trembled as she raised her wine glass once again, and without conscious thought, Dolph reached across and gently squeezed her shoulder. She started at his touch, and he snatched his hand away, his hand—his entire arm—tingling from the contact.

'My apologies,' he said. 'I did not mean to startle you.'

Fool! What were you thinking?

He had finished his meal, and to cover his dismay, he selected a large slice of apple pie from the dish on the table and poured custard over it.

'Would you care for dessert, Miss Thame?'

She nodded. 'Thank you.'

Trust something prosaic like food to restore the equilibrium. Dolph dished out a slice of pie for Leah and then handed her the jug of custard before tucking into his own dessert.

His instinct to reach out and comfort her had shaken him. He must take more care—she had revealed more of her heart than she realised, and that must act as a warning to him to ignore his desires. Leah was happy here at Dolphin Court. She considered it as her home. He would never forgive himself if she felt obliged to leave because he could not control himself. He was her employer; in a position of authority over her. His honour as a gentleman would not allow him to take advantage of such power.

If he were to follow his natural desire and seduce her, the only remedy would be to offer marriage and—quite apart from his own resolve to never wed again—how could he do that to a woman who had just confided in him her ideal marriage was a love match? He was incapable of love. Incapable of making any woman happy.

I would drive her to despair, just as I did Rebecca.

He picked up his glass and tipped the remaining contents down his throat as Leah set her spoon down and rose to her feet.

'If you will excuse me, I am very tired, sir, and so I shall say goodnight.'

He'd noticed dark circles around her eyes had formed over the past week, suggesting she was not sleeping well—was she still troubled over whatever she had discovered at that meeting in Bristol at the end of January? Maybe he would ask her again about it, but not this evening. He would choose a more suitable time and place.

'Of course. Goodnight, Miss Thame.'

Chapter Nine

Leah's cheeks were still burning when she reached her bedchamber. She lit her candle, undressed swiftly, donned her nightgown and climbed into bed, shivering until her body warmed the chilly sheets. What had she been thinking, to reveal so much to Dolph? Her stomach churned and she felt tears scald her eyes. What on *earth* had she been thinking?

Of all the nights for Lord Hinckley to be absent, this must have been the very worst. She had already been unsettled by Aurelia's letter when she came downstairs. Sally, the housemaid, had delivered it to her just as she was leaving her bedchamber, having dressed for dinner, and she had returned to her room and read it quickly, her heart thumping with excitement and hope—and joy at having a sister...*two* sisters...in this world.

But the letter had also reminded her the day was fast approaching when she must leave the children and Dolphin Court. And leaving Dolph—she had found herself, in the weeks since his return, thinking of him by the nickname

George used—would also be a wrench, despite knowing there could never be anything between them, for she already cared for him and she had, in recent days, found herself longing for the right to soothe away the grief that still shimmered in his eyes in unguarded moments.

So by the time she had gone downstairs, her emotions had already been in turmoil with that mixture of joy, excitement, dread and pure misery, and then Dolph had unsettled her further with his teasing questions about the letter and then utterly disarmed her when he had revealed his fear the children would never forgive him. Her heart had gone out to him, and the wine had lulled her, and he had been so kind, so understanding when she'd spoken of Mama and Papa, that she had almost forgotten she was talking to him. To Dolph. Her brooding, handsome, rugged employer. It wasn't until her emotions had threatened to overcome her, and she had felt his hand on her shoulder, offering comfort much as she would do for the boys, that she had come to her senses, eaten her pudding in record time, gabbled an excuse and escaped.

This evening had served as a warning, though. The spark of attraction she'd felt on that first night had not sputtered out but was now a steady flame. Her feelings for Dolph had grown, and she now dreaded saying goodbye.

A feeling of hopelessness washed through her. She had recognised the occasional gleam in his eyes when he looked at her. He desired her, strange as that was to believe. Although she had little experience of men, she did know they seldom found women like her—tall, red-haired and freckled—alluring. Peter and Usk had taught her that when they discarded her after she ceased to be of any use to them— Peter after Papa died, and Usk as soon as he won his wager.

Leah huddled deeper under the bedclothes. She closed her eyes, willing sleep to overtake her, but still her mind whirled with the many changes fast approaching, and her many worries about her future. If she met the conditions of Lady Tregowan's will, then by this time next year she would be wed. What if her husband turned out to be a scoundrel? Was her judgement of the true nature of men sound enough to protect her and keep her safe, and to sort the decent gentlemen from the rogues? Her record to date gave her little confidence—her experiences with both Peter and Usk proved her lack of good judgement.

One thing was certain... Once she was wed, every-thing—her life, her future, her inheritance—would depend upon that one man. Her husband.

But she had no choice but to go to London and to try.

Leaving Dolphin Court, and all the people she had grown to care about, was bad enough, but the other side of that coin was what awaited her in her future. How would the three half-sisters be received in Society? Their wealth would help to smooth their paths—money always proved an excellent lubricant—but, as Aurelia had already discovered, there would always be some to peer down their noses at three down-at-heel gentlewomen joining their ranks.

She almost wished she had never gone to that meeting... Then she could continue her life here in blissful ignorance and would not be plagued by this ceaseless uncertainty.

Except...then I wouldn't have met Aurelia and Beatrice.

Only the thought of her two half-sisters buoyed her spir-its. For the most part. Because even that godsend was two-edged—what if they did not like one another? Or what if Aurelia and Beatrice became friends but disliked Leah? She had been so happy to receive the letter from Aurelia, but a pleasant letter did not guarantee an amicable relationship in person, and Aurelia had struck Leah as somewhat confrontational at that meeting with Mr Henshaw. Beatrice seemed more amenable, although mayhap a touch timid.

Leah could only pray the three of them would become friends because, if not, then her greatest fear might come to pass—that she would leave here and that she would end up alone.

The following day Dolph was in his study, reading a treatise on animal husbandry, when Nicky burst into his study from behind the secret panel that led to one of the secret passages with which Dolphin Court was blessed. Nicky slammed to a halt, his eyes wide with dismay as he saw his father. In his hand he clutched a carved wooden horse: a toy Dolph recalled from his own childhood.

'Nicky…' the breathless voice sounded from within the secret passage '…you *know* you are not meant to come this way.' Leah appeared in the opening in the panelled wall. 'Oh!' Her hand went to her hair, which had worked free from the hairpins that normally held every strand strictly in place, and her cheeks flamed. 'I am so sorry we disturbed you.'

'You are not disturbing me, Miss Thame.' But that was untrue. Loose tendrils of hair formed an auburn halo around her head, enticingly, and an image formed in his mind's eye of her hair tumbling loose around her pale, freckled, naked shoulders. He swallowed, thrusting that image away. 'This paper is so dull I am in danger of falling asleep. Nicho—Nicky…will you allow me to see your horse?' Nicky approached him and handed over his toy. 'I used to play with this when I was a boy.' Dolph examined the carving. 'The saddle and bridle were painted blue, and I called him Thunder. And there was another one, with red saddlery, called Lightning.'

'That is Stevie's pony.'

'Ah, of course; you would have one each. Have you given them names?'

Nicky nodded. 'Mine is Bullet and Stevie's is Peg'sus. He says that's what he will name his real pony when he gets one. But he says I can't have one yet 'cause I'm too little. But I can ride Billy as well as he can.'

'I noticed Old Billy is still around, but I should think he's a bit wide for your little legs, Nicky.' From the corner of his eye he saw a smile flicker around Leah's lips as she nodded approvingly. 'Well…' and he wondered why he had not thought of it before '… I should think it is time for both you and Stevie to have your own ponies—ones the right size for you. I shall make it my priority. After all, it is important for a gentleman to learn to ride from a young age, is it not, Miss Thame?'

'It is,' she said. 'Now, Nicky, let us leave your father in peace. Stevie is no doubt wondering where we can have hidden so successfully.'

She smiled at Dolph. No longer distracted by her hair, he realised the shadows under her eyes were even more pronounced than before.

'Stevie will not ignore my instructions to avoid that passage, unlike this little imp.'

She ruffled Nicky's hair and started to shepherd him from the study as Dolph pushed the secret panel shut with a click and wished he could behave half as naturally with his sons.

'Papa?'

'Yes, Nicky?'

'*I'm* going to be in the cavalry when I grow up. I'm going to fight with the Duke of Wellington and beat Napoleon.'

'Now, Nicky.' Leah flashed a smile at Dolph. 'You know Napoleon has already been beaten, and I doubt the Duke will still be fighting battles when you are old enough to join the cavalry.'

'But I *want* to fight. Stevie doesn't even want to, and he'll only be an earl when he grows up and that's *boring*. Like lessons.'

Dolph bit back a laugh as his younger son's scornful gaze scanned his desk. 'Nicholas. Apologise to Miss Thame, if you please,' he said. 'It is impolite to call her lessons boring.'

Nicky hung his head. 'I'm sorry, Miss Thame.'

'I accept your apology, Nicky. Now come.'

They went out into the hall, but before Leah could close the study door, Nicky peered back around its edge.

'You will not forget about our ponies, Papa?'

'I won't forget.'

'Can I tell Stevie?'

'Yes, of course you may.'

'Hurrah!'

Dolph heard the scamper of feet as Nicky ran off. On the spur of the moment, he called, 'Miss Thame?'

She reappeared in the study, her eyes wary. 'Sir?'

'I should like to speak with you—a matter I cannot discuss in front of the children. Would you arrange for someone to watch the boys for a short while, and come back here?'

Better to quiz her about what was causing sleepless nights here, in the daylight, than risk another too-intimate conversation after dark.

An anxious frown creased her forehead. She inclined her head. 'Of course. I will take the boys up to the nursery. Cassie will watch over them.'

Fifteen minutes later, having left the boys in Cassie's care and scraped back her wayward hair, pinning it ruthlessly in place, Leah descended the stairs and crossed the large entrance hall to the study door. She couldn't quell her apprehension as she paused and smoothed her palms over her hips. Had he noticed her infatuation with him last night? She'd tried to hide it, but that proved trickier without Lord Hinckley to provide a distraction.

Or was he unhappy with the way she cared for and taught the boys? She believed she struck the right balance between work and play—and he'd seemed to take their invasion of his study in good part—but many parents failed to recognise the necessity of physical activity for boisterous lads.

What if he sent her away? She wasn't ready to leave. Not yet. She pushed aside the sly inner voice that whispered maybe it would be for the best if he *did* send her away—from him. He was part of the reason she was still reluctant to leave, but she also hated the thought of leaving the children before she absolutely must, even though they were already more relaxed around their father. That excuse for delay was rapidly receding.

She sucked in a steadying breath, straightened her shoulders, lifted her chin, knocked on the study door and entered.

Dolph was at his desk, writing. He raised his head and smiled briefly. 'Do take a seat.' He indicated the pair of wingback chairs set either side of the fireplace. 'I shall be with you in a minute.'

Feeling calmer, certain if he intended a reprimand he

would do it at his desk, Leah sat as bid. But that sense of calm did not last, as her worries over the future once again scurried around inside her head.

'Have you discussed your dilemma with anyone yet, Miss Thame?'

His Lordship's quiet question interrupted her constantly circling thoughts. His grey eyes studied her, and she saw nothing other than kindness and concern in their depths. Appalled, she felt her throat thicken. Sympathy... She could cope with anything other than sympathy. She swallowed down her emotion and stretched her lips in a smile.

'You are mistaken, my lord. There is no dilemma.'

He raised one brow and indicated Leah's lap. Looking down, she saw her fingers busy pleating and repleating the wool of her gown. She released the fabric and smoothed her skirts, her face heating.

'Or perhaps it is my fault?'

Her gaze flew to his as her stomach turned a somersault. Had he indeed noticed she had developed a *tendre* for him?

'Do I make you nervous?'

'No!' Instinctively, she touched the hard shape of Mama's ring beneath her gown.

A smile played around his lips. 'I thought not, judging by the way you usually speak your mind. Look... Miss Thame... I do not suggest myself as confidant, but I hope you will take my earlier advice and confide in a friend— perhaps Miss Strong? You deny the existence of a dilemma, but my observations of you since my return tell me you are increasingly troubled.'

His observations of me?

Leah's breath seized at the thought he had taken such

notice of her. She moistened her lips and swallowed again, this time to try to quell the fluttering in her stomach.

'I am surprised you would notice such a trivial matter when you have so many responsibilities.'

His smile was puzzled. 'Would you rather I remain oblivious when someone in my household is troubled? Allow me to help. Please. Miss Strong *is* your friend, is she not?'

'Yes, she is.'

'In that case, if you would like to confide in her, you only need to say the word and I shall arrange for one of the servants to care for the boys during your absence.' His grey eyes twinkled. 'I fear, Miss Thame, I shall have to allow you yet *another* half-day off.'

His words kindled a warmth inside her. He was so hard to resist. He was kind. He talked to her as another adult, not as a servant, and he cared. Oh, not in the way she longed for him to care about her, but he did care for those around him. He was a good man. She felt it deep in her soul.

'Thank you, sir. I shall think about it, and let you know what I decide.' She rose to her feet. 'If that is all, I must return to the children.'

After Sunday service the following day Leah noticed once again how Lord Hinckley danced attendance upon Philippa, paying her extravagant compliments, which, to be fair, she appeared to thoroughly enjoy. He also appeared on excellent terms with the Reverend Strong, who, in Leah's opinion, really ought to discourage His Lordship for his daughter's sake—could he really believe an earl would contemplate matrimony with a country vicar's daughter?

Worried Philippa would be hurt, Leah garnered her courage to broach the subject with Dolph.

'I know His Lordship is your friend and guest, but do you see now why I was concerned about his behaviour?' she said, low-voiced, as they stood shivering by the carriage with the boys, waiting for Hinckley to join them.

The temperature had fallen dramatically over the past couple of days, the weather having turned cold and dry with bright, sunny days and a sharp frost every night. The village pond had already frozen over.

'I do, and I admit I share your concern to a certain extent. I fear Miss Strong is unaccustomed to such casual flirtations as are normal within Society, and she might believe George's attention to be genuine.'

Leah frowned. 'He *is* lying to her, then?'

'It's not that simple. Gentlemen in our world are expected to flirt with ladies, and they often pay extravagant compliments that are without substance, but the ladies of the *beau monde* are worldly enough not to attach too much significance to such behaviour.'

The pitfalls ahead of Leah loomed large. She would be seeking a husband among men of a similar character and outlook as Hinckley, and she had already proved she was as unworldly as Philippa. Look at how she had fallen for the lies of both Peter and of Usk.

She watched as Hinckley bowed to Philippa, clearly saying farewell. They both looked rapt as they gazed at one another, and Leah frowned, doubtful all of a sudden. Could she be worrying over nothing?

'They do look smitten with one another.'

'Oh, I have no doubt George *is* smitten...for now. But he is a man who regularly fancies himself in love—it's in his nature—and I have seen this too often to trust his adoration will endure this time. I *have* warned him to take care,

398	The Rags-to-Riches Governess

however, and reminded him of her inexperience in matters of the heart.'

Anger stirred on Philippa's behalf. In Leah's opinion, Hinckley should take responsibility for his own behaviour. He was a grown man... What right did he have to treat Philippa as a convenient way to pass the time, leading her on? Leah liked Lord Hinckley, but this made him appear as no better than Lord Usk when he had fooled Leah into kissing him. Or, even worse, than Lord Tregowan, who had seduced Mama, an innocent, and then offloaded her onto another man like a second-hand coat.

Hinckley finally joined them and, as they climbed into the carriage for the journey home, Leah decided she *would* accept Dolph's offer of time off to visit Philippa. The need to unburden herself to a friend had become almost irresistible, and she could at the same time warn her friend to treat Lord Hinckley with caution.

Chapter Ten

That night sleep again evaded Leah as worries about her future tormented her. The minute she lay in her bed, they surged to the fore, keeping her mind active even as her body craved sleep. With a muttered oath, she threw aside the bedcovers and rose from the bed, pushing her feet into her slippers. She lit a candle, slipped her dressing gown on over her nightgown and left her bedchamber by the connecting door to her sitting room. The fire was not yet dead, so she stirred it with the poker and laid small sticks in a lattice over the hot ashes. In no time, the dry wood caught, allowing her to feed bigger sticks and lumps of coal onto the fire.

When it was burning steadily, she went to the table by the window and pulled her writing slope towards her, running her fingertips over the rosewood surface, her mind travelling back into the past with every familiar scratch and dent. It had belonged to Papa—her *real* father, not the man whose blood she shared—and she treasured it and the memories it evoked; happy memories, of Papa writing his sermons, his pen quietly scratching over the paper while Mama sewed, her head bent over her needle. A lump of pain formed in Leah's throat. She had been so very alone since Papa died...no one to really care if she lived or she died. Dolphin Court had given her a sense of belonging she had felt nowhere else, and now she must leave here and face an unknown future with two half-sisters who were virtual strangers. She must say goodbye to the three children she adored, and how she dreaded that prospect. How would she say those words without dissolving into tears and making her departure even more painful for them? Increasingly, too, the prospect of never seeing Dolph again played havoc with her emotions.

Her head might accept that going to London and attempting to fulfil the conditions of Lady Tregowan's will was the only sensible course of action, but her heart was still not convinced.

Cursing again beneath her breath, she opened the slope to form a writing surface and then took a sheet of paper from inside. She opened the inkwell, picked up her pen and began to reply to Aurelia's letter, hoping the activity would help quell the turmoil of her thoughts. It did not. She pushed her chair back, crossed to put more coal on the fire and then paced the room, her mind still hopelessly alert. After several turns up and down the room, a wail penetrated Leah's constantly circling inner monologue.

Stevie!

She did not take her candle, knowing from experience the light would rouse him more fully and make it much harder to settle him back down. She went out onto the landing and hurried along it to the boys' room. Stevie was thrashing around, whimpers escaping him from time to time. Leah sat on the mattress and stroked his clammy forehead as she murmured soothing words, her eyes growing accustomed to the dark.

'Hush. It's all right. There's nothing to fear, sweetie. Settle down now. I'm here.'

Gradually Stevie calmed, lying still. His thumb stole into his mouth—a habit she still could not break him of at night although he no longer sucked it during the day, long since cured of it by his little brother's scorn. Gradually, Stevie's breathing eased, and Leah stood to go. Stevie's eyes opened, looking right at her, and he mumbled something around his thumb. Gently she removed it from his mouth and asked him to repeat what he'd said.

'I dreamed you went away, like Mama did.'

Her heart cracked in her chest. She could not promise him she would not go. Oh, but how she wished she could give him that reassurance. She stroked his hair back from his forehead again.

'It was just a dream, Stevie. See? I am here.'

She bent to kiss his cheek, tormented even more by the dread of saying goodbye. His eyes fluttered closed and his thumb crept into his mouth once more. He sighed. Leah straightened, watching him; within minutes he was asleep, and Leah slipped out of the room, having left the door ajar. She frowned at a pool of light further along the landing, then gasped, her heart in her throat as a dark shape stirred and stepped away from the wall, resolving itself into the silhouette of a man.

'It's all right. It is me.' Dolph spoke in a whisper. 'I left the candle along there so the light wouldn't disturb Stevie. You did well to settle him down again so quickly.'

Her insides fluttered at the realisation he must have stood in the doorway, watching her. Listening to her.

'Thank you.' Leah stepped past him. 'Goodnight, sir.'

'Wait.'

His hand on her shoulder sent shock waves rippling through her as her breath caught. His fingers closed, not violently but more in a caress. She faced him and his hand dropped away. He was still dressed in his evening clothes, enticingly masculine in black coat and white neckcloth. An evocative mix of citrus, brandy and musky maleness wreathed through her senses, sending a pleasurable shiver racing through her, right to her tingling nerve endings. His breathing sounded ragged in the hush of the night but, rather than fearing him and the subtle tension that appeared to hold him in its grip—or even fearing the alarming leap of her pulse and those tingles sweeping her skin—Leah felt drawn to him, as a moth was tempted to a flame. Even though she knew, as a moth did not, that flames burned. She stood still and waited, hardly daring to breathe.

'I heard floorboards creaking.' His gaze raked her face, and she struggled to blank her expression. 'Footsteps…in your sitting room. Back and forth. For several minutes. Are you still struggling to sleep?'

'Evidently. But it was not I who disturbed Stevie.'

'I do not accuse you of it. It was one of his nightmares, I assume?'

Leah nodded.

'We cannot talk here, and I confess I, too, am not yet tired. Will you join me in a glass of brandy downstairs? It might help us both sleep, and I would welcome the chance to talk to you about Steven and these nightmares.'

Leah's mouth dried as her pulse beat erratically at the thought of being alone with him. She should refuse. But...

'Yes, of course.' She scanned the dark landing. 'No Wolf?'

The dog would at least have provided some distraction for her.

'No. I left him in my room.'

She forced a quiet chuckle, desperate to appear nonchalant. 'That was wise. I'm sure if Stevie caught sight of Wolf, it would thoroughly wake him up.'

From being wary of the dog, Stevie now worshipped him and they were all but inseparable during the day.

Dolph led the way downstairs to the library, where he lit candles on either end of the mantelshelf and poked the fire into life before pouring two glasses of brandy.

'I was reading in here before I came up, so I knew the fire was still warm.' He handed her a glass. 'Have you thought further about confiding in Miss Strong?'

'I have. I shall write and ask when I might visit her.'

His gaze did not waver from her face, and she felt the weight of it...read the concern in his grey eyes.

'I am relieved, and I hope it might set your mind at rest. You look tired, and I know the boys are early risers.'

'I shall cope.'

The urge to be honest with him, to tell him she must leave, rose up within her, but she could not possibly tell him now. Not here, in the dead of night, attired only in her nightgown, with her dressing gown clasped tightly around her and her hair casually plaited. She knew, without recourse to a mirror, her hair would be a mess—it had ever been unruly and required ruthless pinning during the day to tame it and render it suitable for a governess.

Dolphinstone stared at her frowningly before poking the fire again and feeding it with more coal. Then he faced her, nudging the candlestick out of the way to allow him to prop his elbow on the end of the mantelshelf.

'Come. Sit. I wish to discuss Steven.'

Dolph watched as Leah moved to a chair by the fire, her movements graceful and, somehow, measured. She had poise. She held herself in a way many a society lady could only dream of emulating, even though she was attired in plain nightclothes and her hair...her hair... His heart gave a funny little thump at the sight of those fiery tendrils floating around her crown. That fat rope of plaited hair, held loosely in place by a pale green ribbon, draped over her shoulder and her breast—a siren call to a man to tug the bow free and to plunge his fingers through the heavy, shining mass.

For God's sake, man! Stop this fantasy. You told her you wanted to talk to her about Steven.

It had been a lie. He would have said anything at that point, with the scent of warm woman filling his senses, to bask in her company for just a few more moments. Anything to avoid retiring to his cold lonely bedchamber. How had the simple act of returning to Dolphin Court awakened within him this urge for female company? The desire to be held? The drive to hold a warm, willing woman in his arms and to bury himself deep within her heat? He had told himself it was the memory of Rebecca and the echoes of married life, but could that be the only reason for this strange emptiness deep in his soul? He and Rebecca had never been that close. It had been a good enough marriage—they had each passed their time leading their own lives and doing more or less as they wished, no different from so many Society marriages. His political interests and the estates occupied his time and attention. Rebecca had disliked London and its frantic pace of life and had been content to spend her time in Somerset with the children.

But she wasn't content, was she? And I did not even notice.

He shivered as reality hit him, chilling him. He had failed her. He had not even seen the warning signs.

'You wished to speak to me about Steven, sir?'

Leah's quiet question brought his attention back to her.

'Yes. I am concerned about him.' And that was true, even though it had not been Steven in his thoughts when he had spoken. At times, his son and heir seemed so timid...too anxious for a child, far more so than the younger, more rambunctious Nicky. 'He is intelligent and has a quick understanding, but I do worry how he will cope when he goes to school. He is so nervous.' Her brows drew together, and he added, 'He will have to go away to school when he is older, you know that. I should like your opinion as to what we can do to toughen him up a bit. Is there anything we should do to—?' He fell silent at her disapproving expression before continuing, 'I am aware I still do not know the boys very well, but I wish to learn; to be guided by you.' He scrubbed his hand up the side of his face, feeling the rasp of stubble. 'I just want to help my son become the best man he can be.'

She smiled at that. 'You can do that by allowing him to be a little boy. He *is* still only seven, you know. And please do not mistake his sensitive nature for cowardice or timidity. Yes, he is sensitive, but in a good way. He is sensitive to others' feelings whereas Nicky lacks that awareness. *He* is more concerned with his own wants and needs.'

Dolph leapt to the defence of his younger son. 'Nicky does not have a nasty nature. He is just…lively.'

The weight of her luminous gaze settled on him, sending tingles down his spine. The illumination from the candles highlighted the blue-greenness of those beautiful, and intelligent, eyes.

'It was not a criticism of Nicky.' His ruffled feelings were instantly soothed by her gentle words. 'I was trying to illustrate—perhaps a little clumsily—that the two boys are quite different in character, and there is no need to force them to fit the same mould. They each have strengths and weaknesses and, in time, they will hopefully recognise and learn to compensate for the latter.'

'Much as we do for ourselves as adults?'

'Precisely. Although, regrettably, not all adults identify their own weaknesses or, if they do, are not prepared to remedy the flaws in their characters.'

Dolph's eyes narrowed. 'It sounds as though you speak from experience.' Having lived with guilt for so long, he worried her barb was aimed at him. It should not matter what she thought, but he couldn't bear her to think of him as the sort of man who could not—or would not—learn from his mistakes. 'Were you speaking of anyone in particular?'

Her lashes swept down, concealing her thoughts, and her teeth caught at her lower lip. His blood surged at that unconsciously erotic act even as he read her avoidance of eye contact as confirmation that the criticism had, indeed, been for him. His entire body tensed as he awaited her answer.

'Not necessarily,' she said, after a pause. Her tone became acerbic as she then added, 'Although perhaps Lord Hinckley would benefit from a dose of introspection as to *his* behaviour.'

His shoulders relaxed. 'George?'

'Yes. I apologise, because I know he is your friend, but I find it reprehensible he thinks it acceptable to trifle with women's feelings and then shrug off any responsibility. He must know how such behaviour might be misconstrued.'

'But... I explained this to you...' He cringed inwardly at his patronising tone but felt honour bound to defend his friend. 'And I *have* warned him, but these...games, if you will...are constantly played out in Society. It is expected. If a gentleman fails to compliment a lady, he is considered a very poor sort of fellow.'

'And is that how you behave in Society too, Lord Dolphinstone?'

'My behaviour is neither here nor there. We are not discussing me. And do not forget Miss Strong is a willing participant.'

'Willing only because she trusts Lord Hinckley, thinks him sincere and believes him to be a gentleman!'

Dolph straightened, pushing away from the mantelshelf. 'Or willing because she *wants* to believe him. May I remind you that George, as a wealthy earl, is regarded as quite a catch in the matrimonial stakes. The young ladies and their mamas fawn over him at Society events, each of them praying she will be the one to finally ensnare him. Can you categorically deny Miss Strong is any different?'

'Oh!' Leah sprang to her feet to confront him. 'How *dare* you imply Philippa is mercenary.' One finger poked him in the chest as her face tilted up and she glared at him, those extraordinary eyes blazing. 'Is it too hard for you to understand a woman might place the personal attributes of a man above any amount of wealth or status?'

God, I want to kiss her.

He could think of nothing else. She fell silent. Their gazes remained locked. The tip of her tongue emerged to moisten her lips, sending the blood rocketing through his veins. Without volition, he traced those full, lush lips with one finger. Her breathing hitched in the quiet of the room. He moved closer. She did not retreat. Rather, she swayed towards him, and then, before he had time to gather his thoughts, or to consider the consequences, his arms swept around her and their lips met in a searing kiss. She melted in his arms as his tongue penetrated her mouth and he deepened the kiss. Their tongues tangled, and his blood sang at her eager response. All too soon, however, she stiffened and pushed him away.

He reined in his rampaging lust, forcing his arms to release her, and stepped back, thrusting one hand through his hair as Leah stumbled back and covered her mouth with the back of her hand, her eyes huge and round.

'Is this how gentlemen such as Lord Hinckley and yourself treat unwary females?' She spoke from behind the shield of her hand. 'You all appear to believe you are entitled to act as you please, and that we are there for your pleasure: to be dallied with and cast aside at will.'

'What do you mean by *you all appear*? Has this happened before? Were you cast aside by some man?' Anger flared inside him.

She shook her head vehemently, her eyes stricken. The desire to protect her made him extend his hand, but he did not touch her and instead tried to soothe her with his words.

'I apologise. I had no intention... I did not mean for that to happen. It was entirely reprehensible.' What else could he say? There was no excuse to justify kissing her, not even when she appeared willing. He was her *employer*. He had a duty of care towards her. 'I have no intention of casting you aside for something that was my fault, but I shall understand if you wish to leave. I will supply you with a good reference, you need have no fear of that.'

'I...'

She heaved a sigh, her bosom rising and falling. Dolph forced his gaze higher. To her face. Her flushed cheeks. Her glittering eyes. Were they suppressed tears? He felt even more of a scoundrel.

Her voice trembled as she said, 'I must bear some of the blame. I could have stopped you.' She subsided into the chair again. 'I *should* have stopped you.'

There was a sadness in her eyes, and a touch of shame that puzzled him. Again, he wondered if she had experienced something similar in her past, but the air between them seemed too brittle to broach the subject again, so he resisted the urge to bombard her with further questions.

'You bear none of the blame, Leah. I meant what I said—the fault was mine. But I had no intention of kissing you. It took me by surprise as well.'

Her eyes searched his face. 'So...if you did not mean to kiss me, why did you?'

What to say? I couldn't not *kiss you, at that moment, when you looked up at me with your eyes like deep, sunlit pools? I couldn't* not *kiss you because I find you irresistibly alluring, with your long, slender limbs and your red hair and your freckles, that entice me into wondering if—and where—they sprinkle your skin in places hidden from my gaze?*

'I cannot explain it.' He moved again to the fireplace to prop his elbow on the mantelshelf, his heart thundering in his chest. 'I have found it difficult, coming back here... The memories are unsettling. *I* am unsettled. Although that is no excuse for taking advantage of you. I do not know what came over me.'

'You must miss your wife dreadfully.'

Her sympathy penetrated deep inside his soul like a knife and twisted. He welcomed the pain. He didn't deserve her sympathy. Not when he was responsible for Rebecca's death. He had kissed Leah to satisfy his own needs without a thought as to how it might affect her—he was no better than George.

He liked Leah and he admired her courage in standing up to him when she deemed it necessary. But she was a respectable gentlewoman and *he*…he could offer her nothing apart from the loss of her virtue and the ruin of her reputation.

'Dolphin Court is very different without her.'

But I do not miss her. Not like you mean.

And that was yet another reason why he did not deserve to consider his own unhappiness. Why could he not have loved Rebecca as she deserved? If he had, she would still be here now. Was he even capable of love? He stepped away from the fireplace.

'I'm sure I will come to terms with her absence in time. I must bid you goodnight now but, please, stay and finish your brandy. I hope it will help you to sleep when you go back to bed. If you need time to recover in the morning, send word and I shall arrange for the boys to be cared for. Again…' he executed a small bow '… I apologise for my behaviour and I hope we may put it behind us.'

Her mouth twitched into a tentative half-smile that did not reach her eyes. 'Goodnight, my lord.'

Chapter Eleven

As the library door closed softly behind Dolph, Leah allowed her forced smile to drop. She leaned back in the chair,
one hand pressed to her bosom, feeling as though the weight
of the world rested on her shoulders.

'Oh, dear God,' she whispered, closing her eyes. Warm
moisture seeped from beneath her lids. 'Oh, dear God…
what now?'

But the question was rhetorical. She knew very well
'what now'. The luxury of staying at Dolphin Court until
the last possible minute had been wrenched from her. She
must now leave for London sooner rather than later because
she knew neither she nor Dolph could move past this. That
kiss would always lie between them—unspoken and unac-
knowledged, maybe, but it would be there, overshadowing
everything. Muddying their relationship as employer and
employee. Distracting them both from the most important
thing—the happiness and welfare of Stevie and Nicky.

She relived that kiss, the entire surface of her skin tingling as she recalled his lips moving over hers and their tongues dancing together. Never had she dreamed of such a wonderful sensation, and she had—for several enchanting, sensual, *delusional* minutes—revelled in the fantasy that he had fallen in love with her. Her treacherous mind had conjured up a hopeless dream of her and Dolph and the children as a family, living together happily at Dolphin Court for the rest of their lives.

But reality had eventually intruded, thank goodness, although it had taken every ounce of her strength to push him away.

She'd been attracted to him from the first moment they met and, since his return, that attraction had strengthened, and she'd suspected—maybe even hoped—it was not entirely one-sided. But she could not and would not fool herself the glimpses of fire and longing she had seen in him had anything to do with feelings or love. She must face the truth. Those flashes of desire were merely the frustration of a widower with no outlet for his physical needs. He'd all but admitted it.

Dolph was still grieving, and she must not allow herself to become a convenient prop to help him get over his wife's death. She had been used by both Peter and Lord Usk for their own purposes before being cast aside, and she vowed that never again would she allow her foolish dreams to override her common sense in matters of the heart.

Her throat tightened, a painful lump lodged inside as she accepted she must say goodbye to the children and to Dolph within days. But how soon? Tomorrow? Impossible to walk away just like that. Would it really hurt to stay an extra week, or maybe two? But she knew, deep down, she was lying to herself if she tried to pretend the boys still needed her support to become more confident around their father. In truth, their relationship was strengthening every day.

There was no excuse not to go straight away but, for her own sake, she would wait a little longer, just to give her a little more time with the boys... A sob built up in her chest but she managed to gulp it back. She would spend that time storing up memories, and she would avoid being alone with Dolph, for that way lay temptation of a sort that would only give her more heartache. She would delay telling either the children or Dolph about her departure until she was ready to go. A selfish decision, perhaps, but she could not bear the thought of a long, drawn-out painful goodbye. A short, sharp pain would be better for all concerned, but especially for her.

But... Dolph would need time to find a suitable new governess. She pondered that dilemma—there must be a way to stay fair to everyone. Her thoughts flew to Philippa. Philippa...her level-headed friend who loved children and to whom she had already decided to unburden herself about Lady Tregowan's will and that amazing and unexpected change of fortune. Philippa would, surely, step in and bridge the gap between Leah leaving and a new governess being appointed?

So, she would say nothing to Dolph—or to anyone at the Court—until she'd spoken to Philippa and, in the meantime, she would work on creating happy memories for both herself and for the children. The minute she reached that decision, a feeling of calm descended despite the voice of warning in her head that her decision to stay for even one extra day was risking more heartbreak for herself.

She straightened in the chair and reached for her brandy, swallowing it in one huge gulp. She coughed, her eyes wa-

tering. It would take all of her strength, but she would behave as though that kiss had never happened.

Leah had still not visited Miss Strong when, two days
later, the door to the schoolroom burst open while Dolph—
later than usual—was helping Stevie with his arithmetic and
Leah patiently worked with Nicky on his writing skills on
the far side of the room. It was as though that kiss had never
happened. Leah gave no hint of discomfort in his presence,
while Dolph studiously avoided being alone with her.

George—a hectic flush on his cheeks—rushed in with
a panting Wolf at his heels.

'Oh! Apologies, et cetera. But, Dolph, really! Tell me
you have skates.' George executed a hasty bow in Leah's
direction. 'Apologies, Miss Thame, for the interruption to
your lesson, but Palmer told me you were here, Dolph, and
I could not wait.'

'Could not wait for what, George?'

'I have come from the village—the pond is covered in
thick ice, and I've been ice skating with Phil—Miss Strong.
Such fun! The whole village was out there, watching or
taking part.'

'Skating?' Leah said. 'But... Lord Hinckley...your shoulder...'

George had only recently dispensed with using the sling
to support his left arm. He laughed. 'Oh, I took care, never
fear. I wasn't likely to fall, you know, Miss Thame—my
balance is first rate, and there is nothing wrong with my
other arm, so I took particular care to skate on Miss Strong's
left so I could catch her if needs be. Not that I was needed,
for she is an excessively talented skater—pirouettes and

all sorts! She showed up everyone else on the ice, I can tell you.'

'And that is what you have come to tell us, George?' asked Dolph.

'Well, yes. I thought we might take the boys skating to-morrow—I am sure they will enjoy it and Miss Strong is very much looking forward to seeing us all. Tell me you have skates stashed away in an attic somewhere, Dolph. You *must* have.'

Dolph rubbed his jaw, conscious Nicky was looking at him pleadingly. Stevie sat quietly, head bent, making it hard to decipher whether he would enjoy such an excursion, and he noticed Leah give his hand a quick squeeze. But…ice skating. It would be good fun, and it would be an opportunity to spend time with the boys away from the school-room until they found suitable ponies, and they could ride out together.

Frinton—who presided over the stables—had asked around about suitable ponies for the boys, learning of two for sale at a farm some four miles away, but the weather had been too cold and the ground too hard and slippery to go and try them out. So, until then, any time spent with the boys involved lessons.

Leah and the boys still took their daily walk when the weather was dry, but Dolph had avoided going with them, fearing the boys would rush hither and thither and leave far too much time for he and Leah to talk privately. He had taken care to avoid being alone with her since the morning after that kiss, when they'd both agreed it had been a mistake and they would forget all about it. Easier said than done, he had found, for he'd been unable to banish it from his thoughts no matter how hard he tried. Leah, on the other hand, appeared to have shrugged off the incident with little effort.

'*Please*, Papa,' Nicky begged. 'I *love* to skate on the ice.'

'You do, Nicky?' Leah's lips pursed, holding back a smile, but her blue-green eyes laughed, and Dolph's heart felt as though it were performing a slow somersault. 'When did you try ice skating?'

Nicky pouted. 'I skidded on a puddle yesterday. It is *fun*.'

'It's not as easy as you might think, Nicky,' said Dolph. 'You have to balance on a thin metal blade strapped to each shoe. People fall over. A lot.'

'*I* won't fall,' said Nicky. 'But I bet Stevie does. An' he'll cry!'

'Will not!' Steven glared at his younger brother.

'Enough, boys. Yes, we will all go tomorrow. I know there are skates around somewhere from when I was a lad.' He found himself looking forward to it with an eagerness that surprised him and, before he could check his words, he added, 'And I am fairly certain there is a pair for you, too, Miss Thame.'

'Me?' She looked startled. 'I cannot skate.'

'Oh, come now, Miss Thame,' said George. 'Dolph was just teasing the boys. It's not that hard. You will enjoy it.'

'Nevertheless, I shall take even greater enjoyment in standing on solid ground and watching the rest of you.'

'Now, come on, Miss Thame. George is right, you know. It's not that difficult. I'm certain you will demonstrate perfect balance. This is no time to be chicken-hearted, when your charges will both be complete beginners too.'

'Yes! Miss Thame is going to skate too.' Nicky jumped around, waving his arms.

Stevie tugged at her sleeve. 'I will catch you if you fall, miss. I promise.'

She smiled warmly at him. 'Thank you, Stevie. I will think about it, but no promises.' She stood up and smoothed her skirts. 'Lessons are over, boys. Would you like to go now with your papa to find your skates while I tidy up the schoolroom?'

Her eyebrows flicked as she smiled jauntily at Dolph.

There, her smile seemed to say. *That is what to expect if you challenge me. You may have the boys all to yourself.*

Leah awoke the next morning with dread weighting her stomach. Stevie had whispered to her, as she was tucking him in last night, that Papa had found enough skates for them all, but it was to be a secret and the boys weren't to tell Miss Thame in case she refused to accompany them to the village. 'But,' Stevie had continued, 'you *will* still come, won't you, miss? We can help each other.' And, aware he was afraid his younger brother would show him up in front of his father—for there was no doubt Nicky was more proficient in most physical activities—Leah did not have the heart to let Stevie down.

Ice skating. She had never tried it, but she had slipped and fallen on ice before, and it was *hard*. It hurt. And she would fall, she just knew it. She would fall and make a fool of herself. And her fear was greater than Stevie's, for she was an adult. Nobody would turn a hair if a child fell over, but if she were to fall, it would be so undignified. She could already feel the heat of humiliation.

Unable to bear the suspense, she threw back her bedcovers and rushed to the window, tweaking the curtains apart to look at the weather outside. It was still dark, but the ice on the inside of the windowpanes told its own tale. There had been no miraculous thaw overnight.

I can refuse. He cannot force *me to do it.*

But Stevie's anxious expression materialised in her mind's eye. How could she let him down?

It had been agreed they would leave Dolphin Court at eleven, and after skating, they were all invited to the Rectory for soup and sandwiches. Lord Hinckley had arranged it all with Philippa, making Leah wonder if he could possibly be serious about her after all.

Don't be a fool! He is an earl, for goodness' sake... He will look much higher for a wife than a country vicar's daughter. We don't live between the pages of Little Goody Two-Shoes.

Surely Philippa must realise it? Leah couldn't bear to think of her heart being broken or, even worse, that she might succumb to temptation and allow herself to be seduced by Lord Hinckley. After all, it did happen. It had happened to Mama. Leah vowed to warn her friend at the earliest opportunity.

In two hours or so it will all be over. I can cope with that.

But, despite her nerves, Leah could not quell the flutter of purely feminine satisfaction as she had gazed at her reflection in the mirror after dressing in her royal-blue velvet carriage gown, for this shade of blue had always suited her. She did not care that such thoughts were pure vanity and she thrust aside the question of whom she might be hoping to impress.

Eleven o'clock arrived all too soon. Leah donned her warm winter cloak, the blue velvet bonnet that matched her gown, a pair of fur-lined gloves, a woollen scarf and a pair of fur-lined half-boots before collecting the boys—already well-wrapped in warm clothes—from Cassie's care. Tilly, upon realising she was not included in the outing, set up a loud wailing as Leah ushered the two excited boys out of the nursery and followed them down the stairs, her insides heavy with the grim determination to see through the ordeal if it killed her.

'Miss Thame!' Hinckley laughed up at her from the hall. 'Look, Dolph! She looks for all the world as if she's facing the gallows!' Dolph's expression remained indecipherable.

'Cheer up!' Hinckley continued. 'You might find you enjoy skating.'

Dolph's brow furrowed. 'George...' he growled.

Hinckley reddened. 'Oops! Sorry, Dolph.'

Leah descended the final few stairs, striving to keep her expression blank, although she knew very well what they were talking about. Dolph's frown softened as she reached them and her stomach swooped as it always did when their eyes met.

'Well, George has let the cat out of the bag and, yes, there is a pair of skates for you too,' he said to Leah. 'But no one will force you to skate if you do not wish to—the option is simply there if you decide to try.'

Leah felt a hand nudge into hers. Stevie, looking up at her pleadingly.

'I have changed my mind already.' She firmed her grip on Stevie's hand. 'I will do it.'

A smile curved Dolph's lips, his grey eyes warming, and Leah's pulse responded with a pleasurable skip. That almost made up for the fear coursing through her entire body. Almost.

'I promise not to let you fall, Miss Thame.'

Chapter Twelve

Half a dozen villagers were already on the pond by the time they reached the village. The carriage was sent back to Dolphin Court, with instructions to return in three hours to collect them, and the moment had arrived. Philippa glided towards them across the ice, graceful as a swan, and the solid weight of dread that had settled inside Leah stirred, churning her insides, making her feel sick. To cover her nerves, and while the two men greeted Philippa, Leah crouched down to strap on first Stevie's and then Nicky's skates, fixed their mufflers more securely around their necks so there were no loose ends flapping, and made sure their gloves and caps were on.

She stood up, once she was sure her nerves were under control, and greeted Philippa. The men, she noticed, were busy donning their own skates. With any luck they would forget about her, and she could watch them safely from the bank. There were a few wooden chairs set around the edge, presumably for spectators, and they looked far more enticing to Leah than the wide, glittering expanse of ice before her.

'You make ice skating look remarkably easy, Philippa,' she said.

Philippa laughed gaily, her eyes sparkling. 'It is, Leah. It is so...*liberating*, to travel at such speed as a result of one's own skill and momentum.'

Before Leah could respond, a shriek split the air. Stevie! Leah had been vaguely aware of Nicky tugging his older brother towards the ice as she spoke to Philippa, and now she desperately searched the skaters on the ice, looking for Stevie, expecting to see him in a huddled heap. But no. There he was, at the far side of the pond already, and actually skating. He had a little wobble now and then but, in the main, he looked in control, and even at this distance Leah could see the huge grin on his face. The shriek had come from Nicky, just a few feet from the edge of the ice and still on this side of the pond. His legs resembled those of a newborn foal trying to stand for the first time and his arms cartwheeled as he fought to keep his balance.

'We'll help him,' Hinckley said.

He grabbed Philippa's hand and they hurried to the edge of the ice. Within seconds, they had Nicky securely between them, steadying him. Hinckley called back, 'You help Miss Thame, Dolph. We'll stay with Nicky until he finds his balance,' and off they set across the ice, each holding one of Nicky's hands.

Leah sought Stevie again and, if anything, he looked even more adept as he glided in front of Nicky, showing off. Leah couldn't help but laugh.

'To think Stevie was petrified of today, and now look at him.' She glanced at Dolph, who was watching both his sons with clear pride. 'He was afraid of making a fool of himself. Worried Nicky would outshine him, as he so often does in physical challenges.'

'It's a joy to see him so confident.' Dolph turned to Leah. His eyes searched hers. 'It is your turn. Unless you are too nervous to even try?'

Leah tilted her chin. Stevie might no longer need her on the ice, but how could she possibly refuse to try when he had been so brave? She would not allow herself to appear a coward in front of the boys.

'No. As I said, I will try. But I shall not promise to persevere if I fall over.'

He nodded, his lips pursing with a suppressed smile. 'I knew you would rise to the challenge but, rest assured, I shall ensure you remain on your feet. If you sit there—' he indicated a nearby chair '—I shall help you with your skates.'

Her heart in her mouth, Leah sat down and Dolphinstone crouched before her, the brim of his beaver hat concealing his face. Unobserved, she watched him, her stomach fluttering with more than just nerves about the skating ordeal to come as he stripped off his gloves and lifted her booted foot, his grip warm and firm around her ankle, even through the leather of her half-boots. He pushed the hem of her gown up from her foot, to give him access, and tingles chased each other across Leah's back. Although there were people all around, it was as though the two of them existed apart from them, contained in their own separate bubble. She swallowed, clasping her gloved hands together as he fitted the skate to her foot and buckled the straps to secure it in place. He placed her foot back on the ground, and then he tipped his face up, catching her watching him.

Time appeared to stand still as their gazes fused. Now she knew why they had both avoided being alone together since that kiss. This attraction was definitely not one-sided; Dolph felt it as keenly as she. Her heart lurched and her entire body heated. Then he bent his head once more, and she released the breath that had seized her lungs, uncertain of what that moment might have meant to him, although she knew very well what it meant to her.

Fool! Have you learned nothing?

Twice she had lowered her defences to allow a man close. Twice she had been tricked into believing a man's feelings for her were genuine. And the fact still remained Dolph was an earl, and she—although soon to be wealthy, and thus elevated in Society—was still his governess, and baseborn, to boot. If he was ever to remarry—and he had been clear in his snub to Hinckley when the subject had arisen—he would look much higher than Leah, for the sake of his children.

'Now for the other one.' Dolph's voice was firm and emotionless as he strapped on her other skate. But, when he looked up at her again to say, 'Now, Miss Thame. It is time to put you through your paces,' the heat banked in his eyes was clear, even to a novice about men and their desires such as Leah, and her pulse leapt anew.

Dolph stood in one fluid motion. He pulled on his gloves before extending both hands. Leah took them, relishing the feeling as his fingers closed around hers, and his strength as he tugged her to her feet. Her ankles knuckled over immediately; balancing on the skates proved even trickier than she'd anticipated.

'Whoa! Steady! You're not even on the ice yet.'

Dolph released her hands to steady her under the elbows as she straightened her ankles, concentrating on the strangeness of balancing on the thin blade. The effect was to bring their bodies close together, chest to breast, and Leah resisted the urge to lean into him. With an effort, she stepped back, forcing him to relinquish his grip on her elbows. This time, *she* took *his* hands. This was *her* nightmare. She would be in control.

'That's the way.'

His murmured approval was the spur she needed to face the next step. She lifted her chin.

'I am ready.'

There weren't so very many people on the ice, and no one was watching. Nobody—surely—would notice or care if she fell. Besides, Dolph had promised he would not allow her to fall. She would put her trust in him.

They stepped onto the ice, and Leah found her worst fears were nothing compared to the actuality of losing—it seemed—all control over her legs and her feet, which seemed to be trying to slide in every direction at once. Dolph swapped her left hand from his right to his left, and wrapped his right arm around her waist, giving her added support.

'Relax,' he said. 'Allow your foot to slide forward and move with it…keep your body above it. That's it. Right foot first, stay in time with me. I have you. I won't let you fall.' His voice lowered to a deep, throaty murmur. '*Trust* me.'

Leah shivered. *I do.* But she held back the words and directed her attention to her feet instead. She'd trusted other men. Peter. Usk. They'd lied to her. Doubts rose to peck at her.

'Try not to look down at your feet,' he said. 'Look straight ahead. *Feel* your body and its balance as you look where you're going.'

'I cannot. I'm scared if I look up, I will fall.'

'I am here. You can trust me.'

But her eyes remained stubbornly fixed on the ice as her legs continued to misbehave and her feet shot away at impossible angles until a jubilant shout jerked her gaze up to Stevie as he sped past, grinning hugely. Her stomach dived as she saw they were right in the middle of the pond. The bank…safety…looked an impossible distance away.

'Miss Thame! Papa! Look at me!'

Stevie skated a circle in front of them and then skidded to a halt. He wobbled a little, and Dolph's arm firmed around Leah's waist as he brought them to a halt by Stevie. He released Leah's hand to reach out and grip Stevie's shoulder.

'Steady, son.'

'I'm all right, Papa. I *love* skating.'

'And you are exceptionally good at it, Stevie,' said Leah. 'Unlike me, I'm afraid.'

'But Papa will make you like it, Miss Thame, won't he?'

'I will certainly try my best, Stevie. Why don't you go and help your brother?'

Nicky was still in between Hinckley and Philippa but he did look as though he was improving.

'Yes, Papa.' Stevie skated away, full of self-importance.

'Now. Let us try again.' Dolph took Leah's hand again and softened the arm wrapped around her waist. 'Ready?'

She had no time to reply, for he was already moving, and all she could think of was that distance to the edge and to safety. Her feet slid this way and that, and the more she frantically fought to stay upright, the less control she seemed to have.

'Whoa!'

She was vaguely aware, and somewhat irritated, that

Dolph was laughing as he pivoted—all masculine elegance and control—to face her. Before she realised his intention, he bent his knees and in the next instant he swung her up into his arms, cradling her against his chest. Her arms snaked around his neck in a purely reflexive gesture as he glided towards the edge of the pond, and her heart, already racing, pounded still further as she delighted in the sensation of being picked up as though she were a child and cradled against his solid chest.

He halted but, rather than setting her down immediately, there was a pause. Leah sneaked a look at his face. His grey eyes stared into the distance. His expression was inscrutable as his arms tightened and he hugged her closer, his breathing ragged. She wondered what he was thinking—she did not even pretend to believe he was thinking about her.

'My lord?'

She felt his body jerk, as though his mind had been far away. His cheeks flushed slightly, and the thought sneaked into her brain that a memory had struck him... Maybe he and Lady Dolphinstone had skated here together, in the past.

'Now you will accuse *me* of being a wool-gatherer, Miss Thame.' He lowered her carefully to the ground. 'We shall try that again but, this time, please try not to hold your breath while you stare at your feet. Your mind needs to stay quiet. Allow your instinct and your natural balance to control your body.'

'Would you not rather go and skate with Lord Hinckley and Miss Strong?' Leah nodded towards where the pair were skating together, Stevie having taken charge of Nicky, who was now finding his balance. 'I am persuaded you will enjoy yourself more than attempting to teach me. I fear I am a lost cause.'

'Firstly, you are not a lost cause, Miss Thame. And secondly...'

The silence stretched. Leah glanced up at Dolph, to find him staring down at her, his brow bunched in a puzzled frown.

'Secondly?'

'Secondly...' He hauled in an audible breath. 'No. I would not enjoy skating with them more than I am enjoying teaching you.'

Heat flushed up from her neck to wash her face, and that accursed glimmer of hope deep inside her—the one she had been at such pains to banish—glowed a touch brighter. 'I... thank you.' She gulped, before saying, unsteadily, 'Teaching others is rewarding, is it not? That is why I like teaching children—seeing them learn and become more confident.'

His chuckle sounded a little strained. 'Rewarding,' he said. 'Yes.'

He reached across to take her left hand in his left, and again put his arm around her back. Even through her thick cloak she was aware his fingers tightened into her waist for a fleeting moment before relaxing once again. 'Here we go, Miss Thame. Try to look ahead and keep your weight above your front foot.'

She tried. She really did. For half a circuit of the pond she even began to enjoy the sensation of gliding smoothly across the ice, and she definitely enjoyed the sensation of her hand in Dolph's and of his arm around her. But, all too soon, she lost control of her front leg, which shot sideways instead of forwards, and the doubts and fears piled onto her, and instead of her right arm elegantly extending to assist her balance, she reached across to grab frantically at Dolph's forearm, involuntarily spinning to face him and getting in his way. He swerved and lost his balance. Time seemed to slow, his fall taking an excruciatingly long time, and Leah felt herself begin to overbalance too. Somehow, though, he grabbed her and twisted, cushioning her fall. Rather than a hard landing on the ice, she found herself for the second time that morning held tightly to his chest.

'Oh! Oh, my!' Leah just lay there, not hurt but shocked into immobility, her bonnet knocked awry.

'Are you hurt?'

His words seemed as though they were spoken right by her ear. She twisted her head to look at him, but her bonnet brim covered her eyes.

'I'm fine,' she breathed. 'But what about *you*? You broke my fall.'

She felt, rather than heard, the chuckle rumble deep in his chest. 'I did tell you to trust me, did I not? I couldn't quite stop you falling, but I could stop you getting hurt.' He pushed her bonnet back to its rightful position. His face was remarkably close, and his familiar scent filled her as his eyes searched hers. 'I would hate for you to get hurt.'

His voice was low and intimate, there was heat in his gaze, and the hard ridge pressing against her belly confirmed that, physically at least, he desired her. Her heart hammered in her chest as her breasts ached. She became aware of a strange yearning deep inside her and a tiny pleasurable pulse of…something…that beat within the feminine folds between her thighs. She swallowed and waited for a second pulse, but it did not come. Was this how a woman felt desire? She had heard others speak of it, in whispers, but never had she imagined experiencing it herself. She had never felt anything physical for either Peter or for Lord Usk—any attraction on her part had been solely in her mind. She swallowed, knowing that Dolph, too, felt it. But she also knew that male physical desire did not necessarily mean emotional attachment.

A loud swishing, scraping sound broke the spell between them, and two hands thrust unceremoniously under her arms to swing her up and away from her employer's recumbent form.

'Up you get, Miss Thame. You don't want to squash poor Dolph, do you?'

And Leah was plonked unceremoniously onto the ice although, luckily, Philippa was there to help steady her as Hinckley laughingly extended one hand to Dolph and hauled him to his feet.

Chapter Thirteen

Dolph busied himself brushing imaginary slivers of ice from his coat and breeches, as George exclaimed, 'Whoops! I do believe old Dolph here was winded there for a moment, Miss Thame! But how lucky for you he managed to save you from a painful landing.'

Dolph's immediate relief George had noticed nothing untoward was quickly dispelled by his friend's wink—a wink that informed Dolph that George had not only noticed but was thoroughly entertained by the entire interlude. Nevertheless, Dolph gave his friend credit for intervening at exactly the right moment to save Dolph from committing the social gaffe of kissing his sons' governess in full public view.

Whatever had he been thinking? How had he so forgotten himself, and their surroundings, to so nearly be overcome by temptation? He cast a sidelong look at Leah in an attempt to gauge how much she had noticed. Her downcast eyes and the blush tinting her high cheekbones suggested she was fully cognisant of the frisson of awareness that had sizzled between them.

'Indeed it was.' If he kept his tone matter-of-fact, as though he'd noticed nothing, hopefully both George and Leah would soon wonder if they'd been mistaken. 'Think how awkward it would be if Miss Thame broke a bone—who would look after the boys?'

'Perhaps—' and the governess's brisk tone suggested that she, too, was ready to deny that spark between them had ever occurred '—it is unwise for me to try again. As you say, my lord, it would not do for me to fall and break something, and quite apart from the effect on the boys' care and education, *I* have no wish to suffer such an injury.'

'That is entirely understandable, Miss Thame,' said George, soothingly, 'and I am quite sure Dolph has no desire to see you suffer either. But you cannot give up now. You were beginning to enjoy yourself...and do not deny it, for both Philippa and I remarked upon it. Allow me to offer my assistance. With me on one side and Dolph on the other, you cannot possibly fall.'

Dolph clenched his jaw, seeing no alternative but to go along with George's suggestion—damn him and his interference. 'Splendid idea, George. Come, Miss Thame. We will make a skater of you yet.'

And they did. Within half an hour, Leah was skating independently, albeit with both Dolph and George within touching distance in case they needed to catch her quickly. She soon grew overwarm and she discarded her cloak, leaving Dolph to admire her willowy figure, and how the shade of blue she wore complemented her colouring even as he puzzled over his reaction to her. He had met any number of beauties in Europe, but he'd had no interest in them whatsoever and had carefully avoided any hint of entanglement.

Had that been too soon after Rebecca's death? Was this merely a signal that that side of his life was not over, as he'd repeatedly told himself? Had his body simply decided it had been deprived long enough? After all, such urges were natural for a man of his age—surely he would respond in the same way to any attractive female. They were not triggered by Leah specifically.

'I need to rest.' Leah sounded breathless, her cheeks flushed, her eyes bright as she glanced at Dolph, then quickly looked straight ahead again. 'I am afraid to stop... afraid I will fall if I try to slow.'

Almost before he realised what he was doing, Dolph skated close to her and passed his arm once again around her slender waist, even though he could quite easily have simply taken her hand. He excused his action by telling himself she would feel more secure this way, and he steered her towards the edge of the ice. George followed them.

Miss Strong had already left the ice and was sitting on a chair to remove her skates.

'It is starting to rain,' she called as they approached. 'Mrs Hubbard—' she indicated an elderly woman who had hobbled across to the pond, leaning on her stick, and settled onto one of the chairs to watch the fun '—tells me the pond will be half thawed by tomorrow, because the wind has veered to a south-westerly. It is fortunate we took advantage of the ice when we did.'

'Indeed it is.' Dolph peered up at the sky and the grey clouds that had gathered in the short time they had been skating. A fine, cold drizzle hit his face, cooling and welcome. 'It is a good time to stop—that sky looks like it means business. The temperature does not feel much warmer to me, though.'

'Not yet, perhaps, but if Mrs Hubbard forecasts a change in the weather, you can be confident it will happen.' Miss Strong smiled at him, raising her brows. 'I hope you will still join us at the vicarage for a bowl of soup?'

'Delighted to; thank you for the invitation.'

George went to assist Miss Strong while Dolph helped Leah to the chair where he had earlier placed her discarded cloak. His arm was still around her waist and he relished the feeling of her leaning into his support.

'Here.' He shook out her cloak, then swung it around her shoulders and fastened it at the neck, gazing down at her bowed head, her face shielded by her bonnet's brim. A few auburn tendrils had worked free and he admired the contrast of her red hair against the rich blue of her bonnet. She sat, and he knelt before her, his heart hammering faster now than when they were skating. 'Allow me to unbuckle your skates.' His fingers trembled, causing him to fumble the straps, and his mouth felt horribly dry as he scrambled around for something innocuous to say.

What the devil is wrong with me? I'm behaving like a green lad.

Was it the awkwardness of not knowing how to behave with a woman he admired but who was out of bounds? This was not like a mild flirtation with a lady at a ball or a house party. Leah was employed by him. She lived in his house. He was responsible for her. His principles forbade him to flirt with her—let alone anything stronger—unless his intentions were honourable. And they could not possibly be honourable. He would never marry again.

He finished removing her skates and, with a profound

sense of relief, he stood up before bending to remove his own. Only then did he look at her. Her attention was on the boys, who were still out on the ice. The visibility had lessened in even those few minutes since they had stopped skating. Dolph watched his sons with pride—Nicky had clearly got the hang of his skates, but he was nowhere near as confident as Stevie, who was watching over him as they circled the pond. As they neared the side where the adults now stood, Dolph hailed them, telling them it was time to stop.

'You should wear vivid colours more often,' he heard himself say to Leah, his eyes still on the boys. 'They suit you.'

By his side, he heard Leah's gasp, quickly stifled. And little wonder—her appearance was far too personal a subject.

'What I mean is—' he scrambled to save the situation '—there is no need to confine yourself to dull-coloured gowns if you have other garments in your possession. *I* should not object, and I doubt the boys would even notice.'

'That would be…inappropriate, I fear, my lord. I should not like to provoke criticism from others within the household or from any in the neighbourhood.'

'Of course. I understand.'

'Besides, my usual gowns are more practical for caring for the boys, especially when we are confined to the house and play hide-and-seek. Those secret passages are horridly dusty.'

Dolph was saved from having to say more by the arrival of Stevie and Nicky.

'Let me help you with your skates, boys,' Leah said, crouching down. 'Miss Strong has invited us back to the vicarage for hot soup and sandwiches. It will help us warm up again—Mrs Hubbard might declare the temperature is on the rise, but I cannot say it feels any warmer to me now we have stopped skating.'

The party of five tramped across the village green towards the vicarage as the drizzle turned heavy. The vicarage was warm and cheery, and the Reverend and Mrs Strong were most welcoming. The time passed quickly and, before they realised it, a knock at the door heralded the carriage's arrival.

Back at Dolphin Court, Leah shepherded the boys upstairs, still avoiding Dolph's gaze, much as she had both at the vicarage and on the journey home, concentrating on his sons instead. Dolph watched them go, wondering how to deal with the flare of attraction between them.

'Miss Thame, Dolph?'

He started at George's quiet question. 'What about her?'

'You seem...taken with her. Philippa commented on it as well. It's the first time I've seen a spark of interest in another female since you lost your wife.'

Guilt poked at Dolph's conscience and he vowed to take more care to keep their relationship professional, most especially when there were others around. He knew *he* would reap no repercussions should gossip begin to circulate about him and Leah, but her reputation would surely suffer.

'I confess Miss Thame is growing on me,' George continued. 'I have never known a woman I initially dismissed as plain to suddenly appear alluring. When she is animated, she is quite arresting. Most odd.'

Nothing would induce Dolph to admit as much. Her eyes haunted him. Her smile kindled his blood. He'd thought he'd been seized by a peculiar fancy for a woman not his usual type simply because he had not been intimate with a woman for so long. Now…ought he to wonder if there was more to it?

But George's words did prompt Dolph to retort: 'George. You are *not* to flirt with my governess.'

George laughed and held up his hands in surrender. 'Nothing could be further from my thoughts, Dolph. I should hate to upset your domestic arrangements. Just sayin', in case you hadn't noticed. I know what a monk you've become since you lost Rebecca.'

'Well, you and Miss Strong are both mistaken if you imagine my interest in Miss Thame is of a personal nature, George. I admire her ability with the boys. She is good for them, and I appreciate her work. Nothing more.' Dolph led the way to the drawing room. 'You know how it is with governesses—they are more than servants and yet not really part of the family. It is a fine line to walk.'

'Indeed it is. Especially when said governess is from good bloodlines.'

'George! You make her sound like a racehorse. And marriage to *anyone*, as I have repeatedly told you, is not on my agenda.'

'Oh, you know what I mean. Philippa told me about Miss Thame's family—her father was a vicar; a younger son. And *his* mother was a Weston—Baverstock's family, you know.'

The Earl of Baverstock's country estate was also in Somerset. But Leah's breeding made no difference. Dolph remained firm in his resolve to never marry again—never to risk driving another woman to suicide. Besides, she was still his governess—he had no wish to invite scandal onto his family name.

'A bit like Philippa…' George continued, his expression turning dreamy. 'Her parents are from excellent families too. Her father told me he is the grandson of Grosdale, and her mother was a Davenport. All good stock. Very respectable.'

His thoughts dragged away from his own difficulties, Dolph stared at his friend and wondered anew at his intentions towards Miss Strong, particularly after having spent time in their company and seeing for himself the ease with which George made himself at home at the vicarage. If he didn't know George so well, he might well believe he was truly in love this time. But he did know his friend and he had seen all this before. He knew the ease with which his mercurial adoration could shift from one lady to the next.

He changed the subject. 'Talking of racehorses, that reminds me… Frinton knows of a farmer over towards Hewton whose children have outgrown their ponies. If Mrs Hubbard is right, and the thaw has begun, I shall take Steven and Nicholas to view them one afternoon this week. I'll see what the weather is like in the morning, and send one of the grooms over with a note if the ground has softened sufficiently. Would you care to accompany us? You can help entertain the boys on the journey.'

'Delighted, old chap. Will Miss Thame come with us too?'

'Of course not. Buying horseflesh is a matter for us men. We can look after the boys between us.'

And that will leave Leah free to visit Miss Strong and hopefully confide in her about whatever is causing those sleepless nights.

'Now.' He slapped George on the back. 'Shall we indulge in a glass of brandy?'

'Yes, let's.' George, easily distracted, grinned. 'I need something to chase the chill out of my bones.'

Leah brought all three children down to say goodnight later, as had become her routine. Dolph always looked forward to this quiet time, and he enjoyed the chance to cuddle the sleepy Matilda, for, during the day, she was too lively to submit to being held for more than a few minutes before wriggling free. As Leah walked through the door, carrying Matilda, he drank in the sight, his heart twitching with sadness that Rebecca was not here to see her children grow, and that Matilda would never know her mother. Her arms were wound around Leah's neck, and she sleepily fingered a loose tendril of hair. Dolph went to them and held out his arms. For one heart-stopping second, Matilda clung to Leah before allowing the governess to pass her to Dolph, but he noticed, as he sat down, that his daughter's eyes followed Leah as she ushered the boys towards Dolph.

'Well, boys.' He pitched his voice low so as not to rouse Matilda too much. Leah had told him that, often, Matilda was asleep by the time they reached the nursery again. 'How did you enjoy the ice skating today?'

Steven puffed out his chest. 'I loved doing it, Papa. I can spin circles.'

'You were particularly good, Stevie. And you, Nicky… you soon got the hang of it too. Well done.'

Nicky's eyes brightened at Dolph's words. 'I liked it too, Papa. I'll soon be better than Stevie, won't I? And I'm already better than Miss Thame.'

Leah smiled, and their eyes met. His heart jolted as a bolt of energy surged through him. He swallowed hard as she wrenched her gaze from his, blushing.

'Well, I am not sure about that, Nicky,' he said, willing his voice to remain even. 'Stevie seems to have a talent for skating, so, although you might be as good, you may never overtake him, but that is all right, for you have other talents, do you not?'

'I can climb higher than him.'

Dolph had watched from the window one day, his heart in his mouth as his sons both climbed the same old elm he had used to climb as a boy. Nicky had scrambled up, as agile as a monkey, while Stevie had been far more cautious and clearly did not enjoy the experience.

'That is true. And I have good news. The thaw appears to have set in, so, either tomorrow or the next day, we shall go to view those ponies Frinton told us about. What do you think of that?'

'Hurrah!'

Both boys shouted simultaneously, and Nicky jumped up and down, waving his arms, while Stevie grabbed Leah's hand, shaking it while grinning up at her. Their sister stiffened in Dolph's arms. Her face screwed up and, as she let out a wail, Leah sent him a fulminating glare, and Dolph sent her an apologetic look in reply, knowing she disliked the boys getting too excited at this time.

'Quiet, boys.' Dolph tightened his arms around Matilda, cuddling her into his chest. 'Hush, Tilly,' he whispered, and feathered his lips across her soft forehead.

Leah had grabbed hold of Nicky to restrain him and put her other arm around Stevie.

'That will give you both something to look forward to,' she said calmly. 'Now, it is time for bed, children.'

She walked towards Dolph, who stood up and handed Tilly to her. Their hands touched in the exchange, sending sparks sizzling through his veins. How did she have this effect on him? Her eyes remained downcast, but he was almost certain she experienced that same ripple of excitement. He bid the children goodnight and watched as they all left the drawing room, his stomach stirring uneasily as he wondered where this inexplicable attraction between him and Leah might end.

During dinner that evening, Leah appeared subdued, but George was as talkative as ever and appeared not to notice her mood. Dolph buried all his uncertainty beneath a light veneer of conversation, and the meal passed quickly.

'I shall go and practise on the pianoforte, if you gentlemen will excuse me,' Leah said when they finished eating.

The two men stood as she left the room, and they settled down to a glass of port. To Dolph's relief, George did not return to his earlier teasing about Leah and, instead, the conversation veered onto their experiences of estate management and tenant farmers, with the distant piano music providing a pleasant background. Before long, they joined Leah in the drawing room, where Wolf sprawled in front of the fire. She glanced up as they entered, a smile in her eyes, her pleasure in the music plain to see. A feeling of calm settled over Dolph as he sat down, leaning back and closing his eyes to listen. But when the piece ended, George's voice interrupted his reverie.

'My apologies to you both.' Dolph's eyes opened. George had remained standing. 'I am very tired and ready for my bed.' He nodded to Dolph and bowed to Leah. 'Beautiful piece, Miss Thame. Was that Mozart?'

'It was.'

'Good old Wolfgang, eh?'

At the sound of his name, the dog opened one eye and gently thumped his tail.

'Goodnight, then, Dolph; Miss Thame. I shall see you in the morning.'

As they both bid George goodnight, Dolph silenced the inner warning voice demanding he follow suit. With a full belly and after a couple of glasses of both wine and port, he felt relaxed and mellow but not yet ready to sleep. He watched from under heavy lids as Leah rose to her feet.

'Do not retire just yet,' he said. 'Come. Sit down a moment so we may talk.'

A frown twitched between her brows, but she did as he asked.

Chapter Fourteen

Leah knew she ought to follow Hinckley out of the drawing room, despite Dolph's request she remain, especially now she was aware of the risk of their being alone together. Until that moment on the ice, she had persuaded herself that—no matter her own blossoming feelings—Dolph would make certain there was no repeat of their kiss from three nights ago. But his desire for her had been obvious and her own physical response to lying full length on him had been...troubling. A prudent woman would leave, but she was clearly *im*prudent because, heaven help her, she *wanted* to kiss him again.

She chose the sofa opposite the chair upon which Dolph sat. She smoothed the skirt of her gown as she sat and then folded her hands in her lap.

'I wish to speak to you about our plans for tomorrow,' he said. 'It would appear Mrs Hubbard was correct—I spoke to Frinton after the boys went to bed, and the ground has already begun to thaw. As long as it does not freeze again tonight, I shall send a note to Hewton in the morning to tell them to expect us in the afternoon. And, Leah...please take the opportunity to call upon Miss Strong tomorrow, as we discussed before.'

'Thank you.' She was grateful for his discretion, and that she did not have to deny, yet again, that she was troubled. 'And I also intend to set my mind at rest by warning Philippa not to take Lord Hinckley too seriously, even though I know she is far from naïve and he is not the wicked sort who would ravish an innocent and desert her.'

Unlike my real father.

That thought made her feel physically sick, and she diverted her gaze to stare into the dancing orange, yellow and blue of the flames rather than risk Dolph reading her sudden distress.

Although Tregowan did, at least, arrange matches for his three victims.

Why, though, did Mama, and the mothers of both Aurelia and Beatrice, succumb to Lord Tregowan? They would all three have known he was a married man, and yet... The nausea rose to choke her. The only conclusion she could draw was that either her mother had lacked morals, or her natural father had, somehow, forced her mother to...

She clenched her jaw and swallowed desperately.

Was this yearning for Dolph somehow in her blood? Did she take after her mother? No, she could not believe that of her mama—perhaps it was Lord Tregowan's bad blood? After all, he had ruined three young girls' lives... She thrust down any further conjecture, afraid of where it might lead. She had enough to worry about in the here and now, for the time had come when she must ask Philippa to step in and look after the boys until Dolph found a replacement governess. After tomorrow, she would have no more excuse to cling on to her life at Dolphin Court. Her heart felt as though it were being ripped to shreds, but that only confirmed this was the right thing to do. She had lingered here too long.

'Is that what happened to you?'

Leah started at that quiet question, rattled that she had retreated into her own thoughts so completely in his presence.

'You were lost in thought again,' he said. 'As though your words triggered a memory.' He leaned towards her, his grey gaze intense. 'The other night...the night we kissed... At the time, it seemed as though maybe it had resurrected an unhappy memory. Forgive me for asking, but did someone in the past...a man...take advantage of you? Let you down? Desert you?'

Her heart leapt into her throat that he had guessed so much, but she bristled at the idea he might view her as a victim.

'Not in that way,' she said. 'Please do not allow that one kiss to give you the wrong impression of me—I am not a loose woman.'

He reared back, his eyes hurt. 'I did not intend to imply it. My apologies. There are multiple ways in which one person can let down another.' A muscle bunched in his jaw, and he rubbed his hand over it, as if to soothe the tension. 'So many ways.'

Those last three words, spoken so softly, and his suddenly bleak expression prompted Leah's curiosity, but how could she phrase the question she now burned to ask? It seemed too personal for a governess to ask her employer. But...she would soon leave Dolphin Court, and that knowledge encouraged her to speak more boldly than she might otherwise.

'You have been let down in the past?'

His laugh was cynical. 'No. It is I who have been guilty of failing those I love. Those whose welfare should have been my only concern.'

'The children?'

'Not only the children.' He surged to his feet then, his cheeks flushing. 'I beg your pardon. I should not be talking to you about such things.'

'And yet...' Leah paused.

He stared at her for long, silent seconds. Then he raised one eyebrow.

'And yet...?'

'Please sit down again.' Leah indicated his chair. 'I find it somewhat intimidating with you looming over me like that.'

He did so, his brows beetled together as he stared into the flames. The firelight warmed his ruggedly handsome face but also highlighted the signs of strain around his eyes, and the harsh lines bracketing his mouth, and she realised how effectively he normally hid the strain he was clearly under. The only hint until tonight had been his involuntary glance at the cliffs, that first day at Dolphin Bay, and that moment today, on the ice, when the memories seemed to lure him into the past.

'I have no wish to pry, nor to anger you, but as you once advised me to confide in a friend if I was troubled, I feel emboldened to offer that advice back to you. Could you not talk about your feelings to Lord Hinckley?'

He barked a laugh. 'You know little about men, Miss Thame. That is clear. Men,' he added, 'do not discuss their feelings.'

It was Leah's turn to raise an eyebrow, despite the accuracy of his first remark. She focussed on the second. 'Because they have far more important matters demanding their attention?'

'Oh, indeed.' His eyes glinted with amusement...and a hint of admiration.

Her stomach swooped as she took in his rugged good looks—his square jaw, broad shoulders and chest, and strong thighs. That pull of attraction grew ever stronger. How could she not be enticed? He was so big; so masculine; so very, very male.

'You speak as though you feel guilt over the past but, surely, burying feelings...not bringing them into the open... surely that can lead to consequences that might otherwise be avoided?'

Papa—the father who had raised her—had speculated that suppressing worries and feelings could result in mental disorders, an observation born out of years of tending to his parishioners. Dolph's skin had now leached of colour. His grey eyes were stricken, and Leah's heart went out to him.

'I am a good listener. And you may trust my discretion.'

He shook his head. 'I cannot burden you...anyone...with this.'

'Why do you presume it will be a burden? Truly, I should like to help, if I can, by listening. *Truly*,' she emphasised, as he clearly wavered.

He rubbed his hand across his jaw and then propped his elbows on his knees and stared into the fire. How she longed to take him in her arms and comfort him, but she could only offer words.

'Guilt,' she said, 'is a destructive emotion. Do not allow it to fester inside you and taint the rest of your life. And that of your children.'

He stared at her. 'You think it will affect them?'

'It is bound to. It will bring you low, and *that* will upset the children. They are more sensitive to such moods than you might realise. Some children more than others, of course. I am speaking of Stevie, in particular. He is your heir. You do not wish him to suffer because he cannot understand his father's unhappiness, do you? A sensitive child such as he might interpret your unhappiness as a sign of discontent with *him*. He will lose confidence.'

She'd pushed him as far as she could. She could tell it, by the firming of his jaw and the sudden shuttering of his expression. He would not confide in her—hardly surprising, when she was nothing more than his governess. She'd been in danger of forgetting the difference in their status; she'd been close to thinking of him only as a friend in need of help and understanding.

'My children will not suffer. From now on, *they* are my only priority. I am perfectly able to control my mood when I am with them, I assure you.'

There was nothing to be gained by pursuing the topic. She must be content she'd said her piece and that Dolph might reflect upon her words. She burned to know what else he had referred to—who else he had let down—but she doubted she would ever know for sure. She suspected, however, he meant his late wife. Rebecca.

'I doubt not your ability, nor your good intentions towards the children, for you have already made great progress. All children have a need to feel secure and to feel loved, and already both boys are more confident in your company. Tomorrow will surely only help to build upon that foundation.'

He smiled at her then. 'That is my hope. And I plan to take them out riding every afternoon, when the weather allows…always supposing their strict governess will permit such outings.'

Leah laughed to hide the shaft of pain she felt on hearing those words. She would not be here to approve or disapprove, and that knowledge cut deep. She rose to her feet.

'I shall bid you goodnight, sir. It is late.'

He stood too, bringing them face to face. So close she could make out the black flecks that dotted his irises and the silver threads scattered through his dark brown hair. She should step back, but her muscles would not obey her. His musky male scent surrounded her, wreathing through her senses. Her pulse hammered, and all she could hear was the sound of her own blood pounding through her veins. Saliva flooded her mouth, and she swallowed. She wanted to kiss him. Wanted to taste him again, before she left. Without volition, her hand rose to rest on his chest, the silk of his waistcoat cool and smooth to her touch.

His eyes darkened. 'You are a remarkable woman, Miss Thame.' His voice deepened. 'Leah.'

Leah's stomach swooped. She could not tear her gaze from his.

'Your hair…' He threaded one finger into her hair at her temple and lifted it away, working a tendril loose to slide through his fingers. 'It reminds me of the colours of autumn…all the colours interwoven and changing according to the light.' He repeated the action, freeing more of her hair, allowing it to fall to her shoulder and over her breast. 'Stunning,' he murmured, closing his hand around it, lifting it and then allowing it to slide through his grip. Before she knew it, the pins that had secured it were on the floor and her hair was loose, spilling over her shoulders.

Leah's pulse quickened as her breasts grew tender and her

limbs heavy. She stared up at him, captured by the intensity of his eyes, more black than grey behind the heavy lids. She licked lips that had suddenly dried, and his gaze released hers as it moved down to her mouth. His hand cupped her chin and he lowered his face to hers, but the moment before their lips met, he whispered, 'May I kiss you, Leah?'

Her heart tumbled in her chest. She would be gone by the end of the week. She may never see him again...and, God help her, her lips craved his. This need had been building since the moment she had seen him again...his stark masculinity attracting her like no other man ever had. It was nothing more than a kiss... As long as she remembered that and did not allow herself to indulge in foolish daydreams, there would be no harm. And where was the harm if she wanted to taste him before she left? They were both adults. He was trustworthy; she felt it deep in her bones. *He* would not kiss and tell, unlike Viscount Usk.

She nodded. For whatever reason, he found her attractive—red hair, freckles and all—and he wanted to kiss her, and it was a pure thrill for a woman like her to know she aroused desire in such a man.

His mouth touched hers, warm and smooth and tasting of brandy. His arm swept around her waist, supporting her, and she needed no urging to step closer, relishing his solid strength as she moulded her soft curves to his hard, muscular body. Her eyes closed as his fingers curved around the back of her head, threading through her hair, his lips moving over hers. Her lips parted to the nudge of his tongue, and a low groan rumbled through him as he deepened the kiss.

It was a dreamy kiss, a kiss to melt into, slow and sensuous as tongues caressed and lips moved. Despite her best intentions, a myriad of hopes spun through her, overcoming her caution. What if Dolph did have feelings for her, beyond the physical? What if he *could* grow to love her?

Eyes closed, Leah gave herself up to the sensations tumbling through her. Her fingers hooked into his shoulders as the strength in her legs dissolved and pure need flooded her body, thrumming through her with every beat of her heart. A groan vibrated in her throat, and she pressed closer in an attempt to soothe the ache in her breasts. Every nerve in her body seemed to be linked to the sweet spot between her legs, and her hips moved, tilting of their own volition. She met each thrust of his tongue with one of her own, opening to him, responding to a rhythm that came as instinctively to her as breathing.

His hands dropped to her bottom. His fingers spread and gripped, lifting her against him. She moaned to feel his thick, hard length press against her belly, and without volition, she moved, rubbing her body against him, her nipples aching. He tore his mouth from hers, trailing hot, open-mouthed kisses along her jaw. Her head tipped back, and he feasted on the sensitive skin of her neck, nibbling, licking, kissing. Then his hand was on her breast, squeezing, moulding, and the yearning sensation between her thighs exploded, craving more. And more.

But just as her conscience began to reassert itself, with the reminder this was wrong, she must stop this now, Dolph abruptly released her, steadying her with his hands at her waist. Both were breathing hard as they locked eyes.

'I am sorry. I should not have done that.'

'You asked. I said yes.'

'That is true.' Dolph swept one hand over his head, then half turned from her. 'But I had to stop it going any further.

It would be unfair when I can make you neither a reputable nor even an irreputable offer.'

He means as his mistress. Horror flooded Leah. Why would that even enter his head? She would *never* accept such a position, even without the children to consider.

'I pay your wages. You are a respectable female living under my roof and I am responsible for your welfare and your reputation.' He paced the room a moment before halting in front of her, his grey eyes rueful. 'I cannot deny I am attracted to you, Leah—you would not believe me if I tried—but the children are my main concern. They need you far more than I do. I will not risk their happiness.'

How she longed to tell him then she was leaving—that the boys would lose her anyway—but she did not, for the conviction grew that it would make no difference. Dolph had been clear he would never remarry—his love for Rebecca must have been true and strong—and even though, in her fantasies, she had been guilty of imagining a future here as Dolph's wife and as the children's stepmother, she knew in her heart that could not be. Even if Dolph did not still love Rebecca, the fact remained he was an earl and she, Leah, was a baseborn nobody. Besides...would she truly choose to marry a man whose sole purpose was for her to be a replacement mother for his children? Even if she loved that man?

'I understand,' she said.

'I'm sorry. I think we must agree to redouble our efforts to avoid being alone together in future.'

'I agree.' What more could she say?

Tomorrow...as soon as she had spoken to Philippa...she would tell him then. And she would leave immediately. There was no point in further delay; it would just get more and more painful. And though she reminded herself she had a whole new life to look forward to in London, the thought of her future resulted in the taste of ashes in her mouth, and the pain of sorrow in her heart.

Chapter Fifteen

Steven and Nicholas could barely contain their excitement the following morning when their father decreed the ground had softened enough to allow them to go and look at the ponies that afternoon. Leah was exhausted by noon, especially after her restless night. She wondered if Dolph had any idea how demanding they would be on the drive over to Hewton, and how he and Hinckley would cope with two small boys in such a highly excitable state. But Dolph managed the problem by the simple expedient of allowing the boys to sit up on the box seat next to Travers, the coachman, while Frinton—the Dolphin Court head man who was going with them to help judge the suitability of the ponies for the boys—climbed into the carriage with Dolph and Hinckley. Leah watched the carriage drive away and then climbed into the buggy that had been brought around for her to drive over to the vicarage.

Philippa was expecting her, as Leah had sent a note that

morning, asking if she might call upon her, and had received a delighted reply in the affirmative.

'This is delightful,' Philippa said, as she and Leah settled in front of the fire in the parlour with a pot of tea and a plate holding a delicious-smelling, freshly baked apple cake.

Philippa poured a cup of tea for Leah. 'Would you care for a slice of cake?'

'Yes, please.'

Philippa cut a slice and handed a plate to Leah with an impish smile. 'Look at us...social visits and taking afternoon tea like two ladies.' She cut one for herself and bit into it, chewing with a beatific smile on her face. 'You never know,' she continued after finishing her mouthful, 'one day, maybe we *will* both be ladies.'

Leah balanced her plate on her knee as she sipped her tea, ruthlessly crushing the little kernel of hope that had sprung into existence at some point during the long, sleepless night. She was afraid of that hope, for what good would it do? Hope born out of the realisation that Dolph liked her. Desired her. And she must marry someone in the next twelve months. Under *eleven* months by now.

But Dolph was still an earl, still grieving his wife's tragic suicide, still battling his own guilt, and she had heard herself his vehement vow to never marry again. Allowing her hopes to stray in his direction was futile. Besides, she still had her dream of love within her marriage, and she was sure marriage with a man she loved but who could not offer her love in return would be a recipe for heartache.

She longed to unburden herself to Philippa but, now she was here, she didn't know where to start. So she began with the easy—for her—bit.

'May I speak to you about Lord Hinckley, Philippa?'

Philippa's smile disappeared. 'Uh-oh. This sounds serious. He has asked me to call him George, you know.'

'I don't doubt it.' Lord Usk had begged her to call him Harold, too. It meant nothing, but silly females gave too much credence to such matters. 'But…do take care, my dear. Hinckley is an earl, living a very different life from yours. I cannot help but be concerned—'

'That I have fallen under the spell of his silken words and extravagant compliments?' Philippa shook her head and laughed. 'Leah, you goose. Do you really imagine I am such a country miss I do not understand His Lordship is amusing himself with a flirtation while he rusticates in the country? Believe me… I am in no danger of expecting anything more from George than the chance to spend time with an amusing gentleman who, I admit, makes me laugh. I enjoy his company—and I believe he enjoys mine—but I will not lose my heart to a man who will be gone from here in a few weeks with never a backward look.'

Leah stared at her friend, then shook her head, smiling ruefully.

'I have underestimated you, have I not?' Philippa's customary good sense appeared firmly in place where Hinckley was concerned. 'I am relieved you are blessed with such clear sight. Please forgive my interference.'

Philippa reached across and squeezed Leah's hand. 'I appreciate you were concerned enough to warn me. You truly are a good friend.'

Leah then found herself the subject of a searching look.

'And, as *your* friend,' Philippa continued, 'I would be remiss if I did not mention you are looking fagged to death, Leah. What is it?' She moved to sit next to Leah and took her hand. 'Tell me,' she urged in a soft voice. 'Are you... are you ill?'

'No. It is nothing like that. But I do have something to tell you.'

She told Philippa about Lady Tregowan's will, and that she must leave Dolphin Court soon.

'There are conditions to our inheritance. We must all move to London by Easter at the latest, and we must live together there for the duration of the Season, after which we may choose to live either at Falconfield Hall or remain in London. And we must each marry within a year, but we must not marry the current Lord Tregowan.'

'Would he not be your half-brother, though?'

'No. The Tregowans had no children. The current Earl is the son of a distant cousin who fell out with the former Earl over some matter or other.'

'But...' Philippa's brow wrinkled. 'So...you have two sisters you knew nothing about?'

'Half-sisters. Yes, but please do not tell anyone—that secret is not mine alone to reveal.'

'You know you may rely on my discretion. But...why are you still here working for a pittance as a governess now you are wealthy? It makes no sense to me. What has Lord Dolphinstone to say about your good fortune?'

'Ah.' Leah fiddled with her skirts, pleating and repleating the fabric.

'Leah! You have not told him, have you? Why ever not? You must give him time to appoint another governess. You cannot leave him in the lurch.'

Leah bit her lip. 'I know. You are right. But...you were there when I arrived home that day, Philippa. You saw how angry he was. I was afraid he would send me away immediately if I told him the truth, and how could I leave the children at the very moment their father returned? I just wanted to help the boys adjust to their papa being home before I unsettled them further with the news I must leave.' Leah forced her next words through a throat clogged with unshed tears. 'Philippa... I dread saying goodbye to the boys.' She closed her eyes and groped for her friend's hand. *I cannot pretend to myself my heart is not breaking twice over now.* 'And to their father,' she added in a strangulated whisper.

'Oh, Leah.' Philippa hugged her. 'I suspected... I noticed, yesterday...but I did not like to say anything. But His Lordship appears very taken with you, and George said it's the first time he's shown an interest in anyone since his wife died. Is there no chance? After all, your circumstances have changed. You will no longer be a governess but a lady of means. And if you must marry anyway...'

Her voice trailed away. But Leah could not allow herself to believe, not after what had happened in the past and despite that tiny seed of hope still lodged deep inside her heart—the hope that, faced with the fact of her leaving, Dolph might realise he could not let her go. But pride would never allow her to admit as much, not to anyone.

'No,' she said. 'His Lordship is adamant he will never remarry. And although that inheritance will make me more acceptable, the circumstances of my birth will count against me. Except, of course, with gentlemen with pockets to let who will, of course, overlook such unsavoury details.'

Philippa squeezed her hand. 'We are a fine pair, are we not?'

Leah dragged in an unsteady breath and opened her eyes. The time had come. If she stayed, she would only fall more hopelessly under Dolph's spell. She must try to look forward instead, to the new life that awaited her with Aurelia and Beatrice.

'Philippa?'

Philippa tipped her head to one side, her eyes big with sympathy. 'Leah?'

'Might I impose upon our friendship? Would you agree to step in and care for the boys until His Lordship appoints another governess?' There. She had said it. The die was cast. 'I will tell him at the earliest possible opportunity,' she rushed on, 'and then I shall tell the children, and… and… Oh, Philippa!' She gulped back her emotions as they threatened to erupt. 'I could not bear to linger once they all know. It will be too painful.'

'Hush.' Philippa squeezed Leah's hand. 'Of course I will. Just send me word when you know the day.'

Leah forced a smile and squeezed her friend's hand in return. 'Thank you. I shall miss you, my dearest friend.'

Philippa's smile was sorrowful. 'I shall miss you too, and I wish you all the luck in the world when you go to London.'

Leah forced herself to smile back, but her heart was heavier than she had ever known it. She would have a hard task to hide her anguish from Dolph and the boys until she left, but she was determined to try.

'No! For the last time, you cannot ride the ponies home.'

'But… Papa…*pleeeease*.' Nicky gazed up at Dolph with huge, beseeching eyes that grew more teary by the second. 'We will be careful, won't we, Stevie?'

Stevie scuffed his boot on the ground. 'I do not want to. I want to go in the carriage with Papa.'

Thank God one of my sons is biddable. How does Leah cope with this?

The thought of the governess stirred a conflicting mix of emotions, the same mix that had kept him awake long into the night—desire, first and uppermost; admiration and gratitude for how she had cared for his children; shame that he had taken advantage of her. Again. And dismay that the first woman to stir his blood since Rebecca's death happened to be a woman in his employ and therefore under his protection.

I must not lose control again. I cannot risk driving her away... The boys would be distraught if they lost Leah. She's like a mother to them.

He directed a stern look at his youngest son. 'You heard your brother, Nicholas. Get in the carriage.'

Nicky's lower lip thrust forward. Dolph cast a pleading look at George, who grimaced and shrugged before climbing into the carriage. Stevie followed him, leaving Dolph facing his recalcitrant younger son. Rescue came in the form of Frinton.

'Now, then, Master Nicky. You do as your father tells you, and less of your nonsense. That there pony ain't fit enough to be rid one mile, let alone four—they'll both find it hard enough tied behind the carriage. Their little legs'll have to work twice as fast to keep up. Now. Less of your stubbornness. You'll have plenty of time to ride once they're back at the Court, all safe and sound.'

Dolph watched, amazed, as Nicky flushed, hung his head and trailed over to the carriage to clamber up the steps. He turned to Frinton.

'Thank you.'

'You was much the same when you was that age, milord. Far too full of what you wanted and no stopping to think of the wisdom or rights of your demands. *And* you was as easy to steer. You might be experienced with bargaining with politicians and the like, but I'll tell you this for free. You never bargain with young'uns. Never. Or sure as certain you'll be making a rod for your own back.'

Having delivered his homily, Frinton climbed up to the box seat, leaving Dolph to join George and the boys in the carriage.

'I feel sick,' said Nicky.

'The carriage,' said Dolph, 'has not even begun to move. You cannot possibly feel sick.'

Nicky crossed his arms, lower lip once again protruding. 'I don't like being inside. I want to drive with Travers and Frinton.'

'Well, you can't.' Dolph tried very hard to control his exasperation. 'We will be home before you know it. Close your eyes and try to sleep.'

George, he noted, would be of no help, for he had already tipped his hat over his eyes and stretched his legs across the carriage, giving a good impression of a man taking a nap. The slight smirk on his mouth suggested, though, that he was listening to, and enjoying, this test of Dolph's fathering skills.

Nicky wriggled in his seat, kicking his legs, which reached nowhere near the floor. His lip protruded further. 'Not tired. Get sick if I close my eyes.'

'Look, Nicky. Look at the river. There's a heron. Can you see it?'

Stevie cast an anxious glance at Dolph, whose heart clenched. He prayed that, by riding out together daily, Stevie would relax a little more in his company. He still seemed so formal—very different from the boy he saw interacting with Leah. As for Nicky... Dolph heaved a silent sigh. Be-

fore today, he'd found Nicky the easier of his sons to understand, but he couldn't fathom why his younger son was
hell-bent on testing his patience today. He should be happy
at getting a pony of his own but, if anything, his behaviour
had worsened as the afternoon wore on. Dolph now regretted not bringing Leah with them although, after the night
before, he was also relieved not to face an hour's journey
in an enclosed carriage with her.

The memory of that kiss set his blood pounding and his
lips tingling. If only she weren't his governess. If only she
were a lady of his world…then he might… But no. He could
not risk it. Rebecca had been so unhappy with him she had
taken her own life, and he had failed to see any warning
signs. How could he risk putting any other woman through
the same? Especially one he was beginning to care about.

At least Stevie's distraction appeared to have worked, for
both boys now knelt on the seats, peering out of the window at the river snaking through the meadow alongside the
road. Dolph sighed and closed his eyes, trying without success to quieten the thoughts racing around inside his head
as a headache threatened to take hold. He felt more out of
his depth than ever. He had not even realised children could
be so different. In the past, children had, in his head, been
lumped together into one homogenous mass. But his sons
were little people—individuals—and he was determined to
get to know their characters. He'd missed so much of their
earlier years, distracted by politics, business and the estate.
He'd allowed anything and everything, it seemed, to take
precedence over family. He'd barely even noticed his children, other than as a natural step in his life. He'd gone to
school and university, taken over the title and estate when
his father died; married; had children. He'd followed the

The Rags-to-Riches Governess

natural order of life for a man in his position, but he now felt ashamed of his neglect of his entire family. If he'd paid more attention...if he'd spent more time with them... Rebecca might still be alive.

He'd been a bad husband. Not cruel. Not even mean. But careless and dismissive. Rebecca had deserved better. And instead of staying to comfort his children after their mother died, he'd left them in the care of a stranger, more concerned with dealing with his own grief by distracting himself with the negotiations in Vienna. It was fortunate Leah had proved such a good woman. The children clearly loved her.

At least he'd got that bit right, although it was only by luck, not judgement.

Well, it might be too late to make amends to Rebecca, but his relationship with his children was getting better. And now they would have their own ponies, meaning he could spend more time with them outside the schoolroom. Which meant he need see even less of Leah. It was for the best. He must not risk his behaviour becoming a reason for her to resign.

He would not allow his children to suffer another loss in their lives.

'Papa?'

He opened his eyes. 'Yes, Nicky?'

'I don't feel well.'

Dolph studied his son. It was true. His face did have a greenish pallor... Dolph rapped on the carriage ceiling with his cane and it rocked to a halt.

'Papaaaa...'

'Hell and damnation!' Dolph sprang to the door, flung it wide, jumped down—straight into a patch of mud at the side of the road, into which his booted feet sank up to the ankles. 'Grrr!' He tugged his feet out of the cloying mud.

'Dolph!' George's shout was urgent.

He spun around, took in Nicky's face with one look, grabbed him unceremoniously under the arms and swung him out of the vehicle.

'Bleurghhhh…'

All down the front of Dolph's greatcoat. The sour stench of vomit reached his nostrils and curdled his own stomach, but at least Nicky had not soiled his own clothing. About to yell at Nicky—in pure reflex—Dolph managed to bite his tongue in time.

Tears streamed down his son's face as he sobbed, and Dolph couldn't even hug him to reassure him, or they would both be covered in sick. Then Frinton was there. He took Nicky and put him down on the road.

'Best take that coat off, milord, or you'll all be puking with the stink. There's a rug up top. Hi, Travers. Throw down the spare rug, will you?'

The coachman did as bid. Dolph stripped off his greatcoat, handing it to Frinton, who grabbed a stick from the verge and scraped off the worst of the vomit before folding the coat carefully, with the stain on the outside.

'No sense in spreading it over more of the coat than necessary,' he said cheerfully. 'Mrs Frampton'll soon have that sponged clean.'

Dolph crouched down next to Nicky and put his hands on the trembling shoulders. The next minute, Nicky pressed his warm little body into Dolph's chest, and his arms wrapped around his father's neck.

'Want Miss Thame,' he sobbed.

'Shhh. Yes. I know.' Dolph stood up, still holding Nicky

in his arms. 'You shall have her soon. But we must get home first, Nicky. It won't take long, and the next road will be less bumpy than this one.' Dolph looked up at Frinton. 'Have you any water?'

A canteen of water was produced, and Nicky was persuaded to rinse out his mouth before sipping a little.

'Master Nicky can ride up front with me and Travers,' said Frinton. 'How about it, Master Nicky?'

Nicky's head shook vehemently. 'Wanna stay with Papa.'

Dolph's heart lurched, and joy spread through him like warm honey. 'Then you shall,' he said.

He climbed into the carriage and, as he settled in his seat with Nicky on his lap, he noticed George watching him with an indefinable look on his face.

'Never thought to see you so...fatherly,' he said. 'You're a lucky man, with three such fine children.'

'I am,' said Dolph. And was surprised to find he meant it. *Maybe,* he thought, as he cuddled Nicky, lying slumped against his chest, *I can become a good father after all.*

'Papa?'

'Yes, Stevie?'

'What's hell and damnation?'

Dolph caught George's eye and saw the wretch trying hard not to laugh. Maybe he still had some work to do to become a good father.

'It's a special grown-up phrase. It's not for children to use, so you must not say it. Do you hear me, Stevie? Miss Thame will *not* be happy if she hears you repeat it.'

Nicky stirred, lifting his head so his hair tickled Dolph's chin.

'Hell and damnation,' he murmured under his breath.

'Nicholas…' Dolph put as much warning as he could muster into his son's name.

'Sorry, Papa.'

Nicky relaxed again, and Dolph breathed a sigh of relief. Not long now till they reached home. He was exhausted. His gaze settled on his older son, sitting quietly and obediently as he watched the passing scenery. Stevie's lips moved, and Dolph would swear he mouthed, *Hell and damnation*.

He felt the press of failure once again. What sort of a father used such bad language in front of his young sons?

Chapter Sixteen

Dolph could see Leah waiting at the window when the carriage pulled up outside the house, and relief flooded him.
By the time the steps were down, she was outside, her shawl
wrapped tightly around her.

Her amazing eyes widened when Dolph emerged from
the carriage with Nicky still in his arms and the carriage
rug around his shoulders. There had been no further un-
scheduled stops—for which Dolph was profoundly grateful—and Nicky had, in fact, fallen asleep. He now roused,
his eyes drowsy as he looked around. Then he tensed, and
wriggled, as he saw Leah.

'Miss Thame! I puked over Papa!' He wriggled harder,
and Dolph gave up trying to hold him, putting him down
on the ground.

'Oh, no. Poor Papa.'

Her eyes danced with amusement, the low-lying winter
sun catching them and making them sparkle like the sea
on a bright day. Dolph's pulse kicked, and his heart jolted

in his chest. Desperate to disguise his reaction and determined to stick to his vow to allow no repeat of last night's intimacy, Dolph raised one eyebrow in the aristocratic manner he had learned would repress all but the most insensitive individual. Leah bit her lip, but the sparkle of amusement remained in her gaze and Dolph realised how good it felt to be teased, and how nice it was to see Leah in such a light-hearted mood. He recalled her mission today and he hoped her visit to Miss Strong would mean no more sleepless nights.

'I came out to find out if your trip had been a success,' Leah went on. She nodded towards the two ponies tethered to the rear of the carriage. 'I can see it was.'

'Come on, Miss Thame.' Stevie grabbed the governess's hand and pulled her towards the ponies. 'The bay one is mine. He is bigger than Nicky's 'cause I am the biggest.'

'He is very handsome, Stevie. What is his name?'

'He is actually a she,' said Dolph as he joined them. 'And she is called Dolly.' He caught Steven's grimace at the name. Dolph sympathised—it was not a name for a budding knight's charger. 'But she will not mind if you change it to a more appropriate name, I am sure, Stevie.'

'I want to change my pony's name too.' Nicky pushed his way between his brother and Miss Thame and pointed at his pony, a grey. 'She is called Prudence. It's a silly name.'

'Well, I agree,' said Leah. 'No self-respecting young man would want to ride a pony called Prudence.'

'What would you like to call them, boys?' Dolph asked. 'You can choose.'

'Ummmmmm.' The two boys looked at one another, clearly bereft of ideas.

'There is no hurry,' Leah said. 'It is cold out here, and

you do not want your ponies to catch a chill now they have stopped moving. Why not let Frinton get them all warm in their stalls with some nice hay to eat, and we can go indoors to think of suitable names?'

She glanced back at the house, and for a split second, Dolph swore her smile slipped to reveal an expression of misery, but when she looked back at them, she was again all smiles.

'Wolf is waiting inside, full of excitement now you're all home—I had to leave him inside in case he frightened the ponies.'

Dolph couldn't remember her being this talkative. Ever. Either confiding in Miss Strong had lifted an intolerable burden from Leah's shoulders, or she was hiding something.

'When I arrived home,' she carried on, 'poor Wolf was full of sulks and wouldn't talk to me because we all went out without him. He's forgotten his bad mood now, however, and is bounding around full of excitement, as I said. A bit like the boys before you set off.'

Dolph grimaced, pushing to the back of his mind his uneasiness at the thought of more secrets in his household. 'Don't remind me.'

'Come along, boys. Inside the house now, please.'

Miss Thame shepherded Stevie and Nicky towards the front. Dolph watched them go until a nudge from George grabbed his attention.

'Quite the touching family scene, old fellow. If someone was to offer me odds, I'd confidently wager you will end up in the luscious Miss Thame's arms before very long. I trust you appreciated my timely withdrawal last night so you could spend a little time alone together?'

'George.' Dolph forced his words through gritted teeth.

'If you wish to be throttled, you are going the right way about it. So, if you care anything for your health, you will not say another word on that particular subject. It is all in your imagination. Miss Thame is a valued member of my *staff*. She is a respectable woman and has done nothing to deserve you speaking of her with such disrespect.'

George grinned. 'Of course she is, Dolph. I offer you my unreserved apology.'

Dolph stalked ahead of his friend into the house, not trusting himself to say another word.

Leah took the three children down to the drawing room to say goodnight to Dolph that night, only to find George was present—a blatant departure from the norm and, she soon realised, a deliberate ploy on Dolph's part. He'd clearly meant what he said the previous evening: he would risk nothing that might result in the boys losing their beloved governess. There was no opportunity to request a private interview and, if she was honest, she was grateful to put off the moment she dreaded until later.

George dominated the conversation all through dinner that evening, as usual. When the time came for Leah to withdraw, both gentlemen rose as she did.

'Will you play for us later, Miss Thame?' George asked.

Leah caught the expression of dismay that flashed across Dolph's features and—even though she knew he had forsworn marriage and that, even had he not, he would not marry his own governess, no matter how attracted he might be to her—it still felt as though a dagger had pierced her heart.

Stupid, stupid woman. Will I never learn?

It seemed no amount of brutal home truths was enough

to fully destroy her foolish daydreams or her pathetic hope he might experience some kind of epiphany and realise he loved her, and not his dead wife, after all.

'My apologies, sir, but I have the beginnings of the headache and I intend to retire now. I bid you goodnight, gentlemen.'

'I hope you will feel better after a good night's sleep,' Hinckley said.

Dolph inclined his head, with a brief 'Goodnight, Miss Thame,' before sitting again and gesturing at Palmer to pour the port.

As she climbed the stairs, Leah knew she must find the opportunity tomorrow to speak privately to Dolph, to tell him she was resigning her post. She would then tell the boys, and she would leave just as soon as she could.

The worry about how she would tell Steven and Nicholas kept her awake long into the night, but she refused to fret over what she would say to Dolph. He had made his position clear, and she would not waste her time wallowing in self-pity. She had an exciting change ahead of her and she would be a fool not to take advantage of the opportunity fate had thrust in her path.

If she told herself enough times, she might begin to believe it.

The next day—the first day of March—dawned with dark clouds massing on the horizon, and by mid-afternoon, the rain was sheeting down. It was clear to Leah that Dolph was taking even more stringent steps than ever to avoid being alone with her. He visited the schoolroom as normal in the afternoon, taking care to concentrate wholly on the boys and their work. Leah was unsurprised, but it still hurt every time he avoided meeting her eyes and every time she recognised the small manoeuvres with which he ensured they could not exchange so much as a private word. She was still determined to speak to him today about her resignation, however, even if it meant writing to him to demand an appointment. She was relieved when, after his usual half-hour, Dolph stood up—his signal it was time for him to go.

'I must attend to estate matters,' he said, 'but before I leave, I wondered if you boys had thought about names for your ponies yet? It is raining today, but if tomorrow is dry, I thought we might ride out, with me and Lord Hinckley leading you. Would you enjoy that?'

'Yes, please, Papa,' said Stevie, while Nicky beamed.

'Excellent,' said Dolph. 'So, have you chosen names?'

Leah held her tongue. She had discussed suitable names with the boys and suggested maybe the names of birds might be appropriate. Nicky, up to then, had been determined to call his grey mare Wellington, with Stevie favouring Apollo for his bay.

'I have chosen mine,' said Stevie. 'I shall call her Falcon.' He beamed at Leah, and she nodded approvingly.

'That is a good name, Stevie,' she said, 'for some falcons are indeed females, are they not, Lord Dolphinstone?'

He shot her a hard look upon her use of his title. She mentally shrugged. Why should she care? She was leaving. Soon.

'They are, and I agree. It is a good name for your pony, Stevie. Have you decided on a name, Nicky?'

'Swift.' Nicky bounced off his stool. 'Swifts are faster than an arrow, aren't they, Papa?'

'Indeed, Nicky. And falcons are extremely fast as well. I shall have to hope my horse can keep up with two such speedy ponies.' He nodded to Leah. 'Thank you, Miss Thame. I shall attend lessons at the same time tomorrow, following which I shall take the boys out on their ponies if it is not raining.'

'Hurrah!' Stevie, too, jumped to his feet.

'Now settle down again, boys. Miss Thame has not yet dismissed you, and if I hear you have not paid attention after I leave, I may have to rethink our ride.'

Both boys subsided and, after the door closed behind Dolph, they bent their heads obediently to their schoolwork until three o'clock, when Leah decided they had been patient for long enough.

'That's it, boys. Lessons are over. Would you like to play with your soldiers?'

She did not really expect them to agree—with no opportunity for a walk today, they would be itching to be more active.

'May we play hide-and-seek? Pleeeease, Miss Thame.'

Nicky stared up at Leah with a beseeching look she could not resist.

'Stevie? What about you?'

'Hide-and-seek, miss.'

Leah could not refuse. How many more days would she have to play with them? She must make the most of the time they had left together. Their little faces blurred as the reality of saying goodbye to them hit her again, and she turned away to straighten the items on her already tidy desk.

'Of course we can play hide-and-seek,' she said. 'Shall you boys go and hide first? But, I warn you, do not venture near your father's study, for he is busy and will not wish to be disturbed.'

* * *

Dolph put down the letter he was reading as George wandered into his study with Wolf at his heels. He stifled a sigh.

He had so much to do—correspondence to catch up on and various reports on the state of his tenanted farmsteads—but, somehow, he had achieved virtually nothing since leaving the schoolroom. His thoughts kept wandering away from business matters and onto Leah. Her calm acceptance of his attempts to avoid any private talk had needled him, even though he knew it was the only solution. His body, however, paid no heed to his logic. It was a dilemma. One he was uncertain how to resolve, other than to seek out a lonely widow and reach a mutual arrangement, sordid as that sounded.

Dolph knew his friend would only interrupt him for a good reason and so, rather than resenting the intrusion, he welcomed it, telling himself George could be the very distraction he needed to keep his thoughts from Leah.

'What can I do for you, George?'

'Is that claret in that decanter, Dolph? I've just returned from the village and I'm awash with tea. Need something to bolster my spirits and you might find yourself in need of fortification as well, when you hear what I've got to tell you.'

His curiosity piqued, Dolph poured two glasses of the rich red wine and crossed to the pair of green leather wingback chairs flanking the hearth. Wolf sat by his chair, leaning against his lower leg.

'That sounds ominous.' Dolph frowned. 'Is this about Miss Strong?' Had George compromised her? That would create a tangle of worms, for certain.

'Yes. No. Well, it only concerns her in that she let something slip she was not meant to tell me.'

The Rags-to-Riches Governess

Dolph raised his brows and fondled Wolf's ears as he waited for George to continue.

'It would appear, old chap, that you are about to lose the services of Miss Thame.'

Chapter Seventeen

'Lose…? No.' Every muscle in Dolph's body clenched. 'You must be mistaken.'

Leah would never leave the boys. Would she? He thought they'd resolved that kiss… Was that not why they had agreed to avoid being alone together in future? Why they'd agreed to avoid temptation?

'She has not seemed unhappy in her role here.'

'There's no mistake, Dolph.' George sipped his claret. 'Philippa mentioned Miss Thame's visit yesterday, and how much she would miss her. Of course, having said that much, she was obliged to explain further, but she was also surprised I was not aware—Miss Thame told her she would speak to you at the earliest possible opportunity.'

And I have purposely avoided giving her any chance to do so.

Wolf nudged his hand reproachfully, and Dolph absent-mindedly resumed stroking his silky head and ears.

'Evidently,' George continued, 'Miss Thame has come

into an inheritance, and she has asked Philippa to step in to teach the boys until you are able to appoint another governess.' He cocked his head. 'She did not inform you of her plans, then, Dolph?'

'No.' He felt sick. He must think of a way to stop her leaving. Wolf stood up and laid his head on Dolph's knee, watching him with worried eyes.

'And you knew nothing of this inheritance?'

'No.'

The boys... What would this do to them? They adored Leah. Losing her would break their hearts. He knocked back the remains of his claret and placed the empty glass on a side table, his hand trembling as he realised the full impact on the boys of losing Leah.

And what about you? How will you feel if she goes?

Dolph ignored that inner voice. His feelings were not the point. Only the boys mattered. He had nothing to offer any woman. Not after Rebecca.

His fist clenched on his lap, and Wolf licked it with his warm tongue.

'It will be a shock for you, no doubt.' George scratched his head and frowned. 'I thought the two of you were growing close.'

Dolph shrugged. 'Not in the way you're suggesting.' He worked to keep his voice level and light. He was not proud of the way he lusted after Leah. 'We share the common objective of the well-being of my sons. Nothing more.'

'Ah. I see. The *boys*, then, will miss her terribly.'

'They will.'

Unable to remain still, Dolph surged to his feet and paced the room, sweeping his fingers over his hair, almost tripping over Wolf, who was shadowing him.

'Get out of the way, Wolf!' Dolph pointed to the fireplace and was immediately seized by guilt as the dog slunk over and lay down on the hearth rug. 'This is dreadful, George. I have to do something to stop her leaving. I *cannot* allow the children to lose another mother figure—they will be inconsolable. I—I'll do anything to keep her here. Did Miss Strong tell you any more about Miss Thame's plans?'

'I only know she has inherited a house in London together with sufficient funds to provide her with an independent income.'

'An income?' He sank down onto his chair again, that sudden surge of energy depleted and his gut churning. The laugh he forced sounded hollow even to his ears. 'So, there is little point in offering her a pay rise.'

'Is this still about the children?'

The understanding and the sympathy in George's eyes squeezed his gut even harder.

'Of course it is. Don't be ridiculous. But I must do something to persuade her to stay. I will do whatever it takes, but…tell me, George. What *can* I do? What can I offer her to make her stay?'

'You could marry her.'

A startled laugh burst from Dolph. 'Marriage? You are not serious? You know full well I shall never marry again.'

'I know you said you would not, but it would make sense, Dolph. Think about it… The children will have a stepmother they already adore, and you cannot deny you are attracted to her, so bedding her will be no hardship.'

No hardship? It would be a pleasure. Bedding Leah had been on his mind since he had first kissed her. But marriage? The thought had never once entered his head. They had only known one another a matter of weeks. Besides, how could he risk another woman's happiness? What if it happened all over again—the gradual growing apart and the slow sinking of her spirit, until... He jerked his thoughts from following that thought through to its conclusion. How could he risk it? He could not face that burden of responsibility.

He sank down onto his knees beside Wolf and petted him, to make amends for snapping at him earlier. His thoughts continued to whirl.

Although...was marriage such a ridiculous notion? What if he made it clear it was a business arrangement, as so many marriages were? Could that help to steer any expectations away from romantic nonsense and onto the purely practical aspects of a union? If she had no expectations of him, then he could not let her down.

He liked Leah. Found her attractive. Many marriages were built on less.

That's not the point. You do not deserve happiness after what you put Rebecca through. The children, though...

But there was Leah herself to consider, too. She had confessed her wish to marry for love—he could never offer her that. He was incapable of love. He could never make her happy. Could he?

'And consider her inheritance,' George continued, while Dolph's head was still full of conjecture. 'A property in London is not to be sneezed at. It makes all kind of sense. You must see that. It is the perfect solution for both you and the children.'

Burning with humiliation, Leah crept quietly back along the secret passage that stretched from the library to Dolph's study. She'd been so sure she would find the boys here, having been unable to locate them in any of their usual hiding places. She'd been convinced they had disobeyed her and had, after all, hidden in the passage that led to Dolph's study. She'd been wrong. She hadn't found the boys crouched down, giggling, as she'd expected. Instead, she had heard Lord Hinckley telling Dolph of her plans. And Dolph's response.

Why, oh, why had Philippa told Hinckley about her inheritance? Although, to be fair, she had not told him the whole, thank goodness. She could not face the humiliation of Dolph knowing his sons were being taught by a woman whose father had discarded her mother like a worn-out nag once she became a liability to him.

She must go at once to Dolph and resign. She would leave in the morning. Her pride would not allow her to stay a moment longer after hearing that conversation in which Dolph and Hinckley had discussed her as though she were no more than a horse to be traded. Hot fury evaporated any tears before they could even form... How *dared* they? She was a person. With feelings. Not just a convenience to make his life easier by substituting the children's mother.

Although...was not that idea all Hinckley's? *Dolph* had said nothing to suggest marriage was a business transaction. Despite the hurt, a shoot of hope unfurled. What if, now the notion had been put in his head, Dolph realised he loved her too much to let her go? What then?

Don't be an utter fool. Has experience taught you nothing?

She emerged from behind the secret panel into the library and stood irresolute, doubts ricocheting inside her head. She must find the boys first. And then she would go to Dolph.

As she spun on her heel and headed for the door, she was brought up short by a muffled giggle. She tilted her head.

'What is that I hear?' She rotated slowly, her eyes searching every nook. 'Is it a mouse, I wonder?'

Another giggle, and a movement of one of the floor-length curtains. Despite her longing to curl up into a ball and wallow in her pain, Leah ran across to the window and tickled the solid little body concealed within its drape.

'I've got you!'

With a shriek and a burst of laughter, Nicky erupted from behind the curtain. Leah immediately investigated the other curtains in the room and, before long, Stevie too was winkled out.

'Bravo, Miss Thame.'

Leah stiffened at that amused masculine drawl. By the time she faced Dolph, her expression had sobered. He'd kissed her. Twice. And then regretted it. True, she had been a willing participant, but only because she'd stupidly hoped he might develop feelings for her. The triumph of hope over experience! Well, no more. She would not wait for him to broach the subject. She'd had enough of not being in control of her own life. Now was the time to begin. She captured Dolph's gaze and held it.

'My lord. I am glad you are here, as I must speak with you as a matter of urgency. Stevie, Nicky, would you please go up to Cassie in the nursery? I shall be up very shortly.'

Dolph's grey eyes narrowed as he frowned. The air between them appeared to crackle with suppressed energy, and Leah's heart thumped against her ribs as nerves curdled her stomach.

'But what about our game, miss? It is your turn to hide.'

Their gazes remained fused as Dolph said, 'Do as Miss Thame tells you, boys. And take Wolf with you.'

Audibly grumbling, Stevie and Nicky left the room, accompanied by the huge dog, who had come in with Dolph. Leah's nostrils flared as she inhaled, steeling herself, but before she could speak, Dolph held up his hand, palm forward, silencing her.

'Before you say anything, I have something I should like to say. Or ask, rather.'

Leah raised a brow but nodded, her breath growing short.

'This might seem as though it comes out of the blue, but I wish to request your hand in marriage.'

Pain sliced through Leah. No words of love. No hint of any feeling for her. Just a bald proposal. A *businesslike* proposal, made only after prompting by George. She searched his expression, noting the tic of the muscle in his jaw and the compression of his lips. Despite her idiotic hopes, he looked nothing like a man who had discovered he was in love.

'Why?'

'Why?'

His expression was almost comical as his brows shot skywards, but Leah had never felt less like laughing.

'Yes. I have heard you swear never to marry again. So, I should like to understand why you are proposing to me. And why now?'

'Does it matter why now? The fact is, I have no wish to risk losing you, and I fear our recent...um...encounters... my behaviour...might prompt you to leave. The children love you and I'll do anything to protect them against further loss and heartache.'

'Anything?' She could feel tears prickling behind her eyes. 'Including marrying their governess?'

'Yes! No…that is not what I meant. I will do my utmost to make you happy, of course, and not to let you down. Think of the advantages—you will be a countess; I am wealthy; you love the children and they love you. They *need* you.'

She crossed to the window, staring out, desperately trying to quash the hurt that spiked through her. There had been nothing personal in that proposal. He could have been proposing to any woman.

What did you expect, you stupid fool? When will you ever learn?

She had seen marriages where the men viewed their wives as just another possession, someone to do their bidding and to produce heirs. And Dolph would not even need her for that, as he had Steven and Nicholas. She swallowed. If she did not already love Dolph, then maybe such a marriage would work. But he had spoken no words of love, and a marriage where one partner loved and the other did not… *could* not… No. She could not bear such a life.

'Leah?'

With a start, she realised she had not answered him. Slowly, she turned back to the room. She had always been honest with him, ever since his return, and he had seemed to value it. She would not be coy about her reason for refusal, especially as she'd already confessed her silly dream of a love match, so it wasn't even a matter of salvaging some pride. She faced him, her back straight, hands clasped before her.

'As I understand it, you are offering me an arrangement akin to a business transaction. For a practical reason, to keep me here as a convenient replacement mother for your children. My answer is no. You already know that is not what I want from a marriage and, as I can now afford to support myself without working, I should prefer to remain single rather than be trapped in a loveless union with a man still in love with his late wife.'

A flash of something like shock crossed his face before his expression blanked.

'I… I am fond of you. You know I am.'

Are you? Or has any interest in me been driven by lust? No doubt my real father was fond *of Lady Tregowan. That did not stop him seducing and ruining three young ladies.*

'I am sorry. That is not enough for me. My answer is no.'

There was indecision in his face. Silently, she willed him on. *Please. Find out you cannot bear to lose me. Persuade me we can be happy together.* His indecision did not last. His brow lowered.

'You can afford to support yourself, you say?'

'I can. I have come into some money. I no longer need earn my living as a governess.'

That was all he needed to know. She would not tell him about the marriage stipulation—that was still a humiliation, in her opinion. All she could hope for now would be marriage to a decent man with whom she could be content, without any of the heartache of unrequited love. Neither would she tell him about her sisters or their link to the Tregowans—thank goodness Philippa had kept that titbit from Hinckley. Of course, if Dolph was aware she was the illegitimate daughter of Lord Tregowan, he might very well withdraw his offer anyway. So, no. She would tell him none of it. It was *her* business.

'And you have known this how long?' he growled. He began to pace the room. 'No. Let me guess. You have known about it ever since your trip to Bristol. Ever since I came home. And yet you have left it until now to tell me, and you are prepared to leave me in the lurch by giving me no no-tice whatsoever?' He halted before her, towering over her. 'I thought better of you, Miss Thame.'

Leah stiffened and raised her chin. '*That*, my lord, is grossly unjust. I remained here to help the children settle after you reappeared without warning in their lives. But you no longer need me. Besides...' she narrowed her eyes at him '... *I* did not say I was leaving immediately—I have not even proffered my resignation, even though that is my intention.'

His jaw squared. 'I inferred as much from your previ-ous comment.'

Clipped and dismissive. No hint of the man who had sounded so desperate to stop her leaving when he spoke to George. She moistened her lips and her hand rose of its own volition to touch Mama's ring, concealed beneath her bodice, giving her courage.

Her chin lifted higher, pride driving her on. 'Then I con-gratulate you on your perspicacity, sir...at least in *certain* matters. You are correct, and I therefore now tender my resignation, effective immediately. Miss Strong has agreed to teach the boys until you are able to appoint a new gov-erness.'

A single flicker of the eyelid was his only reaction. 'Might I ask why the haste?'

She searched his expression but saw no hint of dismay at the news her departure was imminent.

'You and I both know it is for the best after what hap-pened between us the other evening.'

'Then marry me.' He gathered her hands in his. 'We would not have to deny ourselves. Think of the advantages.'

Yet another blow to her heart and yet another good rea-

son why she was doing the right thing. Better to leave now
than risk falling any deeper in love with him. And if she
were to marry, better to find a man she liked and could respect. She might not experience the highs of love, but at
least she'd be spared the lows.

Her voice chilled. 'I have already told you I have no wish
to be married simply for the sake of your children. Allow
me to add neither do I harbour any ambition to be wed
simply to provide a convenient bedfellow for my husband.
I deserve better.'

His expression shuttered. He dropped her hands and
turned away. Dismissing her. 'I see. Well, I cannot deny
my disappointment you fail to appreciate the benefits of my
proposal. You have made your wishes crystal clear and it
would be wrong of me to persist in any attempt to change
your mind.'

His indifference was proof enough to Leah she had done
the right thing, and it confirmed the glimpses of fire and
longing she had seen in him were merely the frustration of
a widower with no outlet for his physical needs. And that,
to her, was probably a worse reason for marrying a man
than to be a surrogate mother for his children.

There was nothing more to say.

'I will tell the boys now.' Her throat ached at the thought.
How could she explain it to them? She resolutely consoled
herself with thoughts of her new family. 'I shall leave tomorrow, if I may beg the use of the carriage as far as Bristol.'

'How will you get to London?'

He didn't seem to notice she hadn't told him her ultimate
destination. That had come from George. But she had not
the heart to challenge him on that fact. It was all too much.

'I shall purchase a ticket on the London stagecoach, of course.'

'No.' He faced her, his features harsh. 'You will not travel alone in a public conveyance. The carriage will take you all the way. I shall instruct Travers. And you will take a maid with you. You are a respectable woman, and your reputation must be protected.'

The relief was huge—she had quailed at the thought of how she would cope with such a lengthy journey, all alone. She had never in her life travelled so far from the West Country.

'Thank you. I am grateful. I will, of course, reimburse all costs.'

'You will not.' His face softened. 'Allow me to do this for you, Leah. Please.'

She forced her smile. 'Thank you. I accept.' She walked to the door, but paused before opening it. She looked back at him, her heart breaking but, still, that foolish hope flickering deep inside, fanned anew by his urge to protect her on that journey. She could not resist a final challenge. If she never saw him again, what would one more slice of humiliation matter?

'If you should decide you want me for the *right* reasons, my lord, you know where I will be.'

Chapter Eighteen

Leah stepped down from Dolph's carriage and peered up at the town house that would be her home for the next few months. Despite the anguish of leaving Dolphin Court—and the heart-wrenching memories of the tear-stained faces of Stevie and Nicky, and their sobbing pleas for her not to leave—she had worked hard not to dwell on what she was leaving behind during the carriage ride to London, instead setting her thoughts firmly on the future.

Her future. Her half-sisters. The new life that awaited her.

That was the only way to banish the memory of Dolph and his kisses, that awful proposal, and his utter lack of emotion as he bid her goodbye. She was grateful to him for the comfort of her journey, however, so she would not become bitter that a man she had fallen in love with did not feel the same way towards her. That thoughtfulness—to send her to London in his own carriage, with the maid, Sally, to lend her respectability—confirmed her basic instinct that Dolph was a good man. Sally's presence had also stopped Leah brooding, helping her control her misery, and now they had arrived, she couldn't deny the thrill of excitement that raced through her at what was to come.

The coachmen unloaded Leah's trunk as the front door opened to reveal a nondescript man with mousy hair and a prominent nose, dressed in a black tailcoat. His sharp gaze took them all in, and then he bowed to Leah.

'Miss Thame? We have been expecting you.' Before leaving Dolphin Court, Leah had written to Aurelia to tell her she was on her way. 'I am Vardy, your butler.'

Two footmen hurried out past him to collect Leah's trunk and carry it inside.

'I am pleased to meet you, Vardy.'

'Will your people require accommodation?' He eyed the carriage. 'I'm afraid we cannot stable the horses—there's only the two stalls in the mews.'

'Don't you worry about us, miss,' Travers said. 'His Lordship said we was to put up at his town house for the night. It's closed up, but there's a caretaker there and we'll make do for one night, never fear.'

'Thank you.' Leah looked from one to the other, all faces grown familiar to her, and tears prickled behind her eyes. 'I am grateful for all your help on the journey.'

She fumbled in her reticule and withdrew some coins to give to the three. 'In appreciation. Thank you again. And goodbye.'

A parting less painful than that with the boys. Or, even worse, with Dolph—although the memory of his shuttered expression fired her determination to forget all about him as soon as she could. Her heart might have been torn into pieces, but he showed no remorse at losing her. Decent man or not, that proposal really had been all about her staying for the sake of the children. She welcomed the hot flare of anger inside—anger she would need to help her put the past behind her without too many backward glances.

The carriage rattled away, and she followed Vardy along the entrance hall and up the stairs.

'Mrs Butterby and Miss Croome are in the drawing room.' He opened a door off the landing. 'Miss Thame has arrived, ma'am.'

He stood aside, and Leah—her insides a tangle of nerves—walked into a pleasant room with high windows and decorated in shades of gold and green. Her nerves soon disappeared as Aurelia crossed the room with her hands outstretched. She looked altogether different from the gaunt, dull-haired woman Leah had met in the solicitor's office just under five weeks ago. Now her fair hair shone, her hollow cheeks had filled, her skin glowed and her high-necked morning dress with blue bodice and blue and white striped skirt accentuated her blue eyes. She looked every inch the Society lady and Leah felt dowdy in comparison.

'Leah! I am so pleased you are come at last. Come and meet Mrs Butterby, our chaperone. I warn you, she takes her role *very* seriously,' she added in a whisper, rolling her eyes.

Leah peered over her half-sister's shoulder at the elegant grey-haired lady standing by the sofa. The name Butterby had conjured up a plump, motherly figure vastly different from this slender, unsmiling female.

She switched her gaze back to her sister, contentment spreading through her. 'I am happy to meet you again, Aurelia. Thank you for the welcome.'

Daringly, she kissed Aurelia's cheek, breathing in an exotic, spicy scent that conjured up images of faraway lands, colour and sunshine.

'And, Mrs Butterby.' She crossed the drawing room to the lady and, not knowing quite what would be expected, bobbed a curtsy. 'Thank you for taking on the role of our chaperone.'

The lady's smile was unexpectedly sweet, relieving the severity of her face as her eyes crinkled at the corners. Leah immediately felt more at ease.

'I am happy to meet you, Miss Thame. And Aurelia is correct—' a censorious look was levelled at Aurelia, who elevated one perfectly arched eyebrow in response '—I do take my role seriously. It is my ambition to see you all successfully wed by the end of the Season and, to that end, you will both do well to remember I have cultivated the hearing of a bat, the eyes of a hawk and a nose for trouble—essential attributes for a chaperone with three wealthy young ladies' reputations to protect.'

Leah caught a second eye-roll from Aurelia and bit back a smile. Battle lines, it seemed, had already been drawn between them. She could hardly blame Aurelia for being put out when she, like Leah, had been earning her own way in life—she would understandably chafe at such restrictions. For her own part, Leah did not much care. She had no desire to go out there and flirt with various men. Mentally, she wafted away the black cloud that descended whenever her thoughts drifted in Dolph's direction. Soon, she hoped, she would feel genuine enthusiasm for the Season ahead instead of the fake excitement she must project to the world to disguise her inner heartache.

'And, speaking of reputations, I ought to forewarn you, Miss Thame—Lady Tregowan's will, and the identity of the beneficiaries, has been the gossip *du jour* from the moment of Aurelia's arrival. I counsel you to keep the details of your paternity a secret, however. An air of mystery will do none of you any harm and the truth that you are half-sisters might well blight your chances with some of the most eligible gentlemen.'

Leah disliked the idea of hiding her relationship to her half-sisters but, seeing Aurelia's quick shake of the head, she said nothing. For the moment.

'Have either of you heard from Beatrice?' she said instead. 'Do you know when she is likely to arrive in London?'

'No.' Mrs Butterby frowned. 'I hope she will arrive soon—we have all manner of appointments with mantua-makers, milliners and dancing masters, and the later she arrives, the more of a rush it will be to prepare her for when the Season proper begins. As it is, she will miss out on the earlier entertainments. There are already a few families in Town, and I expect invitations to start to arrive as soon as word spreads about three heiresses on the hunt for a husband.'

On the hunt for a husband... What a dreadful phrase. What a dreadful prospect.

'Shall I ring for refreshments? I dare say you are fatigued after your long journey, Miss Thame.'

'Oh, please. Call me Leah. Every time I hear Miss Thame, I am transported straight back to the schoolroom, and I intend to leave all memory of my time as a governess in the past.'

Surreptitiously, she crossed her fingers, praying that if she told herself that enough times, it would be true.

'Leah. Thank you. Although I shall stick to the formalities in public.'

'Of course. Might I freshen up first? I feel decidedly grubby.'

'I asked the kitchen to heat water ready for you. Come. I shall show you up to your bedchamber.' Aurelia headed for the door. 'Your maid will have unpacked your trunk by now, I dare say.'

'My *maid*?'

'Yes indeed.' Mrs Butterby's eyes twinkled. 'If you are to take the *ton* by storm, you will, first and foremost, need to look the part. Unless you wish to spend hours coaxing your own hair into the latest fashionable style?'

'Of course.'

Life would be easier if she agreed to everything until she worked out which aspects of this new life suited her and which did not. It would take time to become used to the fact she was a wealthy woman and, as such, in control of her own life. Until she married, that was. *If* she married. She had already decided she would not wed just any man for the sake of it because, if that was to be her fate, why would she not have accepted Dolph?

Except you already love him. And he still loves Rebecca. That is why.

Nevertheless, she would try to find a husband to suit her—a man she could respect and with whom she could be comfortable. Life might not reach the peaks of excitement with such a spouse, but she would at least be protected from the despair that would result from her loving too much and him too little.

She joined Aurelia and followed her upstairs to the second floor.

'My bedchamber and one other overlook the street, so we put you in that one,' Aurelia said. 'Beatrice's room and Prudence's are at the back.'

The name Prudence conjured up a picture of Nicky and his pony, now renamed Swift. It felt as though a knife stabbed her through the heart, but Leah forced a laugh. 'Prudence?'

Aurelia's blue eyes narrowed. 'What's wrong?'

Leah shook her head. 'Nothing. I—I used to know someone called Prudence, that's all.'

'And is *Prudence* the reason you crossed your fingers when you claimed you wished to leave all memories of your time as a governess in the past?'

I shall have to take care around Aurelia. She is altogether too perceptive.

'I don't know what you mean.' Leah swallowed. 'Is Prudence Mrs Butterby's name?'

'Clever diversionary tactic there, Leah. And yes, although she has not suggested I use it, so I don't call her that to her face.' An impish grin lit Aurelia's face. 'One has to take one's pleasure where one may.' She winked. 'Here we are.' She opened a door. 'My bedchamber is next to yours.'

Leah stepped inside a room decorated with a trailing light pink and green floral-design wallpaper. Two tall windows were dressed with rose-coloured curtains that matched the drapes around the bed and the eiderdown. Matching walnut furniture, including a wardrobe, chest of drawers, washstand and dressing table, was placed around the walls, and a gently steaming jug and a basin stood on the washstand, ready for Leah to wash. Her trunk was already empty, and a dark-haired woman of around five-and-forty was placing

Leah's clothing in the drawers. She turned as they entered and curtsied.

'Good afternoon, miss. I am Faith, your lady's maid.'

Her gaze travelled over Leah from head to foot and back again, making Leah squirm as she imagined the thoughts running through Faith's head. No doubt she would regret not having a rewarding subject like Aurelia to dress. She drew herself up to her full height.

'I am pleased to meet you, Faith.' Leah turned to Aurelia. 'Thank you. If you will excuse me, I should like to wash and to change my gown. I'll join you in the drawing room shortly.'

Aurelia smiled. 'I am glad you've arrived, Leah. I'm looking forward to getting to know you.'

Faith helped Leah to remove her carriage gown. 'Which gown shall I lay out, miss?'

'The green muslin, please.' Leah washed her hands and face, and then, enjoying the warm water on her skin, she stroked the washcloth over her bare arms and legs.

'Have you only just started here, Faith, or did you work for Lady Tregowan before?'

'Mrs Butterby appointed me a fortnight ago, miss. Me and Maria, who will be Miss Fothergill's maid when she arrives. Bet started earlier—she is working for Miss Croome.' Faith had found Leah's muslin and laid it on the bed. 'This colour must suit you very well, miss, if you don't mind me saying? It will bring out your eyes—such a lovely colour, they are. And it'll be a stunning contrast with your hair.'

She handed Leah a towel. Leah dried her face, then patted her limbs dry before handing it back, Faith's words running through her head the entire time.

'Red hair is unfashionable,' she ventured.

Faith cocked her head to one side. 'In my book, to be different is a good thing. All those young misses…they are like peas in a pod! You… Look at you, miss. I count myself lucky to have you rather than Miss Croome. Golden hair? Pah! You are tall. Slim. Elegant. Your hair is stunning, and your eyes are amazing. We will work to make the most of you, and you will end up the toast of the Season. You see if I am not right.'

I don't want to be the toast of the Season. I want Dolph!

Would pain slash at her every time he entered her thoughts? Would she ever forget him? She turned to the dressing table. 'Well, I count myself lucky to have you too, Faith. You have bolstered my confidence no end. Thank you.'

'Ah, bless you, miss. I love my job…' Faith moved behind Leah and began to unpin and then brush out her hair. Leah closed her eyes, enjoying the luxury of someone else teasing out the tangles. 'I used to work for Lady Yeovil,' Faith continued, 'until she passed away. She was also, as they say, not in the common way, but in her heyday the gentlemen buzzed around her like bees around blossom.'

The remainder of the afternoon was spent being lectured by Mrs Butterby on all aspects of tonnish life. Aurelia—having, as she said, heard it all before—soon excused herself, claiming she wanted to read her book in peace. Mrs Butterby watched her go.

'Really! She will be the death of me, that girl.'

'Why do you say that?'

'I know she is your half-sister, Leah, but she is determined not to accept my advice. Headstrong, that is what she is. I fear for her reputation—let alone her virtue—when she is let loose in Society.'

'Do not forget Aurelia has been looking after her own life—and virtue—since her mother died. I am sure she hears what you are saying, even if she appears unwilling to take your advice. I'm certain your fears are unfounded.'

'I hope you are right. I am keen to see all three of you happily settled, that is all. Do not misunderstand me, Leah. I like Aurelia. She has a quick mind and she is a beautiful woman. But she is stubborn; she has a sharp tongue at times; and she is, I find, guarded. Mayhap she will confide more in you, as you are nearer the same age. You might prove a calming influence on her.'

Leah intended to love Aurelia as her sister, whether or not she proved stubborn, sharp-tongued and secretive. She hoped they would also become friends.

The conversation then veered onto the coming Season. Later, when they were dining, Leah broached the subject of their unexpected inheritance.

'Will you tell us about Lady Tregowan, Mrs Butterby? Apologies if you have heard all this before, Aurelia, but I long to understand why she left her entire estate to three strangers. And why those particular conditions were included.'

'I have no objection,' said Aurelia.

'Very well,' said Mrs Butterby. 'Now, let me see… I lived with Lady Tregowan—Sarah—for many years. She took me on as her companion after Beatrice's mother left. Sarah was a semi-invalid following a bout of illness soon after she wed Lord Tregowan, hence her need for a companion. She didn't know the real reason for Beatrice's mother's departure until much later, when His Lordship confessed all to her.'

Mrs Butterby shook her head, her expression one of contempt. '*He* experienced an epiphany when he himself fell ill. He wanted to clear his conscience before meeting his maker, and so he did just that, with no regard for the pain it would cause Sarah. He did not say it directly, but the implication was it was *her* fault he had strayed because she was unable to give him children. And nothing I said could shake her of the belief she was responsible for the ruin of your mothers' lives.'

Always the woman's fault! Sympathy for Lady Tregowan and both anger and shame for her father filled Leah. 'And so she thought to make amends by leaving us money?'

'Yes. Eventually. It was Aurelia's circumstances that prompted her to act.'

'Not that Her Ladyship ever set eyes on me that I know of,' Aurelia said. 'All I knew of her was as a lady who came to our milliner's shop in Bath once. I was not there, but I remember Mama telling me and hoping she would become a regular client. But she never came back.'

'She rarely went out and therefore had little need for new hats,' said Mrs Butterby. 'But that was not when she altered her will. After His Lordship died—eight years ago, now— Sarah discovered the circumstances of all of you and, as none of you appeared wanting, it never occurred to her to intervene. But then she grew sicker. We leased a house in Bath for the winter months in order that she could take the waters regularly and, while there, we learned of Aurelia's mother's death, which had left Aurelia in difficult circumstances.'

Aurelia hunched a shoulder but offered no clarification. Leah hoped to find out more as they became closer.

'You say she altered her will,' Leah said. 'But who were the original beneficiaries?'

'The current Lord Tregowan. He inherited the title and

the entailed estates when your father died, but Falconfield and this house were unentailed and your father left them to his widow.'

'The current Lord Tregowan?' Leah frowned. 'But…she must have experienced a sudden change of heart, for is it not Tregowan we are forbidden to marry?'

'It is.' Mrs Butterby sighed, laid down her knife and fork, and leaned back in her chair. 'It all happened very quickly. One thing on top of the other. Do not misunderstand me— what I am about to say does not mean I disapprove of you inheriting Sarah's estate, but the decision to change her will was made rather hastily.

'After learning Aurelia was in dire straits, she sent a man to find out how both you and Beatrice were faring, Leah. He reported back that the man who had raised Beatrice had died, leaving her nothing, and she now relied on the charity of her brother, and that you, Leah, were earning your living as a governess, and had been dismissed from a previous job after kissing the son of your employers.'

Leah's face heated. 'That was not the whole story,' she protested.

'It never is,' said Mrs Butterby, not unkindly. 'Sarah fretted so, fearing that any one of you—or all of you—would follow in your mothers' footsteps. She became obsessed with how she could stop that happening.

'Then she learned Lord Tregowan was in financial difficulties, and it was rumoured he had substantial gambling debts. You must understand, Sarah loved Falconfield Hall. She grew up there. She brought it to the marriage as part of her dowry, and she spent almost her entire married life living there. She hated Tregowan, which is in Cornwall, and very remote. It was Tregowan where Sarah fell ill and, rightly or wrongly, she always blamed the place, flatly refusing to live there afterwards.

'It was the only thing they ever argued about. His Lordship wanted to sell Falconfield to raise funds to invest in Tregowan, but Sarah stood firm and he, in the end, gave in to her. She was adept at using her poor health to get her own way, and I do believe he felt guilty that she contracted her illness at Tregowan.

'Sarah convinced herself the current Lord Tregowan would sell Falconfield to pay off his gambling debts and to invest in Tregowan, and she couldn't bear the idea after she had fought so hard against it. She hoped one of you would fall in love with Falconfield and would make it your marital home.'

'Is that the reason why we must give first refusal to the others should one of us—or our husbands—decide to sell our share?' asked Leah.

'Yes. She had a new will drawn up straight away. She would not even wait to consult the solicitors who had acted for Lord Tregowan but used a firm in Bath. She signed it and gave it to me to have delivered to Henshaw and Dent in Bristol, but I delayed, fearing she might change her mind again. Two days later, she died, quite unexpectedly even though she had been ill. Her heart, the physician said.' She paused, to swallow some wine.

'And the other conditions?' Leah asked. 'Why were they included?'

'It was her way of ensuring you did not fall from grace, as your mothers did.'

'Fall from grace?' Aurelia's eyes narrowed. 'How dare she? Her husband had a role in every one of those seductions. *He* knew what he was doing whereas my mother, at least, was young, unworldly and innocent. She was seventeen years old when I was born. Seventeen!'

Mrs Butterby held up her hands in a gesture of calm. 'I am aware of it, my dear. Please believe me. But Sarah... As I said, she was somewhat obsessed. She was housebound. Bedridden for much of the time. She had little else to occupy her thoughts.'

'That explains the stipulation we must marry,' Leah said, 'but why the insistence on our spending the Season in London?'

'It was to give you all the best chance of finding a good husband.'

'Good?' Aurelia's laugh was bitter. 'Aristocrats who care for nothing other than their own pleasures; who freely spend money they do not have, and care not how many debts they leave in their wake; aristocrats with their inherent belief in their own superiority over the rest of us. I do not consider men like that to be "good".'

Leah gripped her hands together under the cover of the table. Dolph was not like that—superior, and obsessed with money and status. Was he?

No. He cannot be, or he would not have offered for me, a lowly governess.

Even though his offer was for the wrong reasons.

'They are not all tarnished with arrogance and greed,' said Mrs Butterby quietly, 'just as not all poor people are dirty, lazy and feckless. There are good and bad individuals in every walk of life. Look at Lady Tregowan—would she have even considered your fate if she had been as you described?'

Aurelia lowered her gaze to her empty plate. Leah wondered even more what Aurelia's experiences had been. It was clear there was a great deal of anger locked inside her, and she hoped the challenge of getting to know and understand her prickly half-sister would help to distract her from the fact her heart had been torn into pieces.

Chapter Nineteen

Tomorrow would be one week since Leah left Dolphin
Court but, to Dolph, it felt like a year. Miss Strong had
stepped in to teach the boys, and her father had turned up
trumps when he'd suggested his cousin, Miss Pike, for the
role of governess. Dolph had interviewed her, liked her, and
she was due to arrive tomorrow to take up her post.

Today was therefore Miss Strong's last day in charge
of the boys, and Dolph found himself walking with her to
the stables after lessons had ended for the day—she to be
driven home by a groom and Dolph to ride out with Stevie
and Nicky on their new ponies. The boys had raced ahead
to the stables and were already lost to sight—their daily
ride with Dolph and Frinton had become the highlight of
their days, but they still missed Leah and talked about her
incessantly, oblivious to their father's heartache and how
every time her name was mentioned another fragment was
ripped from his soul.

'Well, Miss Strong—how are the boys coming along with their lessons?'

Dolph had ceased to visit the schoolroom daily, with the excuse his presence at lessons would make Miss Strong uncomfortable. But the truth was that the schoolroom reminded him too much of Leah at a time he strove with every fibre of his being to forget her.

'They keep asking when Leah is coming home, my lord.'

His stomach clenched. 'I have explained to them Miss Thame had to leave and they know Miss Pike is due to arrive tomorrow. They will soon settle down.'

Out of the corner of his eye he saw Miss Strong frown. 'I hope you are right. I am sure the boys will like Cousin Miriam, but that won't stop them missing Leah.'

They reached the stables where the buggy was waiting, and Dolph handed Miss Strong up next to the groom. 'I thank you for all your help, Miss Strong. I very much appreciate you standing in at such short notice.'

She studied him for a long moment, the minuscule lift of her eyebrows enough for him to understand she probably agreed with George he had been a fool to let Leah go, let alone aid her by sending her to London in his carriage.

What else could I have done? I proposed. She refused me. I could hardly force her to the altar!

'Good afternoon, my lord.'

The groom slapped the reins on the pony's broad back, and the buggy set off on the short drive back to the village, leaving Dolph to continue his silent argument with himself. He had only proposed for the boys' sake—his children were his priority now. And although he would have been happy had Leah accepted his offer, he still thought she was better off without him.

I don't deserve to be happy, not after what happened to Rebecca.

'Milord?'

Frinton was in front of him, holding both his own and Dolph's horses, with Steven and Nicholas already mounted on Falcon and Swift. Dolph shook his head clear of arguments, regrets, and memories of both Rebecca and Leah, and quickly mounted up.

Upon their return, as they walked back to the house from the stables, Nicky ran on ahead, but Stevie stayed back to walk beside Dolph.

'Papa? I should like to ask you a question.'

'Go ahead. I shall do my best to answer it.'

'It is about Miss Thame.'

Dolph's heart sank. Was everyone in a conspiracy to ensure he could not forget her? 'What about her, Stevie?'

'Well… I do not understand.' Stevie's forehead wrinkled in thought. 'Mama died and left us, so I know you cannot bring her home again. But Miss Thame did not die. So why did she leave us? Does she not love us any longer?'

'Of course she still loves you, Stevie, but sometimes life changes and grown-ups must do things they would rather not do.'

'Can't you bring her home, Papa? She will listen to you. I tried to tell her not to leave, but she still went.'

'You will have a new governess tomorrow, Stevie. And you will soon love Miss Pike just as much as you did Miss Thame.'

I won't, though.

That thought stabbed Dolph, bringing him to an abrupt halt. He could not catch his breath… Where had that come from? He missed Leah, yes. He'd been attracted to her, physically. He'd enjoyed her company. But...*love*?

'Papa?'

With an effort, Dolph took in Steven's upturned face, his expression anxious.

'Why have you stopped? You look funny. What's wrong?'

'Nothing, son. Nothing is wrong. Come. Cassie is waiting for us.'

Dolph pointed at the front door, where Cassie—Tilly in her arms—was standing with Nicky. Wolf was there too, his tail waving. For one brief second Dolph's mind played a trick on him, and it was Leah who stood there, holding Tilly. Then Wolf barked and bounded to meet them, and the vision cleared.

Love, though. Could it be? Truly?

Dolph placed his hand on Stevie's shoulder and urged him on, even as his spirits soared, energised by that revelation. Was it love he felt for Leah? How had he not realised? Then, as quickly as joy and hope erupted through him, it subsided. What difference did it make? She'd gone. He fended Wolf away automatically as the great dog bounced around him and Steven, and as they reached the front door, Dolph concentrated on his children. *They* were what was important.

But they love Leah, too. If I can persuade her to come home...

No! You don't deserve it. Not after what you did...

He shook his head to clear it again. Tilly was reaching out to him, her chubby cheeks beaming, and his heart flipped in his chest as he took her in his arms.

'Papa!' She squirmed and bent over his arm, her own arms straining towards Wolf. 'Papa. Woof!'

Dolph crouched down and Tilly giggled as Wolf licked

her cheek. Several minutes later, having carried Tilly up to the nursery with Cassie and the children, Dolph—Wolf padding behind him—descended the stairs again. He paused at the foot and gazed around as if seeing the house for the first time. It was still his home, but now it felt as though some of the heart and soul of the place had gone with Leah.

'Dolph! There you are. Why are you standing there like a mooncalf? Come in here. I need to talk to you.'

Glad of the interruption to his melancholy thoughts, Dolph followed George into the drawing room.

'What is it, George?' Dolph took up his customary stance by the fireplace as George sat on the sofa. Wolf stretched out before the fire with a contented sigh.

'The new woman arrives tomorrow, doesn't she?'

'Indeed she does.'

'So you have no excuse not to go to London and persuade Miss Thame to come home.'

Dolph's heart lurched. *Home?* He blanked his expression and stared at his friend. 'What nonsense is this, George? As you just pointed out, the new governess arrives tomorrow.'

'All the more incentive for you to persuade Miss Thame to return as your wife.'

'My *wife*?'

Emotion churned in the pit of Dolph's belly. George watched him patiently, and it occurred to Dolph his friend had changed over the past weeks. He was more thoughtful. Less erratic. More settled, somehow.

'If you recall, I did propose to her—at your suggestion— and she refused me.'

'You must have made a pig's ear of it, old fellow, for it was crystal clear she held a *tendre* for you and you for her. Did you declare your feelings for her?'

'Declare...? No! I was not...am not...in love with her.' His denial came automatically, but his doubts were already mushrooming. 'If you are so eager for a wedding, George, why do you not follow your own advice and propose to Miss Strong?'

George grinned, cocking his head to one side. 'Attack is the best form of defence,' he murmured, before adding, 'Why did you let her go, Dolph?'

'I did not let her go. She went. There is a subtle difference.'

'You could have stopped her.'

'I tried!' Dolph pushed away from the mantel and took a hasty turn around the room, energy pumping through him as he fought the urge to unburden himself of all the contradictory thoughts that tangled his brain. No matter how George appeared to have altered, Dolph needed to work this out for himself.

'Try again. Go to London.'

'And repeat the mistake I made after Rebecca died? I abandoned the children immediately after I appointed Miss Thame. I will not do so again. The children will soon forget her.'

'Out of sight is out of mind?' George stood and brushed his hands down his breeches. Then he sighed and fixed Dolph with a knowing look. 'Any fool can see it's not only the children who are devastated by Miss Thame's departure.'

Dolph stiffened. 'I do not know what you mean.'

'I cannot make up my mind whether you lie to me or to yourself. It is time you stopped blaming yourself for Rebecca's death, my friend. Accidents happen. It was nobody's fault.'

It was! It was my fault.

'Will you spend the rest of your life denying yourself happiness? Do you really imagine Rebecca would want you to keep punishing yourself?'

Dolph shook his head in denial. 'You are talking nonsense. It is the children who are important... It is they to whom I must make amends, for abandoning them in their hour of need.'

'And yet it is the children who are suffering now. Why continue with this pretence? I swear I do not understand you, Dolph.' George gripped him by the shoulders. 'Face up to the truth, man. Even I can see the heart has gone out of you since Miss Thame left. There is no shame in it. If you love her, go after her and tell her before it is too late.' He released Dolph and stepped back. 'There. I have said my piece. I can do no more. I shall go and change for dinner.'

He paused after opening the door and looked back.

'You're a stubborn fool, Dolph. Do not lose this chance for you and the children—*and* Miss Thame—to find happiness.'

He left the room, leaving Dolph staring after him, dumbstruck. George... *George*...had recognised the depth of his feelings for Leah while he, Dolph, had remained blind. He slumped on the sofa. But George did not know the truth about Rebecca. No one knew but Dolph. If only he could understand why she'd taken her own life, maybe he could change. Wolf, who had lain quietly till now, scrambled to his feet. He laid his head on Dolph's knee, and Dolph fondled his ears and smoothed his domed head.

'I miss her, Wolf.' He cradled the dog's head between his hands and spoke to those trusting brown eyes. 'Why is life so complicated? I wish Herr Lueger were here. I wish there were someone I could unburden myself to.' He smiled then, at Wolf. 'Other than a dog, of course.'

Loneliness rose up to swamp him, and he could feel tears scald his eyes. The elderly Austrian's long-ago words sounded in his head.

'You bury your feelings. You shut them away. You believe you have dealt with them, never to bother you again, but I tell you that is not so, my friend. You simply delay the time you must face what happened and the guilt you carry. I was not there. I cannot tell you this is the truth or that is the truth. Only you can know that, and only you can decide to forgive yourself for your part.'

Wolf pressed forward and licked Dolph's chin.

'Only I can know, and only I can decide.' Still those internal arguments raged in his head. 'How can I risk history repeating itself, Wolf? What if I married Leah and then drove her to suicide? Isn't it better for the children—and me—to lose her this way than to risk that?'

He leaned forward to bury his face in Wolf's thick fur, drawing comfort from him but no nearer a solution. After several minutes, he rose to his feet and made his weary way up the stairs to change his clothes for dinner.

In London, the days passed in a whirlwind of shopping, dressmakers, dancing lessons and promenading or driving in Hyde Park in the late afternoon. Leah and Aurelia were introduced to the members of polite society who were already in Town, and invitations to suppers, card parties and soirées began to arrive.

Leah's confidence had grown in the week since she'd arrived—wearing the right gown for the right occasion, and wearing colours and styles that suited her, whether or not those colours and styles were the height of fashion, boosted her self-esteem. Faith had proved herself invaluable, especially with her skill in styling Leah's hair, pinning it up in a soft chignon and allowing gently waving tendrils of hair— '*Not* ringlets, miss. They are not for you!'—to frame and soften her face.

It was all new and exciting, and Leah worked hard to convince herself she was happy. But she could not quite control the skip of her heart whenever she spied a dark-haired gentleman of a certain height, nor the plunge of her spirits when that same gentleman turned to reveal the face of a stranger.

She missed Dolph; missed him with a visceral ache that only deepened as the days passed. She had thought... *hoped*...that pain would lessen. She had thought her memories of him would start to fade—that the novelty of being in London and of meeting so many new people and of participating in so many new experiences would slowly push all thought of Dolph to the back of her mind. She was wrong.

The constant effort of hiding her erratic changes in mood exhausted her, but she told herself it was worth it to escape sharp eyes of her half-sister, who was the one bright spot in her life. The two had grown closer, encouraging and advising one another on their shopping trips, and giggling together—in private, for Mrs Butterby was always on hand to nip any hint of public unladylike behaviour in the bud—at some of the more outrageous fashions and customs of the *beau monde*.

But Leah soon learned her acting skills were not enough to fool Aurelia. She'd known her sister was observant but, as the days passed and Aurelia said nothing, she believed she had succeeded in fooling her as well as Mrs Butterby.

'I *told* you Prudence would find some arrogant lord to introduce us to,' grumbled Aurelia one evening as she and Leah entered the drawing room and waited for the tea tray to be delivered. They had just arrived home from the theatre, and Mrs Butterby, pleading fatigue, had gone straight to bed. 'She watches us like a hawk. There is never any chance to meet any suitors other than those *she* deems suitable. The theatre was the perfect place to meet a wider variety of men, not just overprivileged aristocrats, half of whose pockets are to let in any case.'

Aurelia did not hide her contempt for the aristocracy from Leah, but she was single-minded in her pursuit of a wealthy husband—understandable when she had been all but penniless before inheriting her share of Lady Tregowan's fortune.

'She has our best interests at heart, Aurelia, and she does understand this world better than you or I.'

'Hmmph.' Aurelia moved to sit next to Leah on the sofa and took Leah's hand. 'I am pleased we are alone, for I should like to talk to you without fear she might overhear us.'

She sounded serious, with no hint of her usual slightly mocking tone. Leah waited, hoping Aurelia would finally trust Leah enough to open up about her past. Mrs Butterby's suggestion that Aurelia was not a woman who easily shared confidences had proved correct, and Leah had been careful to curb her curiosity, wary of antagonising her secretive sister.

'I know we are still unfamiliar with one another, Leah, but we *are* sisters, and I want you to know I am here for you, if you wish to talk about whatever it is that haunts you.'

Leah straightened, instinctively preparing to deny it.

'No!' Aurelia raised her hand, palm forward. 'Do not pretend with me. You are unhappy. I see you when you think no one is watching you, so I say it again—if you wish to talk, I am here for you.' She flashed a smile. 'I can be discreet, you know.'

Dolph. Leah longed to pour out her despair. But she could not. It was too raw. Too recent. And Aurelia was too…unknown.

She changed the clasp of their hands, so she was holding Aurelia's.

'And I am also here for you, Aurelia, should *you* wish to confide in *me*. I have noticed how you change the subject whenever your father is mentioned.'

'Ah.' The corner of Aurelia's mouth quirked up. 'The difference there, my dear sister, is I have no wish to share. The past is the past. May it remain there.'

'Very well. I thank you for your offer, and I shall bear it in mind should *I* wish to share.'

Aurelia laughed. 'Touché. And yet…' with her free hand she reached to brush a lock of hair back from Leah's forehead '… *I* am not haunted by my past. I do not retreat into *my* past and long for…something…from there to appear in my present.'

Leah flinched at the gentle understanding on her sister's face. She looked away. 'I cannot. Not yet.' Tears prickled her eyes and her throat constricted. She swallowed hard.

'Then I shall pry no further, my dear. Maybe, in time, we shall both welcome a confidante. Now, in the meantime…' Leah's hand was released. She swallowed again, making sure her emotions were under control, as Aurelia continued, '…*what* are we to do about Beatrice? Do you think we should write to her, despite what she said about her brother? I am worried we have heard nothing from her.'

'As am I. But as to what to do… I am not sure.' They had already discussed Beatrice's apparent fear of her brother. 'She was adamant we should not write to her, and I should hate to cause trouble for her.'

Aurelia sighed. 'I hate having to just sit here and *wait*, but maybe it is too soon to panic—it is still over four weeks to Eastertide. Oh! How I wish she would hurry up and join us. I cannot wait until we can openly acknowledge our connection.' She eyed Leah. 'You do still agree with me we should openly admit we are half-sisters?'

'Yes. Although not, of course, if Beatrice should object.'

They had agreed any acknowledgement must wait until Beatrice joined them and had her say, as any adverse reaction to the news would affect all three of them.

'I have a feeling Beatrice will be as eager as us to show the world we are proud to be sisters,' said Aurelia. 'Even in the face of Prudence's predictions of scandal and disaster.'

Leah laughed. 'She did not use quite such incendiary words, Aurelia. She fears the truth will put off many genuine gentlemen and leave us with hardened fortune hunters from whom to choose.'

'Well, if a little thing like that is enough to put off a gentleman, I do not think he would make a particularly good husband, do you? And it would mean a lifetime of lies to your spouse. Think of that. What if he discovered the truth after marriage?'

Janet, the maid, brought in the tea tray then, and Aurelia sprang up to pour them both a cup while Leah pondered her sister's words. How would Dolph have reacted had Leah told him the truth about her inheritance and her paternity? She absent-mindedly took the cup and saucer handed to her and sipped the hot tea, her head full of Dolph. Would he have changed his mind and withdrawn his proposal?

'There you go again.'

Leah jumped at Aurelia's softly spoken comment, feeling her cheeks heat.

'Where *do* you go inside your head, Leah? It does not make you happy.'

Leah shook her head, fearing if she spoke, the whole might flood out.

'I know I said I wouldn't pry, but…is it Lord Dolphinstone? Did you fall in love with him? Do not think I haven't noticed you dropping his name into the conversation at odd moments—*Dolph says this; Dolph did that.*'

Hot embarrassment flooded Leah. *Do I do that?*

Aurelia sat next to Leah and put her arm around her. 'It is all right, Leah. I know you don't wish to talk about it, but I will say the man is a fool to let such a diamond slip through his fingers, and a fool such as that is not worth a moment more of your regret.'

Leah felt Aurelia stroking her nape, and she realised she had bowed her head.

'You will tell me one day, when you know I may be trusted,' Aurelia whispered.

Leah firmed her jaw, then raised her head, forcing her eyes open.

'Going back to Beatrice,' she said, 'do you think we should go to her brother's house and bring her to London ourselves?'

'I don't know.' Aurelia nibbled one finger, her brow puckering in thought. Then she directed a mischievous grin at Leah. 'This may surprise you, but I think we should discuss it with Prudence. If she agrees, we could all go down to Somerset together.'

Leah laughed. 'I am *astonished* you might suggest we talk to Prudence about *anything*, let alone Beatrice.'

The confinement of this life continued to chafe Aurelia, and her frustration was all too often targeted at Mrs Butterby.

Aurelia huffed a laugh. 'I know our situation is not her fault, but I cannot help being irritated by her determination to see us "marry well", as if good breeding is the only essential measure of a suitable match. I tell you, Leah, I should far prefer a man who has earned his position and wealth than one who merely inherited them, but who is nonetheless convinced of his own superiority, and who will no doubt secretly despise me for the circumstances of my birth. There was no stipulation in Lady Tregowan's will as to what position in Society any husband must occupy, but Prudence is determined we marry into its upper ranks. Well, I do not know about you, but I can do without a spouse who will look down upon me throughout our marriage because of my birth.'

'Is that how your father treated your mother? And you?'

Leah was aware she had been fortunate. Papa and Mama had fallen in love, and their marriage had been happy. Her childhood had been happy.

Aurelia stiffened, her cheeks colouring. 'Did I say that?'

'There is no need to be defensive, Aurelia. *I* do not judge you. How could I?'

'Hmmph. I suppose not.' Her eyes remained downcast.

It was Leah's turn to comfort Aurelia. She put her arms around her and pulled her into a hug.

'We will each tell the other, one day.' She pressed a kiss to Aurelia's cheek. 'On the day we both fully believe the other may be trusted.'

Chapter Twenty

Dolph stared helplessly at Steven's tear-drenched face.

'I must go, Stevie.' He rounded his desk, dropped to his knees, put his arms around his eldest son and pulled him in for a hug. Wolf, who had been snoring by the fire, lumbered to his feet and padded across to join in. 'But I won't leave until the beginning of next week, and I promise I will only be gone a matter of a week or so.'

He had finally accepted the truth. He loved Leah…had for a while, but he'd blinded himself to his feelings, dismissing them as lust, or friendship, or anything rather than admit the truth. And his reluctance to admit the truth was because he did not believe he deserved to be happy, as George had said. And now he had lost Leah, and he missed her more with every passing day. There was little point in regretting he had not spoken of love when he proposed—he had not been ready to confess his feelings to himself, let alone to her. But he was ready now, and the need to see her again and to be honest with her, to declare his love, was near

overwhelming. He'd had to force himself to remain in Somerset—all the time frantic Leah would meet someone new—
until the new governess had moved in and the boys settled
into their new routine. Fortunately, Miss Pike had proved
herself a gem almost immediately but, still, Dolph worried
he'd left it too late or that she would refuse him again.

He took heart from her words: *If you should decide you
want me for the right reasons, my lord, you know where I
will be*, but he also faced the hard truth that, should she refuse him again—if he had hopelessly messed everything up
by not being honest with her, let alone with himself—then
his only option would be to return to Dolphin Court and to
learn to live with his own failure. However much he loved
Leah, he would not abandon his children again by spending
weeks on end in London while he proved his love for her.

'But, Papa...'

A figure darkened the door of Dolph's study. 'Stevie!
There you are. I am so sorry, my lord, but he slipped away
when I was busy with Nicky.'

'It is quite all right, Miss Pike.' Dolph stood up, keeping one hand on Stevie's shoulder. 'Stevie and I have a few
matters to discuss. I shall return him to the schoolroom
when we are done.'

Miss Pike had only been with them six days, but the boys
had taken to her immediately, helped by her one-eyed pet
parrot, Horatio, who could say *Fiddlesticks* and *Stow it*,
fascinating the boys, and who frequently terrorised poor
Wolf, with its swooping, airborne attacks.

'Very well, my lord. I shall return to Nicky, or he will be
up to some manner of mischief, I'll be bound.'

She flashed a smile and hurried away.

'Come, Stevie.' Dolph led his son to the chair by the

hearth, sat down and lifted him onto his lap. 'Listen. It will not be like last time. You have my word as a gentleman I shall return as soon as I humanly can.'

Steven sat still for a few minutes, pouting. Then he scrambled from Dolph's knee and stood to attention in front of him. 'Is it business, Papa?'

Love for his small solemn boy flooded Dolph. 'It is business of sorts, Stevie, yes.'

'In London?'

Dolph frowned. He had the feeling of walking into a verbal trap set by a seven-year-old. 'Ye-es.'

'I am your heir, Papa. I need to help with business. I shall come with you.'

'Stevie. That is imposs…' Dolph paused. It wasn't impossible. 'Do you know something, Stevie?' he said slowly. 'That is an excellent idea. We will all go to London. The whole family. And we won't wait until next week. We shall go tomorrow.'

'Hurrah! We're going to London.' Stevie capered around the room, Wolf prancing at his heels, his tail waving. 'Can we go and see Miss Thame, Papa?'

He should have foreseen it. His heart sank. How would they cope with seeing her again when they were only just getting used to her absence? Stevie halted in front of Dolph and patted his hand.

'Do not worry, Papa. We love Miss Thame, but we know she had to leave us. We won't get upset again, I promise.'

Dolph grabbed Stevie and hugged him close, not only to hide the tears in his eyes but also his grin of pure delight. How had he ever worried Steven was too sensitive and needed toughening up?

* * *

He told George he was going away after dinner that evening, after the servants had withdrawn and while they lingered over their port and cigars.

'I am pleased you are easier about leaving the children now,' said George. 'The boys have certainly taken to Miss Pike and her parrot—I never saw such looks of delight as on their faces when she descended from the post-chaise carrying its cage.'

'I am not leaving them. They are coming with me.'

George stared. 'You're a brave man, Dolph. Don't you remember the horror of that journey back from Hewton with their ponies?'

'Oh, I remember all right. That is why I hoped to prevail upon you to return to London too. I can keep you company in your carriage while the children, Miss Pike and Cassie occupy the other.'

'Ah.' George fell silent, staring at his glass while he twiddled it between his thumb and forefinger. 'The thing is, old fellow… I am not quite ready to go yet.'

Dolph waited, watching a succession of expressions flow across George's face. Eventually he looked up.

'You may take my carriage—it'll be more comfortable than all cramming into yours or hiring a post-chaise. Winters can return here for me. There's no rush…as long as you have no objection to my staying here?'

'Not at all.' Still Dolph waited, until the words burst from George in a torrent.

'You see…the thing is… I didn't expect… I never expected…' He snatched up his glass and gulped the remain-

ing port in one swallow. 'I don't want to leave her, Dolph.
I *cannot* leave her.'

'So…what do you intend to do about it, my friend?'

'I shall ask her to marry me.' George poured another
measure into his glass and shook his head in disbelief. 'It
very much looks as though we are both on the brink of entering the parson's mousetrap, Dolph.'

'In my case, there will be bridges to mend first. I can
only hope I shall succeed.' He raised his glass. 'To you and
Philippa, George. I hope you will be very happy together.'

'Thank you, my friend.' George's glass chinked against
Dolph's. 'And, in my turn, a toast to wish you luck on your
mission to repair those bridges in London.'

Two weeks to the day after Leah's arrival in London, Mrs
Butterby suggested they take advantage of a dry afternoon
by taking a drive in the Park in Lady Tregowan's barouche.

Barely had they arrived in Hyde Park when Aurelia said,
'May Leah and I walk for a spell, Mrs Butterby? The crowds
are sparse enough that you won't lose sight of us.' Only then
did she look at Leah and add, 'If you should like to walk
with me, that is, Leah?'

'I shall be happy to.'

'Of course you may.' Mrs Butterby peered all around
and then tutted. ''Tis most vexing. Lord Sampford assured
me he would ride in the Park this afternoon. Veryan too.'
She sighed. 'Oh, well. 'Tis early yet… I dare say they will
be here later.'

Leah smiled at their chaperone's disgruntled tone even
as she wondered how long it would be before one of their
approved admirers, such as Sampford or Veryan, joined
them. Not long, she suspected—their possession of a tidy

fortune each had guaranteed the persistent attention of several gentlemen of the *ton*. Mrs Butterby was kept on her toes warning the undesirables away, but both Sampford and Veryan had earned her approval as being suitable marriage prospects even though neither Leah nor Aurelia could stand either gentleman, whose conversation appeared to consist entirely of tittle-tattle.

Without warning, Dolph's image materialised in her mind's eye. *His* conversation had never been dull or trite. She sucked in a deep breath, willing her emotions down, determined to reveal no sign of distress as she swallowed past the aching lump in her throat. When would it get easier, this sense of loss? She missed him. She missed the children. She missed her home. This—she cast a sweeping glance around the Park as she and Aurelia strolled, taking in the members of Polite Society who had already returned to Town and who, like them, were promenading in order to see and be seen—*this* was not what she wanted.

'Leah...' Aurelia halted and faced Leah, a tiny crease stitched between her fair brows. 'I wanted to talk to you alone... Oh! Not about your precious Dolph,' she added quickly. 'I promised, did I not? No. It is Beatrice. We can delay no longer... We *must* go down to Somerset to rescue her. I have an uneasy feeling, right here—' she pressed her hand to her midriff '—and it will not go away.'

'Rescue her? Do you imagine her brother has her locked away?'

'I would put nothing past him,' Aurelia said darkly. 'She was scared of him. I know she was.'

'Yes. I know it too. I am sorry. I have been preoccupied— it's almost a week since we agreed to talk to Prudence, isn't it? I quite forgot, I'm afraid.' Guilt curled through her. 'I have been selfish.'

Aurelia tucked her arm through Leah's, and they began to stroll once more. 'As you said, you have been preoccupied. We still have time.'

'Then we shall talk to Prudence today.' Leah's heart sank at the sight of two gentlemen on horseback. 'Uh-oh. Here are Veryan and Sampford. Prepare yourself for another sparkling display of wit and intelligence.'

Aurelia giggled. 'You wicked woman! You know you ought to be grateful for their condescension in even noticing us.'

'Oh, I assure you, I am fully aware of the honour they do us,' Leah murmured.

They curtsied as Their Lordships halted their horses and bowed.

'Good afternoon, Miss Croome; Miss Thame. What a splendid afternoon for a stroll.'

Leah smiled dutifully. 'Splendid indeed, my lord.'

'You have escaped the clutches of the good Mrs Butterby today, I see.'

Veryan's patronising tone set Leah's teeth on edge.

'Not entirely,' Aurelia responded. 'She is being driven in the barouche. Miss Thame and I wished to enjoy a quiet stroll together.' She tilted her chin. 'So, if you will excuse us, we shall be on our way.'

'Now, now, Miss Croome. I know you do not mean it, for I am familiar with your teasing ways. Indeed, I have a fancy to take a stroll myself,' said Sampford. 'What say you, Veryan? Shall we take a turn about the Park with the ladies?'

Aurelia cast a speaking look at Leah as Their Lordships

dismounted and handed their reins to the groom riding in their wake. Leah knew her sister was quite capable of sending this pair of peacocks packing, if Leah did but give her the nod. But even though she resented the interruption to their conversation, she was aware the Season had a long way to go yet, and there was little point in insulting prominent members of the *ton* just for the sake of it.

Their Lordships proffered an arm to each of the sisters. Leah sent a resigned smile to Aurelia before laying her hand upon Veryan's forearm. This might spell the end of their conversation about Beatrice, but she would not allow herself to become distracted from the subject again. How awful if they did nothing and Beatrice was in trouble.

As the four of them strolled, Leah directed her gaze straight ahead.

'Oh!' The exclamation escaped her before she could stop it.

'Are you well, Miss Thame?' Veryan laid his hand over hers and squeezed it solicitously. 'Shall I summon your chaperone?'

'No. Indeed, I am well, my lord.' Leah could not tear her attention from the figure approaching them. His head was tilted down, and the brim of his hat was low so she could not fully distinguish his features, but the set of those shoulders...the power of those breeches-clad thighs striding along... She swallowed, her pulse fluttering. *Could it be?*

Veryan followed her gaze. 'Well,' he tittered, looking past Leah to Lord Sampford, 'Dolphinstone's vow to shun Society did not last long, did it? I wonder what could possibly have prompted him to come up to Town so soon after losing his governess?'

Leah cringed inside. She knew what he implied—she'd

made no secret she'd worked as a governess, most recently for Dolph, and she'd heard the snide comments as to why he had let an heiress such as her slip through his fingers. But she would not gratify Veryan by rising to his sly dig.

Not so Aurelia. 'What is it you imply, sir?' Her eyes snapped fire.

Veryan smiled mockingly. 'Nothing that need concern you, my dear.'

'Then you should not have mentioned it,' said Aurelia. 'It was impolite.'

Leah caught Veryan's barely disguised smirk, and anger at his superiority roiled her insides. No wonder Aurelia resented these arrogant aristocrats. And then her fury was further fuelled by anger at Dolph for breaking his word by leaving the children again.

Dolph nodded at Sampford and Veryan but clearly had no intention of stopping. Then his gaze met Leah's, and shock flashed across his expression before he successfully blanked it. He halted, raised his hat and bowed, his jaw muscles bunched, brows low over frowning eyes.

'Well met, Miss Thame.'

Leah curtsied, determinedly blanking her own expression. 'My lord.'

'You are in good health?'

'I am. Thank you.' She longed to demand why he had left the children, but refrained, knowing any hint of discord between them would only encourage further gossip. 'Will you allow me to introduce Miss Aurelia Croome?'

'Indeed. I am pleased to meet you, Miss Croome.' Dolph's smile did not reach his eyes.

Aurelia curtsied, her smile equally cool. 'I am fascinated

to meet you, my lord, after hearing so much about Miss Thame's life at Dolphin Court.'

Dolph's eyes narrowed and he shot a questioning glance at Leah. Who lifted her chin. Dolph's jaw firmed again.

'If you will excuse me, I have a meeting I must attend.' He studied Leah, and she felt her colour rise. 'I shall call on you if I may?'

Leah dropped a curtsy. 'Of course, my lord.'

She did not turn to watch as he walked away although every fibre of her being screamed at her to do so…to run after him…to know why he was here. Instead, she battened down her emotions and set herself to the interminable exchange of small talk that passed for entertainment in Polite Society.

Chapter Twenty-One

'Are you all right?' Aurelia whispered to Leah twenty minutes later, after Sampford and Veryan delivered them back to Mrs Butterby. They were already seated side by side on the backward-facing seat, opposite their chaperone, who was distracted as she ascertained Their Lordships' attendance at Lady Todmorden's rout that evening. 'You have been so quiet, and you look even paler than usual.'

Leah merely nodded. The effort of concealing her shock from their escorts had left her with a mouth too dry and brain far too jumbled to trust herself to say anything. Aurelia squeezed her hand and Leah desperately tried to calm her breathing as she pushed aside her conjectures—and, to her dismay, her *hopes*—as to why Dolph was here, in London.

'Thank goodness *that* ordeal is over,' Aurelia declared as the barouche pulled away. 'Do you think they have any notion how exceedingly *tedious* their conversation is?'

'Aurelia! Please!' Mrs Butterby indicated Hall, who was

driving the barouche. 'You do not wish for such opinions to become common knowledge.'

'Do I not?' Aurelia rolled her eyes at Leah, who forced a smile, grateful to her sister for diverting Mrs Butterby's attention away from her.

'You really are hopelessly outspoken—it will win you no friends in Society. Please, Leah, will *you* tell her?'

Leah hated their chaperone's tendency to try to get Leah to side with her against Aurelia. She shook her head. 'It is not my place to tell Aurelia how to behave.'

Aurelia squeezed her hand again, and Mrs Butterby spent the rest of the journey delivering a homily to Aurelia on ladylike behaviour. When they arrived home Leah and Aurelia headed straight for the drawing room, and Mrs Butterby said she would join them shortly.

'Really!' Aurelia flung herself onto the sofa. 'She is infuriating. Have you noticed how she constantly tries to set you against me? I can only view her strategy as one of divide and conquer—she no doubt believes we will be easier to manage as individuals than as friends who support one another.' She directed her bright blue gaze at Leah. 'We are friends, are we not, Leah? I know I am sometimes a touch... shall we say, confrontational—' a smile flashed across her face '—but I would do anything for you. You do know that?'

Touched, Leah sat next to Aurelia and hugged her. 'Yes, I do know it, and yes, we are friends.'

'And, as your friend... I know I said I would not pry, but... Leah... Lord Dolphinstone.'

Leah's heart somersaulted in her chest, and her pulse picked up again. Just at the mention of his name.

'You did not tell me he was so handsome.'

When Leah did not reply, Aurelia sighed. 'Well, it is

hard to contain my curiosity, but I *did* say I would not pry, and friends should stick to their word. And sisters, even more so.'

Leah's arm was still around Aurelia, and she hugged her again. 'I am so happy we are sisters,' she said. Then she frowned. 'And I would be far happier to admit that outright. Which brings us back to what we should do about Beatrice.'

'Yes, I shall accept your change of subject,' Aurelia said, nudging Leah gently. 'So, speaking of Beatrice...' She chewed her lip. 'How would we feel if we did nothing, and she simply did not turn up?'

Leah shoved all thought of Dolph from her mind. Beatrice was important too.

'We would regret it. Deeply.'

Mrs Butterby entered the room as Leah spoke. 'Regret what, pray?'

'We are worried about Beatrice,' Leah said. 'We would like to go to her brother's house and bring her back to London before Easter.'

Mrs Butterby sat in a chair and fussed about, smoothing her skirts. 'She has over three weeks yet.'

'But what if she misses the deadline?' said Aurelia. 'You did not see her when she spoke about her brother. She is scared of him. He is a brute.'

'She told you so, did she, Aurelia?'

'She didn't have to tell me. I can feel it here!'

Aurelia clapped a hand to her chest, covering her heart, and Leah puzzled again at the contradictions in this sister of hers. Defensive about her own past, and about her future too, scathing of many people she met, but fiercely protective of Beatrice, whom she barely knew, and of Leah too.

'It does you credit you are concerned about Beatrice,

and I promise we will not allow her to miss her chance. If we have heard nothing by early next week, then we shall all three go down to Somerset and fetch her. Although...' she looked from Leah to Aurelia and back again '...you do realise that if Beatrice fails to arrive in time, you two will benefit from it?'

Leah gasped, horrified it would even occur to Mrs Butterby that she might think such a thing. Before she could speak, however, Aurelia leapt in.

'As if *that* would make any difference! She is our flesh and blood, and that is worth more than any amount of money. Is that not right, Leah?'

'It is.'

Aurelia had again surprised Leah, but had also delighted her because, when Leah looked inside her own heart, she knew exactly how fortunate she was—finding Aurelia and Beatrice meant more to her than any amount of wealth.

Dolph's head spun as he strode away from Leah and her companions.

Sampford and Veryan! What the devil is she doing with that pair of scoundrels? And what *is she doing promenading in the Park anyway? Dressed in the height of fashion, too...*

His thoughts stuttered to a halt. George had told him she'd inherited a house and some money. He'd *assumed* it had been a modest amount—sufficient to enable her not to work for her living.

With a silent oath, he turned for home. He'd arrived an hour ago, tired and stiff after close to five days of travel, making slow progress for the children's sake, although they had travelled better than Dolph expected, especially once they reached the well-maintained road to London. As soon as they had arrived at his town house, Dolph had taken advantage of the dry weather to walk in the Park in order to blow the cobwebs away.

Never had he imagined Leah would be one of the first people he saw. His plan had been to call upon her the next day, after a refreshing night's sleep, and to tell her the truth about Rebecca's death, and to confess his own culpability, and to throw himself upon her mercy and beg her to take a chance on him and to be his wife.

Now he realised he'd never even thought to ask Travers for Leah's address, and he also realised, with a wash of shame, that he'd never *really* believed she would refuse him again, even after he confessed the truth about Rebecca's suicide. He had *assumed*—and there was that word again—she would forgive him because what he could offer her was superior to what she already had.

For the first time, doubts assailed him. She was clearly in better circumstances than he'd imagined. What if she was enjoying her life here in London? *What if she said no?*

As soon as he arrived home, he walked straight through into the mews and asked for Travers. When his coachman emerged from the stables Dolph drew him aside.

'It occurs to me I should pay my respects to Miss Thame while I am in Town, and I shall therefore need her address.'

He gritted his teeth at the amused gleam in Travers's eyes.

'South Street, milord. Tregowan House.'

Tregowan House? What the devil...?

Dolph fought to hide his bewilderment.

'Thank you, Travers. I shan't need the carriage in that case.' South Street was only around the corner from his own house in South Audley Street.

The first thing Dolph saw when he walked into his house was Nicky with Miss Pike's parrot on his shoulder.

'Wolf. Wolf. Say Wolf, Horatio. Wolf.'

'What are you up to, Nicky? Where is Miss Pike?'

Nicky looked at him guiltily. 'She is upstairs, Papa.'

'And where does she think you are?'

'Putting Horatio's cage in her chamber.'

'And is Horatio meant to be *inside* his cage?'

Nicky pouted. 'He has been inside his cage for *days*, Papa. He needed to fly.' He gazed up at Dolph, all innocence. 'He *needed* to blow the cobwebs away.'

Dolph bit back his grin at having his own words recited back to him. 'Go now and do as Miss Pike bid you,' he said, sternly. 'And then ask her how else you may help her.'

'Yes, Papa.' Nicky headed for the staircase.

Horatio suddenly stirred and stretched out his wings. 'Wolf!' he screeched. 'Wolf!'

The click of claws on the tiled floor sounded as Wolf emerged from the parlour and trotted along the hall, ears pricked.

'Wolf! Wolf!' Horatio took flight and dived at Wolf—aiming at his rump, too wise to venture too close to the dog's teeth. Wolf twisted, snapping ineffectually at empty air.

Dolph rubbed his hand around the back of his neck. He needed peace and quiet to think through what he'd learned about Leah. But first...

'Wolf. In.' He pointed at the parlour door. The dog obeyed, and Dolph shut the door. 'Come along, Nicky. Let us go and find Miss Pike. I doubt she will be happy you have taught her parrot to call Wolf—it'll cause chaos.'

Nicky beamed. 'It will, won't it, Papa? Are we going to

see Miss Thame while we are here? Stevie said she lives in London now.'

'I do not know, Nicky.' And he really didn't know. Not now. He didn't know what to think. 'We shall see.'

In the end, with so many unanswered questions whizzing around his head, Dolph abandoned his plans of a quiet evening in, followed by an early night, and ventured out after dinner. A visit to his club elicited the information from the doorman that the foremost event that evening was Lady Todmorden's rout. Dolph knew Lady Todmorden's spouse, Sir Horace, from his governmental work, and so he strolled from St James's to their house in Bruton Street, confident of a welcome despite his lack of an invitation. Here he hoped to find acquaintances who could fill in the gaps in his knowledge as to why Leah appeared to have been bequeathed Tregowan House.

The Todmordens' house was ablaze with light and the road hectic with carriages lining up to deposit their occupants at the door. A cacophony of laughter and conversation drifted through the open windows.

'Dolph! Good to see you again.' Sir Horace Todmorden's magnificent side whiskers quivered in his enthusiasm. 'It must be—what—close on a year and a half since we last met? You fellows did a grand job over in Europe, by the way. Thank God Napoleon got his comeuppance at last, eh?'

Lady Todmorden placed a hand on her husband's arm and smiled at Dolph. 'Welcome, Lord Dolphinstone. We were so sorry to hear of your loss last year, were we not, Horace?'

'What? Oh, yes. Quite. Condolences, my dear fellow. I quite forgot in all the kerfuffle over that bounder Bonaparte. Yes...welcome indeed.' He waved his arm in an expansive gesture. 'Do go ahead and mingle. I'm sure you'll find some familiar faces in there.'

Dolph smiled and then headed for the room indicated by Sir Horace. He paused in the open doorway and accepted a glass of champagne from a passing footman as he scanned the occupants for one of those familiar faces.

The first person he saw was Leah, holding court. Really, there was no other way to describe the scene before him. Leah, surrounded by half a dozen gentlemen—Veryan included—who were clinging to her every word and vying with one another to earn a smile, or a glance from those brilliant eyes. The sparkle was obvious, even from clear across the room, as the men flirted with her and she...*she* appeared to relish the attention.

Fortune hunters. Every one of 'em. They're only after her money. They don't know the real Leah as I do.

Jealousy spiralled up through Dolph at a dizzying speed. His free hand fisted at his side as he forced himself to sip nonchalantly at the champagne and watched, his gaze unwavering.

Her appearance was nothing short of regal as she stood straight and proud. She was inches taller than most other ladies present, but she did not slouch. And her hair gleamed like a beacon... It was braided up behind—bright, glossy, threaded with pearls—to reveal her elegant neck and ivory shoulders. Gentle curls softened her temples. Her gown— the colour of emeralds—clung to every inch of her willowy frame, draping the long, elegant line of her thighs, and the off-the-shoulder wide neckline exposed an expanse of bare skin unmarred by any decoration save for a green ribbon threaded through her mother's wedding ring. Strangely, that ring reassured him that this gleaming, polished lady of quality was still the same Leah he knew and loved.

'Dolph! Back in Town so soon?'

Dolph turned to see his old friend Sir Charles Pidgeon, who claimed a horror of the countryside and lived in London the year round with his wife and family.

'Pidge. Good to see you again.'

'I thought you were determined not to set foot in the place again, and yet here you are, not three months later. Is Hinckley back as well?'

'No, he's stayed down in Somerset for the time being.'

'And you? Why have you graced us with your presence again, so soon? Ah...'

Dolph stiffened as his old friend grinned knowingly.

'Could it, perchance, have something to do with the exceedingly popular Miss Thame? She was your governess, as I understand it.'

Dolph frowned. 'That is common knowledge?'

'She has made no secret of the fact. Neither has Miss Croome hidden that she was in dire straits before Lady Tregowan bequeathed them her fortune.'

'Miss Croome was also a beneficiary? In the same will? Lady Tregowan's will?'

Pidge's brows shot up. 'You did not know?'

'I only knew Miss Thame had inherited a house in London and an amount of money that meant she no longer had to work for a living.'

'Ah. Then allow me to fill you in, my dear chap, although there are still gaps in what we know, and rumours galore to fill those gaps, as you might imagine. One of those rumours is that there is another beneficiary, so no one is quite sure whether your Miss Thame has inherited one half or one third of Lady Tregowan's entire estate. Still, either way, she is a very wealthy lady.'

'*All* of it?' Dolph's brows shot up. 'Including Falconfield Hall? What about the current Earl? He would surely have expected to inherit something?'

'Ah, poor Tregowan. No one's seen hide nor hair of him—rumour has it he's licking his wounds back home in Cornwall. It's to be hoped the blow doesn't drive him to despair… Rumour is his finances are shot.'

Dolph felt a swell of sympathy for poor Tregowan. He didn't know him well, but he hoped his situation wasn't as serious as Pidge implied. And Leah…she had inherited a small fortune, and yet she had remained at Dolphin Court, working, when she could have been a lady of leisure. And that, he knew, was out of the goodness of her heart and from her desire to help the children become accustomed once again to their own father.

'The speculation, as you can imagine, is rife,' Pidge went on. 'Two young women appear from nowhere and take up residence in Tregowan House under the chaperonage of the late Lady Tregowan's companion? Society hasn't had this much excitement this early in the Season for many years. The tattlemongers are busily whispering behind their hands, questioning the link with Lady Tregowan, while the sticklers are already peering down their noses at the ladies in question. I doubt they will be honoured with vouchers for Almack's when it opens, but both *are* of respectable enough breeding on the face of it, and money does have a way of blinding those in debt to such negative connotations, does it not?'

Hence Leah being in company with Veryan and Sampford that afternoon. No wonder she had refused his offer when she had such wealth and excitement awaiting her in London.

'Thank you for bringing me up to date, Pidge.'

Pidge slapped Dolph's back. 'You're welcome, my friend. And if your appearance here has anything to do with Miss Thame, I honestly wish you luck, for she seems a decent woman and she will do far better with you than with any of those chancers cosying up to her. And, if you ask me— which you wouldn't, but I shall tell you anyway—the lady might give a good impression of lapping up all that attention but, in my opinion, her heart is not in it.'

With a final smile, Pidge wandered off while Dolph remained in place, searching the room with his eyes, seeking Leah. Someone was in the way, and Dolph shifted until he could see her. As she came into view—still surrounded by admirers—he battled a primeval urge to drag her away from them, to warn them away from her, to warn *her* they cared only for her money.

Her head turned, as if she felt the force of his gaze, and their eyes locked. He felt the blow as though it were physical. The air shot from his lungs and he strove to refill them, his legs suddenly weak. He could not move but remained as if frozen in place as he watched Leah's reaction. And, of course, there was no artifice. Not for her the coy lowering of her lashes. Not for her the turn of the shoulder to punish him. Not for her the revenge of flirting even more outrageously with her admirers simply in order to prove she had no need of him.

No. She excused herself from her coterie and she crossed the floor to him. Her smile, though, was hesitant. She was unsure, but she would not use that as an excuse to cut him. She had always been forthright and uncomplicated with him, and London had not—yet—changed her. She stopped in front of him and looked up, directly into his eyes.

Chapter Twenty-Two

'Good evening, Leah.' Dolph drank in her ivory skin dotted with those fascinating freckles, and her stunning turquoise eyes. Oh, how he had missed her.

'My lord.' A frown of disapproval creased her brow. 'I was unaware of your intention to come to London. You have left the children? After all your promises to put them first?'

'I had some unfinished business to attend to, but I have brought them with me.'

Her frown cleared at his words. Dolph sent his gaze around the room and saw several pairs of resentful eyes watching them. He crooked his arm. 'Would you care to stroll? I have news for you.'

Leah placed her hand on his forearm and Dolph reined in his urge to cover her hand with his. Her scent wreathed through his senses, in part familiar, and yet her own scent was overlaid with an unfamiliar, evocative floral perfume.

'Did Lord Hinckley accompany you to London?'

'No. He found he could not tear himself away from Somerset.'

'Ahhhhh.' Her lips curved as she sighed with satisfaction. 'He could not leave Philippa?'

'He offered for Miss Strong on the morning we left, and she accepted him.'

'I am delighted. Philippa deserves to be happy.'

They strolled on, through an open door at one end of the room and into another, equally crowded but with one distinct advantage, as far as Dolph was concerned. It did not contain Leah's flock of admirers but instead consisted of an older group of guests, mainly gentlemen recognisable to Dolph as ex-military.

Dolph glanced sideways as Leah spoke. Her mouth might smile but her eyes were sad. Without volition, his hand now covered hers, and he gently squeezed. If George was right about Leah's feelings for Dolph, then he had hurt her. Badly. He'd been a blind idiot not to see what had been in front of his nose.

'We *all* deserve to be happy,' he murmured.

Her head bowed, and he noticed her eyes screw shut for an instant, as though she were in pain. 'Tell me. The children are well?'

'They are.'

'Your business must be exceedingly important for you to come rushing up to London like this.'

'Oh, it is. It is, without doubt, the most important business of my entire life.'

'I see.'

He knew she would question him no further. He needed to explain himself—to throw himself upon her mercy—but this was neither the time nor the place for such an intimate and emotional discussion. She would know everything soon enough, and he would find out if her feelings for him were strong enough to withstand the truth about Rebecca. Frustration bubbled through him. He longed to find a quiet spot, to take her in his arms and to kiss away her doubts. But only a scoundrel would do that before telling her the full truth and giving her the chance to reject him.

Wouldn't he?

Almost without conscious thought, he scanned the library and spied a single door set into the far wall. It was closed, meaning what lay beyond was not open to guests. Dolph changed the direction of their stroll to ensure they passed close by it even as a voice inside clamoured he was being unfair.

'Who is caring for the boys? Have you found a new governess for them?'

'I have. Miss Pike. She is a cousin of the Reverend Strong. And she has a one-eyed parrot. Horatio.'

'A *parrot*?' Her lips quirked, and the memory of their taste, their texture, their eagerness, exploded through him. She soon sobered. 'Then the boys will have forgotten all about me already, I fear.'

'No. *None* of us have forgotten you. Nicky asked only today if they may visit you.'

Leah's fingers tightened on his arm, and Dolph sent her a sideways look, just in time to see the glint of a tear on her lower lashes, and to catch the hitch in her breath.

'I am sorry. I did not mean to distress you.'

'And I did not intend to allow my emotions to overcome me.' Leah touched the corner of her eye with one gloved finger. 'Foolish woman! I do apologise.'

Dolph reached for his pocket handkerchief and moved to shield her from view, although, judging by the general hubbub, the other guests were too engrossed in their own conversation to take much notice of the two of them. He pushed his handkerchief into Leah's hand. She snatched it from him and quickly thrust it out of sight in her reticule.

'Not in front of everyone, please,' she hissed. 'There are already people who look to find fault with every little thing about us—about me and Aurelia, I mean—without handing them more ammunition with a display of *vulgar emotion*, as Mrs Butterby would say.'

Dolph stared down at her. Her eyes still brimmed with tears and, as he watched, one drop spilled over her lashes and slowly tracked down her cheek. She bent her head and another tear plopped to the floor. With a muttered exclamation, he cupped her elbow and steered her to that door, opened it and nudged her through. A glance behind showed nobody taking any notice, so he followed her, shutting the door behind them. The room was dark, but another door, slightly ajar, allowed enough light to reveal they were in a small parlour. Dolph strode to the second door and peered out to see it opened into the back of the entrance hall. He used a tinderbox upon the mantelshelf to light a candle.

'Why do you imagine people are looking to find fault in you?'

A quiet, bitter-sounding laugh escaped her. 'We have seen the looks. Heard the comments. It would appear the purity of our *breeding* is in question. As if we were a couple of racehorses.'

Dolph bit back a laugh at her disgruntled tone. 'You should ignore them. It is pure jealousy and spite, for the most part. They are envious of your good fortune.' His voice deepened as he stepped closer to her. 'And of your beauty.'

She stared up at him. 'Beauty? Now I know you are flannelling me. And I thank you for it, but there is no need to try and make me feel better with false compliments.'

'The compliment was not false. You stand out as a diamond among all the other females here, despite your lack of jewels.' He stroked one finger down the silk ribbon and paused as he reached the ring. 'You still wear your mama's ring, I see.'

Her hand rose to her chest, and her fingers brushed his as she touched the ring. 'It is more precious to me than any jewels. It keeps her memory close.'

His heart ached at the sadness in her voice. She had lost both parents. She had no family. She had been forced to earn her living at what was often a thankless task, and he— the one person who should have protected her against more hardship—had effectively driven her away from where she was happy. Nothing could excuse his behaviour. He hadn't recognised his love for Leah just as he hadn't recognised Rebecca's despair. He truly was a failure, and he was ashamed.

Dolph placed two fingers beneath Leah's chin, tilting her face to his. 'Leah... I—'

The door behind them opened, and they jumped apart as Miss Croome stalked into the room, glaring at Dolph.

'Leah! Mrs Butterby is hunting high and low for you. You had better come with me before she creates an uproar over your disappearance. It is fortunate I was watching you and saw Lord Dolphinstone spirit you away.'

'Spirit me away? Aurelia... I am in no danger from His Lordship, I assure you.'

'Your *reputation* is in danger.' Miss Croome's blue eyes,

flashing like sapphires, scrutinised Dolph from head to toe and back again. 'Why have you come to London?'

Leah gasped. 'Aurelia! Please—'

Dolph touched Leah's arm. 'It is all right, Leah. Miss Croome is entitled to wonder why we are here alone, and to question my motives. I am in London on *personal* business, Miss Croome.'

His gaze sought Leah's as he spoke. A blush stole up her neck to her cheeks, and her fingers sought her mother's ring. Her throat moved as she swallowed.

Her eyes clung to his as she said, 'Aurelia, will you kindly go to Mrs Butterby and reassure her I am found and perfectly safe?'

That suspicious blue gaze transferred to Leah. 'Come with me.'

'I will be right behind you. I promise.'

Miss Croome drew herself up to her full height, meaning the top of her head barely reached Dolph's shoulder. Her eyes narrowed. 'If Leah does not appear in *three minutes*, I shall return, so be warned.'

She stalked from the room.

'I see I have no need to fear for your safety when you have your own personal bodyguard,' Dolph said, with a laugh. 'She is rather protective, is she not? It makes me wonder what you have told her about me.'

'I have told her nothing. She is aware you were my employer, and that is all. I only met Aurelia for the first time at that meeting in Bristol. I do not know her well enough to share confidences...not that there are any confidences to tell, of course. And,' she added, 'you are no longer responsible for me, so there is no need for you to fear for my safety or to concern yourself about anything to do with me.'

'Touché.' Dolph cupped Leah's shoulders. 'Leah…listen… I am aware we do not have much time. That personal business…' He watched her closely. 'It involves you.'

'Oh.' Her smile wavered. 'I appear to be lost for words. Can you enlighten me with more details of this personal business?'

'I cannot. At least, not fully. There are things I must tell you that will take more time than we have available now. May I call upon you tomorrow?'

'Yes. I shall look forward to it.' Her expression belied her words and the tremor in her voice signalled her doubts.

He had caused this. And, all at once, he understood Pidge had been right. Her performance as a queen among her entourage had been precisely that. A performance. And his treatment of her had added to her doubts about her own allure.

Dolph's hands firmed on her shoulders and he drew her slowly towards him.

'I have missed you more than you could ever know, my sweet Leah.' He lowered his face as hers tilted towards him. His mouth brushed hers and then settled. Her response was, as ever, heartbreakingly honest—her lips softening beneath his in a slow, sensual kiss that set his pulse racing. Too soon, she pulled away, her hands flat upon his chest.

'I must go.' Her deep turquoise gaze searched his. 'You should know—my reasons for refusing your offer have not changed.'

Forever honest. He gently brushed back a stray lock of her hair at her temple.

'But my reasons for making that offer *have* changed, dear Leah. However…' he placed his forefinger against her lips as her mouth opened to speak '…there is something I must tell you first. Something you need to understand, before we speak of the future. So we will talk tomorrow.'

He put his arms around her and pulled her close, just holding her. His eyes closed and he breathed in her floral scent. What would tomorrow bring? Would she understand why he had hesitated to admit—or even recognise—his feelings for her? Would she willingly face the risk of being his wife? And yet, even as those thoughts crossed his mind, he began to realise the benign neglect that had dogged his marriage to Rebecca need not be repeated. His future was in his hands. Unlike then—and whether it was because he was now older and more mature, or whether it was because it was Leah rather than Rebecca, and he loved her with his whole heart—he no longer viewed his decision to give up his government business as a sacrifice. He felt as though he would be content to stay at Dolphin Court with Leah for the remainder of his days. He loved her. Never in his life had he felt that emotion so deeply, so naturally, so *passionately*.

With reluctance, he released her.

'Come. Let us go before Miss Croome returns to savage me once again.'

He took her hand and led her to the door into the entrance hall. A swift peek revealed only servants—a footman on duty by the front door and two maids waiting to assist guests with their coats upon arrival and departure. Dolph urged Leah through the door and followed her out into the hall and then into the room in which he had first seen her. It was still packed with guests.

Miss Croome pounced the minute they entered. 'I was about to come looking for you again,' she hissed. 'Mrs Butterby has the headache now, no doubt from all the worry you've caused.'

'Nonsense!' said Leah. 'There is no need to be overly dramatic, Aurelia.'

Miss Croome's blue eyes raked Dolph once again. 'If there was nothing clandestine in your little *tête-à-tête*, why did *His Lordship* not introduce himself to your chaperone?'

'*Aurelia*. Please…'

Miss Croome's expression softened, and she took Leah's hand. 'I am sorry. I am worried for you, and that has sharpened my tongue, perhaps.' She bit her lip and looked up at Dolph. 'I apologise, my lord.'

'You were rightly concerned for your friend,' he said. 'And now, Miss Croome, perhaps you will be kind enough to conduct us to your Mrs Butterby, for you are quite right, and I should have made myself known to her at the outset.'

Leah's smile warmed his heart. They followed Miss Croome through the throng to a slender, grey-haired lady, whose drawn features did indeed give the impression she was in pain.

'Mrs Butterby,' said Leah. 'May I introduce Lord Dolphinstone? My lord, this is Mrs Butterby, who is kindly standing as chaperone for myself and Miss Croome for the duration of our time in London.'

Mrs Butterby curtsied. 'I am pleased to meet you, my lord. I do hope you will call upon us while you are in Town.'

Dolph bowed. 'Thank you, ma'am. I have already asked Miss Thame if I might call upon her tomorrow.'

Mrs Butterby's eyes widened. 'I shall look forward to your visit, my lord.'

Leah took the older woman by the arm. 'Are you quite well, dear ma'am? Aurelia said you are suffering the headache.'

'Oh. Well. Yes, indeed, but it is only very slight.'

'It does not look to me to be only slight. It is unbearably hot and stuffy in here, not to mention the noise. Shall we go home?'

'Well, if you and Aurelia have no objection, I must confess it would be a relief.'

'I have no objection,' said Miss Croome.

'Nor I,' said Leah.

Mrs Butterby scanned the room distractedly. 'In that case, I shall find Lady Todmorden and say our goodbyes while you girls bespeak our carriage and our cloaks. Lord Dolphinstone, I am sorry we must leave, but I shall look forward to meeting you properly tomorrow.'

Dolph bowed and watched her walk away. Miss Croome stirred then. 'I shall order the carriage. I will meet you in the hall, Leah.' And she, too, walked away.

Dolph scanned the crowd and became aware of the many pairs of eyes upon him. Mostly male, and somewhat disgruntled.

'Might I escort you to the door?' Dolph took Leah's hand and placed it upon his sleeve very deliberately—a non-verbal statement as to his intentions, aimed at every last one of those fortune hunters. 'Shall I call upon you at eleven? Will that be acceptable?'

'It will.'

Miss Croome, already wearing her mantle, was waiting in the entrance hall.

'Which is your coat?'

'The green pelisse.' Leah indicated the garment held by the waiting maid.

Dolph moved behind her, holding the pelisse as she slipped her arms into the sleeves. As he settled the coat across her shoulders, the tips of his fingers brushed first the satiny skin of her neck and then a silky curl of hair that had escaped its pin. His breath stirred the soft hairs at her nape, and he saw gooseflesh erupt and felt her quiver in response. His own pulse thrummed, and the blood surged to his groin, causing him to grow hard. He wanted her. *Ached* for her.

Such a simple action, to assist her with her coat, and yet his reaction stirred so many complex needs and worries and regrets and...*guilt*. His old friend guilt. Seizing on a sudden impulse, he bent his head and put his lips to her ear.

'Do not stop believing, my sweet Leah.'

Her shoulders tensed beneath his hands. Her chaperone chose that moment to bustle into the hall, and Dolph took advantage of the distraction to press a kiss to the side of Leah's neck.

'All will be well. I promise you.'

Chapter Twenty-Three

'So,' hissed Aurelia, as she and Leah waited to climb into the carriage behind Mrs Butterby, 'you did not tell me your Dolph is as obsessed with you as you are with him.'

'Is he? Am I?' Leah raised one eyebrow, affecting nonchalance despite the blush heating her cheeks. 'That sounds singularly inappropriate given he was my employer.'

'Tosh. You don't fool me, sister. Or are you in the habit of allowing your employers to make love to you under the cover of assisting you with your pelisse?'

Another shiver racked Leah as she felt again the brush of Dolph's fingers over her sensitive nape, and the sweet, petal-soft touch of his lips upon her neck. She had hoped no one had noticed. Trust Aurelia—nothing much escaped those sharp blue eyes of hers.

'Can you trust him, though, Leah? Ask yourself what he is doing here in London.'

'He has come on business. Please, take care,' Leah whispered urgently. 'Mrs Butterby will hear you.'

A footman handed first her and then Aurelia into the carriage, which immediately set off. Leah resisted the urge to look back to see if Dolph was there, somewhere, watching her depart. What did it all mean? The carefully selected words; that kiss; the fire that smouldered in those grey eyes? He'd said there was something she needed to understand before they could discuss the future. She tingled with excitement. She had prayed he might realise he loved her when she was gone, and she now prayed he could convince her of it, for her resolve was as strong as ever. If she must accept a marriage of convenience—and she was by no means certain she would do so—she would rather it was to a man whose heart was at least free to grow to love her. She would not wed a man still in love with his first wife, for that way lay misery and heartache.

A sharp nudge from Aurelia's elbow brought Leah back to her surroundings. They were nearing home. Mrs Butterby was uncharacteristically quiet, staring out of the carriage window and nibbling absently at the finger of her glove. As the vehicle slowed, she jerked out of her reverie.

'How is your headache now, ma'am?' asked Leah.

'Oh. It is a little better, I believe.' Mrs Butterby massaged her temples as the carriage drew to a stop. 'The noise at the rout did not help, but I have also been thinking about Beatrice, after our conversation this afternoon. I know I said there is still time, and that is true, but... I honestly did think she would be here by now. I know dear Sarah was very worried when she found out how badly her brother treated her.'

She accepted Vardy's hand to help her down the carriage steps and walked into the house ahead of Leah and Aurelia, straight up to the drawing room, where she sat down. 'We shall discuss what we are to do in the morning when my head is clearer. However, I cannot retire to bed without first asking you about Lord Dolphinstone, Leah.'

'What about him?' Leah caught Aurelia's smirk out of the corner of her eye and glared at her.

'May we attach any significance to his calling upon you tomorrow? He is a fine figure of a man and I do know he is well respected in Society. And an earl!' She sighed. 'Quite the catch!'

'I do not know,' she said. 'I hope so. And yet…' She shrugged helplessly.

Aurelia sat beside her. 'Why do you not tell us the whole, Leah? I was right there was something between you when you worked for His Lordship, was I not?'

'You were. We grew close and we kissed.' She smiled, ruefully. 'And I did not mean to, but I fell in love with him, despite knowing he had vowed never to remarry because he still loved his late wife. When I decided I must leave before I fell any deeper for him, he asked me to marry him.'

'He asked you to *marry* him? And you love him?' Mrs Butterby shook her head. 'Why are you here? Why did you not snap his hand off, you foolish girl?'

Leah sighed. 'He only proposed to me for the children's sake, to stop me leaving. I overheard him tell his friend Lord Hinckley that he would do anything to stop me going, and L-Lord Hinckley suggested he marry me. It was not even Dolph's idea. And he made no attempt to hide that it was a practical solution, as far as he was concerned.'

'The scoundrel!' Aurelia patted Leah's arm. 'But he followed you. That is a good sign, is it not?'

'I hope so. And what he said tonight… I told him my reasons for refusing him have not changed, and he said that his reasons for making that offer *have* changed.'

'But…that is wonderful.' Mrs Butterby clasped her hands to her bosom. 'So-o-o-o romantic.'

'But then he said there is something I need to understand before we can speak of the future. And I have racked my brains, but I cannot think what he means. I so want to believe my dream will come true, but I have been fooled before and now I just feel confused.'

'Well…he had the *look* of a man who is enamoured,' said Aurelia, 'but is he to be trusted? You know him best, Leah.'

Leah frowned. She so desperately wanted to trust Dolph, but the memory of Peter and Usk loomed large. Could she really trust her own judgement? *But…this is Dolph. Has he ever given me reason not to trust him?* She felt guilty for even doubting him. She loved him, and surely trust must go hand in hand with love?

'You are right, Aurelia. I *do* know him. He was honest about the reason for his proposal at Dolphin Court and I trust him to be honest with me tomorrow.' She prayed she was right. 'I fear I have allowed conjecture and my emotions to distort my good sense.' She rose to her feet. 'I shall see you both in the morning. Goodnight.'

Despite her resolve to stop trying to guess what Dolph was to tell her, and to trust him, Leah still struggled to sleep. The following morning she awoke with a start as Faith bustled into her room.

'Miss Thame! Miss Thame!'

Leah blurrily focussed her eyes on her maid as she fought the desire to turn over and sink back into oblivion. But the urgency in Faith's voice roused her curiosity.

'What is it?' Leah propped herself up on one elbow.

'It's Miss Fothergill, miss. She has arrived, and…oh,

miss, I knew you would want to know, so I hurried up here straight away.'

Leah frowned. *Beatrice? Here?* 'What time is it?'

'Almost nine, miss. Mr Vardy has put her in the morning parlour next to the fire. She's chilled to the bone, poor thing.'

Leah jumped out of bed and grabbed her shawl, thrusting her feet into her slippers before hurrying from her bedchamber. 'Have Mrs Butterby and Miss Croome been told?'

'Bet has gone to tell them, miss.'

The door to the morning parlour was ajar and, from within, Leah could hear the snap of the fire. She paused outside the door.

'Thank you, Faith. Please ask the kitchen to send up a warm drink and something to eat for Miss Fothergill.'

'Mrs Burnham is already seeing to it, miss.' Faith bobbed a curtsy and hurried away. Leah bit her lip and pushed the door open, wondering what she might find.

Beatrice was sitting on the chair nearest the fire, huddled over and seemingly talking to a wicker basket by her feet. Her head snapped up as Leah entered and her fearful expression changed to one of sheer relief. She leapt up and rushed across the room. For one moment, Leah thought Beatrice would hurl herself into her arms, but her half-sister abruptly halted when just a few feet away, her fingers plucking nervously at the skirts of her lilac gown.

'Leah! I cannot tell you how happy I am to see you again.'

Her attempt at a smile tugged on Leah's heartstrings. She cared not for societal norms of behaviour. Beatrice was her half-sister—her flesh and blood—and Leah's instinct was to touch...to offer comfort. She smiled warmly, opened her arms and drew Beatrice close in a hug. Her cheek, when Leah kissed it, was cold.

'And I,' she said, 'am delighted you have joined us at last. Come, sit by the fire again. You are shivering.'

She urged Beatrice to sit back down and then tugged another chair alongside so she could keep hold of her sister's icy hand. The basket rocked and an unearthly yowl sounded from within.

'What on earth is in there, Beatrice?'

'Oh, dear. I hope it is all right. It is Spartacus. My cat. I *could* not leave him behind.'

'Of course you could not. Is it time to let him out of there, do you think?'

'He is hungry. I—I asked Vardy to bring something for him from the kitchen. Is that all right?'

'Beatrice…my dear…this is your home. Yours and mine and Aurelia's. If you wish to bring your cat, and to give an order to the butler, you are perfectly entitled to do so.'

Leah was rewarded with a smile that revealed dimples in both Beatrice's cheeks. 'I am sorry. I worry… I—I do not wish to take advantage, or to upset anyone.'

'Trust me. You will not upset any of us. Everyone will just be happy you have arrived, I promise.'

Another furious and long-drawn-out yowl emerged from the basket as Mrs Burnham, the housekeeper, entered, carrying a tray laden with a pot of chocolate, two cups, a plate of fragrant, gently steaming fresh rolls, and two dishes, one of meat scraps and one of water.

'Thank you, Mrs Burnham.' Leah moved a side table to within Beatrice's reach. 'Place it here, if you please.'

Mrs Burnham poured the chocolate and then placed the

two dishes on the floor, at the edge of the carpet square. 'For the cat,' she said.

'Thank you.' Beatrice knelt by the basket and unbuckled the straps. Before she could open the lid, a huge black cat pushed it up and squirmed through the opening. He hissed loudly, ears flat to his head, before streaking across the room and scrambling onto the windowsill where he glared malevolently at the three women. 'Oh, dear.'

Leah bit back a smile and judged it better to ignore Spartacus's antisocial behaviour for Beatrice's sake.

'Thank you, Mrs Burnham. And would you arrange for water to be heated for a bath for Miss Fothergill, please?' Leah smiled at Beatrice. 'A bath will warm you up, and we can eat a proper breakfast afterwards with Aurelia and Mrs Butterby, if you are still hungry.'

As soon as the door closed behind the housekeeper, Leah handed one of the cups to Beatrice, who wrapped her hands around it and sipped, her eyes closed. Leah took advantage of the moment to study her sister. She looked thinner than she remembered from their meeting in Bristol eight weeks ago, and some of her bloom had faded.

'I presume by your early arrival you travelled up on the mail coach, Beatrice? You must be exhausted. I...' Leah hesitated to pry, but she could not resist saying, 'I am surprised your brother allowed you to travel all this way unescorted.'

Beatrice slumped in her chair, closing her eyes as she rubbed the middle of her forehead, effectively shielding her expression from Leah.

'He did not know. I—I had to run away, you see. Percy... he's my brother...he found the will and he insisted he would bring me to London himself. Well, him and his wife, Fenella, and *her* b-brother...but, oh, Leah... I could not bear them to taint my new life, and so I *had* to leave when I got the chance but, the whole way, I was so scared he would catch me and spoil everything.'

She hung her head and heaved in a shuddering breath, and Leah recalled Beatrice's agitation when she had mentioned her brother after their first meeting in Bristol. She couldn't wait to hear the whole story of what had happened, but she curbed her curiosity.

'At least you are here now, and you are safe from him, Beatrice.'

Beatrice shook her head despondently. 'You do not know my brother. He will not give up so easily.' Then she fell silent, catching her lower lip between her teeth before releasing it and straightening in the chair. 'He is not my brother, though, is he? I ought not to feel guilty for running away. And I have another family now. He can no longer tell me what to do.' She turned a pair of huge blue eyes—so like Aurelia's but trusting rather than wary—to Leah. 'Can he?'

Leah squeezed Beatrice's hand. 'No, Beatrice. He cannot. You are a wealthy young lady now, and we—Aurelia and I—are your family.'

Beatrice set her cup down, picked up a plate and took a roll. She bit into it and chewed, her forehead creased in thought. Then she swallowed and sighed. 'But he knows this address, Leah. He will follow me here, I know it.'

'Let him come, then. You need never be alone with him— I, or Aurelia, will be with you.'

Beatrice smiled. 'Thank you.'

'There is no need to thank me. We are sisters. We will all look after one another. And, look…even Spartacus has made himself at home.'

She pointed at the cat—the biggest she had ever seen—

who was crouching over the dish and wolfing down food as though he hadn't seen a feed in a fortnight.

'All will be well,' she added, and her heart leapt as she recalled Dolph saying the exact same words to her last night, and as she remembered he would be here at eleven o'clock.

Chapter Twenty-Four

While Beatrice bathed, Leah returned to her bedchamber to wash and dress. Faith told her Aurelia and Mrs Butterby were both awake and would see her in the morning parlour for breakfast. When a knock sounded at Leah's door, it was Maria, Beatrice's maid, with Beatrice herself, her hair still damp and smelling of lemons, and dressed in an ill-fitting yellow-sprigged muslin gown and a threadbare shawl draped around her shoulders.

Leah frowned. 'Are you warm enough dressed so scantily, Beatrice?'

Beatrice turned pink. 'I did not bring many gowns with me. Only what I could carry.'

'Faith? Fetch my paisley shawl, will you, please?' Leah smiled at Beatrice. 'I could not forgive myself if you catch a chill with that damp hair. Please oblige me by borrowing one of my shawls—the weather is hardly warm enough for such lightweight clothing.'

Beatrice hung her head. 'I am sorry. I didn't think. My

sister-in-law likes big fires at Pilcombe Grange, and it is often stifling indoors.'

'And do *not* keep apologising.' Leah tucked her arm through her half-sister's. 'My comment was not a criticism but concern for your comfort. You will soon have a new wardrobe, and then your clothes will be suitable for London and for this house, and you will forget all about that brother of yours. Now, come. Aurelia is impatient to see you again, and Mrs Butterby is longing to be introduced.'

Later, as the four women sat at the table in the morning parlour, breaking their fast, Leah had to bite her tongue on more than one occasion as Aurelia and Mrs Butterby questioned Beatrice. Really! She might as well not have wasted her time in trying to reassure Beatrice and ease her fears because, by the time they rose from the table, her sister was as anxious as ever. Mrs Butterby, talking non-stop as she tried to prepare poor Beatrice for her new life in the bosom of the *haut ton*, walked ahead with Beatrice to the drawing room while Leah and Aurelia followed behind.

'That brother!' Aurelia shook her head. 'I should like to meet him. I would soon send him packing, I can tell you.'

'I do not doubt it. But, Aurelia... I do think it will help reduce Beatrice's anxiety if we avoid talking about her brother too often.'

Aurelia stopped and frowned. 'What do you mean? I am trying to give her some backbone—she needs to stand up for herself.'

'I know. But her confidence needs building up first, and if we keep reminding her of her brother, it will take her much longer to accept she is safe from him.'

'You mean if *I* keep reminding her of him. But I want to know what he did to her to make her so...so...*meek*. I cannot wait for him to call here.' Aurelia's dainty hands balled into fists. 'How dare he turn a beautiful woman into this… this…*blancmange*?'

'Come…' Leah linked her arm through Aurelia's and continued towards the drawing room. 'You and I are not going to quarrel over this, are we? It is far too soon for Beatrice to cope with all these questions, let alone Mrs Butterby's warnings of disasters waiting to befall the unwary newcomer to Society. The poor thing must be exhausted.'

'You are right.' Aurelia shook her head. 'I do not admit this lightly, but even if Beatrice did not fear her brother, I would distrust him. I find it hard to trust the gentlemen of this world.'

'I had noticed,' said Leah, dryly. 'But at least now Beatrice is here we can finally discuss whether or not we publicly admit to our relationship.'

'You know my opinion on that. I think we should announce it and be damned.'

'As do I, but I can also understand why Mrs Butterby advises caution.'

'Caution?' Mrs Butterby queried from where she and Beatrice sat on the sofa. 'About what did I advise caution?'

'Whether or not to openly acknowledge the three of us are half-sisters,' said Leah. She sat on a vacant chair—Spartacus, busy grooming himself, having commandeered the seat closest to the fire—and smiled at Beatrice. 'We agreed to wait until your arrival, as the decision will affect you too.'

Beatrice straightened, frowning. 'Why should we not admit to our relationship?' Her gaze darted between the other three women. 'I am *proud* to have you as sisters and I care not who knows it.'

Aurelia—standing next to Leah's chair—nudged her. 'There. Beatrice agrees with me.'

'But…you do not understand, Beatrice,' said Mrs Butterby. 'By openly admitting you are the offspring of the late Lord Tregowan, you are exposing your mothers' morals to the censure of Society.'

'Speculation is already rife,' said Leah.

'Ah, but speculation is merely that. Once you acknowledge the truth, there will be no going back. And there will be suitors, and families, who will not even consider an alliance if there is a hint of a taint in your bloodlines.'

'If I am not good enough for a man to marry based upon my own merit, then *he* is not good enough for me to consider,' said Aurelia.

'And I, too, am proud to call you both my sisters,' said Leah. 'So I agree we should acknowledge our relationship, for, as Aurelia pointed out, to keep it secret would mean a lifetime of lies, and surely there can be nothing worse than starting out married life upon a lie.'

And I shall start with telling Dolph the truth. Her pulse quickened at the thought he would soon be there.

'Well. If you are all determined…' Mrs Butterby paused, heaved a sigh, shook her head, and then, unexpectedly, she smiled. 'May I say… I applaud your courage and your integrity. And I am also slightly envious you have one another. I hope you continue to support each other, and that you become lifelong friends as well as sisters.' Her voice faltered over the last few words, and she took out her handkerchief and blotted her eyes. 'There! I have turned all maudlin! Beatrice, my dear, you must be exhausted… Why do you not go upstairs to rest now? And—' She shot to her feet. 'Leah!

In all the furore of Beatrice's arrival, I quite forgot! Lord Dolphinstone arrives shortly. Oh, my goodness.'

'Lord Dolphinstone?'

Leah blushed at Beatrice's quizzical look. 'I will tell you all about it later. Mrs Butterby is right... You do look exhausted. Go and get some rest.'

Beatrice's expression changed to one of anxiety. 'Oh, no. I couldn't possibly... What if Percy comes here?'

'What if he does?' Aurelia went to Beatrice and hauled her to her feet. 'We are here to support you, and he no longer has any authority over you.' She hugged her, hard. 'You are safe, Beatrice. Come along, up the stairs with you. And perhaps you'd better take that monster with you.'

She indicated Spartacus, and Beatrice, blushing, scooped him into her arms, saying, 'Oh. Of course. I'm sorry.'

Spartacus put his ears back and grumbled, but he made no attempt to escape. Aurelia glanced back at Leah as she shepherded Beatrice out of the room.

'Be sure of what *you* want, Leah. Do not allow him to bamboozle you with sweet words that disguise an empty heart. You deserve to be happy and you need not answer him straight away if you are unsure. Trust your instincts... They will tell you if he is sincere.'

'She is right,' said Mrs Butterby when the others had gone. 'If His Lordship has truly discovered deeper feelings for you, he will be prepared to prove it and he will wait for your answer. *You* need to be certain. Aurelia never ceases to surprise me. Here was I, thinking she is as hard as nails with not a romantic bone in her body, but she clearly does believe in love.'

'For others, maybe,' said Leah, 'but I am not so sure she believes in it for herself. She appears to regard her marriage as a purely business transaction. I cannot see her ever surrendering her own heart to a man.'

'Well. Time will tell.'

'Thank you for supporting our decision, Mrs Butterby. It means a lot. I know you are eager for us all to make the best matches we can.'

'I feel it is my duty to dear Sarah's memory, but I would not see any one of you marry unwisely, my dear. I want you all to be happy in your marriages.'

'As do I. Do you know, I always hoped that one day I would marry for love, just as my parents did.' Leah frowned. 'Or so I thought. It was a shock to discover their union was an arranged marriage. May I ask… I understand why my mother agreed to the marriage, but was my father's incentive a purely mercenary one?'

'Not entirely. All three of your fathers were paid handsomely, of course, but there was also promotion, in your father's case. He was a curate, and Lord Tregowan arranged for him to take over the living at the church in the village where you grew up.'

So Papa wed Mama as a means to an end? He used her—and she used him, to give her respectability. But they still fell in love.

Her understanding of the complexities of relationships shifted, and hope bloomed in her heart. Hope for her and for Dolph.

At that moment, Vardy entered the drawing room and bowed.

'Lord Dolphinstone has arrived, ma'am, and requests an audience with Miss Thame.'

Leah's stomach lurched.

'Thank you,' said Mrs Butterby. 'Please show him up.

Leah, do you wish me to stay with you, or would you prefer privacy?'

'I should prefer to speak to His Lordship in private, I believe. Thank you.'

Mrs Butterby smiled and hurried out of the room.

Dolph followed the butler upstairs to the drawing room, his stomach tied in knots. Last night, when he was with Leah, he'd been convinced she would forgive him and accept his proposal. But various conversations and comments by others at the rout had rocked his confidence—his simplistic view that her admirers consisted solely of fortune hunters had been shattered as it became clear he was not the only man who admired her for both her appearance and her character. How had he been so blinkered as to believe no other men would see her appeal? He'd lain awake half the night fretting he'd left it too late to win her.

Now he must not only confess the truth about Rebecca and his blame for her suicide, but he must also convince Leah that he truly loved her. Would she believe him—and forgive him—after he hurt her so badly with that clumsy proposal at the Court?

The butler showed him into the drawing room. Leah's expression gave away nothing of her feelings, no hint of what her answer might be, her lovely blue-green eyes guarded. He longed to fling himself at her feet and to beg her to forgive him and to accept his love and his heart, but he could not. First, he must tell her the truth.

'Good morning, my lord.'

Dolph drank in her willowy form, clad in a simple primrose and white striped gown. Her shining red hair was loosely pinned, and she glowed with health. How had he been so slow to realise how much love he held in his heart for this woman? Love that now filled every cell and permeated every thought. How could he bear to lose her now? He would move heaven and earth, mountains included, to make her happy. To keep her content. So much he wanted... *needed*...to say. He opened his mouth, tightly reining in all that emotion swirling through him.

'Good morning, Leah. I believe you are aware why I have sought an interview with you this morning?'

Dolph bowed, cringing at his own stiff formality. He sounded as though he were about to interview her for a job. But what else could he do but revert to the manners expected of a gentleman? He did not want to place too much pressure on her. He owed it to her to help her understand everything before he placed his heart and his future happiness in her hands.

'There is something I need to tell you first, however...'

He fell silent as Leah held up one hand.

'May we sit first?'

'Yes! Yes, of course.'

Dolph gestured towards the sofa. Leah glided across the room and sat down. About to move to a nearby chair, he changed his mind and sat next to her. She—almost imperceptibly—inched away from him, plaiting her fingers in her lap. His heart sank as she shot him a sideways glance.

'There is something *I* must tell *you* first,' she said. 'It might change your mind about your intentions.'

He bit back his instinctive denial that anything could change his intentions. She was deadly serious and he owed her the respect to listen to what she had to say first.

'Very well. I am listening.'

He could not tear his gaze from her restless fingers as they fidgeted in her lap.

'We spoke yesterday about my good fortune and about the third beneficiary of Lady Tregowan's will.'

'I recall.'

'She arrived this morning. Miss Beatrice Fothergill—'

'Fothergill? Any relation to Sir Percy Fothergill?'

'Yes. No.' She sighed. 'That is what I wish to explain. Aurelia, Beatrice and I have agreed to openly acknowledge the reason Lady Tregowan bequeathed us her entire estate.' She captured his gaze. 'You will be the first to know. We are sisters. Well, half-sisters, to be precise.'

'Half-sisters? You mean... Lady Tregowan was your mother?' How had *that* remained a secret in Somerset society, especially when Lady Tregowan had never given Tregowan a child?

'No. Lord Tregowan fathered all three of us. He arranged marriages for our mothers before any of us were born. M-my papa was not my father. I am illegitimate.'

He'd noticed that hitch in her voice before when she spoke of her father—the man who raised her. And now he understood.

'And this is what you discovered at that meeting in Bristol?'

'It is.' The look she sent him was frank. 'As you may imagine, it took time to take in all the implications.'

'Indeed.' No wonder she did not race off to London straight away, quite apart from the added complication of him arriving home the very same day. And no wonder she had appeared distracted.

'If you think this changes my mind about you, Leah... about wanting you as my wife...you are mistaken.'

'But... I am illegitimate.'

'Not in the eyes of the law or Society. Your parents were married when you were born; your father raised you as his own child. No one knows.'

'But they *will* know. We intend to acknowledge each other as sisters. Mrs Butterby has counselled us against it, but we are as one on it. It will cause a scandal.'

'A scandal?' Dolph laughed and shook his head. 'At first, maybe, but it will not endure. Society will absorb the news, gossip about it for a while and then move on to the next juicy titbit.

'Leah—' he took her hand and raised it to his lips, pressing them to her warm skin, breathing in her familiar fragrance of lavender-scented soap '—this sort of thing happens more often than you can ever know. The morality of many in the *haut ton* can be summed up by one phrase: *don't get caught.*'

'But we will be caught, by our own admission.'

'And your mothers' reputations will be picked over and some will visit your mother's sin upon you. But it truly makes no difference to me. Now...tell me about your new sister. What is she like? Does she look like you or more like Miss Croome?'

'She resembles Aurelia, but she is a gentler soul. Aurelia is a little...prickly...at times.'

'Really? I cannot say I noticed.'

Leah's eyes crinkled in amusement. 'Aurelia may be fierce but she has a good heart.'

'I shall take your word for it.' Dolph's pulse picked up speed and his mouth dried. The time had come... He could put it off no longer. 'Leah... I still have my own confession to make.'

She shifted so she was half facing him, her face serious. 'I am listening.'

'You know of my vow to never marry again.'

'I do.'

'I allowed you... George...*everyone*...to believe it was because my love for Rebecca was too strong to be replaced. That was never the reason. The shameful truth is that I did not love Rebecca. At least, not enough. Ours was an arranged marriage—I was fond of her, and we were not unhappy.' He stared at his hands, gripped together on his lap. 'I believed that, at least. After she died, however, I discovered exactly how unhappy she had been.' He raised his eyes, forcing himself to meet Leah's gaze. 'My neglect of Rebecca—my selfish complacency—caused her death.'

Leah frowned. 'But...her death was an accident. Are you telling me you were there when she died?'

'No. But if I had been there...maybe it would not have happened. Leah, what I am about to tell you is known to *nobody* else. Rebecca killed herself.'

Chapter Twenty-Five

'She...? Oh, *no*. Poor, poor lady.' As her initial shock subsided, Leah's voice lowered. 'And poor you. What a dreadful thing to happen, and how hard it must have been to keep it to yourself.'

He searched her face, his brow wrinkled. 'You immediately express sympathy with no sense of shock when many would condemn her for committing a mortal sin. And you a vicar's daughter, too.'

'Papa—' again, she felt that dull ache when she spoke of him '—was the least judgemental man I have ever known. He understood that, at times, life becomes too hard to bear and, if a person is determined, there is little to stop them, short of locking them away for their own protection.'

Dolph bent his head, clenched fists pressed to his eyes. His back heaved. Leah laid her hand on his back, circling gently...soothing the only way she could, for she doubted she could conjure any words that might comfort him. But she could listen, and help him deal with the grief revived by speaking of what happened.

'I feel so guilty.' He mumbled slightly, his hands still covering his face. 'I should have noticed her mind was so disturbed, but I thought she was still recovering from Matilda's birth. I thought nothing more of it, other than trying to jolly her out of it. I had no idea...but that is no excuse! I should have known...should have realised. I should have *stopped* her.'

Leah's thoughts ranged into the past, to the years after Mama's death, and to the times when Papa would return from visiting parishioners in need of spiritual guidance. At times, he would unburden some of the weight of his own inadequacies, talking to Leah as though she were another adult instead of a girl.

'It might comfort you to know Papa had a theory that some mothers suffer greatly after childbirth.' She blushed at speaking boldly of such a subject to a man, but the urge to ease Dolph's distress outweighed her embarrassment. 'Papa noticed it in several new mothers, and he became convinced it was a biological occurrence. He told me he had seen too many suffer from abnormally low moods, and that status made no difference. A duchess was as likely as a peasant to succumb to that depressed state of nerves. For some it lasted but a few days and was quickly shrugged off. For others, though...' She paused, thinking back, picking her words carefully. 'He heard of young mothers who were committed to mental asylums for their own safety, and also of others who successfully hid the extent of their distress from their families. Sometimes for years.'

'I never made the connection before, but Rebecca's mood was also low for a month or so after both boys were born.

And your father noticed the phenomenon several times, you say?'

'Yes. Papa felt keenly for all those poor souls—not only new mothers—who suffered and did his best to counsel them. Occasionally, though, there would be a person who could see no release other than to take that final, drastic step.'

Leah became aware Dolph was looking at her, hope in his eyes.

'Anyone's death by their own hand is hard to bear,' she said, 'but it must be particularly so when it is the mother of your children.'

'I longed to understand. She left a letter, but it did not explain why. That is what I found so difficult, and I felt so guilty that I let the children down by not realising how unhappy Rebecca had been. I swore to myself I would not put another woman through what she went through because I believed it was my neglect—my preoccupation with politics and government—that had made her so very unhappy. I returned to Dolphin Court determined to make it up to the children for losing their mother, and for my abandonment at the very time they needed me. I told myself my needs were unimportant...that I did not deserve happiness. I would get my satisfaction from making my children happy and running the estate.'

He sighed and gathered Leah's hands in his. 'I had no contingency plan for meeting a woman like you.'

'A *contingency* plan?'

He winced. 'That's not very romantic, is it? But it's the truth. You shattered my carefully constructed idea of what my life should be. Leah...my darling...'

Dolph hauled in a deep breath and leapt to his feet, tugging Leah upright to face him. The words burst from him. 'Dolphin Court is not the same without you. Our family is not the same without you. I know I am asking a great deal when you are the toast of Society but, please...come home with me. Tomorrow! Be my wife. I promise I'll make you happy. I'll get a licence. We can be married right away, here in London. Or we can wait until we get home if you prefer. All I know is that I cannot wait to take you home where you belong. I love you. I should have told you that the first time I proposed, but I made the most spectacular mull of it, didn't I?' He dragged in a fractured breath. 'Tell me I'm not too late.' Agony and hope warred in his expression. 'Please tell me you will trust me to make you happy.'

Leah gazed into his stricken eyes, and she dared to believe there could be a happy ending for them after all.

'Of course I trust you.' She caressed his cheek, marvelling that she could touch him whenever she wanted to from now on. 'And I know we will be happy.' Any doubts had evaporated and those painful experiences with Peter and Usk were now just distant memories. 'But... I did not tell you about the conditions attached to my inheritance, one of which is that all three of us must reside in London for the entirety of the Season and remain under Mrs Butterby's chaperonage until we marry. I did not think to ask if that condition means I must stay in London even if I do marry.'

'What happens if it does mean that and you do not stay in London?'

'I forfeit my share of the inheritance.'

Dolph frowned. 'What would then happen to your share?'

'It would be divided between Aurelia and Beatrice and,

other than an annual allowance of two hundred pounds, I would lose everything.'

A smile spread across his features. He grabbed her hands and cradled them to his heart. 'You will not lose me, sweetheart. You will not lose the children. Marry me. Come home to Dolphin Court and allow your sisters to take your share. You will still have them, too. I don't *care* about the money. We won't need it. I will settle a sum on you so you are protected should anything happen to me. I just want you, and for us to go home together.

'Please, Leah. Say yes. Say you will marry me.'

'Oh, yes, my darling.' Leah pulled her hands free to cradle his face, and she kissed him thoroughly, joy cascading through her. 'Yes. Yes. Yes,' she whispered against his lips.

Then she pulled back. She had just found her sisters. She loved Dolph, so very much. But...

'What is it? What is wrong?'

'Oh, Dolph! I cannot leave. Not yet.'

She braced herself for a tirade of words aimed at persuading her she was wrong.

'Tell me why.'

And there, she realised, was another reason she loved him. He would listen to her doubts and not dismiss them because they did not suit him.

'It is Aurelia and Beatrice. We are still strangers—especially Beatrice—and I desperately want to get to know them better.'

'They can come and stay with us at Dolphin Court. Any time.'

She sighed. 'But...they might need me. Here. In London. Dolph... I did not tell you of the other conditions in the will.'

Dolph sat on the sofa and tugged her down next to him. 'Tell me now.'

'The most important one is that each of us must marry within a year if we wish to keep our inheritance. I... I am sorry, but I cannot abandon my sisters when they have such momentous decisions to make. I really do need to stay.' She searched his eyes.

'Then stay we shall. All of us, the children too. My town house is in South Audley Street, just a five-minute walk from here.' He hugged Leah to him and then kissed her. Very thoroughly. 'We can marry, and you will still be here for your sisters. In fact, you will be in a better position to help them as Lady Dolphinstone.

'Now...enough talk, and kiss me again, my beautiful bride-to-be.'

A shiver of delight ran through Leah at his words. She had never considered herself beautiful, but Dolph thought her so, and his opinion was all that mattered to her. She surrendered to the magic of his lips, pressing close to his firm body, barely believing her good fortune. This man, whom she loved so very deeply, loved her in return, and she could not wait until they were man and wife. As their tongues entwined, however, a thought penetrated the sensual haze surrounding her. She eased her lips from his, ignoring his protesting groan.

'Can we tell the children? Today?'

Dolph's chest vibrated as he laughed, a delicious, deep rumble of a laugh. He pressed his lips to her hair.

'Yes, we can tell the children. We will go now. I insist upon it.' He leapt to his feet and pulled her up. 'In fact, we will tell the whole world, for only then will I fully believe this is real and not a fantasy conjured up by my mind to taunt me.

'I want the entire world to know how much I love you, my beautiful, kind and clever Leah. And the sooner, the better.'

Two days later

Glorious anticipation flooded Leah as she and Dolph climbed the stairs of his town house hand in hand.

It had been a perfect day, beginning with their wedding ceremony at St George's, Hanover Square. The children had been on their best behaviour while their father had exchanged vows with their former governess, whose new half-sisters and erstwhile chaperone had shed a tear or two. The wedding breakfast had been a celebration of their union and an opportunity for the two newly merged families to get to know one another better after two days spent on feverish wedding preparations.

Leah recalled, with a happy glow, the children's excitement when they were told she was to be their new mama. Stevie and Nicky had understood straight away and had flung themselves at her, jabbering nineteen to the dozen. And Tilly—although it was clear she didn't really understand—had been determined not to miss out and had squirmed her way into the middle of that group hug. Aurelia and Beatrice had been just as happy and excited for her, as had Mrs Butterby, and Leah prayed they, too, would marry the men of their dreams, just as she had.

After the wedding breakfast, a walk in Hyde Park for the entire clan had ended a memorable day in style. Now, finally, the newly-weds were alone.

Leah walked ahead of her new husband into his bedchamber and turned to him as he closed the door. He opened his arms, and she stepped into his embrace. He heaved a sigh.

'Happy?' she asked, although she knew the answer from the big smile that had adorned his face for most of the day.

'You do not know how happy, my darling.' He kissed the tip of her nose before leaning away to study her. 'Have I told you today how stunning you look?'

'Oh…' She gave him a playful smile, and her pulse quickened as his gaze dropped to her mouth. 'Once, maybe…or, maybe, a thousand times.'

She tiptoed up and kissed him, rousing a hunger within her shocking in its intensity. She'd yearned for this moment for so long, and the taste of him…the thrust of his tongue… the feel of his arousal trapped between them sent shock waves through her entire body. She ached for him…craving the moment their bodies were joined as their hands and their hearts had earlier been joined in church.

Dolph trailed open-mouthed kisses across her jaw and neck as his fingers thrust into her hair. Before long, it tumbled over her shoulders and down her back, and he lifted a handful to his face, breathing in deeply.

'So beautiful. You smell divine,' he whispered, as he gently turned her, his fingers getting to work on the buttons down the back of her gown.

The gown slid from her shoulders, and gooseflesh rippled across her back as he untied the ribbon that held Mama's ring and kissed her nape.

'Have I ever told you I adore your freckles?'

His fingertips danced across her shoulders before his tongue traced a path from nape to shoulder as he unlaced her. She caught her breath as her corset fell away, her heart pounding in her chest. She turned to him, clad only in her shift, and searched his grey eyes.

'Leah?' His hands skimmed up her arms.

'Dolph?' she murmured, before allowing her lips to curve in a knowing smile. She reached for the buttons of his waist-coat.

Dolph's head tipped back, and he closed his eyes, his breathing harsh as she pushed his coat and waistcoat from his shoulders and unwound his neckcloth, exposing the strong column of his throat. She pressed her lips to his warm skin, breathing in his beloved scent as her fingers played among the curls of chest hair visible in the open neck of his shirt.

Dolph groaned, muttered something unintelligible, stepped back, and in one swift movement, he ripped his shirt over his head, flinging it aside before kicking off his shoes and reaching for his trouser buttons. Leah stepped back, her eyes raking his chest and lingering over the bulge in his trousers. Deliberately, she licked her lips.

Dolph paused. His eyes narrowed. 'You minx,' he growled.

Leah held his gaze and gave him a teasing smile as she gathered her shift, raising it. His chest heaved and another groan, tormented, shuddered from him. She stripped her shift over her head and felt her hair spill across her bare shoulders and breasts, and she stood naked beneath his gaze as he appraised her body. She felt no embarrassment; rather, she felt confident and powerful as never before at the effect she had on this magnificently virile man.

And he is mine. All mine.

She could feel the heat radiating from his body and his intoxicating musky scent filled her. Her body felt heavy and warm; her skin tingled; her breasts ached; and that wonderful and irresistible physical yearning filled her, urging her to act.

But she stayed still. Waiting. Until Dolph raised his eyes to hers. Their gazes locked, and something intense flared in his eyes and she felt her own involuntary response. In one swift movement, they came together, lips meeting and tongues tangling with a savage intensity that stole her breath. His trousers were discarded. He guided her hand to him, and she gasped into his mouth as her fingers wrapped around his hot, silken, solid length.

Dolph's entire body stilled, and then his head dipped. She gasped again as his mouth closed around her aching nipple. Fiery darts of need radiated through her and she felt that same tiny pleasurable pulse beat within the sensitive flesh between her thighs.

Too soon, Dolph raised his head.

'Now, my dazzling Countess,' he growled. He nipped her earlobe. Then he backed her towards the bed. 'Allow me to prove to you how much you mean to me.'

Later, as Leah—sated and complete—lay in her husband's arms, sprawled across his muscled, hair-roughened chest, Dolph heaved a sigh sounding of pure contentment. Leah raised her head and studied him sleepily.

'I love you, Lord Dolphinstone,' she said, simply.

He met her eyes and smiled lovingly before framing her face with gentle hands and kissing her—a slow, sweet, savouring kiss. She felt him slowly grow hard against her thigh.

'I love you too, my Lady Dolphinstone,' he whispered against her lips. 'So very, very much.'

She had nearly lost him—afraid to believe hope might ultimately triumph over experience. But it had, and now she meant to savour every minute of every day—and every night—of their life together.

Her hand stroked down his magnificent body and closed around his solid erection.

'Do you care to prove again how much I mean to you, my lord?'

In one swift movement, he flipped her over onto her back, pinning her to the mattress as he settled himself between her thighs. She relished the weight of him, her entire being throbbing with anticipation.

'You mean the world to me,' he avowed as he filled her. 'And I will never stop proving it to you.'

* * * * *

Keep reading for an excerpt of
Billionaire's Second Chance In Paris
by Rebecca Winters.
Find it in the
Bestselling Authors Collection 2023 anthology,
out now!

PROLOGUE

*Causcelle Estate, La Racineuse,
eastern France, ten years earlier*

FOR ONCE, seventeen-year-old Fleurine Dumotte had the house to herself. Her out-of-control father would be working at the Causcelle dairy until late, thank goodness. Her sweet, wonderful mother had gone to town in La Racineuse with her two siblings to shop. She'd be gone a long time. Fleurine had volunteered to do the laundry for the five-member household in order to be alone.

Knowing there wasn't a moment to lose, she did her chores in record time. Then she got busy making bread, shaping pieces of it into five-inch boy figures. Normally she placed raisins down their tummies to look like buttons. But these were for Raoul Causcelle, so she baked the figures without adornment.

After they cooled, she put tiny dobs of frosting for buttons and added little *pépites de chocolat*. She'd made his favorite milk bread *mannele*. He loved the chocolate on top. It would be her going-away gift to him, but no one could ever know about it. Not even her mother. Her terrifying father forbade her from being with any boy, so her feelings for Raoul had always remained a secret from everyone.

He'd seen her in town helping with the marketing yesterday and had asked her to meet him at the west hay barn at the end of his work today. They could talk one last time while he did his chores, but her excitement was swallowed up in despair. The day after tomorrow he'd be leaving home with his brothers to go to college in Paris hundreds of miles away.

Fleurine had been born and raised on the Causcelle estate. All the kids in the area had gone to the same schools. She and Raoul were eleven months apart. Over the last two years he'd found dozens of ways to meet her accidentally at school and on her way home after the bell rang.

The knowledge that Raoul was leaving had become unbearable, and she'd wanted to do something for him. After wrapping the *mannele* in a bag, she cleaned up the kitchen so her father would never know what she'd done. Next, Fleurine hurried into the bedroom she shared with her thirteen-year-old sister, Emma. Their eleven-year-old brother, Marti, had his own room.

Fleurine had no choice but to put on one of her ugly white dresses that fell below the knee. It had long sleeves that looked like a nursing uniform from a hundred years ago. He'd never seen her in anything else. She wished she were allowed to go to mass like her friends and wear something pretty. How she hated her brown shoes that laced up to the ankles. So many wishes had never been fulfilled…

The women in their household weren't allowed to wear makeup or perfume or cut their hair. All she could do was brush hers that hung down her back. She'd been forbidden to use ribbons or barrettes. Modern styles of clothes were out of the question. She could still hear her father say, "Fleur and Emma Dumotte, you'll live in my house like proper daughters of the Jura-Souboz where your ancestors came from and obey my rules!"

His despotic eighteenth-century rules!

Not wanting to feel pain today, she raced out of the house with her gift and climbed on her bike. Raoul had always been a hard worker and obeyed his nice-looking widower father, who everyone knew had high expectations for him and his brothers. The country's renowned billionaire Louis Causcelle kept his children close. Fleurine had seen him on several occasions but had never met him. She was pained by her father's hatred for the patriarch of the Causcelle dynasty and his family, especially his triplet sons.

On her approach, she saw Raoul's bike outside the barn. She rode hers around the back. She didn't dare leave it where her father could see it from the road on his way home from the dairy.

"There you are, Fleurine," she heard Raoul say while she rested her bike against the barn. He'd walked in through the back to find her. "I hoped you'd be able to make it." His smile lit up her universe.

No one knew her as Fleurine. Only Raoul had started calling her that name last year. He'd said it was because her eyes reminded him of the violet flowers growing in the northern pasture. To her mind, her eyes were a boring gray with tinges of violet. But since he'd given her that name, she'd begun thinking of herself as Fleurine. He'd made it sound beautiful.

"Let's take your bike inside." They walked to the front with it and went in the barn where he shut the big door.

Raoul was fun and exciting. He was also so handsome it made her breath catch. His dancing black eyes and black hair thrilled her as much as his smile. Sometimes he resembled a dashing pirate. She'd always felt insipid around him by comparison.

No young men in school, let alone France, matched the looks of the tall, gorgeous and well-built Causcelle triplet sons. Her girlfriends had told her their pictures had been in all the newspapers and magazines and on TV, but her father didn't allow radio, TV or printed matter in their home.

"I had to do the laundry first, or I would have come sooner. Here." She handed him the bag. "I baked these for you."

His intense gaze made her feel warm all over. He opened it

and pulled out one of her treats. "Let's find out if you're still the best cook in France."

Heat crept into her face. "Don't be ridiculous."

"I swear I'm telling the truth. I've eaten your treats before. You could run your own five-star cooking school." On that note he took a bite and ended up devouring the whole thing with those perfect white teeth. "Yup. You deserve the grand prize for these. Let me thank you properly and give you whatever you want."

Whatever she wanted? Would that Fleurine had the temerity to tell him she wanted the one thing he could never give her. Her father had forbidden her and her siblings to have anything to do with the Causcelle family. If they ever did, they would pay the ultimate price. He terrified them. What an absurd, foolish girl she'd been to have secret dreams about a life with Raoul.

Fleurine had been dreading the moment when he would leave the estate. The end of their childhood had come. To a degree, childhood had been the common denominator that made a more equal playing field for them to be together, but no longer. There wasn't a thing she could do about this parting of their worlds, and already she was dying inside. To face a day without Raoul meant no more adventure or wonder. No more feeling alive.

"Mind if I thank you in the way I've wanted to for a long time?"

Something in his tone sounded different. "What do you mean?"

"Have you ever been kissed by one of the guys around here, Fleurine? Really kissed? I've noticed Remy and Thomas. They never leave you alone."

"They're just friends." Her heart pounded in her throat.

"Do you put me in the same category as *just a friend*?"

She averted her eyes. "A good friend. Are you trying to embarrass me?"

"Anything but. I'd like to know if there's some guy you're interested in on the estate you've kept secret from me."

"How can you ask me that?" Her voice shook. "You know my father."

"Forget your father for a minute. Is there someone you care about and have been alone with?"

She shivered. "That's private, Raoul."

"So there *is* a guy—" He sounded upset.

Her head flew back. "What if I asked you if there's a girl on the estate *you've* kissed?"

He shifted his weight. "Do you want to know the answer? Or aren't you interested enough to find out?"

Fleurine shook her head. "I wouldn't dare ask you. It's none of my business."

"Maybe it's because you're frightened of the answer. Yes, I've kissed a few."

"I think I'd better go."

She turned to leave, but he grasped her arm. "You *are* frightened."

"Please, Raoul. I don't know what you want from me."

He inhaled sharply. "The truth. Nothing more, nothing less. For once in our lives, we're truly alone. I know you're frightened of your father, but he's nowhere around to hear us."

"What truth?" she cried, not understanding him. Something was wrong.

"That you love me as much as I love you!" The interior of the barn resounded with his declaration. "Isn't love the reason you came at the risk of your father finding out? Isn't love why you brought me this gift?"

A gasp escaped her lips. She backed away from him. "E-even if the answer were yes," she said, "you couldn't possibly love me, Raoul Causcelle. Not *you,* who could have any girl, I mean *any* girl, in the world. Are you telling the Dumotte daughter, who's been told to go back to the dark ages where our family belongs, that you love *me*?"

"Don't talk about yourself that way, Fleurine."

"You haven't lived in my skin, Raoul. I'm the offspring of old man Dumotte who lights fires and would have been the first to set a torch to Jeanne d'Arc. Did you know *he* and the demented friends in their cult were the ones who set fire to the monastery when he was a young teenager?

"He helped murder all those monks to get rid of your father's brother-in-law Gregoire. My father was taught to hate every Catholic before his family moved here from Switzerland and started working for your family. He's forbidden our family from ever stepping inside a Catholic church."

"I've suspected it for a long time."

"He's insane, but most of all he hates your father for marrying your mother."

Raoul moved closer. His black eyes flashed. "What do you mean?"

"He wanted Delphine Ronfleur for himself, but she wanted your father and married him. My mother broke down one day and told me everything. She lives in fear of him. So do I. If she tries to leave or expose him, he has threatened to kill the whole family. Lately he's been watching me."

"I knew that was the reason why you've tried to be so careful around me," Raoul murmured.

"Then, you should know there's never been anyone else for me but you, and there never will be. But you're the son of the man my father despises. I'm afraid *you're* another object of his hatred now. Run to Paris while there's still time and stay safe! He mustn't ever see us alone together. I'm a nothing who's not worthy of you, Raoul."

"Don't you ever say things like that, Fleurine." He reached out and crushed her in his arms, holding her until her thrashing stopped, but her body kept heaving sobs. "I've always loved you and have sensed deep down you felt the same way. Let me kiss you so I can show you how I feel. We'll deal with everything else later."

Fleurine couldn't believe this was happening. Raoul honestly loved *her*?

"Right now, we need this time together before I have to leave. Once I'm gone, we know letters and phone calls will be impossible." He lowered his head. First, he planted soft kisses near her mouth then her lips. She kissed him back the same way. Slowly they melded.

Their kisses grew deeper and longer. She threw her arms around his neck and clung to him, exhilarated by new sensations of being kissed and held in his arms. If only this could go on forever.

"I love you, Fleurine. I can't remember a time when I didn't."

"I won't be able to live without you!" she cried, kissing him over and over again.

"All these years we've shared everything but this. I have plans for us. When I come home at Christmas, you'll have turned eighteen the day before. I'll make all the arrangements, and we'll run away immediately to get married at the church in Paris. Your father won't know what happened until it's too late."

"Oh, Raoul. *Your* father would never permit it."

He kissed every feature. "Don't worry. He married my mother in their teens and won't be able to raise an argument. We'll live in Paris in an apartment. You're the smartest girl at school and can start college. We'll go together, and I'll pay for it, and after graduation we'll buy our own home while I work for the family business. We'll be away from your father and live the rest of our lives the way I've always dreamed."

"If I thought that could happen…" She returned his kisses with shocking hunger.

Suddenly the barn door lifted. In the late-afternoon light she saw her father, a tall, powerfully built man with a ruddy complexion and beard. He held a hunting rifle aimed at Raoul.

"Get your hands off my daughter or I'll shoot you dead this instant."

Fleurine pulled out of Raoul's arms. How had her father known she was here? "We weren't doing anything wrong!" she cried in absolute horror. "I was just saying goodbye to him."

She heard him cock the rifle. "Get in the truck, Fleur."

"Don't hurt him!" she screamed.

"Do as I say. If I ever catch the two of you together again, you'll both be dead. You've shamed me, daughter."

Knowing what he was capable of, she ran out of the barn to the truck. Before she got in, she threw up, terrified of what he'd do to Raoul. As she heaved her trembling body into the truck, her father got in on the other side. He put the rifle on the rack behind their heads.

When she looked back, she saw Raoul standing at the barn entrance.

Dieu merci he was still alive!

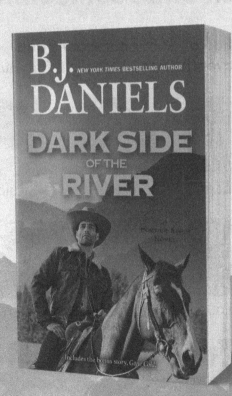

MILLS & BOON

Want to know more about your favourite series or discover a new one?

Experience the variety of romance that Mills & Boon has to offer at our website:

millsandboon.com.au

Shop all of our categories and discover the one that's right for you.

MODERN

DESIRE

MEDICAL

INTRIGUE

ROMANTIC SUSPENSE

WESTERN

HISTORICAL

FOREVER
EBOOK ONLY

HEART
EBOOK ONLY

f @millsandboonaustralia   🐦 📷 @millsandboonaus

ubscribe and
all in love with
Mills & Boon
eries today!

ou'll be among the first
 read stories delivered
 your door monthly
nd enjoy great savings.

WE
SIMPLY
LOVE
ROMANCE

MILLS & BOON

JOIN US

0419856828

Sign up to our newsletter to stay up to date with...

- Exclusive member discount codes
- Competitions
- New release book information
- All the latest news on your favourite authors

Plus...
get $10 off your first order.
What's not to love?

Sign up at **millsandboon.com.au/newsletter**